LAZARETTO

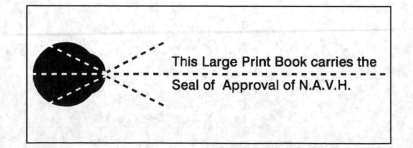

This Large Print Book carries the
Seal of Approval of N.A.V.H.

LAZARETTO

DIANE MCKINNEY-WHETSTONE

THORNDIKE PRESS
A part of Gale, Cengage Learning

Farmington Hills, Mich • San Francisco • New York • Waterville, Maine
Meriden, Conn • Mason, Ohio • Chicago

GALE
CENGAGE Learning®

Thorndike Press® Large Print African-American.
The text of this Large Print edition is unabridged.
Other aspects of the book may vary from the original edition.
Set in 16 pt. Plantin.

LIBRARY OF CONGRESS CATALOGING-IN-PUBLICATION DATA

Names: McKinney-Whetstone, Diane, author.
Title: Lazaretto / by Diane McKinney-Whetstone.
Description: Large print edition. | Waterville, Maine : Thorndike Press, 2016. | Series: Thorndike Press large print African-American
Identifiers: LCCN 2016037156| ISBN 9781410495389 (hardcover) | ISBN 1410495388 (hardcover)
Subjects: LCSH: African Americans—Fiction. | Large type books.
Classification: LCC PS3563.C3825 L39 2016b | DDC 813/.54—dc23
LC record available at https://lccn.loc.gov/2016037156

Published in 2017 by arrangement with Harper, an imprint of HarperCollins Publishers

Printed in the United States of America
1 2 3 4 5 6 7 21 20 19 18 17

LAZARETTO

PART I

1

The dimly lit room smelled of sage and mint and boiled cotton. A lone candle high on a whitewashed mantel threw off just enough light to illuminate a space on the wall above it where a picture of Abraham Lincoln hung. The sight of him with his top hat and wry smile seemed to calm Meda as she pushed and moaned, her legs spread wide apart. Fourteen-year-old Sylvia gently slid her hands between Meda's legs into what felt to Sylvia like the center of a volcano.

"How many fingers can you insert?" asked Dr. Miss, the midwife directing Sylvia.

"My entire hand," Sylvia said, as a low-pitched cry of pain rumbled out of Meda and Sylvia quickly pulled her hand back.

"Your hand is not the cause of her discomfort this moment," Dr. Miss said. "This is her first, and there is no history to draw on with the first to help them when they push."

"Yes, ma'am," Sylvia said. This was also Sylvia's first. She'd worked here going on a year as assistant to Dr. Miss, and right now her duties had taken a monumental leap. She and Dr. Miss had exchanged places, and instead of dabbing Meda's forehead and speaking encouraging words in a soothing voice, and otherwise doing what Dr. Miss requested, Sylvia now sat on Dr. Miss's stool at the foot of the cot, taking the lead in delivering a baby.

"Now, tell me what you see."

Sylvia looked over at the waning flame of the candle that was struggling to stay alive. "I believe I need more light," she said as she got up to retrieve the candle.

"Did I say you need more light?" Dr. Miss snapped, as if to remind Sylvia who was who.

"No, ma'am, you did not."

"Your hands should be your light."

"Yes, ma'am. But you generally employ more light at this juncture. I am just trying to determine if there is a reason —"

"I know how to do this in the absence of light, and you must as well, because another occasion may require it. Leave the candle and return to the stool."

"Yes, ma'am," Sylvia said, then held her tongue as she walked back across the pine

10

floor that had been painted white, the way everything in this room was white, from the cot to the stool to the hearth to the frame that held the president's likeness. Sylvia reasoned that the preponderance of white in this room was Dr. Miss's attempt at coating a swath of purity over the various situations that found their way here. Though Dr. Miss prided herself on delivering the babies of literate, well-to-do black parents attracted to her because her father had been a respected intellectual, a Freemason, and a barber who dispensed fiery diatribes against slavery right along with the perfect cut and shave, there was an underbelly to her practice that she kept hidden from her respectable clientele, where she expertly removed formations eight to twelve weeks along, before a woman started to show. "Troubled formations" Dr. Miss called them when a woman was not legally betrothed, or too young, or too old, too fragile, or, as in the case of Meda, escorted here under the cover of night by a wealthy white man in a two-horse carriage. Dr. Miss had become well known in the whispered circles of rich white men as a viable medical solution to the consequence of their indiscretions. Meda was supposed to have been such a case. But once Meda was out of her cape, even Sylvia could see that though this young woman was small, and carried small, the formation she carried had already dropped, was already in a prone position, and, troubled or not, was a full-term formation ready to be born.

The candle's light was down to a wisp as Sylvia returned to her place on the stool. She was about to insert her hand again and see what she could see, but then Meda let out a growl of a sound followed by a hard grunt that expanded like a cyclone, growing longer, wider. And Sylvia gasped, because suddenly she could almost see the head.

"Crowning?" Dr. Miss called, standing over Sylvia now.

"I believe so, uh, yes."

"Cup your hands — and take care, it will be slippery."

Sylvia did, surprised that her hands were not shaking because all of her insides were as she watched the head push out and actually turn itself around as the shoulders squeezed through. "Uh, uh, uh" was all that Sylvia could manage to say, because with all of the other births she had been tending to the mother at the other end of the cot. She'd never before witnessed this instant. And then, stillness, everywhere in the room it seemed, except for the silence that replicated itself in pulses of non-sound. And already her hands were holding the baby. And the baby's cries pushed through the silence. And Sylvia was both laughing and crying, and now the candle flame had died completely, and between the darkened air and her own tears she could barely see enough even to determine whether the baby was a girl or a boy. She tried to piece through the darkness, but before she could, Dr. Miss covered the baby with a white square of a blanket and snipped the cord. Sylvia lifted the baby to her then. She moved her hand under the blanket to rub its back. Its skin was warm and slick. The tiny curls of its breath tickled her neck; the pat-pat of its heartbeat thrilled her. And then a cold space of air as Dr. Miss took the baby from her arms and Sylvia felt the sudden absence of its warmth. Then her eyes cleared and she focused on the miniscule hand that was the palest pink with just a hint of yellow, like the first light of dawn reaching through the black air. It seemed to be reaching for Meda's voice as Meda called out, "My baby, give him to me. Please, let me have my child."

Generally at this point, Dr. Miss would inspect the baby, then place it on the mother's chest. She did not this time.

"Warm her, please, she's getting chills. Then deliver the afterbirth," she said to Sylvia. "Rub her stomach in circles to help it along. Then pour a cup of calming brew and get her to sip."

"Yes, ma'am," Sylvia said, looking through the air to try to find Dr. Miss's face. Dr. Miss was tall and thin and dark, made even taller and darker by a white cloth wrapped around her head and piled high like a queen's crown, the rest of her essentially lost in this black-aired room. Sylvia often thought that with all of the medicinal plants growing around here and the concoctions brewing, if Dr. Miss had not been such a skilled midwife she could have certainly succeeded as a witch. She thought that now, as Dr. Miss seemed to turn a deaf ear to Meda, who was trying to sit up, her calls for her baby having grown louder, more insistent. The baby's cries were full throttle now, too. It was as if the baby and Meda were engaged in a charged call-and-response, the space between them widening as Dr. Miss walked away with the baby, her long white dress flouncing as she moved through the door, leaving Sylvia to contain Meda, who was trying to get up from the cot to go after them.

Sylvia delivered the afterbirth and sedated

14

Meda per Dr. Miss's instructions. Then she went into the parlor, where Dr. Miss was in hushed conversation with the man who'd escorted Meda there, Tom Benin, a powerful Philadelphia attorney — though he seemed anything but at that moment, as Dr. Miss motioned Sylvia in and he turned and glanced at her. He seemed as if he'd been winnowed down by shame and remorse, his skin whitened, his eyes red, his manner delicate as he listened to Dr. Miss's report. "She arrived months too late for the other procedure," Dr. Miss said. "I am sorry that she was so good at keeping it cloaked. She is a small woman after all."

He looked down, away from Dr. Miss, as if he were a chastened schoolboy being reprimanded by the headmaster. He even stammered over his words as he asked Dr. Miss if she was certain that there had been no other option.

"If there had been, I assure you we would have exercised it." She snapped the ends of her words.

"And the baby was born alive?" he asked, as if he hoped that by phrasing the question directly he might hear a different response.

"I have already said yes. Born alive. Full-term." The edge to Dr. Miss's tone increased the more she spoke.

He pulled out a pocket watch, a gold watch decorated with bridges, the likes of which Sylvia had never seen. "I am just not prepared for such a result at this time," he said, talking more to the watch than to Dr. Miss.

"Neither were we. But we are accustomed to adjusting to unexpected results."

"So you have had this situation prior?"

"We have, and have handled it with discretion."

"And if you handle this likewise, what will be its disposition?"

"We think it best that the fewer details you have, the better for all concerned."

"And how is she?"

"Meda, or the baby, because the baby is actually —"

"Her, her, Meda," he said, his hushed voice straining with agitation now.

"I assure you that Meda will pull through expertly in body, though the heart is slower to recover."

He swallowed hard and placed his hands on the edges of Dr. Miss's ornate oak desk as if to steady himself, as if to keep himself from collapsing into tears. And Sylvia balled her fist, to steady herself, too, to resist the wave of compassion for the man trying to bowl her over. She disliked about herself

16

the way that she could be affected by a thin vein of good in a person who was otherwise despicable, wished right now that she was blind to this man's complexities.

He squared his shoulders then, suddenly remembering his status. "On second thought, I will see to its disposition myself. Ready it, please. My carriage is waiting along the side of this structure. Deliver it to me there."

"Sir?" Dr. Miss said, as if she'd not heard him.

"It occurs to me that I have several options."

"But, sir, I already have a suitable resolution in mind." Dr. Miss's sharp tone was replaced with a softer, pleading one. "A young Negro couple of the highest caliber —"

"I have said I have other options in mind."

Now it was he snapping the ends of his words and Dr. Miss was the one looking away, looking down as she breathed deeply several times, and the only thing in the room that seemed to move was her chest, rising and falling. "As you wish," she said. "And we should tell Meda . . . what, sir?"

"Tell her her baby girl died," he said, already out of the parlor.

Dr. Miss sank in her chair, her face ashen,

as if all the blood had left her. Her head wrap had begun to unravel and hung along the side of her face. She spoke more to the thick velvet draperies swagged around the parlor's doorway than to Sylvia. "The woman I had in mind would have been the perfect mother. I've been treating her barren womb. Now . . . who knows what he will do."

Sylvia's heart was beating double time as she swallowed the urge to cry. "Was it a girl, ma'am?" she asked in a whisper.

"Did you not deliver it?" Dr. Miss's voice was a mix of agitation and reprimand.

Sylvia clasped and unclasped her hands. "The candle died, ma'am. Uh, it was dark, and then you covered it, uh, the baby. You covered the baby and I did not see —"

"Let that be a lesson to you. I told you that your hands should be your eyes."

"Yes, ma'am," and then Sylvia could no longer hold it in and she started to cry. "You do not think he means the baby harm, do you?" She said in a cracked voice.

"I do not know what he will do. He does not even know what he will do. He is not in his right mind; the shock of a live birth has left him incapable of clear thought."

"Well, we can tell *him* that the baby died," Sylvia said, her voice screeching as she tried to contain herself. "We can take the lie that he is prepared to tell to Miss Meda and turn it right back on him. Then you can give the baby to the woman as you had planned."

"That is preposterous, Sylvia."

"But, ma'am, you said he is incapable of clear thought. We should think for him, then, for the sake of the baby —"

"And what if he asks to see the corpse? That is his child —"

"But is the baby not also Miss Meda's? Is Miss Meda his property? In Philadelphia, in 1865?"

Dr. Miss stood and rewound her head wrap back up high. "I will cover the baby in a balm that will protect her against evil intentions. And you, Sylvia, must accept that most Negroes do not live the prosperous life that your parents are able to give you. It is best for Meda that she believes her baby died. She will grieve, she will recover, she will be better than most in her situation. It is my understanding that the Benins' live-in help enjoy excellent accommodations."

"And yet she has come to us carrying his —" Sylvia stopped herself then. She had gone too far; she knew by the way Dr. Miss squared her shoulders and focused her eyes like spears trained on Sylvia. "Forgive me, ma'am," Sylvia said as she looked down at the planked hearts-of-pine floor. "It's just that that baby was my first." She swallowed hard to hold herself from crying again. "Shall I ready the baby and deliver it to his carriage?"

"I will do it," Dr. Miss said. "And you best mind your mouth, Sylvia, or find a different training ground for your nursing aspirations."

"Yes, ma'am," Sylvia said, but Dr. Miss had already left the parlor. Sylvia sank into the chair where Tom Benin had just been. She was remembering the feel of the baby's head finding the crook of her neck and nestling there. "A girl," she whispered to herself. "It was a girl. It was my first."

Hours later a brilliant burst of sunlight ushered Meda to full consciousness. She'd dozed, on and off, after her baby was born, and the spate of time following was a blur. Whatever it was they'd made her drink had invited a fog to settle inside of her head. She'd barely been aware of their comings and goings as they piled blankets on her, and packed her insides to stop a threatening hemorrhage, and squeezed her breasts to relieve the buildup. Each time they entered the room, she'd call for her baby. Dr. Miss at turns ignored her, instead whispering instructions to Sylvia, or she'd just gently touch her fingers to Meda's forehead and tell her to hush. "Get some rest, and hush."

She was certain, though, that she'd given birth, believed it to be a boy, because the president told her so. She'd focused on Abraham Lincoln's likeness during the time she was in labor. His picture hung above the only lit candle in the room and in her throes of her pain she thought she saw his lips move, thought she heard his whispered voice as he encouraged her and told her that she was doing well, even alerted her when she was crowning. "Fine boy you've got there, Meda," she thought she heard Lincoln say just before the candlelight died, and then she couldn't hear him anymore.

She studied Mr. Lincoln now under the blazing sunlight. He was no longer talking to her and returned to being just a picture in a frame on a wall. Now here was the young girl, Sylvia, coming in, a pleasant-looking brown-skinned girl in a crisp white dress. She held a bucket; towels were draped over her arms; her dress pocket bulged with a cup that would catch the milk she'd press from Meda's breasts. And now Meda could see that her face was tear-stained.

Meda sat straight up. "You've been crying," she said in a matter-of-fact tone. "It is my baby, is it not? My baby's dead?"

"No, ma'am — I mean yes, ma'am," Sylvia said, confused. "Dr. Miss didn't tell you? I mean, I am so sorry, but it is the president. It seems — I am so sorry about your baby, Miss Meda. Yes, I thought Dr. Miss had told you that your baby succumbed — but . . . also the president."

"They killed him?"

"Yes, ma'am," she sniffed. "They did, they killed him."

"They killed my baby. I knew they would."

"Oh! No! Miss Meda, no, not your baby. I mean, your baby's gone, but your baby — of course I am so, so sorry about your baby, and yes my tears are for her, too, but also for the president. Mr. Lincoln, the president, is dead."

"The president? They killed the president?"

"Yes, ma'am. While he watched a play, shot in the head. Mr. Lincoln, the president, is dead."

"And you said 'her'? Are you saying my baby was a girl?"

"Yes, Miss Meda, I am so sorry, I thought Dr. Miss told you."

"Not a boy?"

"No, ma'am, a girl."

"Might I see her?"

Sylvia set the bucket on the floor and hung her head as if in prayer. "I am sorry, Miss Meda. Forgive me, please. I am generally far better with my composure, but with learning of the president, uh, and your sweet baby. Uh, no. I am afraid you cannot see the baby. Mr. Benin arranged for a swift burial that has already taken place."

"Did you see her?" she asked then. Her voice was flat.

"I did not. Dr. Miss whisked her away while I was with you, trying to tend to you, you were bleeding quite a bit, and, uh, Miss Meda, my heart is breaking for you this instant."

"But he told me it was a boy, a fine boy."

"Who, Miss Meda? Who said such a thing?"

"I —" Meda stopped herself. She couldn't tell Sylvia that Mr. Lincoln had watched from the wall and congratulated her on the birth of her son. "It must have been my imaginings," she said, and as she looked away, Sylvia approached the bed.

Meda offered neither resistance nor assistance as Sylvia pulled her gown from her shoulders to ease the pressure in her breasts. She had lost the capacity to feel; thought that the channels that carried sensations

23

throughout her body had been crushed under the weight of this dual tragic news, that her baby had died, and the president, too. Thought right now that it was a blessing that she could not feel. She shrugged as Sylvia apologized for the hard coldness of the cup against her breast. Then Sylvia made a buffer out of the towel and told Meda that her hope was that her baby girl and Mr. Lincoln had found each other in the sky and flown away together, Heaven-bound.

2

Good thing for Sylvia that the city, or at least her tidy block of well-to-do black people on Addison Street above Eighteenth, her comfortable home filled with books and fine china and parental scrutiny, was in an uproar over the president's death. She didn't have to force herself to say all was well when her mother, Maze, asked her how she'd gotten along at Dr. Miss's — she'd never let on if her hours with the midwife were traumatic because she feared her parents wouldn't allow her to continue working there. But today she didn't have to hide her deflation. Didn't have to pretend to laugh at her father's, Levi, jokes about how all the babies Dr. Miss delivered came feet first — Dr. Miss had in fact delivered Sylvia, who herself had threatened to come feet first, but Dr. Miss had managed to turn her around and later informed Maze and Levi that Sylvia bore close watching because such children were known to be troublemakers for bucking the tide; Levi had whispered to his wife that Sylvia had just been trying to delay the instant when she looked on Dr. Miss's godforsaken face.

But there were no jokes today. No need for Sylvia to make excuses for her puffy eyes or lack of appetite. As soon as she walked through the door, Maze pulled her in a hug and held on. And even though her father had always maintained that Lincoln could have much sooner initiated much bolder moves to resolve the issue of the enslaved, right then he showed signs of having wept.

By the next day, Sylvia had replayed that image of the baby's hand pushing into the air in that whitewashed room so often that it sapped her of all vitality. She was so listless that her parents didn't pressure her about attending Easter Sunday services as they prepared to go themselves.

She gathered books once they left, *The Scarlet Letter* and *Narrative of the Life of Frederick Douglass,* and sat out back on the steps and tried to force her mind in other directions. Before now she'd mostly been able to manage the complex of emotions that came with the job of assisting Dr. Miss. She aspired to be a nurse, and she knew that her tenure with Dr. Miss was proving a remarkable training ground. But Meda's situation had been different.

She looked up from her book at that moment and watched their next-door neighbor, Clo, walk into the yard. Crazy Clo they called her behind her back, for her penchant for obsessively tracking her husband's every move. It surprised Sylvia that she was actually glad to see Clo; she might at least be the distraction that Hester Prynne had not been.

Clo was dressed for church, her crocheted gloves on her hands, her bonnet sitting high atop her upsweep of a hairdo. She'd adorned the bonnet with replicas of fruit made of plaster of Paris, bananas and pears that Sylvia thought hideous. Her face was practically lost under the hat. Clo was thinner than she should be, and Sylvia's mother maintained that Clo was so busy chasing after that philandering husband, she didn't nourish herself as properly as she should. Sylvia felt sorry for Clo all of a sudden, for the ugly hat, for what showed of her hungry, lean face, her eyes red, her voice trembling as she asked Sylvia if she would assist her in an important task.

"Of course, Miss Clo," Sylvia said as she jumped up from the steps, thinking that perhaps Clo needed help packing up collations to take to church, then regretting that she'd agreed when Clo told her what she wanted: namely, for Sylvia to travel with her to Fitzwater Street to coax a woman from her house so that Clo could have a conversation with her.

Sylvia asked, "What woman? Why?"

"Some strumpet of a woman Seafus has taken a liking to, and I need to nip it right now."

Sylvia protested that she didn't really want to get involved. Plus, gambling houses were in that neighborhood; her mother would be mortified if she knew. Clo persisted. Reminded Sylvia of all the times she cared for her when she was younger, allowing her parents the flexibility to concentrate on their thriving catering business. "You ought to give me my due, Sylvia," she said. "Weren't for me, you and your people might be relegated down there on Fitzwater." Sylvia knew there was no truth to that. But she also knew that Clo wouldn't otherwise leave the yard until she relented. So she did.

Nevada, the woman Clo wanted to talk to, had just moved to Philadelphia and had already earned the nickname Clam Buster for her ability to crack a man's illusions of himself and render him spineless, soft, have him flopping about after her with his dignity nothing more than a trail of droppings. Clo told Sylvia that she had picked Sunday knowing that most on that block were likely late-sleeping heathens, and those who were up at a decent hour were probably at church. The front steps would be empty of sitting-outs who might notice her and get to Nevada first and warn her. Clo hung back at the corner, prepped Sylvia to draw Nevada out of her house by saying that she was girlfriend to Seafus's brother, that Seafus had a surprise for her waiting at the corner.

Sylvia had not challenged Clo on the logic, though she thought if she were Nevada, she certainly wouldn't fall for such a story. She watched the door to Nevada's house edge open. An older woman appeared in that slice of opening, and Sylvia took in a deep breath. The aroma of baking cornbread wafted out and surprised her. She hadn't expected such a righteous aroma; had expected a whore's heavy perfume, or gin, stale coffee even, but not cornbread. Nor had she expected to be eyed by the likes of this wild-looking woman, whose hair was out and unrestrained, her feet bare; she made clucking sounds as she raised her eyebrows at Sylvia. "Well?"

Sylvia mustered up the sweetest smile she

could feign. " 'Scuse me, ma'am, I'm here to call on Nevada."

"You friend to my granddaughter?"

"Like to be, ma'am," Sylvia lied. "We made acquaintance the other day at Freidman's on Reed Street where I was looking at white muslin blouses."

The woman let go a half-whistle, half wolf-howl of a laugh and Sylvia jumped back. "Hold on," she said finally, as she closed the door.

Sylvia looked down to the end of the block; she could see the bananas of Clo's hat edging around the corner. She thought about leaving. The woman could just as soon be going to retrieve a butcher knife as she was to be calling her granddaughter to the door. She was about to turn to walk down the steps when the door opened all the way and the smell of cornbread returned and there Nevada stood.

Sylvia was shocked by Nevada's appearance. She wasn't much older than Sylvia, with an innocent-looking roundness to her face. Her coloring was more red than light and a clump of freckles trekked from her right eye in the shape of a teardrop. Her mound of brown bushy hair had come out of a braid, and Sylvia could see nothing about her that justified the clam-buster characterization. Not even in what she wore, a simple pale-blue, ankle-length dress held closed with a wide sash; her feet, like her grandmother's, were bare.

Nevada smiled then, "Good day," she said. "I know you?"

"My name is Sylvia; I live on Addison —" The sound of the grandmother's laughter crackled from deep in the house, interrupting Sylvia.

"Oh, that's just my grandmom, everybody calls her Miss Ma. She just breaks out into laughter for no good reason. I hope she don't scare you much."

"Well, as I was saying, I live on Pine Street next door to Clo. You know Clo, do you not?"

Nevada stared directly at Sylvia, the smile gone from her face. "Cain't say I do."

"Or will *not* say that you do?" Sylvia matched Nevada's stare with a defiance of her own. Deep down, Sylvia knew that what Nevada did, and with whom she did it, was none of her concern, but just the week before she'd assisted Dr. Miss with a procedure on a young woman about Nevada's age who was carrying the child of a married man. She was farther along than she should have been and had almost bled out, but they'd managed to save her life and afterward Dr. Miss told Sylvia that if more young women who had a say-so were witness to the things Sylvia was while in her employ, they'd not fall swoon to the falsehoods a man lets flourish when his nature rises. Sylvia had thought about Meda, who'd had no say-so. "I believe you know her husband," Sylvia continued.

"Which one is he?"

"That many, you got to ask which one?"

Nevada's expression was unchanged as she stared at Sylvia, though the tear-shaped clump of freckles seemed to slide farther down her face.

"Small wonder Miss Clo calls you a strumpet," Sylvia said then.

"What she call you, her bootlicker?"

"I am nobody's bootlicker."

"Well then, you and me got a lot in common. We both pleasing to the eye and now we both know how it feel to be called something we not."

Sylvia flinched when Nevada said she was pleasing to the eye. She thought her smarts and her sincerity her best qualities, not her looks. She was oak-toned of complexion with a pouty mouth and polite nose and slender build. She had a wide smile that opened her lean face and rounded the severity of her cheekbones. She was often complimented on her smile. Still, she thought her appearance average; certainly didn't think herself pretty like Nevada was pretty in the way that grabbed men by the collar and said keep your eyes peeled on me Mister Sir.

"Why you knock on my grandma's door with your dinging mess?" Nevada squinted her eyes at Sylvia. "What it to you whether I know Seafus or not?"

Sylvia looked away, looked at the window frame that was rotting around the sides, thought it just a matter of time before the window fell completely from its casing. Felt sorry for them that they lived in such a house. Hated that she was so quick to feel sorry for people. Feeling sorry for the hungry look on Clo's face that had gotten her in this imbecilic situation. Thought back to the way Tom Benin's hand had trembled the day before when he'd asked about Meda and then had to steady himself on Dr. Miss's desk, and how she'd felt sorry for him. She shook the feeling now, met Nevada's glare, and returned it. "Actually, I don't give a crow's caw who you know."

"Then why you show up here?"

"I'll tell you why." Sylvia decided she owed no allegiance to Clo. "Clo lives next door to me and she helped my parents years ago and used to keep me for them so that they could travel overnights to their catering jobs, and I guess she thinks that gives her the right to persuade me to lure you out of your house so she can talk to you, and she was only able to persuade me because I am tired, I am distraught over the president, and I just put in hours at a place where the work tugs at my heart." She stopped herself. "I don't know why I knocked on your door. All I know for certain is that Miss Clo is hiding down at the corner and waiting for me to bring you down there, likely to whip your hide."

"So why you spilling the beans?"

"In truth, I do not know why about that, either."

"Look, Sylvia," Nevada said then, "I am not really studying Seafus in that way, he much too old."

"Well then, why do you give him the time of day?"

" 'Cause he spends nice on me, that's why. And I'm up north trying to help my grandmother. She not able to work as she once could. She got this malady that you just privy to that spur her into fits of laughter that she cain't stop herself of. It get worse as she's get older and the lady she work for tired of it and cut her hours and her pay and I'm up here to work in her stead, and they pay me half of what they did my grandmother, so she still lacking."

"So I'm supposed to cry for you and your grandmother? For all I know you could be gumming me."

"One thing you must know about me, Sylvia, I don't dwell in the dung from a hog or a cow or ox or no other mammal whether it got four legs or two. I confess to letting a already-spoken-for old man like Seafus whisper in my ear and press a quarter in my palm, but I do not want that man for keeps. Furthermore, his wife got the duty to keep him home. I aren't paid to do her duty. Now you can signal her to come on down here if you want, but my grandmom keep a pouch full of lye ready to throw. And you can catch a weasel sleeping 'fore you can find me where I cain't land a punch in my own defense." Nevada stood up taller, squared her shoulders. "So if she coming down here, I hope she got more than you with her if she think she winning the battle for my, pardon my wording, Sylvia, 'cause you seem proper and all, but, for my ass."

Sylvia's mouth flew open. Shocked that Nevada would let such a word pass through her lips, on a Sunday no less, an Easter Sunday, an Easter Sunday when all were mourning the president.

35

"That right, I said it, *ass.*" Nevada repeated it.

Sylvia squared her shoulders, too. "Number one, it would just be Clo. Knocking on your grandmother's door is one thing, but I am not looking to fight on Clo's behalf. And number two, you not so special 'cause you can speak the word 'ass' out loud. I can as well. Ass, ass, ass." Sylvia didn't know what it was about this sudden use of profanity that felt so good. But she could feel her whole chest opening as she repeated the word. Felt almost giddy. Wondered if she was on the verge of a breakdown.

"Hmn," Nevada said, pursing her lips, trying to keep a smile from showing. "Well, in that case, my grandmother got cabbage and cornbread hot and ready to serve. You welcome to some. Just know I am not trying to pay you off. Just being polite."

"Well, I am just being polite in accepting," Sylvia said. "Not as if I am trying to be your friend."

"Suit yourself. But if you was my friend, I sure wouldn't have you putting yourself in harm's way for some no-count man."

"And if you were my friend, you would have enough sense not to be spooning with a man married to the likes of Clo."

Nevada sucked the air in through her

teeth and ushered Sylvia in, and Sylvia ended up staying the better part of the afternoon. They bickered back and forth over cornbread and coffee — Sylvia declined the cabbage. In between, Nevada told Sylvia uproarious stories about Seafus and several other men she'd come to know. Sylvia was doubled over she laughed so hard. Then Nevada asked Sylvia what kind of work she did that tugged at her heart.

"I put in hours at a midwife's establishment. We lost a baby yesterday."

"Awl," Nevada said. "Sorry to hear it."

Sylvia shrugged. "I'll be well enough about it."

"Really? Look to me like a good cry is in order."

"Well, that proves you don't know half of what think you do," Sylvia said. Then she did cry. It was a continuous cry. She made loud hawking sounds that overrode the noise of Miss Ma's intermittent laughter bursts coming from the other room.

Nevada spooned up a bowl of cabbage and set it in front of Sylvia. "My grandmother puts a secret ingredient in her cabbage known to heal a broken heart. She made a extra good amount on account of the president's death and done already sent it up and down the block. No harm in sampling it."

Sylvia took just a forkful, and shortly she was slurping it down. It was warm and slick, soothing. Nevada had started on another story about another man, and Sylvia sat back and braced herself for the laughter waiting to come.

3

A week and a day after Meda gave birth, the same day that the president's casket was slated to arrive in Philadelphia, Dr. Miss declared Meda well enough to leave. Meda presented Sylvia with a parting gift, a sketch of the president wearing a playful face, winking his eye. Sylvia was impressed; Meda could tell, as Sylvia giggled and asked Meda why she chose to render him in such a way.

"Because he is my father," Meda said.

"Ma'am?" Sylvia said, thinking she'd not heard her correctly as she looked at Meda standing there in her crisp frock, her hair pulled back in a neat bun; how pretty she was was more apparent now as her face had begun to recover from the changes pregnancy brings about; her pert nose no longer stretched wider across her face, the splotches erased from under her eyes, her eyes big and dark and innocent like a doll baby's eyes. Her posture, like her speech, was of the girls who'd been to finishing school, though Sylvia had learned during their talks the past week that Meda had been educated by the Quakers, as her mother worked for them, cleaning penitentiary cells. She appeared perfectly sane standing there, and yet she'd just made an outrageous claim.

"I served him tea when he was in Philadelphia for the Sanitary Fair June past," Meda said to Sylvia's confused expression. "His ill-tempered wife had just yelled at him in the most horrid way and brought him to tears. I sat with him and he talked with me and it calmed him. He called me Daughter, said that if he could have been so graced to have had a daughter, he would have hoped that she would have had my comportment. And I thought that perhaps I am his daughter."

"But what makes you think perhaps?"

Meda turned to look at the picture of Abraham Lincoln hanging over the mantel that had helped her as she'd pushed her baby into the world. She didn't try to explain to Sylvia how, when she'd asked her mother who her father was, her mother told her, "Pick a one; pick a good one and just say he be the one." And over the years, when Meda would relay her choice of a father,

40

her mother most always grimaced. But just before her mother died, Meda told her that she'd chosen Mr. Lincoln for her father. "Say so? Hear tell he got some black in 'im," her mother had said, and then she blushed. Meda thought it the blush of a woman smitten. She wondered about the blush, the possibility the blush suggested. Allowed the possibility to settle in, thinking who could know for sure anyhow.

She said that to Sylvia's confused expression now. "Because of the way things are, Sylvia, who can know for sure?" She watched the confusion on Sylvia's face slowly dissipate. Meda knew Sylvia would understand, she was a smart one. Meda, thinking now that had her baby lived, she would have given a similar reply when the question of a father came up: pick a one, pick a good one.

Sylvia did a half-curtsy. "I shall cherish this sketching always, Miss Meda. It will bring me comfort in these longs days that we must suffer through without President Lincoln, to know that there was such a playful side to him, and that you had the privilege of serving him tea."

Sylvia hugged Meda then, and helped her into her cape and saw her through the door into the April air that was unseasonably warm.

The air was still warm and smelled of horse manure and sweet corn outside of Independence Hall, where Meda stood. Church bells rang and clashed. A cannon pulled rank with its gusty boom. Soldiers stood in formation. And under a black and silver sky that matched the casket going in, men in well-cut suits with vest-pocket timepieces gathered to view Abraham Lincoln's remains. The mayor had set aside the hours of ten in the evening till one in the morning for the city's elite to spend time with the corpse among only themselves. The presence of the soldiers held the everyday people at bay. But Meda was determined to get in, too.

This would be her only chance, as she'd just learned that Tom Benin had loaned her out for the next two weeks to an orphanage for poor white boys as part of his charitable contributions. If she would have a turn at viewing the president's remains, she'd have to figure out a means to wrestle the time away. So she proposed arriving at the orphanage that night instead of in the morning to get a jump on whatever her duties there would be, and when Tom Benin agreed, she'd taken a detour to finagle her way into Independence Hall.

She surveyed the line and tried to keep her emotions in check: partly she felt rage at this assemblage of rich white men getting exclusive time with the fallen president who'd preached equality; partly she felt grief over the sagging void where his sense of fairness had once lived and breathed; partly she felt the thunderous pressure in her breasts as if her monthly curse had come on like a cloudburst, except that it wasn't her monthly curse, it was just her breasts that ached as if all the hurt she'd ever known in her nineteen years had crowded there for an uprising that pulsed and squeezed. She pictured her hands reaching through the darkness in Dr. Miss's procedure room, reaching for her baby.

She managed through the boisterous crowds of mourners into the exclusive area where invitation-holders waited more patiently. She advanced through the line by cutting in and saying, "Beg your pardon, need to get an urgent message to the mister," over and over, like a chant until she arrived at the archway into the hall and a blue-sleeved arm came out and blocked her progression.

"Who would that be?" the man asked her, as he puffed his breath in her face, and she felt as if she'd been slapped.

"Mr. Tom Benin," she said, struggling to keep her temper in check. She looked up at his lips, which appeared to move in slow motion. She balled her fists and thought what a great relief it would be to land one in his mouth, thought that such a move might even help ease the pain and pressure that she felt deep in her breasts, but she had the elegant posture of a ballerina and knew she'd damage herself more than him, so she unfurled her hands and played along.

"Point this Mr. Tom Benin out to me," he said, and Meda looked up and down the line and each man appeared to be an exact replica of the one in front, the one behind, the one in conversation with the one adjacent. It was as if the bowels of the earth had opened in an extended torturous labor and pushed out him after identical white him, fully formed and dressed for this occasion.

"I cannot say exactly where he is."

"Well, then I cannot exactly let you in now, can I?"

"You could if you so choose." She stopped herself and coughed lest she call him a devil's bastard. She looked down. "His wife has taken ill," she half-whispered.

"Let the girl in, for blazing sakes," someone called from behind them. "Or move it

44

to the side. You're holding the rest of us up now."

He twitched his nose and then pulled Meda from the line and into the grand hall where the Declaration of Independence had been signed. She'd been in here once before when the Quaker women who'd schooled the colored children of those hired to clean the penitentiary brought them here to allow them to touch for themselves the crack in the Liberty Bell. The air was markedly cooler and smelled of bergamot, from the men's eau de cologne, and wet cowhide. Orchestral sounds of sad, slow hymns rippled just above her head as they walked next to the line and the blue arm cautioned Meda that should she be unable to point out Tom Benin, he would see that she spent the night in jail for committing perjury to an officer of the court, such as he was. "Yes-suh," she said, although she had no intention of pointing out Benin; she hoped he'd already come and gone. She just wanted to get close enough to look on Mr. Lincoln's face, was all. She knew that face by heart. She'd seen the president up close once and had memorized every detail of his face down to the mole on his cheek. She'd dreamt of him afterward and filled pages upon pages of parchment with her sketched renderings.

She was almost at the front of the line when she heard Tom Benin call her name the way he'd always say it, with a question at the end. He never barked at her the way his wife sometimes did, though his tone was more grating because it gave her the illusion that she had a choice. Meda? Please tell them to ready the carriage, or Meda? Please deliver my boots to be shined, or Meda? Mrs. Benin is under the weather and asked me to relay that she declines her evening snack. Meda? Meda? Meda? and she'd want to shout at him, just declare my name, please, do not give it the shape of a question when we both know that you are spouting directives, not options.

She walked toward the space where her name still dangled in the air, the rise at the end of her name. "Mr. Benin," she said as the blue arm that had dictated her path retreated in exchange for the blue of Tom Benin's eyes that stared at her straight on. He was near to the spot where the men stopped to allow the one in front a few seconds alone at the president's side, and Meda went and stood next to him.

"Meda? Has something happened? Is that why you are here?" His whispered voice was urgent.

46

"Yes, sir, something has happened."

"And that would be? Meda? Has something gone wrong with Mrs. Benin?"

"No, sir, not Mrs. Benin," she said, slowly, hoping to drag out this back and forth with him until the white-gloved soldiers standing stoic at the foot and the head of the black and silver casket motioned that it was Benin's turn, which one now did, and Meda seized it as her turn, too.

And just like that she was looking down on the president and she gasped at how lifelike he appeared, as if he were still breathing. She blinked back tears as she studied his features and could see that his eyes remained sealed, not a quiver anywhere in his long frame. His face looked exactly as she remembered it except that he was darker now, dark the way she'd made him when she'd colored in her rendition of him on the parchment paper. Especially around one cheek, a spot on his forehead. She sobbed openly now, "Poor Mr. President, I am sorry, so sorry."

Tom Benin had already moved along. Muttered rumblings of complaint pushed into the small of Meda's back. She ignored them and focused on the orchestral "Bread of Heaven" hymn that fell over her like rain. They were at the part that says "feed me till

I want no more." She felt a warm wetness spread out along the front of her frock, and she wasn't sure if it was from her tears or if her breasts had been unable to contain all the hurt gathered there and just overflowed like a cresting gully. It was her breasts spilling over, she could tell. She pulled her shawl closer around her to hide the deepening stain, then felt a gentle tug on her arm and looked up. A tall soldier leaned toward her. "Ma'am," he said. In all of her nineteen years she could count the other times, precisely, when she'd been called "ma'am" by a white man. Exactly once. When she'd met the president, before he'd called her Daughter, he had called her ma'am. The soldier extended his gloved hand. "May I see you out?"

He had one glass eye and one real one. The real one was a dusky gray and seemed to twinkle, and she wondered if he'd known President Lincoln in life; he seemed the type the president would have wanted to have around him. She took his hand, and with her other hand clutched her shawl to cover the place on her frock where her breasts had leaked their fullness. She didn't know which was warmer, the feel of his hand through his glove, or the wetness settling against her chest.

She exited through a side door into a near riotous bedlam as Philadelphians of every stripe — save the moneyed, who were being allowed into the hall — shouted and cursed and threatened to storm the cordon of soldiers and police. She didn't even look around for Tom Benin; she knew that such a scene would have rankled him and that by now he had hurried into his carriage and was halfway to his Germantown mansion. She was relieved that she didn't have to go back there tonight. Her hand still tingled from where the soldier had held it, and she wondered if he had been with the president's body on the train and through all the cities, wondered if, as a result, he'd caught a bit of Mr. Lincoln's spirit as it flew away, wondered if he'd transferred it to her through the gloved hand. She started walking in the direction of the orphanage.

4

By the time Meda reached the orphanage she had decided that she would not be cleaning ash from beneath a dirty stove, or hard-rubbing muslin shirts up and down a washboard, or beating mites from a braided rug. She didn't even clean at the Benins', beyond a little light dusting, and turning down their beds. She was more their personal help: taking dictation for Mrs. Benin's notes, keeping their clothing in good order, preparing their breakfast and lunch and snacks, as they had a special cook for dinners. No, she certainly was not doing any heavy cleaning here. Besides, she was in mourning, she told herself as she stood in the foyer with the house matron. She introduced herself to the woman and apologized profusely for waking her — the matron, a woman much younger than Meda expected, was in her nightcap and sleeping gown, with a shawl pulled over her shoulders. She

50

began ticking off a list of tasks for Meda which included cleaning the badly coal-stained foyer floor. She was in the process of explaining that many of the regular cleaning chores had lately gone undone, when she was interrupted by the appearance of a squat woman with a red nose and large ears who ambled into the foyer. "Not another wit a infant, Ann," she said in a brogue so thick that at first Meda could not even understand her. "Please yer know hardly can carry along wit the two new we got." Ann shook her head, said no more babies, and the woman disappeared, as Meda's ears perked at the mention of the infants.

Meda decided then that she would claim her own duties here, which would be nothing but tending to the infants. She looked up and caught the matron's eyes so there would be no mistaking her position. "Mr. Benin said that he had on good authority from one of your benefactors that you just took in several babies, and now she's just said the identical thing, so his instructions were correct" — she paused and swallowed — "that I was to come here to help with the caretaking of the babies, especially tomorrow, to give you and the others leave to view the poor dead president." She pulled her cloak closer around her with a snapping motion. Then she looked down, lest the woman detect she was lying; she stared at the floor and traced the outline of the worst stain.

"Two newborn, just two," the matron said, and Meda noted that her tone was not harsh, and she had not flinched when Meda looked at her directly the way that some white women did. In fact, as Meda glanced at her now, she saw her face soften, as if she was further inviting Meda's gaze. "An infant arrived last week," she said. "The other two days ago. But there's a host of other duties for you to undertake."

"Yes, ma'am, I understand. And if that be your position, and again, I understand if it is, but still I 'spect I'll endeavor to find my way back to the Germantown mansion, seeing as how Mr. Benin was direct about my undertakings while I'm here, and being acquainted with him as I am, I know he does not suffer lightly the misappropriations of his charities." Meda had not censored her word choices as she suspected this woman was the rebellious type, likely an abolitionist, likely fighting for women to be allowed to cast a vote; the type of woman who would not be put off by her learned speech. She braced herself for her verdict.

"Ah, does he not?" the matron said on a laugh as if the notion amused her. She pulled her sleeping cap from her head and let her hair tumble out. It was dark and thick and suited her eyes, which were likewise dark, and Meda thought her a pretty woman, tall and lithe.

"But you should know that we do not spend a lot of time rocking the babies."

"I understand, certainly," Meda said, sensing victory. "But they surely need much more than rocking."

"And Tom Benin's charity aside — and I certainly do not begrudge it — what those newborns really need is a wet nurse."

"Well, no offense to him, ma'am, but since he is of the male persuasion, he likely thinks that any of my kind might be capable of performing those duties at the drop of a crumb as if we are a sort of cow. Those men are most intelligent, even as they are so ignorant of certain things it befuddles a lady's brain." She watched a smile form at the corners of the matron's mouth, and so she took full advantage. "I have maintained since I was old enough to understand that if gentlewomen ruled the world it would be a more satisfactory place."

"I am inclined to agree," the matron said, "though we would no longer be gentlewomen if we were to try to keep the boorish men in line." She allowed a complete smile to open up her face, though her face was long and slender like the rest of her. She asked Meda her name, and told her hers was Ann.

Meda curtsied. "A pleasure to meet you, Miss Ann."

"Just Ann will suffice," she said as she showed Meda where to hang her bonnet and her cloak and shawl and pointed out the lay of the house: the older boys slept on the third floor on mats; the ones not yet ten years old were crammed into the largest room on the second floor. And the parlor on the main floor, where Meda would stay, was saved for the infants, since it was the easiest room to keep warm and just steps from the kitchen, where their food was. Ann extended her arm, directing Meda into the parlor, though she herself paused at the threshold. "I myself try not to get too attached at this age, because often they do not make it to six weeks, which is why I personally do not rock them, or even hold them."

Meda nodded. "How are they being fed?"

"I'm told that the blue-eyed one has a fairly steady appetite and takes the feeding bottle without complaint. The dark-eyed one is more difficult to satisfy, he wakes more often, has a more cantankerous nature."

"Well, they both seem to be sound sleepers right about now," Meda said, as she held herself back from peering into the cradles. She looked at the fainting couch instead. An expression of longing, she guessed, attached itself to her face at that moment because Ann told her to help herself to a seat.

"Do they have names?" Meda asked, not moving. She wouldn't risk ruining the connection she'd made with Ann by sitting while Ann was still standing.

"They've not been assigned names yet."

"Any knowledge of who their parents were?"

Ann lowered her head, and her voice, as if the babies could hear and understand, and told Meda that one of the babies was found by a constable trying to nab a tax cheat. The constable had hid in an alley where river rats nested and heard the gasping cries of the hours-old baby. Thinking it a rat, he reached for his billy club and in the process dropped his lamp, and that illuminated the baby's face, which was still shrouded in placenta.

Meda placed her hand to her mouth, horrified. "I know," Ann said. "It is difficult to imagine. The other at least came hand-delivered and swaddled the way a newborn ought to be."

Meda wanted to ask who had delivered them, but she did not press. It was not as if one or the other was her child. Her baby died. And anyhow, her baby had been a girl. She did, however, ask Ann if names for the boys should occur to her was she free to call them such.

Ann told her to take the liberty to call them what she wished. She would adjust the notations in the log to reflect whatever names Meda selected. She backed out of the parlor doorway, saying that since it was well past midnight, she'd need to get at least some sleep before venturing out to pay respects to the president, and that Meda would find the feeding apparatus in the kitchen; and as for herself, she could use the couch for her bed.

And just like that, Meda was alone with the silent breaths of the newborns, which smelled sweet and sour like half-curdled cream. She pulled back the thick, knotty drapes to let in the silver starlight. She wanted to laugh out loud that she'd actually maneuvered time off from cleaning this house. She started moving toward the fainting couch, but one of the infants was beginning to stir and the cradle made tapping sounds, and then she could hear the screeches coming from the back of the baby's throat that cut through the air and made her chest hurt. She went to the cradle and lifted him up. As Ann had foretold, it was the dark-eyed boy. She held him at arm's length as he tried to twist himself into the shape of a ball. "You got eyes like Mr. Lincoln," she whispered. "That's what I'ma name you — Lincoln." She pulled him in closer and let him rest against her arm as she walked to the other cradle and peeked in. The other baby was still as death and she leaned her face in to make sure he was breathing. "You not too bad-looking yourself," she cooed into the cradle. "Fact is, you kinda pleasant-looking. I'ma call you Abraham." The one she'd just named Lincoln was moving spastically and pushing his fist into his mouth, and Meda began unbuttoning her frock at the top and went to the fainting couch. She finally sat. This sit felt so good, as if she'd gone to Heaven and was sitting with Jesus, except that Lincoln had worked up a cry that was shaped like a twister. She'd completely undone her frock at the top and now she reached in and down and lifted out her breast and touched it to Lincoln's cheek. He turned his head with such a ferocity that it made Meda giggle. He clamped down and sucked hard. Meda winced at the initial stab of pain that cried in her breasts, and then the aha, the relief, the sweet, sweet relief as this baby drank and drank. "You a hungry something, aren't you, Lincoln?" she whispered as she covered the soft spot on his head with the flap of her frock. She cuddled him even closer as the black and silver air tunneled in through the window, and Lincoln took her milk until he was satisfied and then fell asleep against her breast.

5

After Meda left Dr. Miss's and finagled her way into Independence Hall and cried over the president's corpse and her breasts leaked — after she made her way to the orphanage and configured her chores there to tending exclusively to the newborns — she came to understand the meaning of the phrase "peace that passes all understanding." She should have been raging over her twin tragedies — the president's death and the loss of her own newborn — but instead she felt an astounding sense of peace, velvet-smooth and deep as she fed the babies and rocked them and hummed and sang to them. She even felt giddy at times when she laughed at the sound of their burps, or at the contorted face one or the other made. She shortened the names she'd given them, Lincoln and Abraham, to Linc and Bram, and she enjoyed the feel of their names cooing off her tongue.

On the morning a few days before her last day at the orphanage, Meda and Ann were having tea in the foyer right off of the parlor, as they'd done daily since Meda's arrival. Ann still refused to walk all the way into the parlor and had confessed to Meda that infants did not take to her, such that she avoided their closeness at all costs. Meda pressed Ann to explain, and Ann told her that whenever she'd attempted to care for the infants placed there, the babies died shortly after. It had happened on three separate occasions, and she held herself responsible for their demise, said that she was a type of infant bad-luck charm. Meda told her that could never be true, that she sensed her goodness, and was sure those babies had as well, that Ann had likely sweetened their brief time on earth. Meda thought that she'd actually seen Ann blush when she said that, though Ann was not the blushing type.

Meda appreciated their interruptions for tea, appreciated Ann's quick sense of humor, her relaxed manner, the way she'd pull off her cap and unpin her hair and let it fall, and had encouraged Meda to remove her cap, and also her top frock if she chose because why must they always be so layered and constrained. She'd train her eyes on

Meda and listen intently to what Meda was saying as if Meda was the most important person in the world. Meda told her things then. Told her how she'd once served the president tea, even describing the gold-flecked draperies in his hotel suite; though she'd held back her belief that Lincoln had fathered her — or her hope, sometimes she confused the two. She did tell Ann about her brother, Buddy, whom she loved dearly but who ran card games in his living room and had had the same opportunity as she had to be schooled by the Quakers, but his only desire for education was to learn his numbers so that he could better count his playing cards. Ann had laughed, said their brothers might be related, because Buddy sounded like her brother in Connecticut.

The house was at its quiet time as they sipped their tea. The older boys were at their lessons, the younger ones down for their naps, the aides out of the house doing afternoon errands. And after they chatted about Ann's women's rights meeting the night before, Ann suggested that Meda request of Mr. Benin that she be allowed to stay on for an additional month, and when she did leave, that she be allowed to take the babies with her to be raised in the Benin household.

Meda laughed. "Benin would never allow such a thing, and even if he did, his wife would protest."

"Why should he not allow it? Does he not owe you?"

Meda put her teacup on the half-moon table lest she splatter it. Though Ann asked the question in a matter-of-fact way, her tone had a knowingness to it that made Meda's hands go to ice. "Owe me in what way, Ann?"

"Well, Meda, the day before, as we sat here and the baby cried and you rushed into the parlor to feed him, I noted that both feeding bottles were in the kitchen, all cleaned up and ready for use, and I concluded that you had recently given birth."

Meda looked away. Though she'd been careful to nurse in secret, and only had to nurse Linc, the finicky dark-eyed baby, because Bram had a calmer nature and took the feeding bottle with ease, she had in fact erred by leaving the readied bottles in the kitchen. "It was recent," she said, surprised at how relieved she'd felt saying it. "She did not live long after she was born."

"Really? A daughter?" Ann's voice rose as a stream of surprise hung on her words, even as she squeezed Meda's hand, and then whispered, "Needed in Heaven, I'd say, to make Heaven a sweeter place."

Meda nodded and tightened herself against the wave of grief rolling in, then asked Ann why was she surprised that it had been a girl.

"I had a theory," Ann said, as she retrieved the teapot from the half-moon table and refilled Meda's cup, and then her own. "Part of it was that you had recently given birth, which you have confirmed. Part of it was that Benin was the father, which you have not said, but which I have figured out regardless —"

"Benin? The father?" Meda cut her off.

"Well, *is* he?" Ann asked it with an insistent tone, even as her eyes went soft the way Meda always felt Ann's eyes go soft when she looked at her.

"What makes you think that he is?" Meda asked, stalling, not ready to admit to having lain with Benin because the shame was so large. If she just resisted more when she heard the grunt of air as he pushed open her bedroom door, and the shriek of air as he called her name with a question; if she just searched herself more to determine what it was about her that invited it; if she could just figure that out, she could change that thing about herself and he would leave her alone.

"He has sent messages daily asking about you . . ."

"And from that you claim to discern that I, I — for goodness sakes, I am part of his household staff, of course he would inquire —"

"And besides that, we had never before benefited from his benevolence."

"He prides himself on his charity, he has lists of causes that he —"

"I am sure he does. And perhaps we may have eventually landed on his list as well. But not in such a haphazard way. These things are usually handled in a more formal way. I mean, Benin actually showed up here."

Meda's mouth dropped. "Showed up here? When?"

"Earlier in the day before you arrived. He and his fine carriage and beautiful horses and ostentatious pocketwatch. I only noticed the watch because everything else about him was so refined and the watch was out of place and he kept pulling it out and looking at it and my thought was if time is that much of a concern, why are you here? Why not send a messenger? And he seemed to read my mind because he got straight to the point and asked if we had infants in our care."

Meda clasped her hands in her lap lest they start shaking.

"He said he wanted to make a donation in honor of our slain president," Ann continued, "but he wanted to know that boys who may have lost fathers fighting for the Union would be the beneficiaries. I stretched the truth and told him that we'd just taken in two infants who'd lost fathers in the war. That's when he asked to see them and I pointed him to the parlor, and he actually walked in. And then he said that his help would arrive the next day in the form of his best employee. That he could allow her here for two weeks. And I told him plainly, 'Mr. Benin, we do appreciate you sending your help, but we could also use support in the form of funds,' and I proceeded to list for him our major needs, including a new water pump. Shortly he sent over a considerable donation, which is why we now have running water and all of the boys are in new shoes. And later that night you arrived, Meda. You carried yourself with such grace. But there was an undeniable aura of grief that hung over you."

She paused and set her teacup on the half-moon table next to Meda's cup. Meda took in her expression as she waited for her to continue. Ann's hair was swept behind her ear on one side; the other side hung along her face and practically hid her eye. Her head was tilted and her face, which generally seemed ready for laughter, had a pointed intensity about it. "I pondered the cause for your broken heart. I know now the cause since you have told me that you recently lost your newborn. And I think I have correctly put it together that Benin fathered your child. But the last part of my theory has gone awry as I thought that one of those babies in the parlor was actually the one you bore, since Benin took an interest in looking at them, but you have told me that it was a girl" — she whispered the word "girl" — "who is now a beautiful angel. So I rather speculate that Benin simply searched out an orphanage serving infants. And sending you here to care for them was merely his fumbling attempt to clear his conscience of his unconscionable behavior that left you bearing his child."

Meda looked at the coal-stained floor, at the half-moon table where their teacups touched each other at the rims, then she looked at Ann. Ann had pushed her hair back from her face. Her dark eyes drank in Meda's presence, and Meda knew that it would be impossible to deny what Ann had already reasoned.

"He did not expect a living, breathing baby to be the outcome," Meda said in a voice that trembled, and Ann took both of Meda's hands in her own and squeezed them. "He accompanied me to the midwife thinking the midwife could just wash things away. She is apparently known in his circles for doing such things. But I had hid it the whole while, and I was much too far along. I suppose my hope was that once I had the baby, and held it, that other options would appear. But that was not to be."

"Aha, that explains his urgency," Ann said. "He had not been prepared for the result. I still think the man is a reprehensible boor, but perhaps slightly less so now, since at least he did a favorable thing in sending you here. He knew that caring for the babies would ease the pain of your loss a bit."

Meda nodded as she thought about Linc and Bram, what a beautiful distraction they had proved. "I have gotten quite attached to them."

"And not to me?" Ann asked

Meda felt her heart race. She looked away, looked down again at the coal-stained floor. There opened a gaping silence between them, and after what felt like a decade, Meda sputtered, "Uh, well yes, you, Ann, yes, the babies and you." She felt dizzy, first as the words left her mouth, then from the heat of Ann's body as Ann leaned in and propped her hand under Meda's chin and tilted it up so that they were eye-to-eye. She moved her face in so close to Meda's that Meda could almost taste the tea clinging to Ann's breath, which smelled of ginger and berries. "I was hoping it was me also that you got attached to," Ann whispered.

Ann kissed her then. It was a soft, insistent kiss that lingered. Meda thought that she might cry that this woman was kissing her mouth the way her mouth had only ever been kissed by a man. And the most recent man's kiss, Benin's, had made everything about her, even down to her essence, recoil. She didn't recoil, though, from the press of Ann's mouth; she was confused and also ashamed that she did not recoil. And then she felt something else beyond the confusion and shame. She didn't have a word for that something else, or maybe she didn't want to assign it a word because that would contain it, diminish it; she just knew that this wordless thing felt the opposite of confusion and shame. She pulled away. She covered her mouth as if her mouth was a naked part of her body caught exposed. "Uh, uh," she said, and then she jumped up.

"It's all right, Meda," Ann said. "I promise you it is."

Meda shook her hand loose. "The baby, I hear the baby," she said, as she ran into the parlor and closed the door.

Linc was still sleeping and Meda woke him to feed him. Then she woke Bram and fed him, too. She had to keep busy to shut down her complex web of feelings. She started making a list for the next person who would be charged with caring for Linc and Bram. She wrote that Bram had sensitive skin and should not be left in the sun for long. Linc's skin, on the other hand, gobbled up the sunlight. Bram liked to be left alone to fall asleep. Linc needed to be held closely and rocked first. She vacillated between compiling the list and thinking about Ann. Tried to shake off that feeling that had no name, telling herself that she was a human being, and a human being might have a hundred different feelings in the course of a day.

Linc was starting to make that scratchy sound that was a precursor to his cry. Meda didn't know why, she'd just fed him, dried him. She guessed he sensed that she would soon leave. She was certain that Linc would cry nonstop for her, that he would refuse to drink from that rubber tube. Bram would

69

fare better in her absence; Bram was easy, adaptable. But Linc was irascible. And though his nature charmed Meda, the next caretaker might not be so easily won over by him the way that Meda was; the next caretaker might just allow him to cry non-stop, might allow his needs to go unmet. She felt her eyes spill over. She laid the pen down and covered her face and sobbed into her hands. Her sobs grew in intensity and stretched to accommodate the grief over her own dead child that being here with Bram and Linc had assuaged some. Linc had worked himself up to a full-throttle cry. Meda remained where she was, sobbing in her hands. He needed to wait; needed to get accustomed to her absence. And she needed to get accustomed to his.

A tap on the door and Meda heard Ann calling her, projecting her voice over the sound of Linc's cries. Then Ann cracked open the door and peeped in and asked Meda if she could please enter. Meda sniffed, but otherwise did not reply, and Ann eased the door all the way open, walked all the way into the parlor, straight to the cradle where Linc was now hollering almost convulsively. "Is he fed? What is it?" Ann asked as she started to reach her hand into the cradle and then pulled her hand back as if she had stuck it into a flame. She pressed her eyes shut and leaned all the way in and lifted the baby awkwardly, holding him at arm's length — and his cries grew even louder.

"You can cuddle him," Meda said, as she dried her face and got up and walked to where they were. Ann's expression was so filled with terror that Meda had to keep herself from either grabbing the baby or hugging Ann. She settled on spreading a length of cotton over Ann's shoulder, and gently nudging Ann to bend her arms. Ann pulled Linc all the way to her chest, and there Linc rested and, just like that, sighed contentedly and settled down.

"Oh my goodness, will you look at that," Ann whispered excitedly. "He rather likes me holding him — don't you think?"

"I think he just desired the feel of your closeness," Meda said, looking away as she spoke, gazing out on the foyer where their teacups nestled together on the half-moon table. Deciding then that she would ask Tom Benin to allow her another month here.

6

As Ann had predicted, Tom Benin consented to the additional month. So Meda had time to begin to wean Linc, time to further grieve the loss of her own child. Time to find a word for that feeling that Ann had stirred up in her, that feeling that was too complex to name; it was wearing too many layers, each layer with its own row of buttons, each button difficult to undo. She'd unfastened them in stages: maybe while in the yard, stretching diapers across the line, and a breeze caught her face; or in the parlor, opening the thick drapes at night to let the moonlight in; or while hurrying back from the market stall with the milk that Bram preferred and sudden storm showers soaked her to her skin. She picked through the layers, gave them names — resistance, fear, agitation, excitement, esteem, affection. She'd not moved beyond affection.

Then, late one night, Ann tapped on the parlor door and invited Meda to join her in the foyer for tea. She was distraught because one of the boys had suffered a devastating fall during playtime at school. Ann had just left the hospital and said his condition was grave, that if the swelling in his brain did not go down, he would likely succumb. "They have endured so much at the start of their young lives to be without parents, to be so poor that they must rely on the charity of strangers such as we can amass here to give them at least a semblance of the innocence of childhood, and with all of that to then have a random tragedy such as this . . ."

"Sh, sh, sh," Meda said. She touched her finger to Ann's lips to quiet her as she watched the feeling finally conjure up a word. Desire. It had been there all along as a shimmery glaze over each of the layers Meda had heaped on, hoping to hide the word from herself. She pulled Ann into a hug, then pulled her all the way into the parlor. She was astounded now at the simplicity, the smoothness of desire as she at last allowed the feel of it against the bareness of her skin. She was simultaneously bold and timid: like a charmer, a vamp, powerful and seductive; like a shy girl just

73

needing softness, just afraid to ask, to accept. She'd never known she could be . . . what? Again there was no word, just a feeling she'd never known, of total release because how could she know it when from the time she was thirteen she'd had to keep it covered, keep it hid, because everything else was taken from her against her will, even her baby, and she believed that had she held her baby, she would have lived. But right now, here with Ann, Meda didn't have to protect her capacity to totally let herself go. For the first time in her life she was untethered, felt as if she were floating outside of herself, unmoored and glittering. If the parlor ceiling were not there she was sure she would have touched the tender ocean that was the night sky, and gone further still, until the shimmers came in waves, and then Meda reached out for Ann and held on.

When Meda's extended stay at the orphanage was approaching its end, they received word that Mrs. Benin had vehemently opposed any arrangement that allowed for the boys to take up residence in her house. Meda was not surprised. Benin's wife was a woman concerned with pedigree and would not have her home sullied on a full-time basis with almshouse orphans. Ann persuaded Meda not to accept that as the final word, insisting that in some particulars Meda had more sway over Benin than she realized, that Meda should use that power to her advantage. "In every instance once you return to that house —" Ann had said, and then she stopped herself and cringed as if the thought of Meda back at the Benins' pained her. And Meda promised her that she would.

So Meda posited to Benin that she spend Thursdays into Fridays at the orphanage, and then pack the babies up to stay with her at the Benin house over the weekends and extended holidays. She'd considered it a victory when Benin said no to Thursdays, but consented to the rest of the arrangement. She was able to further arrange her errands — she'd suggested a new milliner for Mrs. Benin, one that was closer to the orphanage, as well as a more convenient bootery and haberdasher — enabling her to procure time in between her work duties to check in on the boys. She managed time, too, to steal away with Ann, time that seemed to speed by in an instant, even as it seemed to stand still.

That first weekend back in the Benin house felt like Christmas to Meda as she made up

Linc and Bram's sleeping space in her bedroom. She had the best sleep she'd ever had in that house. Even though her sleep was interrupted when they cried to be fed, the air in the room was like velvet, as soft as their quiet breaths — the air not disturbed by her watching for the glass doorknob to turn. Tom Benin never made his way into her room when Bram and Linc were there. It was as if they were her protectors, especially Linc, who still woke more often with his fussy self, his dark eyes always open and shining, the sight of which made Meda giggle as she'd offer him milk. "Save some for your brother," she'd whisper. She'd decided then that they would be brothers. Even though their looks grew more opposite the older they were. Linc was dark-haired, dark-eyed with ruddy skin and hard-edged features that gave him a dramatic appearance. Bram was blond and freckled with a polite nose and thin lips and ocean-blue eyes. They were close. Babbled to each other before they could even talk; always aware of the other's presence; always looking around to know where the other was. And always looking for Meda.

When they were old enough to question how they could be brothers and only days apart in age, Meda concocted a fairy tale of a history. Explained to them that they'd been fathered by the same man whose young wife — Bram's mother — was with child when he deployed for battle in July of 1864. He'd taken cannon fire and was being cared for at the home of Union sympathizers and in his delirium mistook the young woman tending to him for his wife. He begged for her to lie down with him, and when she would not — Meda would allow her eyes to mist up at this point in the story — he wailed so plaintively that even the sparrows flocked to the bedroom window, wishing that they could stem his suffering. In the hours before he died, when she was cleaning his wound, she was so taken by the longing in his eyes that she could not deny him. And so, Meda said, as she'd stop as if trying to choke back sobs, he died peacefully that day, leaving another seed — Linc — who would become his second son. Both of their mothers, Meda told them, had died in childbirth.

She could not tell them the truth of their early hours, that one of them had been put out with the trash and almost mistaken for a river rat, and the other came from who-knows-where. So she'd imagined for Linc and Bram a history that they could latch on to, related that history to them over and over as they grew into young boys. Over time, she made that tall tale of a history so real for them that it became part of their fiber, and in the process, part of hers, too, understanding as she did the tragedy of a life with no history at all.

7

It had been two years since Sylvia ushered Meda's baby into the world and that image of the baby reaching for its mother still haunted her, lying dormant for months at a time and then emerging, rankling her. It helped that she stayed busy. Between school and hours with Dr. Miss and the social commitments that her mother insisted on, the teas and cotillions and gatherings sponsored by her mother's Ladies' Literary Society, her father's Pythian Baseball Club, her attendance at the grand wedding and anniversary affairs that her parents catered, she had little idle time. And when she did have time not otherwise spoken for, she'd visit with Nevada, to her mother's chagrin, because Maze didn't think Nevada had sufficient pedigree. But even Maze had to concede that Nevada's free-spirited nature might be good for Sylvia, who tended toward the serious. And their affection for each other was palpable. They were close and confiding one minute, sniping at each other the next; they were sisters, without the bloodline.

Right now Sylvia and Maze were in the yard, retrieving clothes from the line. Sylvia had just handed her mother the white gloves her father wore when he set up the tea service. Maze had just placed the gloves in the basket of the folded garb when she gasped and let the shirt Sylvia was handing her fall to the ground. Maze's brother, Mason, had just stumbled into the yard. He dangled a baby, a practical newborn, though to his credit he managed to support the infant's head. "You got to take her, Maze," he said, hysteria running through his voice. "Her mother's no good to her, no good at all."

"What — who — what the —" Maze matched his hysterics with her own. "Where did you get this child, Mason? Who's the mother?"

"Some ole gypsy gal I took up with over on Ridge Avenue. I swear it, Maze, she don't wanna do nothing but drink rye all day long. Liked to roll over on the baby and dern near crushed her. You gotta take her. Please, you gotta help me, just till her mother rights herself, or I figure summin

80

else out. Please, Sister, please."

Maze's first instinct, before she even considered the baby, was to comment on her brother's diction. She hated that he talked like those black people who'd recently migrated from the fields, even though he was Philadelphia-born and -raised. She'd taken special pride in the fact that the only dirt her hands pushed into was on this patch of backyard land that she and her husband owned that grew the flowers that filled her window planters out front and were the envy of the block. But this situation, with this baby, superseded even his cringe-worthy dialect. "Mason, you are insane," she said, hands on her hips, as Sylvia hunched her shoulders and gave her uncle a playful, you're-in-trouble-now look. Sylvia was mostly amused by her uncle, and by the ire he was so good at arousing in Maze. "I cannot just take in a baby," Maze continued.

"You godda, Maze. I swear to you, her momma tain't right in the head."

"First of all, there is no such word as 'tain't' used the way you just did. Secondly, Levi and I are preparing for a large job, and this infant certainly cannot join us, and Sylvia has her lessons, and her work with the midwife, which means we are not positioned to help you. We just cannot. How do I even know this child is your blood? Looks like a white child to me."

"Don't look at her coloring, Maze. Look at her features." He turned the baby so that her face was fully visible. "Say hello to your aunt Maze, Vergilina —"

"Vergi-*who?*"

"Vergilina Mayella," he gushed as he looked at the child and kissed her forehead.

"Leave it to you to come up with such a country name."

"Forget about the name, Sister, just look at her." He tried to thrust the infant into Maze's arms, but Maze kept her arms wrapped tight across her own chest. "You cain't deny she my flesh and blood," he persisted. "Means she yourn, too, Sister."

The baby flapped her legs and swayed and even in her new life seemed to be laughing. Maze could see that the baby and Sylvia had identical mouths, dark and full. The resemblance softened her, and she thought about what she would do. Only one thing she *could* do. She snatched the baby from her brother. She was careful not to let the newborn-scent catch her nose, because she knew that was such an irresistible scent and she might well jeopardize the catering job that was to be especially lucrative and instead stay here to hold and rock and feed and coddle this apparent niece of hers.

She quickly passed the baby to Sylvia. "She's yours," she said. "Until your daddy and I return. Perhaps Dr. Miss will allow her to accompany you during your hours there."

Sylvia took the baby as her uncle bolted from the yard and was halfway through the alley calling out "Thank you" and "Love you" as he went. She sat on the steps under the shirts still hanging on the line and rocked the baby and kissed her forehead and thought back to how old Meda's daughter would be now; two, she would be just about two years old. "She died. The baby died. She died." Sylvia repeated it to herself now, the way Dr. Miss had made her repeat it over and over until it became a truth that settled into her fiber the way it apparently had for Dr. Miss. As she sat on the steps now, swaying and rocking this newborn cousin, the drying shirts flapping back and forth in the morning breeze hiding the sun and then allowing its warmth to swipe against her forehead, she fought the urge to cry.

"New life will bring tears to your eyes," her mother said then. "You can go ahead and allow yourself to get attached. My sense

is that your uncle won't be returning anytime soon to permanently claim his child."

Sylvia did get attached. Spent every minute
of her time with Vergie when she wasn't
otherwise occupied with school, or work
with Dr. Miss, or the social obligations that
her mother insisted upon. Nevada visited
frequently, and she fell in love with Vergie,
too. Vergie's father popped in with regular-
ity, squeezing his hat between his hands as
he apologized for taking so long to work
things out. He'd toss Vergie in the air and
laugh at her squeals and plant a penny or
two in Sylvia's hands, promising more next
time, promising also to soon relieve her of
the burden of caring for his child — though
Vergie was far from a burden to Sylvia, with
her bouncy disposition and her wide smile.
She had a sass about her that amused Sylvia. Once Vergie learned to string words
together — earlier than most children —
Sylvia would have to chastise her for pub-
licly mocking people. But later, when she
was away from Vergie, she would remember
the way, for example, Vergie would pretend
to be Clo and plant her hand on her hip,
poke out her mouth, stretch her neck the
way a turtle does as she imitated the way
Clo called up and down the block when her

husband went missing. "Seafus! Seafus!" — her voice would rise with each incantation of the name — "now where that dern man done gone and went?" Sylvia would have to stem fits of laughter when she pictured Vergie's antics, especially if she was in class, where she'd dare not jeopardize her reputation as a stellar student.

There was a problem, though, with Vergie the older she grew: she hated her coloring. She was much lighter than Sylvia's mild honey shade; she was even lighter than Maze, who was a blend of yellow and tan. Her hair was thick but straight. "She got white — people hair," she'd heard so often that she would go into a tantrum, crying that she didn't want white people's hair, or white people's skin. She wanted pretty skin, like Sylvia. Her family often complained of their treatment by white people, and Vergie was afraid that one day her aunt and uncle and Sylvia would tire of her white skin and straight hair and put her out with the trash. She needed reassurance from Sylvia that such a thing wouldn't happen and would cry to Sylvia when she heard people whispering about how she looked. Sylvia would console her, tell her to ignore people when they said such things, that her family loved her just the way she was, and would love her even if she was polka dot. Vergie would laugh at that. Then Nevada would add that most of them teasing her were jealous because they wanted to look like her. "They the type that if they can't be white, they'd settle for mulatto. Want to be anything than what they are, which is colored. But you standing on a higher rung than most of 'em, Vergilina, 'cause you proud that you colored. So anybody try to tell you otherwise, you tell them that you got as much claim to the race as Blue-Black Bob." Vergie would ask who Blue-Black Bob was, and Nevada would say she'd never made his acquaintance but he had a heck of a name.

Vergie wanted to be with Sylvia all of the time. She'd try to follow behind her whenever she left the house. Sometimes crying for extended periods after, especially if she had to spend the time with Clo. Her consolation for Sylvia being away for extended times came when her father would show up to take her on week-long fishing trips on the banks of North Carolina, or Virginia Beach, or wherever his newest wealthy lady friend lived. She was in heaven then. Her other consolation came when she could stay with Nevada.

Nevada was a natural consideration to keep Vergie when Sylvia had to travel to

Boston on a three-day excursion with the Society for Negro Girls with Promise, when it coincided with an event Maze and Levi were putting on in Connecticut. Maze agreed to the arrangement, but with reluctance. Though Nevada had managed to endear herself to Maze — despite Nevada's reputation as a clam-buster — and Maze even gave in to allowing Sylvia to take Vergie onto Nevada's block, where there were known gambling houses and otherwise undesirables, she was apprehensive about Vergie spending an entire three days there. Plus, she wasn't at all fond of Nevada's grandmother. Not only was Miss Ma unchurched, Maze didn't want Vergie exposed to Miss Ma's uncouth ways: walking through the streets barefoot, her apron wrinkled, her hair not captured in a bun or braid, not even combed through, just out and wild. "Is she mute?" Maze had asked Sylvia once. "I saw her in the fabric store and she communicated more in sighs and grunts than she did with words." But Sylvia had assured her mother that Miss Ma was harmless; Nevada had been persuasive, too, promising a suitable list of activities for Vergie that included studying her musical scales.

Vergie's excitement was uncontainable.

She loved Nevada as if she were her aunt by blood, and she was fascinated by Miss Ma. She'd heard her aunt Maze say that Miss Ma had a mouth shaped like a pipe and Vergie would stare at her, waiting for hot ash to spew from her mouth. She especially looked forward to Miss Ma's fits of laughter, which formed an uninterrupted stream of sound and seemed to come from different places in her throat so that they reminded Vergie of the soprano section of the children's choir mixed with the off-key baritones. Vergie also liked that the laugh came with no provocation. Miss Ma would be sitting in her chair, hemming a petticoat, and out of nowhere would come the laugh, occasioned by whatever was going on in her head alone. Vergie would sit next to Miss Ma and laugh along with her, until Nevada called for Vergie to help snap peas, or practice words for the spelling bee, or have a dish of cream and berries. "Careful around my grandma," Nevada would caution. "She doesn't really like people."

On the final morning of her stay, Vergie woke to the sound of Miss Ma's laughter. She eased through the bedroom so as not to wake Nevada and followed the sound out to the backyard, where Miss Ma sat on the step, cutting a swath of burlap. The air had a cottony feel as Vergie squeezed in next to her on the step and Miss Ma's laughter hung unfinished in the air as she acknowledged Vergie with a grunt, though she did shift herself to allow Vergie room to sit. "What you cuttin'?" Vergie asked.

"What it look like I'm cuttin'?"

"Looks like a sack."

"Then why you askun if you know aready?"

"Why do you not like people?"

"Like some people."

"Do you like me?"

"Don' care much for white folk."

"I am not white."

"You look it."

"Well, you look mean."

"I *am* mean."

"Why?"

"Just made up that way."

"Well, I am not made up white," Vergie said, as she pulled at the ruffled hem of her night slip. "People ought not to say that about me."

Miss Ma turned to study Vergie, and Vergie thought that her face softened. At least her mouth wasn't as poked out as it usually was. "You got nits in your hair?" Miss Ma asked her.

"Ugh, no! Sylvia and Aunt Maze keep my

hair clean."

"Bet you gonna have nits. All white people get nits in they hair one time or nother, though a nit can't live on no colored scalp."

"Then they cannot live on mine," Vergie said with conviction. She folded her arms across her chest and pouted.

Miss Ma laid her scissors in her sewing basket on the next step down. "Lean your head in, lemme see." Vergie did and Miss Ma ran her hand through Vergie's hair to the scalp. "Now this sure do beat the drum, your hair sure is nappy at the roots. I guess you got some colored in you after all. Anybody call you white gal from here on, you just prove 'em wrong and show off the roots of your hair."

"I want to show off my roots all the time."

"Only way to do that is to cut all your hair off," she said as she reached into her sewing basket and pulled out a spool of thread and a thick embroidery needle.

Vergie eyed the scissors resting in the basket. "I wish my hair was cut all the way off."

"You talking crazy talk, you got a nice suit of hair, let it be. You cut it off, you end up looking like a bald-headed boy." Miss Ma concentrated on guiding the thread through the needle's eye.

"Not if I wear a dress. Could you cut it for me? Please, please, Miss Ma, could you cut my hair off? That way people will know I am really a little colored girl."

"Stupid people in the world," Miss Ma said as she licked the end of the thread and then pressed it between her fingers to close the fray. "Can't go cutting your hair off 'cause they wasn't born with sense. Further, I don want your siddity people gettin in my craw 'bout cutting your hair."

"I could cut it myself," Vergie said as she eased over to the other side of the steps, closer to where the scissors gleamed in the new morning air. "Could you teach me?"

"Nuttin' to teach. You either know how or don't. Main thing is keep your fingers out-nin the way."

Vergie touched the scissors and then pulled her hand back as if Miss Ma would strike her hand, but Miss Ma was concentrating on the thread; she'd managed to edge the tip just through the needle eye and she barely breathed as she worked her fingers to pull it all the way through. Vergie took full advantage of Miss Ma's absorption and reached in the sewing box and grabbed the scissors and darted into the crawl space under the steps. She sat on the ground. The dirt was soft and warm under her. Her hair hung around her shoulders in crinkled waves. She took a deep breath and pulled a fistful up and snipped it. She was surprised at how easily it separated as she watched it fall, much of it landing in the lap of her slip. She stretched out another section and cut at that. She moved through her hair, randomly cutting, imagining that when she was finished she'd finally look like the rest of her family and not have to worry about things happening to her like what had happened to her two weeks before.

She'd just returned from spending four wonderful days with her father on the Chesapeake, where her father's newest gal lived. Sylvia had planned that she and Vergie would spend the entire Saturday together to make up to Vergie for giving her practically no attention because Sylvia's schoolwork had demanded her unwavering focus of late. She dressed Vergie in her prettiest clothes, and Vergie was ebullient as they left the house in the carriage Nevada had arranged through her special friendship with a man who worked at Brown's Livery. They would start at the Haberdashery Fabric store, one of Vergie's favorite places owing to the way the bolts of fabric lined the shelves that seemed to stretch for miles. She'd simultaneously practice her numbers and colors as she walked from one end of the block-long store to the other, counting all the bolts that were red, then blue, then yellow. By the time she got to white, Sylvia was generally finished having the fabric she was purchasing measured and cut. But this day the store was abustle; the clerks were unusually slow; Vergie had gotten to the other end of the store for a third time and had to figure out a new color to count when a tall white man approached her. He was smiling and complimented her on her gloves. "They have a pink border," she said, proud that she had learned her colors so well. "They match the pink ribbons on my hat."

He asked her name and she told him, and then he asked her if her maid was treating her well today. She, thinking it a joke, laughed.

"Isn't the colored lady you are with your maid?" he said and stooped so that he was looking in her eyes.

"She is my cousin. Sylvia. I do not have a maid," she said, as if he were a silly boy who needed correcting.

"You do not? Well, a pretty lass like you deserves her own maid, you could come home with me and have a maid and a pony, and you could swim in the lake every morn-

93

ing because my house sits right on the lake."

"Where do you live?"

"I live in a place called Poughkeepsie."

Vergie giggled at the sound of the name.

"So what do you say? Would you like to visit Poughkeepsie? We could teach you to swim." He stood and held out his hand.

Vergie stared up at the man. Her father had already taught her to swim when he'd take her on fishing trips from the time she could walk. He had complimented her on her swimming just last week, complimented her generally on how proud he was of how smart she was getting. He'd said he admired how she was learning to call on her good senses, and that as she got older, and started moving around in the world without Sylvia or Maze or him to guide her, she would find times when she wouldn't know for sure which direction to tell her feet to carry her. When that day comes, he said, you just say, "Come on, good sense, show me the way." Vergie had laughed at the prospect of literally calling on her good sense like that, though she thought that's what she should do in that moment as the man whispered for her to take his hand so that they could sneak out of the side door. But then her good sense was clouded when he mentioned the pony again, and she asked him what was

94

the pony's name.

"Well, of course it doesn't have a name; it's waiting for you to give it a name when it belongs to only you. You may take it for walks and feed it blocks of sugar and brush its back and it will go 'Neigh, neigh, thank you, Vergie.' "

She gushed at the thought as he told her that the pony was right outside. "Do you want to meet it?" he asked. She looked down at the other end of the block-long store where Sylvia was awaiting her turn in line. "Your cousin will not even know you are gone," he said as Vergie allowed him to take her hand and pull her into the shock of the outside light. A carriage waited, and at first Vergie thought that it was the same carriage she and Sylvia had taken to get there. The horses were stamping their hooves as if saying "Hurry, we're past ready to run," and then Vergie realized that this wasn't her carriage, and she heard her good sense tell her to yank her hand away from this man and run back into the store. But it was too late as she felt herself swooped up into the air. She yelled and kicked, and people passing by stopped and turned in the direction of the commotion, but with the way Vergie was dressed this morning, in her high-society outfit, she appeared perfectly suited for this carriage, for this prosperously appointed man handing her over to a woman who opened the door to the carriage and stretched her hands out and grabbed Vergie, a woman in a wide-brimmed hat with pink feathers and a veil that seemed to match the pink fringes on Vergie's petticoat. The few people who had turned in the directions of Vergie's screams resumed their activities, counting Vergie as just another indulged little rich white girl resorting to her usual tactics to get her way and her parents were getting the response they deserved.

The husband was up on the box and the horses answered his commands and clopped away. The woman held on to Vergie with desperate arms as she pressed the little girl's head against her chest so hard and close that Vergie could smell the vanilla rising off her skin. "I am your mother now," she yelled over Vergie's screams.

"You are not! No you are not!" Vergie hollered back at her and managed to push her head far enough away from the woman's chest so that she could spit in her face.

The woman slapped Vergie with such force her nose began to bleed. "Yes, you are my daughter now, and you should be grateful I'm delivering you from a nigger's life."

Vergie continued to scream and holler and

she clawed at the woman's face and tried with everything in her to wrestle herself free. She felt like the caught fish last week that had struggled so long on the end of her father's pole for a much longer time than she thought it ever could. Her father had cut the line and let the fish fall back into the bay. He'd said that anything with that much will to live deserved another chance. She gasped and writhed as she had seen that fish do. She began to hyperventilate, and the woman yelled to her husband to stop. "She is turning blue."

"Well, calm her," her husband yelled back.

"She is too wild. Untamable. We have to let her go."

"After all of this, are you now saying let her go?"

"Please, yes, she is impossible. This is impossible."

He stopped the carriage and Vergie had already pushed the door open and was about to jump, not even caring how far it was to the ground, but before she could, he had caught her. "Are you bleeding? Why is she bleeding?" he asked as he put her down and reached into his pocket for a handkerchief. But Vergie had already taken off at a run. She ran and called for Sylvia. She wasn't even sure if she was headed toward the fabric store, but it was away from that carriage, so she continued to run. She heard someone call her name, it was Nevada's friend from Brown's Livery, whose carriage had brought them to the fabric store.

"What happened to you? Where is Sylvia?" he asked, as he leaned down and wiped the blood from her nose. She gasped. She could barely talk, she just cried and called out Sylvia's name. He picked her up and told her it was okay, he would take her to Sylvia. He asked again what had happened, how did she get a bloodied nose. "I fell" was all she said, when she could talk again. "I came outside to skip and I fell." She told the same thing to Sylvia, the same thing to her aunt Maze and uncle Levi, the same thing to Nevada, even to her father. "I came outside to skip, and I was skipping and skipping and I didn't know how far away I skipped, and I fell." Over and over she told that story because she was ashamed that she had been foolish enough to let a strange man lead her away from the fabric store, from Sylvia, from her life with her family. Ashamed, too, because she thought she'd caused the man to try and snatch her, something about the very essence of her was so flawed that a white man would just walk up to her and try to whisk her away. She didn't understand it as shame that day, didn't understand it as shame this morning as she sat in the dirt under the crawl space at Nevada's house and cut away at her hair. The shame had already begun to be covered up with anger. She was already showing a sassiness toward white people, resentment toward black people who thought her white, disgust toward anyone who treated her as if her appearance was some sort of gift. Already a whiff of vanilla, like the scent rising off of the woman's skin that day, caused her to vomit, such that Nevada had to withhold vanilla if she was baking cake when Vergie was over.

A heap of hair had accumulated on the dirt under the steps as Vergie continued cutting. She thought she must be getting close to her edges because she could feel patches of scalp. She heard Nevada calling her, Nevada's voice coming from deep in the house. Miss Ma's voice, too, as Miss Ma started with her high-pitched laughter. Vergie moved the scissors as quickly as she could. Now Nevada's voice could be heard shouting over Miss Ma's laughter. "Where is she, Ma? Look at me and tell me where she is."

Vergie responded to Nevada's frantic tone. "I am hiding from you under the steps," she said in a singsongy voice.

"You are, are you?" Vergie could hear the relief in Nevada's voice as Nevada matched the rhythm of Vergie's speech. "Well, come on now, time for us to make breakfast. You want to form the dough for the biscuits, don't you?"

Vergie emerged slowly from the crawl space. She stuck one leg out and then the other. The lap of her night slip was filled with hair and she shook it out as she maneuvered into the sunlight in the backyard. It seemed warmer suddenly, and even before she looked at Nevada she felt the change in the air; now it had an itchy feel, like the edges of the crinoline slip she'd had to wear for an entire day the past Easter as, it seemed, every child in the world gave a recitation about the Risen Lord.

"Here I am," Vergie said as she emerged fully from the crawl space and walked into the center of the yard.

There was a sharp intake of air from Nevada. It was so loud that it penetrated even Miss Ma's high-pitched laughter and left her suddenly quiet. Vergie looked from Nevada to Miss Ma to see if she could tell from their faces whether she'd done a good job getting to the roots of her hair. Their expressions were identical: frozen, horrified.

Vergie patted at her hair. There was a section across the front where practically no hair remained, but just next to that a thick clump, and then, beyond that, an irregular swath of scalp. The pattern repeated itself across her head and she thought that if she'd just had more time they wouldn't be staring at her now as if she were a monster. She thought about trying to finish the job but Nevada seemed to read her mind. "Give me the scissors, Vergilina," Nevada's shaky voice said.

Vergie handed Nevada the scissors, and when Miss Ma's laughter started anew, Vergie wondered if it was really laughter at all; maybe all this time those high-pitched sounds were actually Miss Ma crying. Nevada continued speechless as she stared at Vergie, and now she shook her head back and forth in disbelief. "Your hair, Vergilina. Dear God, your hair . . ." The yard felt suddenly dark, and Vergie ran to Nevada and wrapped her arms around her waist and pressed her head into her stomach. Then she cried. She didn't understand why she cried, but she was overtaken with that feeling again that she'd not yet understood to be shame. It was a shrill feeling that started deep in her stomach and spread out from there even as Nevada patted her back and told her it would be okay; her hair would grow in before she knew it. The feeling had already found an opening in her chest, and settled there.

Over the next months, Vergie grew bolder, brasher — her aunt thought that her behavior bordered on rudeness — but she was severely needy, too. She stayed as close to Sylvia as she could. They'd have to distract Vergie for Sylvia to be able to leave the house without Vergie throwing a tantrum. Which happened one day when Sylvia's parents were preparing for a big catering job, and Sylvia needed to make a quick trip to the wharf to pick up their last-minute supplies.

She rushed to return home with the crate, worried about Vergie's sudden change in temperament. Even Nevada had remarked on it. "She act like a little puppy dog, nipping on the heels of whoever happens to be caring for her. Did something scare her?" Nevada had asked. "It would be a sin for her independent streak to go awry." So Sylvia was preoccupied with thoughts of Vergie as she ran along the wharf, her crate loaded with onions, molasses, peppercorn, and whey. She didn't hear the man calling out to her until he was practically yelling. "Miss

102

Lady, might I offer you a hand?" And when she stopped and turned around, he was right there, smiling. He told her that his name was Carl, and that he had seen her on other occasions but had resisted, till now, the urge to offer his how-do. "This time I said to myself, 'Carl, that pretty miss could sure use a hand.' "

Sylvia thanked him politely but assured him that she could make her way unaided. His teeth were too small, she thought, his ears too large, his face too wide, his hairline already receding. She was picky when it came to men. Nevada tried to convince her that she feared love, and that she only feared love because she was unsure of herself. "For all your smarts, you cannot see it?" She'd challenge Sylvia. "If no one can suit you, then you never have to risk all that a person risks when they allow their feet to leave the ground."

Carl took the crate from Sylvia anyhow and the sudden absence of the weight told her how heavy it had been. She didn't realize that her arms were bleeding from the rubbing of the splintered wood. She generally didn't leave the house with her arms exposed, but she'd left in a hurry, before Vergie could try to follow. Carl noticed the blood before she did. "Ah, what you do to those pretty arms?" he asked, as he put the crate on the ground and pulled a handkerchief from his back pants pocket and dabbed at her arms. His eyes were tender, brown like syrup. His touch was light as air. "If that crate wasn't necessary for toting your haul to wherever you headed, I would crush it with my bare hands as punishment for scraping your pretty arms." He laughed and his laugh caught in his throat and Sylvia realized that he was nervous. She'd not known that her presence could bring out nervousness in a man. The knowledge bolstered her, changed her, and she and Carl began keeping company.

It was a comfortable courtship, Carl was easy about Sylvia's educational pursuits, even encouraged them. He had a decent income, working as a pipefitter at the shipyard, so he won her parent's approval — at least her father's, as it was difficult to satisfy Maze, who was intent on Sylvia being linked with a man of the social class to which her mother aspired. But Carl had won Nevada over with his sincerity. And Vergie adored him since he was always happy to include her in his visits with Sylvia. Which pleased Sylvia greatly, because Vergie was one of the joys of her life.

8

Just as Vergie was Sylvia's joy, Linc and Bram were Meda's. Though a sun didn't set when Meda had not spent part of the day thinking about the baby she'd lost, the boys' presence in her life lifted her up in ways that even Ann's friendship did not. And every time she'd say their names — Bram and Linc — she'd think that she was honoring the president, the father she'd lost.

Mrs. Benin was not so taken by the boys. From the beginning she'd been reluctant about the arrangement of Meda bringing the boys into their home for weekends and holidays. But her husband had overruled her. Said that the infants had lost their fathers to the war, and since he himself had not donned a uniform or fired a gun or given his life on the Union's behalf, at least he could be charitable to the sons of men who had. She'd countered that he could just make a deposit of funds in the orphanage's account. Why must her home be tarnished by the presence of such ragamuffins? Her friends were beginning to whisper. He stood firm, suggested that she buy them the necessary clothes, school them in the manners that her friends might find acceptable.

Though resentful about the arrangement, Mrs. Benin did make available for the boys finely constructed clothing. And by the time they were four years old, she did try to introduce them to music, tried to teach them piano, at which she herself was quite skilled.

Bram showed a proclivity for the piano. He would sit next to Mrs. Benin for long stretches, fascinated by her ability to make music, wanting to be able to make such sounds himself. She began to allow incremental affection for Bram; told him that he had the most beautiful hands, that his long, slender fingers were well-suited for the piano. Linc was also drawn to the music, but he had no patience for the painstaking instruction; found it impossible not to fidget when he sat on the bench next to Mrs. Benin. Plus, he didn't have Bram's hands, as Mrs. Benin explained to him repeatedly. His hands were short and stubby, she said, ill-suited for the keyboard. She'd shoo him away when he came near, tell him he was wasting her time. Linc would slide from the piano bench, and Bram and Linc would touch elbows then — their private gesture of greeting, saying hello or goodbye to one another, their way also of saying, without anyone else being privy, you are my brother and I love you like life itself.

After he was banned from the piano, Linc would find Meda; his preference was to be with Meda, anyhow. He would sit at the foot of her chair and scribble on scraps of paper she'd hand him and listen to her hum as she inked Mrs. Benin's notes. He'd run back and forth through the Benin bedroom as Meda arranged the clothes in their closets. He'd sit at the kitchen table as she prepared the afternoon snack. His favorite times were when she'd read aloud to him, whatever it was she happened to be reading, even something as mundane as a letter to Mrs. Benin inviting her to an event for which Meda was tasked with drafting a reply. They'd take seats on the back porch, and he'd lean his head on her arm, and it was as if he could feel her voice vibrating through her arm. It was the best feeling in the world to him, the sound of her voice even better than the sounds Bram made with the piano keys, which would filter through the house and were growing more and more accomplished.

Tom Benin stepped out onto the porch on one afternoon while they were out there and Linc instantly jumped up. "Sir," he said. Benin nodded in his direction, then stood there, waiting for Meda to look up. She did not. He cleared his throat, and Meda continued reading aloud, though she'd taken her volume down to a whisper, and Linc was confused. Meda had taught them that they had to give Tom Benin the highest respect, even greater than the respect they gave to his wife because it was Mr. Benin who allowed them time away from the orphanage to be with Meda. He thought that Meda must not be aware that Mr. Benin was standing there. So he leaned down and nudged her, "Meda," he said in a loud whisper, and she looked up at him and smiled the softest of smiles.

"What is it, my dear Linc?" she said.

He made his eyes go big and moved them in the direction of Tom Benin, trying to tell her that the man of the house was there, that she was being disrespectful. She still didn't acknowledge Tom Benin. She pulled Linc to her instead and smooched his cheek and told him that he was a most handsome boy. Tom Benin left without a word. And Linc asked Meda why did she not give her hello to him.

"I have my reasons," she said. "Mine alone — you are still obligated to mind your manners when he is about."

On another afternoon, not long after, it happened again. Again Linc stood and said, "Sir," as soon as Tom Benin appeared on the porch. Tom Benin nodded as Meda continued her reading, and then Tom Benin called her name. She looked up then. "Evening?" she said, making it a question rather than a salutation. He reached into his vest pocket. "My watch needs to be cleaned, will you see to it, please?"

She opened her hand and he placed the watch there, and Linc moved in to get a closer look at it, and said, "Ooh, what's that, bridges?"

Tom Benin picked the watch up. "Be careful," he said, "it's irreplaceable. Let me show you." He sat down on the chair that faced Meda, and Linc stood in front of him and Tom Benin told him those were in fact bridges on the watch. "Go ahead, you can touch it," he said. And then he explained to Linc how valuable the watch was, that it was one of the first of its kind to be made, that it had been shown at the exposition in Paris, though he'd actually owned his for several years before that, because the watchmaker was a family friend. Linc squeezed into the chair next to Tom Benin and asked how many bridges were there, and Tom Benin said, "Let's count," and they counted the three bridges.

"He can count higher than that," Meda said, without looking up from the paper she read. Then Tom Benin asked Linc to count for him.

Linc counted to twenty, then applauded himself the same way Meda would clap when he and Bram showed off what they could do. A smile broke on Tom Benin's face, and Linc nestled in closer to him on the chair and pulled on Tom Benin's hand to show him the hand game that Meda had taught him. Tom Benin laughed as Linc chattered away, and then Benin's laughter hung unfinished in the air. Mrs. Benin stood in the doorway. Said that she would like a word with him. He cleared his throat and stood and handed his watch to Linc and asked him if he would deliver it to Meda. As he walked from the porch, Linc gave the watch to Meda and she slipped it in the pocket of her frock. Linc sat next to her again as she resumed reading out loud.

The following weekend, as Bram sat on the piano bench, waiting for Mrs. Benin to come down to start with his lesson, Linc wandered into the room and Bram motioned him to the piano and said listen to this, and proceeded to play the piece he was learning, Bach's minuet in G Major. He told Linc to sit next to him and he would teach him, and then Mrs. Benin would see that Linc also had talent and would once again be willing to give him lessons. Linc tried to follow Bram's example but ended up hitting all the wrong keys, and then he made a game of it, pretending to be a concert pianist, and Bram laughed, and then he froze because there was Mrs. Benin.

"Get up from there this instant," she said, and both boys scrambled to get up. "Not you, Bram, you remain seated," she said as she grabbed the pointing stick from the piano and told Linc to spread out his hands. When he did, she struck his hands with the stick, over and over, until Bram started to cry on Linc's behalf. She hit his hands and called him names — urchin, undisciplined, uncultured, with his rat teeth and eyes so dark and sneaky they looked to have been visited by Satan. Said he had the ugliest hands she'd ever seen, hands that had been spawned by an ape. She seemed to lose all control as she berated him and smacked at his hands till his knuckles began to bleed and Bram, hysterical now, ran to find Meda.

Meda rushed into the room and then stopped at the threshold as she saw the bloody stick going up and down through the air, and Linc standing there, stoic, streaming tears but otherwise not making a sound. "Lord Father God," Meda said under her breath, though her faith had always been wobbly at best. Maybe there was a God, maybe not, was her stance on religion, even as she'd call on the Lord just in case. But she got some confirmation as to his existence when she grabbed for the marble bust of Caesar — or maybe it was Marcus Aurelius, she'd get the two confused — and before she could lift it in her hands, she felt something wide and deep and powerful surround her and pin her arms to her sides, preventing her from picking up the bust and ramming it into Mrs. Benin's head equal to the number of times she'd hard-landed that wooden stick against Linc's hands. Her voice at least still worked, and she screamed, "You evil, wretched cow! Hit him again and I will kill you." At least that's what she'd tried to put forth. But it was as if the same force that had paralyzed her arms snatched at her words as they were passing from her lips, re-forming them. "I need to retrieve Mr. Benin's riding boots that have been resoled. I would like for Lin-

112

coln to accompany me" was the reconfigured version of her words.

She pulled Linc into the kitchen with her. She hugged him and kissed his hands and held herself back from crying. She cleaned away the blood as gently as she could. She coated his battered fingers with a thick layer of honey and overspread that with lard. She loosely wrapped his hands in cotton and they left the house and took a streetcar into town.

Linc considered his battered hands a small price to pay for a streetcar ride with Meda, his only regret being that Bram wasn't with them, too. She asked him every other minute how his hands were. "Better," he said, though all of his fingers still throbbed with a burning sensation. And they were better as he felt the honey oozing into the rawness, setting up a barrier. Plus the motion of the trolley, and the sound of the horses' clop-clops was a comfort as he allowed his head to fall against her arm. The nubby wool of her shawl was scratchy against his cheek, but he could feel a pulsing through the shawl that he thought was her heart beating, so he nestled his head closer in and tried to get his heart to beat in time with hers.

They walked along Market Street, busy

113

with shoppers and peddlers alike, and Meda stopped at a stall and bought a ladle of pepper pot soup that she blew on to cool and then offered to Linc. The flavor exploded in Linc's head, and he asked if next time he could share with Bram. Meda said, "Surely, when all is said and done, you and Bram have only each other to lean on." Linc nodded, though the memory of her heart beating against the side of his face was too recent for him not to consider always having her to lean on, too.

They headed south and ended up at Fitzwater Street where the people were all dark like Meda was dark, and though Linc thought them mostly pleasant-looking, none were as pretty to him as Meda, with the way that her face opened up when she smiled, the way her big droopy eyes crinkled at the corners, the way her cheekbones fell away leaving soft brown blossoms; and even when she wasn't smiling, even when he'd catch her staring off into space with a sadness so heavy hanging in her eyes that he'd want to reach up and pluck it away, even then was she the prettiest to him.

Meda said "How-do" to the people as they moved up the street, and Linc was entranced by a woman sitting on her steps making a loud sound that was a mix of a ship's steam whistle and a wolf's howl. The sound matched her appearance: her hair was uncovered, wild and spikey; her feet were bare; her shoulders moved up and down almost convulsively. It was Miss Ma, Nevada's grandmother.

"What's wrong with her?" Linc asked.

"Near as anyone can tell, not a speck of anything," Meda said. "Miss Ma just breaks out into laughter for no good cause. How are your hands feeling?"

"She is *laughing*?" Linc asked.

"Yes, and only she knows what about. How are your hands?"

"Better," he said. The surprising sight of Miss Ma had trumped the throbbing in his fingers, and he kept turning to look back at her, mesmerized; mesmerized, too, by the fact that everyone they'd passed on this street seemed to know Meda, though they all called her Sister, and Linc asked her why.

"That is just how I am known here. My brother has always called me Sister and I suppose the name just attached itself to me. Linc had never thought of Meda's existence outside of Benin's, or the orphanage, where she still came to help out on Fridays, before she packed them up to spend weekends with her.

They stopped in front of a house where

115

the door was cracked and the air jumped with the fast talk and laughter of men with deep voices. They stepped into that raucous setting, which was her brother's living room, though converted into a gambling parlor on a Saturday afternoon where the card table was the centerpiece and food and spirits and the sounds of a banjo and a harmonica spilled out from the dining room.

Meda walked Linc to the table crowded with ferocious-looking men. "Tell me, Buddy, have you ever seen a more beautiful pair of hands," she asked, her voice finding an interstice between the high and low notes of the harmonica and the booming voices that laughed and cursed.

The one she called Buddy was the color of the hens the cook roasted on Sundays, part red, part brown, part black where the seasoning clumped and burned. One of his eyes hung lower than the other and only opened halfway; the other was a full circle that seemed amused by whatever it saw. He fixed his good eye on Linc, then raised a finger to halt the play of cards. "Commere, liddle white boy, lemme see what you got." Buddy's hands were thick and calloused and surprisingly tender as he unwrapped the rag from around Linc's hands. He let go a long whistle when he saw Linc's scarred, swollen knuckles. "Whose ass I need to kick for fucking up the liddle white boy?"

Meda slapped him in the back. "Just answer me, please, Buddy. Tell him how beautiful are his hands."

"Well, hain't never seen nothin' of beauty in another man, truth be spoke, and y'all must forgive me about Sister's diction, but she been taught by the Quakers, and they say strange things like is a boy's hands beautiful. But I must say" — he turned Linc's hands over and looked at his palms, and then closed his oversized hands over both of Linc's and gently squeezed — "you got 'bout the finest hands I ever seen on a liddle white boy. Colored, too, for that matter." He winked at Linc with his good eye and the harmonica did a double note as if to punctuate Buddy's pronouncement, and Linc felt the sound resonate deep in his chest as if something essential had been moved around to accommodate the sound, to lock it in place.

"You always hold on to this, you hear me?" Meda said, as she thumped Linc's forearm. "The ugly is in her, not you. Never let another make you feel shame when the shame is their own for judging you with no eye trained on justice."

117

The trips to Buddy's house became a Saturday-afternoon ritual for Meda and Linc after that. Bram would remain at the Germantown mansion and take piano instruction from Tom Benin's wife, and Meda and Linc would ride the trolley into town and eat hot roasted peanuts as they walked to Fitzwater Street, to her brother's house.

Linc imbibed the atmosphere at Buddy's house. He couldn't decide which he favored more, the tempo of their talk, which was like a creek rushing in a storm, or the way the blend of the banjo and mouth harp would sift inside of him and nestle, or the richness of their skin colorings, the varieties; he would study his own skin after he left there, hoping that if he looked at the inside of his arm long enough, a brown-tint would show through. Everything about being at Buddy's was a thrill to him, even when the air rippled with danger.

And it was dangerous. Men filled with rye swore that they'd been dealt marked cards. The youngest of the regulars, called Splotch owing to a birthmark across one entire side of his face that looked like a massive ink spill, would glare at Linc whenever he was

118

in the room. Meda was watchful over Linc when Splotch was around. And this day she pulled Linc into the dining room and positioned his chair under one of the sketches she'd traced of Abraham Lincoln that Buddy had affixed to his wall. "You would think old Abe Lincoln was Jesus," Buddy's wife, Nola, teased Meda. "His likeness hanging there 'sposed to protect the boy?"

"The boy already white, how much protection he need?" said Miss Ma. "Furthermore, you got ole Abe looking like a colored man on that picture of him you drew. You saying Jesus was a colored man, too, Sister?"

"I say Jesus is the color of everyman and no man," Meda said, as she grabbed her hooded shawl from the hook. "And Jesus just reminded me I failed to order my biscuits from Lorraine for that Benin woman to have with her fried apples tonight. And even Jesus wants no part of her wretchedness when she is denied her requests."

"You still got that Benin woman thinking you bake her bread by your own hands!" Nola laughed.

"Well, my hands arrange it on the plate, so I aver that I am responsible for her enjoying them," Meda said, as she tied her hood under her neck and then told Linc that she was going around the corner to pick up biscuits, and to sit there with Mr. Lincoln and the fine ladies until she returned.

She hurried out the door. The February air had teeth and her hood was pulled low on her face and tied so tightly under her chin that she could barely move her head. She thought that she had the appearance of the grim reaper as she tried to look up and say how-do to the woman hurrying past her, but a blast of cold air made her lower her head, though she did stop and turn around after the woman returned her greeting with a quick *good afternoon.* The sound of the woman's voice went right to Meda's core and shook her, momentarily rearranging her so that she was no longer standing on her brother's block as the cold gnawed through her winter garb but instead was back in that room where everything had been painted white and Abraham Lincoln spoke to her from his picture on the wall. She turned now and called out to the woman who had hurried past her. "Sylvia? Is that you, Sylvia?" But the wind swallowed up her voice as she watched the woman's back float farther and farther away, and she started to chase after her, but then she did not. What purpose would it serve, she asked herself, to barrage Sylvia with questions that she could not answer back then and surely could not answer now? Questions such as what had caused her baby to succumb? Did she suffer at all? She stopped herself. Sylvia's responses — or lack thereof — about her baby could not bring her child back to life. She started walking again. She wrestled with the terrible sadness that the sound of Sylvia's voice had unleashed in her, the twin tragedies of losing her baby and the president on the same night. She consoled herself that she now had Linc and Bram in her life. She had Ann; she cherished her time with Ann, limited though it was, and soon likely to be curtailed altogether because Ann had received an unpromising report about her mother's health: she had developed palsy, and, depending on how it progressed, Ann might need to return to Connecticut. But she had Ann at least for now, and although Linc and Bram and Ann could never completely repair the jagged rip in her heart from the death of her baby girl, their presence did soothe and soften the edges of it and allowed a seam to grow so that it was no longer a gaping hole.

She turned the corner, focused again on getting to Lorraine's house and procuring the biscuits. Told herself that likely it had not been Sylvia anyhow, as she couldn't

121

imagine the situation that would have the likes of a refined one such as Sylvia down here unescorted in this neighborhood so close to sunset.

It was Sylvia. And she couldn't believe herself that she was down here so close to nightfall. Her mother would be livid if she knew — her mother, her entire family still reeling from the brutal assassination of Negroes in the fall elections, Octavius Catto among them, whom her father knew well. But it was Nevada's birthday, and Sylvia's mother had made a multilayered coconut cake for Nevada, and Sylvia had left the house intending to deliver the cake hours ago because she knew that Nevada was expecting a gentleman to call late afternoon to favor her with an evening recital at First African, and a dinner down in their fellowship hall. Sylvia planned to surprise Nevada with the cake, along with the hand-drawn card Vergie had made, which amounted to an arrangement of ink spills because Vergie had not yet mastered letters. The streetcar, though, had been late owing to the extreme cold temperatures, and then she'd stopped in Strawbridge and Clothier to warm up and had noticed a silk scarf swirling with color and she imagined the scarf draped around Nevada's shoulders, so she decided to purchase it. But it had taken her the better part of an hour to pay for the scarf because once the clerk learned that Sylvia was not buying the scarf at the behest of some lady-of-the-house for whom she worked, he claimed to be holding it for another customer, which provoked Sylvia's defiant nature, and she insisted she would wait and see if the customer returned and if not, then he would have no option but to sell it to her. He looked at the space she occupied as if she had become invisible. A rage brewed in her chest, and she walked away in a huff. She planted herself at the Market Street door. She placed the handled bag that contained the getting-heavier-by-the-moment cake on the floor next to where she stood. She called on her innate sense about people as she watched the mostly white people coming and going. They glanced at her as if they were glancing at a barrel, a cart, a post, some inanimate thing that did not breathe or think or feel. She waited; she would not be thwarted; the situation had expanded beyond the scarf as she felt bits and pieces of her rebuked self coalesce and strengthen. The times she'd been mistaken for the maid when she'd accompanied her parents on catering jobs; the job she'd quit at Pennsylvania Hospital after she'd been relegated to cleaning spittoons, though she'd been more than qualified to assist the nurses when they dressed wounds, or prepared soaks, or even coaxed the indolent to swallow; the being made to wait while a white person was serviced first at the vegetable stall, or the fabric shop, or the cobbler to have her shoes resoled. She waited, trying not to allow their sudden blindness to her presence join forces with the rioting bits of her past kicking up dust in her chest. She waited a full half an hour before she saw him, or, more importantly, before he saw her, saw her for what she was — just a person, just a normal living human being. He was, paradoxically, half-blind. He was tall and walked with the slightest limp and had one glass eye that stared straight ahead, while the corners of the other crinkled as she nodded, and he nodded in return and touched the tip of his hat.

"Sir," she said, as she grabbed up the bag containing the cake and moved in closer to him as they walked side by side, farther into the store.

"Ma'am?" he replied, stopping and turning so that he could focus on her completely with his working eye.

"I have a situation," she said. "And I beg

your indulgence as I explain it and ask for your assistance in a way that I hope you think not inappropriate."

"Go ahead, please," he encouraged.

She told him then of her attempts to purchase the scarf for her dear friend, told him how the clerk withheld the scarf. She focused on his working eye; it was a river shade of gray and flinched a few times during her recitation; otherwise his reaction was muted. "I do not profess to have vision into another man's heart," she said. "I can only assess his actions, and, sir, forgive me for saying, but his actions reveal his belief that a Negro miss is not worthy of a beautiful scarf, and so he chose to use his considerable power to deny me, when really the only thing that should matter is my ability or not to pay the price that the scarf commands." She reached into her cape pocket and pulled out her silk purse. "I am fully capable of paying the price of that scarf." She took a deep breath. "So my request of you, if you be so inclined, is to please purchase the scarf on my behalf." She pulled a neat fold of dollars from her purse, but before she could count them out he raised his finger to stop her. He asked her to point out the clerk, and the scarf, which she did.

She hung back as she watched him walk

in the direction of the counter. His limp was more pronounced, but still he managed to wave at the several people he passed who seemed to know him. She'd chosen well. The clerk held this gentleman in high regard, Sylvia noticed by the mammoth smile that tried to soften the harsh angles in the clerk's face. He leaned in and spoke to the clerk, and Sylvia attempted to read the clerk's face, but he turned too quickly and busied himself behind the counter. She shifted the bag containing the cake from one side to the other. She measured the time of day by the slant of sun pushing through the window. She would barely catch Nevada before Nevada left for her birthday night out on the town, if she caught her at all. She'd wanted to see Nevada's expression when she opened Vergie's card, and when she saw the detail on the cake Maze had crafted. Nevada worried that Maze thought her without the proper pedigree to be such a close friend to Sylvia, but Sylvia was eager to point to the cake as evidence that her mother did have sufficient affection for her. She stopped her thinking as she watched her well-chosen stranger walk toward her. He extended an expertly wrapped package, and Sylvia tried to exchange it for her neat fold of dollar bills.

He waved the money away. "The lad insists that you accept the scarf as his gift as evidence of his sorrow for his ill-chosen behavior."

Sylvia gasped, but she didn't protest. Her mother always told her to accept a kindness with a simple thank-you. To do otherwise would rob not only her of the benefit of the gesture, but would steal also the joy of the one trying to do a good deed. So she said thank you, and curtsied slightly, and he bowed and said good day, and just like that he limped away and Sylvia stood there for a moment and caught her breath. She placed the package in the bag on top of Nevada's birthday cake and proceeded into the dwindling afternoon sun.

Her legs felt like blocks of ice by the time she reached Fitzwater Street. She was certain Nevada was long gone by now, but at least she could warm herself at Miss Ma's fire before she started her journey back home. She walked up the few steps and was about to knock on the door, but there was a note on the door that directed any callers further down the street to Buddy's house. She said "Drats" into the wind and checked herself from saying more. She hated to go down there. Her mother would be mortified if she knew that Sylvia dignified a gambling house with her presence. Even Nevada did not go there, though Nevada's avoiding the place had nothing to do with the card games. "Too many women spruce around the dining room and kitchen for my liking," Nevada had once told Sylvia. "And I do not know why my presence brings out the ugly in a bunch of women congregating and cackling. They sneer at me and shoot daggers at me with their eyes as if I am there to invite their husbands to knock skin with me."

"Well, are you?" Sylvia had asked her, half-joking, which meant that she was half-serious, too.

She reluctantly started in the direction of Buddy's house, since she couldn't leave the cake out here on Miss Ma's steps; nor was she was about to lug it all the way back home.

She held the cake close to her as she walked, cursing the clerk in her head for causing a simple purchase to take the better part of an hour, even as the thought of the glass-eyed man softened her. She concentrated on the house numbers so that she would not bypass Buddy's. She'd been looking for the numbers when Meda passed her and she'd returned her greeting with a distracted "Good afternoon." She'd had a delayed reaction, though. Something about the woman — her greeting, her demeanor — had made Sylvia turn back around, but when she did, Meda had already rounded the corner and was out of view. And, anyhow, Sylvia had finally located the house.

The door was cracked and she could hear men's booming voices, and she thought, *I do not think I am going in there.* She decided to knock on the door and just hand the cake to whomever answered and tell them it was for Miss Ma's granddaughter and quickly leave. But then she thought she heard a child scream; it was a terrible scream, so she did go in, she pushed the door all the way, and walked in — and gasped at the scene playing out.

Linc had disobeyed Meda's instructions to remain in the dining room and sit under the sketch of Abraham Lincoln. Once Meda was out of sight, Buddy winked at Linc, and Linc ran to stand beside him as he shuffled the cards. Buddy had Linc point to which card he should play next, and the man they all called Splotch suffered a hard-to-take loss that hand. Splotch squinted at Linc, then told him, "Commere, lemme show you something." When Linc did, Splotch grabbed him by the collar and with a quick move produced a switchblade. "You lil cheatin' white sum-bitch, I outta slit your throat," he said.

Linc screamed and the room went quiet as the women sucked in their breaths and the last note of the harmonica hung and then fell to the floor with the thud of a body dropping, and Linc could feel the chill of the blade against his neck. That's when Sylvia stepped through the door, though nobody noticed her as Buddy pushed back from the table. He spoke to Splotch in a measured voice. "Turn him loose, Splotch. Right now."

"He cheatin'." Splotch spit his words. "He passing signals cross the table, I seen it."

"You saying cheatin' going on in my house?" Buddy said. "Then you got a dispute wit me, not him. Now drop the blade and fight me like a man."

Sylvia's total focus was on the knife against the child's neck as she watched a trickle of blood drip between the fingers of the one holding the knife. She gasped as she readjusted the cake and lifted it and held it against her chest as if it were a piece of armor, a breastplate. She did the only thing she could do. She threw the cake in their direction. She grimaced at the sound of her mother's good crystal cake plate shattering, though the sound it made did cer-

130

tainly have the intended result of distracting the man for an instant, enabling Linc to pull away from him.

Linc ran to the dining room, clutching his neck, and sat in the chair under Meda's sketch of Abraham Lincoln. He was shaking as Sylvia followed quickly behind him, calling for a swath of cloth, and some brandy or gin or rye — "Any sort of spirits will do," she said. She pressed her handkerchief against Linc's neck, relieved to feel no gallop of blood pushing back.

"Beg your pardon, but who are you?" Nola asked, as she produced a jug and a wad of cotton and Sylvia asked her to please douse the cotton with the alcohol.

"She friend to Nevada, aspire to be a nurse," Miss Ma said. "Do what she askun of you. She siddity from way up there on Addison Street, but she know her trade."

"I was hoping to deliver Nevada's birthday cake," Sylvia said, concentrating on exchanging the handkerchief for the alcohol-soaked rag.

"Well, that was one smashing delivery," Miss Ma said as Linc let out a little yelp at the feel of the alcohol.

"Stings, I know," Sylvia said to Linc as she pulled back the cotton and leaned in to peer at Linc's neck while Buddy's wife held a lamp over her to give her more light.

"It appears to be just a flesh wound," she said, as she closed her ears to the profanity-laced tirade emerging from the living room, the sound of a table turning over, of grown men wrestling.

"Well, thank the Lord for that," Nola said. "Just like my Buddy is in there right this instant whipping Splotch's hind parts, I do believe Buddy's sister woulda killed Splotch by now with her bare hands had Splotch done for-sure harm to this shere boy."

"Say it true," Miss Ma said.

"Does she take care of him?" She tilted Linc's neck from side to side to inspect the wound from different angles.

"In a way, I suppose," Miss Ma said.

"Though it appear to be more complicated from what I gather," Nola said. "The people who employ Sister allow her to cart him and another little white boy back and forth. Befuddling to me, but I do not speak much on it 'round Buddy. He sensitive 'bout his sister."

Sylvia continued applying pressure to the cut on Linc's neck. Then she told Linc to open his mouth and motioned for the lamp again as she looked inside. "Can you swallow for me, sweetie?" she asked Linc.

Linc nodded and swallowed, and she

asked if it hurt to swallow, and he shook his head no, though his attention was really trained on the living room. Buddy had just stood from where he'd been on top of Splotch, pummeling him, and Splotch picked himself up from the floor; his mouth leaked blood and he cupped his hand under his mouth as he spouted off his attempts at an apology. "I never said you cheated, Buddy, I just cannot figger how you lall this white boy in here anyhow. Like to raising a baby monkey. One day it not gon be so cute. It'll be a full-grown ape that's gonna snatch your balls off right from between your legs and eat 'em for breakfast, and then make you watch while he turn your woman into his wench." He had backed all the way to the door and in one swift move pieced through the broken glass of the cake platter to retrieve his switchblade and what was left of his dignity and then was out the door.

Miss Ma had just let go a stream of laughter as Buddy's wife went into the living room to survey the damage. Linc held himself stiffly and choked back sobs. Sylvia could tell that he was trying not to cry. "Can you count from one to one hundred?" she asked Linc.

He nodded, and she lifted his hand and put it against the compress she was holding

133

firm against his neck. "I want you to apply steady pressure just as I am doing. I want you to count very slowly from one to one hundred while you do. Keep the cloth right there until you get to one hundred. Are you able to do that?"

Linc nodded again, grateful really for the distraction. He wanted Meda to be back, he wanted to lean his head against Meda's shoulder. But now he squared his shoulders because Buddy was walking toward him. Buddy was the next best thing to Meda, though in a different way. "How you faring, partner?" Buddy asked him.

"Just a nick," Miss Ma gasped out, her laughter ending as suddenly as it began. "My granddaughter's friend claims it, and she studying to be a nurse, so what she claims to be, is."

Buddy glanced at Sylvia for confirmation. "It does not appear to be serious," Sylvia said, as she watched Buddy's expression spread out in relief. "It looks as if he was holding the child's skin between his fingers so that avoided severing a vein." She gathered her cape hood around her. "I apologize for the mess I made," she said, as she started for the living room.

"I made a bigger one," Buddy said. "And besides, I owe you. Feel free to call in your debt anytime you need sumpin, anytime, anything. My sister love that little boy."

Sylvia was back in the living room. The musicians and the other card players were righting the turned-over furniture, and Nola began sweeping the debris. Sylvia leaned down and fished up the wrapped scarf. She slid it into her cape pocket and mumbled out a "Good evening, all," and then pushed out into the air that was darker now, though suddenly not as cold.

Linc didn't tell Meda the truth of how he'd gotten the scar on his neck. Nor did Buddy or his wife, Miss Ma, the music-makers, or the men who'd been gathered around the card table that evening. Buddy concocted a tale of a fall, and Meda was satisfied that Linc seemed none the worse as a result. Linc did tell Bram about it, though, the way that Linc told Bram everything that happened at Buddy's house. When Linc got to the part about Splotch talking about Linc growing up to be a full-grown ape who would snatch Buddy's balls off, Bram gasped and grabbed himself between his own legs. "You said nothing in retort?" Bram asked him.

"I had no words," Linc said. Then he added that he actually did have words, "but by then the miss who would be a nurse was having me open and close my mouth, and I was mad, I mighta woulda cried."

"Ah, no, Brother," Bram said as he lowered his head. "Crying in front of Buddy would not be good if he's how you describe him."

"But he is," Linc insisted. "Buddy says that men never cry, nor boys who plan on becoming men." He went on then to describe all else that had happened at Buddy's that day, allowing Bram to feel as if he'd been there, too. Already he'd taught Bram how to curse the way the black men at the table did, showed him how to let a toothpick dangle from the corner of his mouth, how to tell if an opponent across the table was bluffing, how to throw a left hook.

The fighting instruction was particularly useful now at the orphanage, where they were constantly taunted by the other boys because they were favored by Ann, who'd never made a secret of her special affection for them. Ann had held them, after all, and they had not died. They'd been the reason that Meda had walked into that coal-stained foyer, walked into Ann's life. Every time Ann looked at Linc and Bram, she was grateful to them for that. And though Ann was as quick to hug all of the boys as she was to reprimand them, she'd hug Linc and Bram more, reprimand them less. And they reciprocated in kind. If Meda was like a mother to them, Ann was like a favorite aunt. But then, she left.

Meda had prepared herself for Ann's leaving as much as she could prepare herself for saying goodbye to the person with whom she could shed all of the varieties of skin she'd wear in the course of a day. The only other adult person who'd even come close was her brother, but she'd had to keep that part of herself that had lain with Benin, the part of her that grieved the loss of her infant, hidden from her brother. Ann knew all of that, knew about her claiming Lincoln for her father, knew how'd she'd talk to her mother when she cleaned the penitentiary and her mother would be inside the cell sweeping the floor and Meda would be on the other side looking in and it would feel that one or the other of them was caged and Meda couldn't tell which. "You both were, sweet lady," Ann had said as they sat close together on the fainting couch in the parlor. And now, almost ten years later, she was telling Ann goodbye and they were both visibly shaken at the ordeal of it. Ann promised that she would send word when Meda could visit. Meda nodded, even though she understood how the world worked, North or South, it did not matter. There was no other space that would accommodate them like this parlor in this orphanage had: expanding and contracting the way Meda reasoned the universe likely did, forming stars out of vast gusts of nothingness to lend sparkle to the night, laughter, a swath of joy, whispers that glittered. A bolide's gleaming fragments. And after that it was time for her to go.

9

Ann was not the only one leaving. Sylvia was, too. But Sylvia's leave was cause for celebration, not heartbreak; a grand send-off, not secret kisses; accolades, not whispered promises that would be difficult to keep.

Sylvia had received an offer for employment to fulfill the position of assistant to the nursing staff at the Lazaretto, the city's immigrant processing and quarantine station that jutted into the Delaware River and connected to Philadelphia at its southern-most point. She thought the position beneath her abilities, she was a fully trained nurse after all, but the possibilities inherent in the position enthralled her. Since every ship hoping to enter the Port of Philadelphia had to be cleared through the Lazaretto during the summer months, she might see firsthand the exotic diseases she'd only read about. She would live there for months at a time. She especially welcomed that. The Lazaretto might prove an escape hatch from a conventional life.

Carl and Sylvia had been keeping steady company since they'd met that day on the wharf. Though there was a period when, at her mother's urgings, she was called upon by a young man, John, more fitting of her attention, or so her mother insisted. His parents owned a prestigious school in Virginia and he was handsome in the most classic way that a black man could be and still be black with his light skin and light eyes and lightly textured hair. His touch was light, too, and initially it was a thrill for Sylvia to have him escort her to the concert hall, or a public reading, or one of the lavish affairs catered by her parents for a well-to-do's wedding reception, or graduation celebration, or cotillion ball. Though as Sylvia's feelings grew in intensity, she noticed John's seem to recede. He no longer stroked the nape of her neck as they took a carriage ride, or clasped her hands as they walked along the oval. When she confided his turnaround to Nevada, Nevada said she thought Sylvia too good for him and his mulatto-loving people. That he was not the prize, Sylvia was the prize. And then she said no more, until Sylvia pressured her, and then Nevada told her that his parents were likely the cause of his faltering passions; she knew of the highfalutin school his parents ran, and that they measured the color of every child hoping to be admitted to the school against a rub of ground ginger: darker than that and the parents received an I-am-sorry-but letter.

Sylvia, with her middle-of-the road complexion that was neither light nor dark had not really suffered the impediments that she knew shackled the darkest-toned of her race. She was well-educated, cultured — and her father now was a regular lecturer at the Institute for Colored Youth on how to assess catering fees based on the services offered. Her parents owned their own home in the most affluent part of the Seventh Ward. And yet, because she was slightly darker than a rub of ground ginger, she could not pass muster. "I am sorry to hear you report that, Nevada," Sylvia had said, defiantly. "Fuck them, fuck him" — though she'd only ever used profanity before in her head, or once or twice whispered such a word when no other living thing was in earshot, or if so only Nevada — and then she let go a profanity-laced tirade about John and his family. Said that the Negro race would never progress to its fullest

141

potential because of people like them, who had copied the worst practices of bigoted whites. Nevada laughed, enjoying the sound of Sylvia's cursing as she told Sylvia that Carl stood head and shoulders above John, above most men, regardless of how her mother felt.

Sylvia knew that part to be true. Carl was certainly a prince of a man. He was loyal, sweet, giving. But her heart did not pound double-time when she thought of him; her world did not spin faster when he approached; his touch was warm, soothing, but there were no explosions, no electric currents running through her at his touch. She loved him as one loves a dear, dear friend, not with a passion; though she could not even claim that she ever loved John with a passion. It was her work that she truly loved. In her most recent position as nurse at the Blockley Almshouse, she felt her whole self involved in what she did. When she was away from work, she was thinking about work, wondering how the one with the broken wrist was faring with the sling she'd fashioned, or had the ginger and garlic soup solved the other's intestinal distress, did the slippery elm relieve the hoarseness, the lavender work for the hysteria. She'd get a rush at times when she'd conjure up a cure, often absent the doctor. She thought that marriage, keeping house, would hinder her ability to work; might curtail it completely. Though Carl seemed encouraging enough now, she feared he might have a change of heart, might insist that, once married, she not work at all. And since she thought Carl such a decent man, she believed that he deserved a woman who saw him as her primary source of passion; he should not have to play second fiddle to her vocation.

Nevada tried to convince her otherwise, "You a loon, Sylvia, if you do not know what you got in Carl. You best hold on to him, he will honor you with all his heart, and allow you your nursing duties besides."

Sylvia wanted to believe as true what Nevada purported. So she'd tried to deny Carl without causing him to go away completely. When he'd first asked for her hand, she'd replied, "Let us delay such plans until I have completed my schooling." When she had graduated, he asked again and she said, "I should rather secure employment first." He was respectful, patient, and then brokenhearted when she'd begun spending time with John. And now, on this day that she was to report to duty at the Lazaretto, she sensed that he would likely propose again.

She enjoyed the grand send-off at the dock, even though Vergie cried inconsolably and Nevada fought tears, too, as she joked with Sylvia to keep an eye out should a position open up that she could fill since she could use a season's respite from her grandmother's craziness. Sylvia's mother and father hugged her tightly. And then Carl, dear Carl, helped her onto the boat, his boat, as he was doing the honors of escorting her there.

The boat pushed off, and Sylvia waved her handkerchief up and down until those she was leaving appeared the size of stick figures. She settled in next to where Carl steered the boat. The sky hung low and gray; the river slurped excitedly. Carl looked straight ahead toward the seam the sky and river made, and just as she'd sensed that he would, Carl asked Sylvia again for her hand one more time, told her this would be his final ask.

Sylvia cleared her throat, and he held up his hand to stop her. "Listen to me, sweet cakes," he said. "If it is not the response I been praying on, then please say nothing. At least I can go through the rest of my life with the knowing that although you never said yes, you also never said no. But answer me this: Is it another mister caught your eye?"

"No, no, no, I promise you it is not. It is, is, how shall I say it?"

"By just saying it."

"It is my work, Carl. I am devoted to it, and you deserve a wife who is devoted to you in kind."

"Your work? Not some dandy —"

"My work," Sylvia said as she looked away and watched the river snapping by.

"Your work?" Carl asked again. "How that can be? Curing a fever? Nursing a cough? I am not intend to belittle your work, but, uh your work, Sylvia? Do your work have a beating heart and big old shoulders for you to rest your head on. Do it?"

"No, Carl," she said and stammered for words to explain. Tried to make him understand that her work had her in situations where she stared down death, and death had won, and she had to respect its power. That through her work she had ushered in new life, and that that had never lost its thrill. But that it was larger even than life and death. "I am able to witness, more than witness, Carl; I am able to participate in the fullness of what it means to be a human being, the shadings and the textures and the variations of life. I am meeting life often at

145

the place where body and soul converge. People at the precipice, a life's course altered. I get lost in the experience of it."

Carl's brow was wrinkled, his eyes pointed, as if he were trying with his whole being to grasp exactly what she was saying.

"It is not against you, Carl, I promise you that," Sylvia said. "You are about as perfect a man as I could wish for, but —" She stared at the river as she spoke, hypnotized by the rhythmic splashes; the push-pull of the undercurrent, the aroma of cedar and cod. "I delivered a baby once, it was my first," she said, as the river egged her on and she was talking now as much to the river as she was to Carl. She described how the pretty, brown-skinned, petite woman was already in the early stages of labor when she'd arrived at the midwife's that day. "She was much too far along for the services that that white lawyer who had escorted her there had requested."

Carl was listening intently, and he sighed and shook his head. "One of those situations," he said.

"One of those," Sylvia repeated, as she went on to detail how excited she became when Dr. Miss directed her to sit on the stool at the foot of the cot, which meant that for the first time she would take the lead in delivering a baby, and how she'd wanted to do a holy dance as the baby turned its shoulders to come into this life. "Ah," she said as she stopped to catch her breath, the telling of it had made her breathless.

"I could not see. There was just a scant light from a solitary candle. The light flickered and died completely, probably from my excited yelps that stirred the air in the room. The room went black, and in the portion of a second that it took for my eyes to adjust, the midwife had already covered the baby."

"Well, there goes a crime: you deliver your first and you do not get to hold it."

"Oh, but I did get to hold it. I held it to my chest. I slipped my hands under the blanket and cradled the new skin on its back, its first breaths pushed out against the crook of my neck. They were the sweetest breaths, and then the midwife whisked the baby from my hands and instructed me to tend to the mother; she was bleeding quite a bit, and afterward I met with the midwife and the lawyer and they were discussing the outcome, and he was shaken. He did not expect the result of things to be a live birth." She went on to describe Tom Benin's manner, his meticulous attire, his gold watch that he kept pulling out. Told Carl how at first Tom Benin seemed perfectly willing to allow the midwife to decide on the baby's disposition. But then, just as quickly, he reversed himself. "He told us to tell the mother that her baby girl had succumbed."

"Son of a white Satan," Carl said, anger jumping in his voice.

"He instructed the midwife to deliver the baby immediately to his carriage. And I will be always haunted by the tiny pink hand reaching for its mother as she cried out for her baby. The poor baby wanted to answer its mother's cry, wanted to lie against its mother's breast, and I felt as if it was fighting with that reach, fighting to get to its mother, and I was powerless to help the baby, to help the mother. But I was present in that moment, Carl. I was there, and I did what I did, and if faced with that situation today, perhaps I would handle it differently. But every fiber of my being was engaged. I just always want to be available, to be present in that way. Always."

"Whew," Carl said, when she had finished. "I suppose I should take solace that just as I can't compete with that, can't no other man, either. That was stage drama all right, whew. But tell me this, what happened to the mother? Did you stay in touch with her?

Or try to?"

"I did not, I would not. In fact, it has been the opposite. What purpose would it serve beyond opening wounds. Not as if I would be at liberty to tell her what truly happened. Besides, it would have been unprofessional to befriend the women who came to the midwife for professional services. And then there is the guilt. My guilt. But I do know that the mother of the baby was quite taken by President Lincoln," she said, her voice lighter now.

"Name me a Negro who was not, though I must say my brother was not obliged to speak favorably of him after he was paid a lot less than the white soldiers doing the same diligence fighting for the Union. And my brother had to pay from his own purse the price to purchase his own uniform. He faulted Lincoln for not fixing up that situation straightaway as he could have done as the great commander and chief."

"My father has said a similar thing. I suppose Mr. Lincoln was filled with contraries, as are we all. But this woman seemed almost, dare I say, to posit that she and the president shared a lineage."

"Really? She look to have white in her?"

"Not to my eye, but if I did not know better, I would think part of her believed that

Mr. Lincoln was her father. And, sadly, she gave birth to the baby the same night the president was killed."

"For true? Two heartbreaks in one night. That hardly seems fair."

Sylvia went into her satchel and pulled out a notebook and from it slipped a single sheet of parchment. "She gave me this," she said, as she leaned in and showed him the sketching of Abraham Lincoln.

"Whoa," Carl said, "who sketched that?"

"She did. Is it not quite good?"

"I'll say. Looks like a true artist drew it."

Sylvia laughed. "To imagine him winking as she has rendered him here, such a playful expression on his face. She served him tea once, or so she said."

"Well, was it imaginary tea?"

"Carl, do not be naughty!" Sylvia laughed.

"I mean, she thinks Lincoln is her daddy, who she say her momma is? Queen of Sheba?"

They both laughed then. It was hearty laughter — laughter Sylvia needed that came from a deeper place. The river gurgled in time to her laughter, seagulls made merry in the sky. She laughed so hard until she cried. When she had recovered herself, Carl asked what of the baby girl?

"What of the baby?" Sylvia said, feeling

her voice tighten.

"Well, what happened to her?"

"I do not know."

"So you don't know where the lawyer took her? Was she raised white or colored?"

"Carl, I do not know," Sylvia said in a determined voice. She was quiet then. Most everything else had quieted, too, except for a single gull that called across the sky, its pitch going from squeals to low moans; the water's hard splashes against the side of the boat; and the heavy thud that was the sound of Sylvia's not-knowing dropping in the boat between them.

10

Linc and Bram missed Ann as much as Meda did, though in a different way. Ann had always made sure that their mats were closest to the hearth in the winter, that their stew came from the top of the pot, that their chores rarely included climbing down into the chimney to sweep it clean. She'd get in between them and the jealousy of the other boys, who'd resented Linc and Bram for their favored status, for their being able to leave the orphanage every weekend and return with the contented expressions of having eaten well, having slept in a soft bed. Of late their spats with their housemates were turning violent; when one or another boy teased them about their "nigger wench maid," Linc and Bram joined forces, and though it was just the two of them against sometimes five or six, they won as many fights as they lost. Buddy and his gambling cohorts had taught Linc the art of boxing, which Linc in turn passed on to Bram. Though they were not quite eleven, the strength of Linc's swing, the power in his punch, was that of a much older boy.

For the next two years, they suffered through replacement after replacement of house matrons. Each one worse than the last. The new matrons either exercised no authority and the boys ran wild, or they ruled with iron-clad dictates that let in no light. None were like Ann, who'd balanced regulations with flexibility, agitation with affection, a rear-end whacking with a kind word and a pat on the head. But bad as Ann's replacements were, they all allowed Meda access as she continued to come in on Fridays and spend the day and help out however she could until evening came and she left with Linc and Bram in tow to spend the weekend in the Benin household.

But then a new head arrived. This one male, Robinson, who had the whitest skin, the silkiest hair, the smoothest hands. He was meticulous about his living quarters, which he expanded, so that more boys than usual were crammed on the second floor. He separated Linc and Bram who, from the time they shared the parlor as infants, had always been roommates. Now Bram's cot was in a room on the third floor, Linc's on the second. He also rearranged the chores Linc and Bram had always done together. Linc was now responsible for cleaning the latrines, and Bram for keeping Robinson's quarters dust free. He reversed the long-standing policy of not indenturing boys of a certain age, as was common at larger establishments such as the Orphan Society of Philadelphia. Dictated that at thirteen, the boys would be indentured. Bram and Linc had just turned thirteen. He collected any jewelry in the boys' possession because he said that it was unfair that some had, and some had not. For Linc and Bram that meant relinquishing the silver rings Meda had given to them the Christmas past. The rings had their first initials engraved inside, and it pained them to hand the rings over. And as if all of that had not hurt enough, they also lost their greatest privilege — time with Meda. Robinson stopped Meda's long-standing practice of coming in on Fridays; he issued a new directive that banned overnight stays away from the house, apart from exceptional circumstances that would nevertheless require his preapproval. That one had been the death knell.

On her last visit with them, Meda promised that she would speak to Benin to see what he could do to ease the situation; but

Benin was overseas, traveling to Europe and then to Asia, so it would be at least several months before he would return, but she asked the boys to please be patient, to stay safe and out of trouble until Benin returned.

She had decided then that she would use Robinson's threat of indenture against him by persuading Benin to use his influence to have the boys farmed out to the Benin mansion. The barn needed restoring, the parlor could use new floors; and Bram was so adept at the piano now that Mrs. Benin could certainly keep him busy performing at one or another of the events she organized and participated in. Meda had it all figured out. She just needed to convince Tom Benin. Ann had always maintained that Tom Benin owed her; that Meda should call in that debt whenever she needed to. Meda had, and it had gotten her a life with the boys, so far. She didn't know how much of that debt was left to dangle. Didn't know if she'd have to make him owe again. Decided that if she had to, she would. Whatever it took to persuade him, she was willing to do. She would invite him into her room if she must. She would wear a half-smile; let her eyes fall to half-closed; she would put on the moan-filled sounds of a cat in heat; she wouldn't judge the rightness or wrongness of it; she had pushed past shame. For the boys, she would do what she had to do. But then they ran away before she could.

They hadn't planned to run away. They had planned to be patient, knowing that Meda would pull strings for them once Tom Benin returned. Their personalities were suffering as a result of being separated from Meda; Linc had turned more excitable, always bracing for a fight. Bram was now more withdrawn, as if he'd grown layers over his true self. Bram had also begun to develop stomach distress, and fevers that would appear out of nowhere and baffle the doctor who came by once a week. But then he would rebound and be well, until the next time.

One night Robinson told Linc that he was not doing an adequate job with the latrines. Linc countered that he was doing the best he could, and, besides, each one should be responsible for cleaning up his own shit. Bram had tried to intercede, said that he would clean the latrines for Linc. Then Bram gave Linc a look, telling him with his eyes to tame down. Linc returned the look, told Bram to toughen up. Linc was taken to the shed that night for a severe flogging. Though the other boys had not heard Linc cry out, they had heard the whirring of the

156

whip moving the air, then the slap of it against skin. And Bram's hard breaths as he held himself back from screaming out in pain on his brother's behalf.

Linc had, shortly after, been hired out as a bricklayer; Bram was kept back for duties around the house. Now they barely saw each other until the end of the week, Friday nights, when they'd sneak down to the cellar with another pair of brothers — these two biological — Matt and Chris, to play cards.

This night Matt had pilfered a carafe of Communion wine and they passed it around and told dirty jokes that Linc had heard from the bricklaying men. They delighted at the sound of new profanity spewing from their mouths. They mocked the walks and accents and eating habits of their other housemates. They told "Robinson stories" and imagined what they'd like to do to him — tie him up and pour cream on his toes and unleash a peck of hungry rats, said one; drench his undergarments in invisible lye, said another; fill his shoes with hot nails, said a third. They had to muffle their laughter when Bram stood and raised his hands and motioned for quiet. He heard footsteps overhead; he knew they were Robinson's because they were so deliberate, so particular, the way everything about Robinson was.

"It's the Worm," Bram whispered, using their name for Robinson. All levity was immediately sucked out of the room; even the pleasurable sensation of the wine splashing around in their heads came to an abrupt stop. They ran to hide the carafe and the cards. Matt's younger brother started to cry, and Linc punched him and told him to be a man. Bram got very still then. A resignation covered his face like a slow-moving shadow and Linc asked what was the matter. "Nothing." Bram spit the word out as he listened to the door at the top of the cellar stairs creak open.

"Bram? Are you there?" Robinson called down.

"Sir," Bram said, as he motioned the others to be still and started walking in the direction of the steps. "Uh, yes, I have come to put away my cleaning supplies."

"Well, do not be in such haste to do so. Ready your supplies this instant and come make a repair of your haphazard sweep of my quarters."

"Yes, sir," Bram said, as the other boys remained motionless until they heard the cellar door close, the footsteps retreat.

"We owe you for that one, you bloke,"

Linc said, as the two others came back to life as well and the wine resumed its whirl in their heads and they started to laugh again and imitate Robinson's walk. When Bram had gathered his cleaning supplies, he told them to get ready to kiss their pennies goodbye because he would be back directly to win them away.

Linc and the two others returned to their cards, and after more than an hour had passed, and the carafe was empty, Linc wondered out loud what was taking Bram so long.

"Maybe he's went straight to his cot and passed out from the wine," Matt said. "I am about to do it, too."

"Me, too," said Chris. "Bram always takes such a long time doing a sweep of the Worm's room."

"Does he now?" Linc asked.

"He got him from his sleep the other night. His mat is next to mine and it woke me." Matt pulled his brother up from the floor, told him to get up to his bed before he was the next one flogged. They planned to repeat the escapade the next night at the same time as they separated to their various sleeping quarters. Then Linc crept up to the third floor and peeked into the room where Bram now slept and saw that Bram's cot was still unoccupied. He felt teeth in his stomach then, biting away. He went back to his own room and stepped over the sleeping boys to get to his cot. He sat and started to pull his shoes from his feet, but then he did not. He ran from the room instead, back up to the third floor, then right to the suite that Robinson had turned into his own kingdom.

He did not know what to do at first as he stood at Robinson's door, gasping. Moonbeams pieced through the cobweb-covered skylight in the hallway and drizzled over him, and he was torn between knocking and just barreling in. And then he didn't have to decide because the door opened and there was Bram, quickly pulling the door shut behind him. He looked stricken, his faced blanched as if no blood flowed there, his eyes red, his lips swollen, his neck welted as if he'd just had a bad case of hives. "What the dickens happened to you?" Linc asked in a whisper. "Why were you in there so long?"

Bram didn't answer. He just stood there, breathing hard as scattered moonbeams gave his face the appearance of a jigsaw puzzle. He tried to speak, but his words were garbled coming out, and he felt as if he were choking, and then he started to vomit instead. He coughed and spit up as

Linc looked on and felt his own stomach start to spin.

"Bram, what the devil?" Linc asked, desperation coating his words.

"Shit," Bram said, when he could gather himself enough to talk. "Now I have to clean this up, too." He tried to move farther down the hallway, but Linc blocked his path.

"Tell me, Bram, what's happening?" Linc said, slowly, pointing the ends of his words.

"It's Robinson," Bram whispered, as he pushed his hands in the center of Linc's chest and moved him still farther down the hallway. "He tried to turn me into a fucking missus."

"What?" Linc asked.

"You heard me, as I was cleaning under his dratted bed — he — he —"

"What, Bram? *What?*" Linc's voice rose, and Bram shook his fist to quiet him.

"He told me I was beautiful," Bram said and then leaned against the wall, as if the saying of it had weakened him. He appeared to be sliding down the wall and Linc grabbed him, shook him. "What did he do to you, Bram? What?" And then he let go of Bram. He ran toward Robinson's room as Bram tried to pull him back, whispering, "No, Linc, you can't, no . . ."

But Linc had already opened the door,

161

had already walked through the sitting room into Robinson's bedroom. Robinson was there in the chair next to his bed, his satin slipper dangling from the foot of his crossed leg. He nestled a globed-shaped glass of brandy in his hand and shook it in slow circles, causing a silent typhoon in the glass. He looked up at Linc, his eyes glassy drunk. "I thought you might be Bram returning," he said, then laughed a slurred laugh.

"I know what you have tried with my brother, and unless you want the world to know, too, this is how things will be from now on —"

"How will they be?" Robinson asked, as he took another sip of brandy and sat up taller in his chair.

"For one, stay away from my brother. For two, I am not cleaning another latrine. For three, we will be allowed to spend the weekends with Meda again — and short of that, the world will know of you and your revolting intentions."

Bram had come into the room. He stood next to Linc, his shoulders squared every bit as defiantly as Linc's were. "I have up-chucked in your hallway, and I will not be cleaning that, either," Bram said.

Robinson's cheek quaked in and out; he touched his finger to his cheek as if to still it. His fingers were long, his knuckles encircled with tufts of silver hair. He looked from Linc to Bram, his head moving slowly, precisely. "I am trying to decide," he said, "which one of you will be sent upstate to work in the mines? Which one on the chain gang?"

"You do not understand," Linc said, squaring his shoulders. "*You* are the one who will be on a fucking chain gang!"

"And *you* do not understand," Robinson said, as he uncrossed and recrossed his legs. "You are a pair of waifs, nothings, thrown-away-at-birth little shits, spawned from alley rats, from what I have heard. Who will give you an audience with your imaginary spews?"

"We will be eager to find out, then," Bram said, though Linc now fell silent. Linc was watching Robinson's face, which suddenly swelled with self-satisfaction, his chest, too, even the silver hair poking over the shirt that remained unbuttoned at the collar and two buttons beyond puffed up the way a cat's hair does when the cat has caught a mouse. Robinson wasn't bluffing, and though they weren't, either, Robinson held the better hand. Buddy had warned Linc about such a thing, about making a wager that he couldn't cover. Buddy would call

163

this killing time. Nothing to do, he'd say, but back your way out of the door, bargaining if you can, fighting if you can't, running if you must.

Bram picked up Linc's thoughts, through osmosis, it seemed, as he began to bargain. "Well, sir, what say you if we just drop all mention of any of this and just return to the way things have been before today?"

"But the cat is already out of the bag now, is it not?" Robinson said, as he focused on Bram, and his eyes went suddenly dreamy. He took another sip from his glass and then, slowly, deliberately licked a drop of brandy that hung on his lips.

Linc didn't know which move unleashed the rage coiled in the pit of his stomach, didn't know if it was the way Robinson looked at Bram, or the slow swipe of his tongue across his lips, or maybe even him saying that they'd been spawned from alley rats. But the rage was there, immediate and uncontainable, forming his hands into mammoth fists that gained strength as they moved through the air and then crashed into the sides of Robinson's face, one time, then another, then a third, just the way Buddy had taught him.

Bram squared off ready for Robinson to jump up and try to take them both on. But

Robinson just sat there as the satin slipper on his crossed foot fell gently to the floor. His head was tilted and fixed askance on his shoulder; his eyes squinted as if he were trying to see something far away, or maybe figure out the meaning of life. A thin creek of blood flowed from one side of his nose and followed the slant of his head and found a place to pool on the open collar of his shirt.

Linc and Bram ran then to the separate rooms where they'd been relegated. They stepped over the huddled figures of their sleeping roommates, each to their own sections and searched their piles of belongings for what they thought they could not do without. For Bram it was his sheets of music, and a barely decipherable sketch torn from a magazine of a blond-haired woman. The sketch had been given to him by Meda, who said that the woman may have been his mother near as she could tell. For Linc it was a spare deck of cards — he tossed aside the sketch Meda gave to him of the black-haired, dark-eyed woman who was supposedly his mother; he'd stopped believing that story several years ago, like he'd stopped believing in Saint Nick, though he loved Meda all the more for the gesture, the attempt to give him worth. He did, though, snatch up the rendering of Abraham Lincoln that Meda had drawn for him. Lincoln at least had been real. And had been drawn by Meda's own hand.

They ran into the dark outside. The night air was busy as it shook off the last of summer so it could make space for autumn cool. *Fuck, you don't think he's dead, do you? Holy shit, we will be hung, put to a firing squad, sent to the fucking gallows,* they called back and forth as they ran with the night. They had few provisions and no plan. But they didn't cry, though Bram was close to tears when he said that they should have gone back to Robinson's room and retrieved the silver rings Meda had given them. "He had no right to take them, they were ours and he had no fucking right," he shouted as they fled through the streets of Philadelphia, not knowing where they were headed; and then Bram knew, as he followed Linc's lead. Though he'd never been there before, the description of the block was seared in his memory the way Linc had described it: they ended up at Buddy's.

A game was still going on in Buddy's living room, Linc knew by the yellow lamplight pushing against the window, and the barely cracked door, and the sounds of a harmonica mixing with high and low laughter. Bram started up the three steps and Linc pulled him back. "We cannot go in now."

"But I thought you said Buddy would welcome us."

"It is not Buddy who concerns me. There is no telling who is in there."

"None who would take Robinson's side over ours."

"Did he not always brag about his connections? Who knows his reach. And there are some men, such as the one who tried to slit my fucking throat, who would rather see me put on trial." His voice shook, and Bram lowered his head. Then he said, "Come on," and he motioned for Bram to follow him, and they went around the corner and through the alley, and Linc counted off the houses until they were in back of Buddy's house. They crept into the yard and found a corner adjacent to the house where the moonlight did not follow. They huddled there and breathed hard and were comforted by the vibrations coming from inside, the laughter and the music that seemed to make the frame of the house bounce to the beat.

They fell asleep waiting for the house to empty and woke to the sun's first glimmer and the siren song of the iceman making his way through the alley: *"Ice here, so nice, my ice be. Fom da Knicker-bocker House a Ice."*

Nola stuck her head out of the back door. "Yoo-hoo, I will have a block, please," she called, as the iceman limped into the yard. One of his legs was half the length of the other and the horse he pulled seemed crippled, too, as it dragged crates of ice behind it.

The iceman seemed not to notice Linc and Bram as he unhooked a crate and lifted out a square of ice and met Buddy's wife at the door. The horse, though, took a couple of slow clops until he was standing in front of Linc and Bram. They pressed further against the side of the house as the horse looked down at them while the iceman did his transaction. When he was finished, he turned and called to the horse. "Come a here. Let dem boys be for my wares meld down to wader."

"Boys? What boys?" Nola said, as she called into the house for Buddy. "Iceman said boys back in the yard. You best come see."

Bram nudged Linc so that he could take the lead in announcing them, but the horse was right over Linc now, leaning in until they were practically eye to eye. "What's his problem?" Bram asked, trying to edge

168

farther away, even as Linc — part frightened, part enthralled — returned the horse's stare.

"He no danger," the iceman said as he walked to where they were and yanked the horse's reins. "Old mare just spoilt rodden, tis all. Tink she special cause she da one what led Ole Abe Link's castit trew all da steets of Phileydelfi."

Buddy had stomped out into the yard. "Humph," he said on an extended breath as the iceman turned and said, "Mornin', Mr. Buddy," and tipped his hat, and the horse seemed to follow suit as it appeared to bow its head in deference to Buddy and then backed up, allowing Linc and Bram to come into Buddy's view. The horse let go a loud and long neigh, and then a snort, as it turned and followed the iceman from the yard, shaking its head up and down as it walked away.

Buddy looked at Linc and Bram, his good eye squinted, the other practically closed. "A pair a runaways if I ever seen it. You know that mare laughing at you," he said. "Horse 'bout the smartest creature on four legs, and it appear she smarter than the two of you put together 'cause she woulda had enough sense to come on into the house."

Bram pushed his elbow into Linc's side as

if to say I told you so.

"And I suspect you Bram, the brother Linc and my sister go on and on about."

"Yes, uh, sir," Bram said, jumping up and extending his hand.

"My name is Buddy, but you can call me Buddy," he said, as he shook Bram's hand. "And I see someone been throwing around a left hook." All eyes went to Linc's hands, which he'd not even realized were swollen, bleeding. He looked at his hands as if they were suddenly disassociated from the rest of him, even as he remembered the feel of his fists smashing against Robinson's head. His hands looked ugly to him, misshapen in the new daylight. He thought now that Mrs. Benin had been correct when she'd told him that he had the ugliest hands she'd ever seen.

"Well, let's see if Mrs. Nola can put a piece o that ice to good use and get your hands back to their right form," Buddy said, waving Linc and Bram toward the back door. "Come on, git in there quick, 'fore Sister show up here and start getting sterical 'bout what happened to your pretty hands. Tain't never heard of such a thing myself as a man wit pretty hands — you, Bram?" He shoved Bram's shoulder, playfully.

"No, sir — I mean, uh, Buddy," Bram said as he followed Linc into the house. Though Bram had just heard such a thing from Robinson, who'd told him that his hands were beautiful, as were his hair, his eyes, his legs, his back.

11

Linc omitted the awful truth of what Robinson had tried to do with Bram when he told Buddy why they'd run away. "He was a tyrant, Buddy," he said, as Nola put a pot of ice chips on the table and situated one, then the other of his hands in. "I finally stood up to him and a fight was the result. I believe he would have killed us if I had not defended myself."

"Mnh," Buddy said. "And how about you, Bram? You look none the worse. Least your hands not showing wear."

"I was all prepared, Linc has taught me your moves, but then Linc went at him with such speed, I did not have the opportunity to put the instruction to use."

"Is that so?" Buddy said, his good eye twinkling with amusement. "Show me what he did."

Bram took the stance and jabbed four times into the air in quick succession. They were forceful jabs as he imagined that it was him, not Linc, going after Robinson in that chair.

"Good form," Buddy said. "You teached him well, Linc. So I figger these was all body blows."

"No, each one to the head," Bram said.

"Well, answer me this, how tall do he stand? As tall as me?"

"About," Linc called from where he sat at the table, alternating his hands in the pot of ice.

"That so? Well, how you get to his head? What he do, lean forward and give you a invitation?"

"I think Linc's first punch caught him right in the gut so he did lean and on account he couldn't cover his head." Bram rushed his words.

"So who threw the first punch?" Buddy asked, looking from Linc to Bram.

"Robinson," they said in unison.

"Where did it land?"

"Got him right about here," Bram said, as he pointed toward his stomach area.

"So who threw the first punch?" Buddy asked again, looking directly at Bram, all play gone from his good eye.

"Robinson did," Bram said, trying to return Buddy's stare, but unable to do so, so he focused on Buddy's cheeks, which were peppered with tiny black moles, and his complexion, which was the same red and brown as Mrs. Benin's piano. He missed that piano suddenly, the feel of the keys under his fingers, the way he could lose himself in the music he played.

"Who threw the first punch?" Buddy asked yet again, and the room was silent, save the soft footsteps of Nola leaving the room and the ice clinking on the side of the pot as Linc moved his hands around.

"Linc did," Bram said.

"And what was this here Robinson doing when Linc threw the punch."

"He was threatening to send us away."

"But what was he *doing*? Where was he at?"

"He was in his quarters."

"Doing what?"

"Sitting in his chair like the king he thought he was."

"So you and Linc barged into his quarters? He sitting in his chair, and Linc punches him in his head?"

"We did not barge in," Bram said.

"Only I did," Linc said from the table.

"I had been ordered in there already."

"So he ordered Bram in to tell you he was gonna send the two of you away?"

"He ordered me in," Bram said, "but not for that." And this time he returned Buddy's stare. "It was under the guise of cleaning his dratted quarters and he put a awful proposition to me and I said no, and I left half-dazed and then Linc showed up with his hot head and barged in there." Bram tried to control the way his voice shook right now, but he could not.

"Mnh," Buddy said, as he seemed to reel back and forth even as he held himself straight and tall.

"What was he like when Linc was done wit im?"

"He was out cold."

Buddy snorted, then he turned to leave the room, saying as he did that he would get Mrs. Nola to prepare them a meal. He stopped under the archway between the dining room and living room. "I hope you killed him, Linc," he called over his back. "I hope you killed him dead. Save me from having to do it."

Nola got the swelling down on Linc's hands. Then she prepared for them a king's breakfast of peppered cow's brain and cornbread. After they had filled themselves, she sent them down to the cellar closet to gather the heavier quilts and winter clothes that she'd stored there during the warmer months. They heard footsteps coming down and they found each other's eyes and dared each other not to cry. These footsteps were light as a ballerina's, because she'd always carried herself like one with her straight back and slender neck and slight build; and even before they wrestled each other to be the first one through the closet door, they picked up her scent that was like ginger and mint. "Meda!" they said in unison, as they tried to push through the door at the same time and landed in a huddle on the floor. "Meda. Meda. Meda."

Right now they sat in the shed kitchen, which looked out over the backyard made golden by the retreating daylight. Though the air over the table was chalky and gray as Meda unfolded a posting, which she showed first to Buddy. "Whew," Buddy said on an extended breath. "Nuttin' good about this here. Nuttin' at all." He straightened his shoulders and read aloud what was there. He read slowly, stopping to sound out the words. "Orphan bludgeons housemaster in vicious attack. Blunt weapon used. Orphan on the run. Reward for his apprehension or information leading to his apprehension." He turned the paper around. "See, got your likeness taking up the rest of the page."

Linc glanced at it and then looked away.

"So they do," he said.

Meda took her voice down to a whisper and lowered her head. "They tell me he is in a hideous state. He is not even able to form words. And the situation is worsened because he has apparent connections to people in high places. His uncle is a magistrate, his own brother, a constable."

"Whew," Buddy said, as he shook his head back and forth. "That do make it worse, but if he got no bility to talk, how he fingering Linc?"

"From what I have gathered," Meda said, as she looked from Linc to Bram, "when Linc's name is put to him, he releases an awful sound. So all the way here I have been pondering what could have happened exactly to cause Linc to be in such a fight with the man?"

"Do not matter worth a crumb what happened exactly," Buddy said. "If the law say this here is what spired, then far as anybody that matters is concerned, this here what it says on this paper is what took place."

"But what led up to it, had he first beat you, Linc?" Meda persisted.

"Not exactly," Linc said.

She looked at Bram then. Bram's face had gone completely red. "Did he beat *you*, Bram? Is that what happened? Was Linc defending you?"

"Do not matter," Buddy said again. "Leave that part of it alone, Sister. Whatever the man did or did not do, I am willing to wager my life that he mustta earned the whupping Linc put on him."

"But we need to know what happened if Linc is to mount a proper defense," she countered.

"Sister, you been breathing that air at that mansion much too long if you think Linc got a defense." He waved the paper around. "And if that Robinson is truly connected to people in such high places, it is only a matter of time for the law come breaking in my door. No secret that Linc was accustomed to spending time here."

Linc pushed back from the table and stood. "We don't want to cause you trouble with the law, Buddy. They will do what you're saying, maybe worse."

"Did I ask you to be concerned wit my affairs?" Buddy said.

"No, but —"

"Well, till I invite you into my business, you stay outta it."

"Sir," Linc said as he sat and rested his palms on his knees.

"Now, this is how it will be, till it is otherwise. You and Bram will stay here till we plans out your next move."

"But you just said they'll kick your door in —"

Buddy held up his hand to stop Linc. "And since we know that will be the move, we prepare for it. That closet in the cellar where the missus store her extras mighta saved a life or two of colored people born to be free who went after their birthright, and stopped in Philadelphia on their way to Canada, 'cording to what I been told. Or, it mighta held escaped convicts, I heard that about it, too. History can be twisted into the shape of a confused tree root depending on the one telling it. But the certain fact is that there is a fake floor in that closet that opens up and leads down to a hole big enough to 'commodate two good-size men. Not the Harrity Hotel, but it got air for breathing. You stay here till we put a plan in place. They show up, we store you down there till they leave."

"That is how it shall be, then," Meda said. "Until we can arrange for your safe passage to a place where you will not be wanted men."

"Not too often Sister agree so readily with my assertions," Buddy said. "So I must be getting smarter."

"Or I am getting dumber," Meda said to

179

the sound of Buddy's snickers, and a half-laugh from Linc. Even Bram offered up a smile.

They were there for over two weeks without consequence. During the day, before the living room filled with nighttime gamblers, the boys moved the heavy furniture around at the direction of Buddy's wife so that the floors could be thoroughly cleaned. They sanded away the dried candle wax and charred ash embedded in the floor around the gambling table. They climbed into the chimney and swept it to newness. They turned the soil in the backyard and planted bulbs. They took down the dead tree and chopped it into manageable-sized logs of kindling. They kept the fireplace free of ash, the windows free of sediment, the tables free of dust. They were happy to do whatever Buddy or his wife asked, since their home was serving as their haven for now. Plus the expense of energy gave their physical selves the chance to release the fear and anger that otherwise had no outlet.

The arrangement had its downside. Though they had the run of the house when it was just Buddy and Nola and the visitors they trusted, such as Miss Ma, they had to remain unseen when card games took over the living room. They'd keep to the shed kitchen or the corner of the yard or the cellar. The sound of the cards, when he could hear them being shuffled, was a torture for Linc, since he could not sit at the table and be a man with the other men. And Bram wanted more than anything to set up the xylophone he'd found in the cellar, and stand next to the one blowing the harmonica, and the one plucking the fiddle, and hold down the melody with his own strikes upon the crudely fashioned instrument.

On the nights when the Indian summer warmth made it possible, they slept in the backyard and on more than one occasion woke to the iceman's song and the clop-clop of his horse; the horse would come to stand in front of Linc and stare at him as if he knew him in another lifetime. Bram complained that the horse spooked him, though Linc had gotten so comfortable with the animal that he'd offer her crumbs of cornbread, and on the mornings when Linc had none, the horse seemed just as content to lick away at Linc's empty palm.

In the meantime, Robinson's condition neither improved nor deteriorated. The blows to his head had reduced Robinson's life to that of a house plant, dependent on others to water him, to drain him, to turn him so he might face the sun. He could not speak, and there was disagreement about his ability to comprehend when others spoke to him, except when Linc's name was mentioned; his eyes would bulge and he'd unloose a sound from his throat that was like the mating call of a bull frog.

Better for Linc if Robinson had died. His family's quest to find Linc and avenge the assault might have dissipated if they'd had the chance to sit in front of Robinson's draped casket and listen to a eulogy reminding them of the power of forgiveness. Instead, Robinson's kin were daily reminded of the attack on him each time they wiped the foam that accumulated around his mouth, or changed his shitty pants, or listened to his high-pitched squeals, which seemed to come out of nowhere, and which they swore were his attempts at forming Linc's name. So between the constable brother and the magistrate uncle, there was pressure all across the legal system that justice should be served on Robinson's behalf. They threw money around. They upped the bounty. And then it happened just as Buddy predicted: they kicked in his door.

Miss Ma, who lived near the corner and had first sight of people coming and going, ran to her backyard and projected her voice in the direction of Buddy's house and started singing from Handel's *Messiah* "And He Shall Glorify." She'd told them to listen for her voice, she couldn't commit exactly to the tune she would sing when she saw them, but it would be loud, she said, and so pleasant they might be tempted to tarry and listen. But run instead, she'd cautioned.

Bram heard it first. He was leaned over, arranging wood chips around the rhododendron bush he'd just planted. He tossed the shovel and yelled, "She's singing!" and that brought Linc from the shed kitchen, where he'd been whitewashing the walls. They took the cellar stairs in two jumps and pushed into the closet and lifted the floor the way Buddy had instructed and squeezed themselves into the hole. Nola followed quickly behind them and spread out the boxes that they'd pushed to one side to lift up the floor. They heard the thud and crash that was the sound of Buddy's front door hitting the living room floor. Yelling and cursing and feet stomping working their way through the house. "Where is he?"

"Who?"

"You damn well know who."

"My door, look what you did to my door."

"Do the same thing to your face if you don't tell me where he is."

"Who? I got a right to know who you talking 'bout."

"You got no rights, nigger. Where is he?"

"I got a right to a front door on my house."

"You got a right to a billy club against your head, like he did to my brother. Where is he?"

"Lord Jesus," Nola said. "Is this about that white boy what assaulted the man in the orphanage. I saw a posting of it. I truly wish I did know of his whereabouts as certain as I could use the reward money."

"Yeah, to buy a new door."

Miss Ma had come in — Linc and Bram could tell by the whistling, howling sounds of her laughter.

"What's so funny, you loony wench? What? Is this funny?"

"Leave her be, please, she has a condition —"

"Well, make her shut up, crazy loony wench, put her in the fucking circus, but tell me where the fuck he is."

Their voices rose and fell as they moved through the house, up the stairs, then back down, through the kitchen, the shed, the whole time spewing profanity and insults and threats.

Linc and Bram stopped breathing as they felt, more than heard, the cellar door being flung open. Footsteps rushing down, to the front, to the rear, to the corner where the closet was. The door opening, opening, opening, in slow motion it seemed, the sounds of its creaking like their own chests cracking. The boxes kicked at, pushed aside, like thunder blasts in their own heads. Muttered complaints, cursing, and cursing some more. And then a slow, slow silence snaked in; they couldn't trust the silence, so they remained as they were, crouched in the hole, blackness all around them. Bram's head was in his hands, and Linc reached out and pushed at Bram's hand. "Did he?" he whispered to Bram, hoping with everything in him that Bram would reply, *Did who? Did what?* But Bram's response was first a sniffing sound, as if his nose was filled with liquid and he was trying to hold it in, to keep it from running down his face, to keep it from showing. "He promised he would return our rings," he said then. And the impenetrable darkness all around them got blacker still.

12

They would go to Yonkers in New York, where Nola had a cousin who worked at the new Glenview mansion. On the morning they were to leave, the iceman came at the usual time, but today his mare was hitched to a carriage where Linc and Bram would hide until they reached the ferry that they would take to Trenton, and then the train to New York. They stood in front of Buddy with their shoulders squared like grown men and thanked him for saving them from years on the chain gangs, or worse. They bowed and kissed Nola's hands and Linc said that if fortune favored him, he should land a miss as perfect as her with whom to share his life.

Buddy laughed. "You been 'round me too long, 'cause you even picking up my lines."

They went out into the backyard to wait for the iceman. They both wished for Meda, even as they understood that she could not arrive there so early in the morning. But there she was anyhow, sitting next to the iceman as he stopped the carriage in the alleyway at the entrance to Buddy's backyard. As contained as Linc and Bram had been with Buddy, they spilled all out of themselves with Meda, as they both ran to her, and practically knocked her over, tussling to hug her first.

She squeezed them hard and then they climbed into the back of the carriage, and she covered them over with a blanket to hide them. As she covered them she thought of how she'd covered them that night she'd first met them, when their skin was new and they did not yet have names. She stood there remembering the feel of Linc's head as it found the crook in her neck, how Bram had not cried at all that night, how she'd had the deepest, purest sleep as she'd rocked Linc to settle him. The remembering fell over her and held her motionless by the carriage. Then Buddy called to her from his perch on the back steps. "Let them go, Sister," he said.

"I will, I already have," she called back, a defiance running through her tone as the iceman whispered something to his horse and it turned its head around and looked at Meda, a longing in its eyes as if it was giving a look by proxy on behalf of Linc and Bram.

After Linc and Bram hugged Meda good-bye, they took a slow boat to Trenton, and after that a train to the Island of Manhattan, which was denser than Philadelphia; dirtier, too; louder, livelier, more corrupt, more options, lonelier, sadder, more sensual.

They were met by Black Mary, Nola's cousin, and they accompanied her on a Ferry ride along the Hudson to the majestic Glenview mansion.

"I was expecting colored," said the one doing the hiring, who had a bulbous red nose and breasts like a woman. "But Black Mary say you got good words put out for you, and that you know hows to plant a tree and prune a bush, and keep the grass even. And come snow, you gotta keep that cleared."

They nodded enthusiastically as he continued to list their duties. They were only thirteen, though they claimed to be sixteen. They settled into the routine of it. They worked hard, and ate well at the end of the day. They began to relax about being found. But after a year, they felt a snaking misery working its way to their bones, killing them: boredom.

They wound their way back to New York City to the growing Italian district of Greenwich Village. "We could be Italian for all we know," Linc said. Bram agreed as they picked up the accents and replicated them and gave themselves Italian surnames and invented pasts of having watched their parents die on the voyage over from a plague that killed half of the adults but seemed to spare all of the children. They made no mention of having ever lived in Philadelphia. They picked up odd jobs selling newspapers, working at fruit and vegetable stalls, even shining shoes. They missed Meda with an ache that neither expressed. They sent letters back and forth addressed to Miss Ma to avoid the law tracking them through their correspondence. They were kept up to date of the happenings in Philadelphia. And then they received a post that contained the very sad news that Nola had succumbed to a lung illness. Meda cautioned them not to try to return to Philadelphia, as she knew they would certainly want to pay proper respects to Buddy. But Robinson's condition had not improved, nor had he died, which meant that his family's thirst for revenge had not died either, and they would surely be nabbed if they were to try and return. She would come to them, she promised.

In the meantime Linc could not contain his desire for the tables. And Bram said that his fingers were itching for the feel of piano keys. They made their way farther uptown to the Tenderloin district and the area dubbed Satan's Circus.

The area fit its name and Linc found a proliferation of card games and made some income at the tables, and supplemented it with work in the building trades. Bram played at any of an array of the music halls and concert saloons frequented by the inebriated rich, and the pay was decent and the tips even better. On more sedate evenings, he'd sit in for pianists at the upscale Fifth Avenue hotels, such as the Brunswick. On Sunday mornings, he played at Episcopal churches, where they paid nicely for his talent.

Occasionally, on Sunday mornings, Linc would fall in on one of those church services on his way home from an all-night card game. He'd ease into a pew that felt unyieldingly hard, and the imposing structures, with their mile-high cathedral ceilings, made him feel small and disconnected, and he'd think that if he had to get beyond those ceilings to get to God they'd never make each other's acquaintance. But then Bram would play, and the sounds of the piano would fill in the void created by those soaring vaults. When Bram saw Linc sitting there, he'd start to improvise. He'd go off music and the young chap sitting next to him turning the pages would look at Bram as if to say, Where are you? What are you playing? I am lost about when to turn the page.

The improvisation would transport Linc to his childhood and the way, when Mrs. Benin wasn't around, Bram would go up-tempo with the hymns he played to suit Meda's ear. He'd allow the music at the church to move through him then. He'd pick up Bram's eyes and nod, thanking him for the music, and for evoking the memory. Bram would extend his elbow out, symbolically, saying, "Anything for you, Brother."

Over the next several years they lived relatively wild but honest lives, falling in and out of favor with one woman or another. They eventually moved to separate houses within a block of each other. They were still close, convening most nights after Bram performed. They talked loud and laughed hard and swore and smoked hemp and drank rye with the rest of the band.

One night they were in a back room at Koster and Bial's Music Hall, passing around a pipe jammed with hashish; it was potent and went straight to Bram's head after only one inhalation, stunning him, stunning all of them. They laughed in slow motion and cursed about how good it was. The pipe seemed not to be lit when it got back around to Bram. He reached for the brass holder where the taper candle blazed on its thick wick. He put the pipe to his mouth and leaned the candle in to reignite the hashish. He sucked in hard and the smoke swam around in his brain and he said, "Uh, *shit,*" not realizing at first that his bangs had gotten in on the act, that the hungry flame was devouring his hair. The bass player sitting across from Bram was the first to notice, and he grabbed a container that he thought to be water and threw the liquid at Bram's head to douse the flames. Except that it was lamp oil, and Bram felt the sudden heat as his hair raged and he shouted out in pain and it took time for them all to realize that he was on fire, their reaction slowed by the hashish. Linc noticed first. He ran to Bram and started beating the flames with his hands as he yelled for a blanket; someone threw him a topcoat and he covered Bram's head and snuffed the fire, and he could smell the burnt flesh even through the coat.

Bram's recuperation was tough as gristle. After weeks at Bellevue Hospital, Linc moved him into his room because he still needed constant watching. He slept on the floor so Bram could have the bed. At points he'd have to tie Bram's hands down because he would rage with fits of delirium and try to tear off the bandages.

Meda traveled to New York and bought a room for a week in a tidy neighborhood that was a short walk to the blocks where Bram and Linc kept rooms. She moved the picture of Abraham Lincoln that she'd given to Linc from the space over his desk to the wall at eye level opposite from where Bram lay. When Bram would wake and yell out in pain-fueled hysteria, and converse with people in the room only he could see, Meda wondered if Abraham Lincoln was talking to Bram the way he'd talked to her the morning her baby died. She put cool compresses around his wrists and whispered to him the way she did when he was an infant, and it seemed to calm him.

After what felt like an eternity, Bram grew clearheaded again. It was the day before Meda was to return to Philadelphia and Linc brought in a banquet-sized breakfast of corn muffins and fried fish and tomatoes. He pulled his desk to the center of the room and borrowed two more plates and utensils from boarders down the hall. He spread a freshly laundered tablecloth over the desk and set a bouquet of flowers in the center. He held Meda's chair out for her, said, "My favorite lady, please have a seat." Meda giggled the way she used to when they were young boys and had done some silly thing. Bram took halting steps to the table and sat, and laughed, too, as he watched Linc push Meda's chair in and lean down to smooch her cheek. Bram was facing the window, and the sun had miraculously found a way to slant between the adjacent brick structures and steal into the room. He realized, just as he had every Saturday during the years when he'd remained at the Benins' while Meda and Linc left to visit her brother, that he had never been as close to Meda as Linc had been. The sun made his eyes water and Linc asked if he was all right and Meda told Linc to pull the shade down, that the sun was making Bram squint, and that it likely hurt to squint, given that squinting involved the forehead, where new skin was still trying to come together.

"Ah, Meda," Bram said, "I would wink at you right now, but that hurts, too. You are my favorite lady," he said, and then felt shy after he'd said it, so he bit into a corn muffin so he could look away. The muffin was still warm and had been saturated with butter, softening it on the inside, so it went down easy.

Meda chatted on about the recent happenings at Buddy's house. Told them that the one who'd played the harmonica at all of the gatherings at Buddy's had died.

"The one called Harmon?" Bram asked.

"That's the one."

"There goes a loss, the way he pushed those notes out, his tempo, his precision. The man had talent."

Linc put another corn muffin on Bram's plate and passed around the tomatoes as he described how the music would drift down to the cellar when they were hiding out at Buddy's and he could tell that Bram was itching to go upstairs and be a part of it.

"Buddy took his passing hard," Meda said, as she bit into the fish, and her eyes shot way open in that way that signaled she was enjoying something intensely. That had been one of Bram's greatest rewards for enduring those grueling piano-practice sessions, watching what Meda's eyes did when he played for her. "But Buddy being Buddy," Meda continued with her story, "he extended use of his house for Harmon's wake. Miss Ma attended, and she laughed the entire time, which was not out of custom for her, but it did spur a bit of a kerfuffle because Harmon's family was not acquainted with Miss Ma's propensity for laughter, and considering the occasion, Harmon's widow took exception and told Miss Ma to quell her laughter or else."

"And she laughed even louder?" Bram asked.

"She did indeed. But not only that, her granddaughter, Nevada, had accompanied her, and Nevada did not take so kindly to witnessing her grandmother being berated."

"Oh no," Bram said, as he swallowed another bite of the muffin.

"Oh no indeed," Meda went on, "because Nevada and Harmon's widow got into quite a spat, and Buddy leaned on the side of Nevada, because I do believe Buddy is sweet on Nevada, which I am happy to see because she brightens his mood since Nola's passing. And Harmon's wife said that she would not remain in such a place and be disrespected, nor would Harmon. So she gathered her people, including a couple of her strapping nephews, and prepared to leave and told the nephews to bring Harmon, too. So the nephews started to lift the coffin, and then Buddy says that he bought and paid for that coffin, so the coffin stays."

"They carried him out with no coffin?" Linc asked, incredulous.

"Yes they did. One of them slung Harmon over his back, and the — excuse me for saying this — but the, the pants they'd dressed Harmon in were oversized, and they came slipping down, exposing poor Harmon in a most unimaginably dreadful way, and then the nephew tripped over the pants and he fell over backwards, and poor exposed Harmon landed on top of him —" Meda stopped and dabbed her lips with her napkin. "I have never in my life seen such a sight." Her eyes watered and her voice cracked and she could no longer contain herself and she laughed. Then Linc laughed, too. Bram sat back and closed his eyes and listened to them laugh: Meda's soprano; Linc's deep bellowing; their pauses and breaths in a lively counterpoint; their laughter was beautiful with its blend of pitches, its starts and stops. Bram hated to say what he was about to say.

"I have quit the piano," he blurted, and his words got in between their laughter and tripped it up, and they both turned and looked at him with their faces wrinkled with confusion.

"What did you say?" Linc asked.

"I do believe I have misheard," Meda said.

"I had visitors —"

"What *visitors*?" Linc asked. "I been with you, there was nobody else here —"

"I been visited," Bram said again as he left the table and stretched out on the bed. "I been visited by the dead."

Linc was speechless. His mouth hung and he looked at Meda. Meda stood and pulled her chair across the room and placed it under the sketch of Abraham Lincoln. She sat and folded her hands in her lap and Bram was struck again by how poised she was with her straight back and graceful way of moving. "And what have the dead said to you during these visits, Bram?" Her voice was soft, almost a whisper.

"That I was born to be a spiritualist, that I need to be their intermediary. That I must quit the piano."

"You cannot!" Linc said, trying not to yell, but yelling nonetheless.

"I cannot which one?" Bram asked. "Become a medium? Or turn away from the piano?"

"None of them. You can't quit your music. Linc stood and walked from one end of the room to the other. "And besides, what does your playing the piano have to do with talking to some dead people. That is not *possible,* anyhow. Unless you actually die

198

yourself and join them — then you can talk to them, talk to them all you dratted want. But while you are living, you talk to the living, and you play the piano for the living." Linc had worked himself up to shouting for real. He surprised himself at the desperation he felt over the notion that he might no longer hear Bram play.

Meda told Linc to lower his voice. "Who has come to you exactly, Bram?" she asked.

"For starters, my mother."

"Truly, Bram," Linc said on an exasperated breath, "it was the pain, I promise you, Brother, it was. Tell him, Meda. He was close to death. Anything alive will imagine a visit from its mother when it has one foot in the dratted grave —"

Meda held up a finger to quiet Linc. She herself had thought about her own mother so often of late that it sometimes seemed that her mother was in the room with her. She wondered how close to death she herself was. "How did she appear?" Meda asked Bram. "Your mother. What was she like?"

"She was" — his voice faltered — "she was beautiful."

"And who else has come to you, Bram?"

"There have been scores of souls, Meda, I promise you there have been."

199

"Have there been babies?" Meda asked. "Infants only minutes old?"

Bram closed his eyes as if trying to remember. He was hitting on something then, something only he knew from having spent Saturday after long Saturday in the Benin house when Linc and Meda would travel to Buddy's. The sounds would sift through the walls and he'd hear them between the notes he played. He'd hear Mrs. Benin's anger, so shrill that it attached itself to her face. And when she'd return to the parlor to take her seat next to him on the piano bench, he found it difficult to look at her, her profile was deafening with its shrill outline. Mr. Benin's anger bounced rather than sifted. It was concrete and lent itself to words that pushed on through the walls and hung over the piano, where Bram played faster and faster to shorten the silence between the notes so that he couldn't hear him, but still he did hear him. "I will not tolerate this from you," Tom Benin's voice would boom. "I demand that you stop it, stop it right now, once and for always. The baby died. She *died.*" That argument seemed to replicate itself Saturday after Saturday with different words spoken in a different order, but the essence of it that reached Bram was always the same. Once when Mrs. Benin returned to the parlor, and Bram stole a glance at her, he could see where Tom Benin's handprint had penetrated the shrillness and bruised her face. He played a long, slow melody then, Stephen Foster's "Beautiful Dreamer." He sang the words as he played. It was smooth and uncomplicated, and also soothing. She hugged him afterward. He allowed it, and even hugged her back, though he felt he was betraying Linc and Meda because she was often so wretched to them. It was a brief hug and then she pushed him away and cleared her throat and told him to move on to the Chopin Prelude in D flat major.

He looked across the room now at Meda. "I don't recall a infant," he said. "Though if I knew one to summon, I do believe she would appear."

"She?" Meda said, then looked away.

Bram closed his eyes again. He could hear Linc's hard breaths, and Meda's softer ones that were like sighs. He felt the salve oozing under the bandage running toward his eye. Before he could lift his own hand Linc was already standing over him, dabbing the salve away, and Meda was next to him, telling him not to rub too hard because the new skin on his forehead was still forming, still tender, still not healed.

201

■ ■ ■ ■

Bram went on to make a handsome living as a medium. People trusted him. His eyes were a milky blue, like ink mixed with cream, suggesting childhood and innocence. His manner was easy, patient. And the burn scar only seemed to help. The skin on his forehead was now fused together like hardened spills of melted wax, as if he'd been struck by a lightning bolt of insight that gave him his powers. And he was an honest broker. Even Linc, who could manage no belief in such a thing as talking to the dead, saw how earnest Bram was in his own belief. He'd seen Bram return advances made to him when he'd felt he'd been unable to reach beyond; he knew that Bram was meticulous in the pre-work he conducted before actually trying to hear from the dead. In addition to interviewing the decedent's family and friends, Bram would study their journals and other documents they'd left. Bram maintained that he enjoyed a level of success that many practicing his discipline in a more haphazard way did not because the dead respected his efforts to know fully who they had been while alive. "That's all any of us wants" — he'd push his point with

Linc — "to be known fully by people who purport to care." Linc would counter that such a want must happen after death, because from what he could see, most living people put great effort into trying to cloak their true selves, even from themselves, and the behavior of men at the card table — the bluffed expressions to force an opponent's moves — was a small version of the workings of the world. They'd volley back and forth then the way that close siblings did, critical on the one hand, indulging the other's hobbyhorse on the other. Bram now protested Linc's penchant for the card table, yet he'd still advance him money when he ran short; and Linc declined to consider the possibility of communiqués from the dead, yet he'd spend hours listening to Bram's recounting his spiritual exploits. Though they'd both feared that Bram's new avocation would prove a wedge between them, their bond was, in fact, strengthened, the way it can be when one person changes profoundly and the other makes a sincere effort to understand, and new circuits are formed between them as a result, reconfigured, firing with possibility.

Bram began to experience episodic bouts of an unnamed malady where he'd vacillate between fevers and chills. He'd vomit, and at its worst he'd turn yellow with jaundice, sometimes even becoming incoherent as if suffering from some sort of brain-wasting disease; other times he'd descend into a trancelike state. Linc hammered him to seek medical attention after the first time. But Bram recovered quickly enough, with no apparent lasting effects. Each recurrence seemed less drastic, being that much more familiar. And then Bram revealed to Linc that the sudden onset and departure of his mysterious ailment was merely a consequence of his work, and that he chose to see it as a positive benefit. "It means I've gotten success, it means they're inside of me," he said, referring to the dead. "I know it with the first taste of a dry mouth, a chalky taste, I know then that it's begun and that I'm reaching them."

"Better if you knew the truth, you stupid bloke, that a chalky mouth means a body needs a drink," Linc said. "You could nip it before you got shitty sick by guzzling water — or, better still, gin."

They went back and forth, then, the way they always had with one another: Bram trying to convince Linc of the merits of his new occupation; Linc straining to convince Bram of its folly, hoping to convince Bram to seek help for his medical condition, insisting that if he did not, he would *actually* be talking to the dead because he would soon be joining them. Bram waved him off, then commenced to detailing his most recent case for Linc. Linc settled in to listen. Not believing in the possibility of it, but listening nonetheless.

13

Meda hadn't thought it would be so easy to get into the parlor of the orphanage, where she'd not been in almost a decade. She'd concocted a story of having been sent by her employer to inspect the parlor for new furniture he was planning to donate. But the door to the home was unlocked, and she walked in and stood in the foyer and took in the air that smelled of garlic and thyme. The charcoal stain was still there on the foyer floor after all these years, and she was glad that it was. She cleared her throat and whispered a hello, and hearing no reply, assumed that it was still the quiet time here, when the older ones were at their studies and the youngest down for naps and the staff disappeared on breaks. She made her way directly into the parlor and closed the door and stepped back in time because not a thing had changed. Same velvet fainting couch, same brocaded draperies — blue with flecks of gold — same boxy writing desk with the missing drawer pull. She looked at the space where the cradles had been that first night she came here, and the space was empty save for the dust beams twirling in through the tall window. She sank into the couch and leaned back and kicked her shoes off and swung her legs around and closed her eyes. She felt at once beautiful, the way she'd felt when she and Ann shared this space, and also the sense of fulfillment that she'd get when she sat here and nursed Linc and knew that she was connected to something larger than herself. She nestled deeper into the couch and thought of church.

Dr. Miss had suggested church when Meda saw her earlier in the day. Dr. Miss, like this room, had not changed: still in that high head wrap and long straight dress that hung more like a robe, as if she were a sort of high priestess. She had not been able to tell if Dr. Miss remembered her, she didn't act as if she did, but then Meda thought she was likely an expert liar. This time Dr. Miss examined Meda in a room that was painted yellow, not white like the room where she'd lost her baby. She'd looked around for a picture of Abraham Lincoln on the wall and was disappointed that there was none, and she suddenly missed him with an ache as Dr. Miss inspected her breast — pressed it, turned it, apologized when Meda pulled in her breath sharply from the pain. Meda had tried to read Dr. Miss's face, but she could not. Reasoned that years of doing what she did had molded Dr. Miss's face so it better resembled an ebony carving than something of flesh and emotions. Not that she needed Dr. Miss's face to tell her what she already knew. The thunderclaps of pain in her breast had already told her; the gradual disfigurement; the way that her breast leaked, which Meda thought of as tears; reasoning that her breast was so sorry for what it was doing to her, for eating away her life, that every now and then it broke down and cried. She'd caress her breast then, forgive it, everything deserved forgiveness.

After Dr. Miss had completed her examination, Meda watched her lips move; it seemed that her mouth and her words were not in time with one another. At the point when the words reached her ears, she'd already deciphered them as they pushed through Dr. Miss's mouth. The words were grating to her ear with their redundancy. So she sifted through them. *Cureless, pray, church* — these were the words that she allowed to register as she assembled herself back into her corset. She fastened the word "church" along with her corset so that it lay against her skin.

She'd not gone to church much as an adult. But during her childhood she'd regularly experienced two types of religious services. One was the Meeting for Worship that was a daily part of the routine at the Quaker school, where they'd sit in silence, and anybody moved to speak, did. There was generally more silence than speaking, and Buddy would look at her and mouth the words "Tain't doing dis." Then he'd lean down and scurry the length of the long, hard bench and sneak out to find his relief in the noise of the streets. Meda, however, would luxuriate in the silence. Sometimes the air whispered to her that it loved her, and then she would sit up straighter and let it kiss her forehead the way her mother did when she thought to. Her other churchlike experience was the one she partook of with her mother when the workers would assemble in the courtyard of the prison at the end of their shift. Someone would strike a tambourine, another would let go a throaty hum that grew into a song; Bible verses would flow like stormy rivers; prayers that moaned mixed with dancing, shouting, and convulsive shakes; and handkerchiefs tossed in the air floated through the courtyard, lending grace and softness to the grand display.

Dr. Miss had said "church" like a question, and Meda had come here because didn't people go to church to find God? Had she not found God here in the purity of those infants' soft breaths that first night; in the trembling righteousness of Ann's touch; in the honest laughter when the babies fixed their faces like clowns; in the thoughts that sifted in with the stillness? She'd know things all of a sudden as she'd sit here, and sometimes the knowing made her cry, like the time the knowing floated in with the light of day that had been gray with clouds and she realized that her mother had not been cleaning the penitentiary, that she had in fact been jailed there. Sometimes the knowing made her sigh, like the time she'd seen Miss Ma's granddaughter parading up Fitzwater Street with a little girl who looked white and she'd asked Miss Ma about her, and Miss Ma said she was kin to Nevada's siddity friend whose people were big-time caterers and she herself was studying to be a nurse. And Meda asked about her people, did her people look white. " 'Bout as mixed up as any colored folk, though not white,

white like that child. Hear it told from
Nevada that all they know 'bout the mother
is that she was some kinda gypsy that didn't
want to be no mother." Meda had kept Miss
Ma on the subject until she called Nevada's
friend by name, Sylvia. Sylvia. She'd wondered about that little girl for weeks. Maybe
that was her little girl. Maybe Sylvia had
taken her infant that morning and pretended to have gotten her from a relative.
Even though the ages were off by two years,
she could have lied about the little girl's
age. But the knowing of that came to her
finally; she was certain that was not her
child. That's the knowing that made her sigh
the most.

And sometimes the knowing made her
laugh, like right this instant as she watched
the dust beams assemble where the cradles
used to be, the specks gathered so closely,
dancing so hard they appeared to be standing still. She doubled over with laughter
now, enjoying the feel of the laughter pulling from way deep in her breast, where the
sickness couldn't reach. The dust beams
twirled and showed hints of color, a little
blue, a little yellow; they sparkled. She
laughed harder still at this particular knowing, so tickled by the knowing that the pain
in her breast went away. My, my, my, she

said when she had recovered herself. This one had been the best knowing of all.

14

The letter was addressed to Linc. His hands shook as he opened it. His eyes glazed over as he read the words, even as he tried not to comprehend the words. It was from Nevada. She introduced herself as Buddy's dear friend. Said that Buddy was too distraught to write himself, and anyhow his penmanship was less than legible, so she was writing, she said, to give him the sad, sad news that Buddy's sister Meda had passed away, that she was likely already buried by the time this letter arrived, that Buddy was heartbroken, but on the mend.

Linc had been unable to say the words out loud, Meda's dead. So he went straight to Bram's room and simply handed the letter to Bram so that he could read it for himself. They stood in the middle of Bram's room, refusing to look at one another because the pain on the other's face would be unbearable. Their world shrank then to the size of a dot, a dot too small to contain them both. Bram said that he needed to go to Philadelphia right then, he needed to inhale the same air that Meda had when she took in her last swallow of air.

Linc just stood there, dazed; his chest felt as if it were collapsing in on itself. What good was Philadelphia without Meda? What good was anyplace without her? He told Bram that he was engaged in a big bricklaying job and could not travel just now. "Just as well that you don't," Bram said. "Robinson's people must still have it out for you. But with my scars they will not know me."

Linc felt a rage brewing then. "To hell with Robinson's people. Weren't they the cause for us having to to run away like rats without a hole? Weren't they the reason we were separated from Meda in the first place? They will not keep me from" — he stopped himself, asked himself *from what*? From Meda? She was dead. Dead! "They will not keep me from at least kneeling down at Meda's grave and telling her goodbye. Thank her for being, for being —" For being what? he asked himself. Just for being, he thought. That was enough, her being. He wanted to see Buddy, too. He wanted to stand in front of Buddy dry-eyed, shoulders squared, and tell him he was sorry for his loss. For their loss. "Let Robinson's people come after me; I'll give them what I still owe Robinson." Bram lowered his eyes when Linc said that.

Linc and Bram made arrangements to meet the next afternoon at McGillin's Olde Ale House on Drury Street in Philadelphia. Bram left. Now Linc had the time and space he needed for a proper breakdown, such as no other man should be witness to, because men just did not cry the way that Linc needed to cry. And he did cry. He cried and cursed God, he cried and called out Meda's name, he cried and wished for the faceless, nameless woman who'd pushed him out into the world, the father who could have been a prince or the devil himself for all he knew, cried that he did not know. And after that, he just cried.

15

By the time Bram arrived in Philadelphia he was already feeling sick. He'd already experienced that predictive dry mouth, sweating already, and then shivering, already losing his coloring. He traveled to Buddy's house but no one was at home, no one on the entire block, it seemed. Then a young girl sitting outside near the corner told him that Buddy had gone fishing 'cause his sister died and he was hurting.

He ended up at the Benins'. He was greeted by a pleasant brown-skinned woman, this one not in a uniform, just as Meda had never worn a uniform, though the rest of Benin's house staff did. He wondered if this was Meda's replacement. Taller than Meda, and meeker, she looked down, away, not directly at Bram. When he told her who he was, her eyes shot open. "I have heard of you from Miss Meda! You are quite the virtuoso. Mrs. Benin speaks of you often, as well." She ushered him into the music room and left to summon Mrs. Benin.

There stood the piano, just as before, that elaborately carved Schomacker. It appeared now less like the mountain it had when he was a child. He touched it, then drew his finger away lest his touch cause it to crumble and collapse down upon him in an avalanche. Then he heard Mrs. Benin's voice behind him. She said, "Why, hello, Bram," and the avalanche began in earnest as his craggy emotions loosed and the foundation no longer held and the precipice toppled and his eyes flooded. They were soft tears, for Meda; he covered his face and cried into his hands for Meda. "Bram," Mrs. Benin called his name again, and his cry went stormy because now it was for Mrs. Benin. It was a hard cry because it was unexpected. He fought this cry, tried not to cry for her, even as he did, so this cry rankled him as it forced its way out. He sensed Mrs. Benin tighten as she stood behind him, the way she would tighten when he'd pour everything he had into a piece of music, when it would even be a moment of transcendence for him, she'd tighten lest she be forced to feel. He pulled a handkerchief from his pocket and covered his face and wiped it dry. Then he turned to regard her. She looked as she had when he'd last seen her, more than ten years ago, same globed-shaped face, same pert nose and thin lips, just a measure hardened.

He saw her gasp; she raised her hand toward his face and then pulled it back quickly. He remembered his burn scar then, and he put his own hand on his forehead, almost as if he was doing it on her behalf. "It looks worse than it is, actually. I got into a tussle with a candle and the candle won the first round." He forced a laugh, then cleared his throat and apologized for the display of emotion he'd just unleashed.

"It is somewhat understandable. Meda showed you inestimable affection."

He nodded. "If I may, I'd like to visit her room."

"There is nothing there. Her brother's people have collected her belongings."

"Did she take her last breath here? In this house?"

"You should of course know that I permitted —"

"Did she take her last breath here?"

"She did."

"Was she alone?"

"Her brother's lady friend had come to see her, she was with her. Good Lord, Bram," she said, as she moved toward the piano and took a seat at the bench, "is this an interrogation? I did not keep a log of her visitors, after all." She ran her fingers along the keyboard. "And as I was about to say, before your rudeness prevented me, I allowed for her to remain here for weeks after she was no longer able to perform her duties. I saw to it that she was comfortable. Mr. Benin even arranged that she be examined by his best physician. I was not obligated to do any of it, but I did."

"That was kind of you," Bram said. "I am glad you had the opportunity in the end to make up for the times when you were not so kind to her." He was sorry as soon as he said it, the way her face seemed to break up like a shifting jigsaw puzzle. He slid in next to her on the bench. She started playing Beethoven's Sonata in D major, their favorite duet, which formerly had served as his reward for a good practice session. He allowed her to play alone at first. Then he found his way — more likely his fingers found their way — to the keys, and he picked up his spot and started to play. She called out "decrescendo," then "piano, piano," encouraging him, instructing him as if he were still ten.

When they were done, he moved from the piano and bowed toward an imaginary audience, the way she'd taught him. She applauded. She stood then and cleared her throat and said, almost in a whisper, that there had been complicated situations with Meda that he wouldn't understand. He thought he saw a pleading in her eyes and he nodded, sensing that he'd freed her some with the nod, and it had cost him nothing after all. She asked him then if Linc had returned to Philadelphia with him.

"No," he said, stiffening at the question. "Why do you ask?"

"Robinson's family is still looking to bring him to justice."

"So they have not relinquished their hunger for revenge?"

She held up her finger. "Bram, you cannot deny that Linc has caused that man — caused his entire family — horrendous suffering."

"Mrs. Benin, just as you aver that there are things I do not understand about your situation, trust me, there are things that you do not understand about ours."

"Well, I suppose we can agree on that much," she said with a half-laugh. They stood there awkwardly, then she pulled Bram into a quick hug that caught him off guard, and then promptly departed, leaving him free to go to Meda's room.

Bram was leaking sweat by the time he reached McGillin's, where he and Linc were to meet. His insides felt charred, each breath so heated that exhaling burned his throat, his nostrils. Even when he used the necessary, the thin stream leaving him was boiling hot. Then Linc arrived and they settled in at a table.

"You look like shit, worse than the black death," Linc said to him, as he ordered a glass of ale and a shaved pork sandwich, and Bram said that he would have the same. "This is the worst I've seen you, you need to get to a dispensary."

"I will be well soon enough, as always," Bram said.

"This is not some dead ghost inside of you, Bram, no matter what you believe. You're truly ill — are you such a flaming dunce that you don't see it?"

"I went to Meda's room . . ." Bram tried to talk over Linc, but his voice was thinning.

"Look at you, even your eyes look like piss —"

"I felt her while I was in her room. I felt her spirit —"

"And I'm sure you have no appetite, as usual." Linc stopped then, as he realized

221

what Bram had just said. "You felt *whose* spirit?"

"Meda's. If you calm down —"

"Brother," Linc said, as he looked directly at Bram, though it hurt to look at him in such a state, "Meda is dead, she is not coming back to talk to you, or me, or anybody else, because the dead do not return." As Linc said it, he realized all over again that Meda was dead, the realization of which had been coming to him in rough waves. One minute he was going about his business, and the next drowning again. Afraid that he might not be able to contain a fresh display of emotion, he got up, said that he had to relieve himself.

He was halfway to the back door that led to the alley of the pub when he turned around, sorry now for the harsh way he'd just spoken to Bram, realized that he was speaking to himself as well as Bram in that instant. Realized that he wished he could believe as Bram did that it was possible to hear from, to speak to Meda. But he could not believe it, and he envied Bram's capacity to trust in things that he could not see. Bram was looking down at the food that had just been set in front of him when Linc called his name. As Bram looked up, Linc extended his elbow, that gesture that they'd had from childhood was between the two of them only, and it said: You are my brother and I love you more than life itself.

Bram extended his elbow, returning the gesture. He smiled, though it hurt even to smile. He watched Linc walk away from the table and if he'd had the strength he would have called him back and told him just to sit for another minute. But he barely had the strength to call out, used what strength he had to lift himself from the table and take the few short steps across the sawdust-covered floor to the tavern's front door. He just managed to get to the outside where the blazing sun was no match for the heat roiling inside his stomach, moving up past his chest, forming a ball in his throat, choking him. He leaned. Then he gagged. He spit up an ocean of black-colored blood. He fell then against the red-colored cobblestone pavement. It felt good to rest here, as he pulled his knees to his chest as if he were five years old again and curling up on Meda's bed to take an afternoon nap.

Linc settled the clouds in his chest and was on his way back to the table when he saw a woman in the alley struggling with a container of trash. Her cheeks were red, her swollen ankles peeking from under her skirt, and he guessed she was the age his mother would have been as she huffed and puffed, and there was no way he could not help her, and so he offered his arm to escort her back across the alley. She pushed him away on a laugh: "With those charming looks, go break the heart of someone closer your own age. Try my daughter, she's not spoken for, you know. Yoo-hoo, get here, Maggie!" she called, and a younger woman sauntered toward them with cheeks as red as hers, though she had markedly slimmer ankles. Linc was polite. He took the younger woman's hand in a gentle press between his own, called her "my lady" as they embarked on the timeless two-step of him pretending that she was the most beautiful woman he'd ever seen, and she with lowered eyes, fingers pressed over lips to suppress a giggle as if she'd never been addressed in such an unfathomable way. He was not aware of the commotion out in front of the tavern, of the shrieks and then the urgent clang of the emergency wagon. Workmen had been laying tracks for the new horseless trolley, so there were bursts of that earsplitting noise; otherwise his senses were engaged back in this alley, where the air was hot and close and smelled of granite dust and rotten peaches. Pigeons circled overhead dropping white smatterings, butchers on a break two doors down argued loudly, and Linc felt himself weakening under the sway of the young woman's shyness. Though it was feigned shyness; she was a forward one, he could tell. She asked him if he was Black Irish, as his lovely eyes and hair were so dark, and he told her that his mother died birthing him, his father had been killed in the war, and that he was likely a mongrel. Her cheeks bloomed even redder as she whispered that she had a mongrel dog once that loved to be stroked, and she'd taken great pleasure in obliging. "Such great pleasure," she said as her voice dipped into a moan and her hooded eyes opened wide for the briefest moment as she looked at him directly. He went into a tug-of-war then with his own arousal — on the one pull of the rope was the thrill of being enticed into her softness, on the other was past experience, which told him that she'd soon make demands that he'd be unable to meet. But as she talked, he realized that she was hinting that she wanted no other time than this time. She was smart, he could tell. And their repartee got hot as the sun back there as he looked around for her mother. "Mum is left," she said then. "Put in her day's work and gone to make her cabbage stew. I like cabbage thrust in the hot pot until it softens. You?" she asked.

"I confess, I do," he said as he felt his discretion fall away such as it had never done while in a sober state. She put her fingers to her lips, motioning for him to be quiet, and led him to the end of the, by then, desolate alley, where a broken-down carriage with three wheels sat propped on its axle. She climbed into the seat and pulled him to her. He expected at that moment for her to name her fee. Reasoned that the one she called her mum was but a poor excuse for a madame. But it didn't matter at that point. He'd already crossed that line where he'd grown two more legs and lost the use of his rational mind. She curled her finger, demurred a "Come on here," as they squeezed into the floor of the carriage, at which moment she took complete control. Controlled the moves and the tempo, controlled when he squeezed and arched his back and even covered his mouth to quiet the *uh,* the *ah,* all gaspy sounds he made. She took care of things the way no woman ever had, rendering him a sap with no spine, no constitution, no brain to speak of. He was just an explosion of sensation, whipped round and round, and she owned him completely.

Afterward, he was dazed, lying on his back on the floor of the carriage, watching the cumulus clouds point down and laugh. He didn't move at first, too drained and satisfied to move. When he felt the blood flow back into his head, his brain, when he was thinking relatively clearly, he gathered himself, pulled his clothes back together, and stumbled out of the carriage.

The alley was eerily empty. He felt his pocket then. His billfold was gone. He yelled out, "Hey, Maggie, you dirty thief!" He ran from one end of the alley to the other. Then stopped himself, reasoning that she and her so-called mum likely did this all the time, surely they had an escape route. He started walking toward the back of the tavern. Felt a lump of rage in his throat at her, at himself for being such an ass. The lump exploded in an unexpected eruption of laughter. He thought he was on the verge of hysteria, he laughed so hard; he was out a week's wages, and still he laughed, the laughter seeming to come from the same deep place that throbbed painful over the sad fact of Meda's death. Remembered suddenly how Meda used to tell him that although she wasn't wholly certain at all times that there was a God, she was pretty sure about the matter — when in the midst of heartache there was suddenly presented a reason for laughter.

He stepped back into the tavern, where the air was cool the way that stone buildings felt cool. He would tell Bram about what just happened to him, give them both some reasons for laughter.

But the table was empty when he returned. He looked around now and noticed suddenly that the entire tavern was empty, just the wide slats of dust hanging in the air. Bram's ale glass had been tipped over, its contents puddled on the sawdust-covered floor. Linc just stood there, the thought trying to nudge into his consciousness that the commotion out front — a large crowd had gathered — had something to do with Bram. But what were the chances of that, he asked himself, meaning to settle himself, as he picked up his satchel from the chair, stepped outside, and looked around for Bram — even called his name as he moved through the crowd, asking "What's happened out here?" of no one in particular.

16

Bram had already been scooped onto the emergency wagon by the time Linc stepped outside of the tavern. Linc was still calling Bram's name, his anxiety beginning to mount when he asked a waif of a boy who was standing in the crowd what had happened.

"I looked over and he was leaving the tavern with a staggering gait. His body shook, and I thought he was laughing. Then he bent and upchucked a ocean. See?" He pointed toward the ground. "Must be everything that was in his gut."

"What was his appearance?" Linc asked, trying not to see the black-colored blood seeping into the cobblestone.

"Blond hair, it was pulled back in a ponytail. And he had a scar on his crown like this," he made a W shape with his fingers and Linc felt as if a cannonball had formed in his chest and dropped all at once to the pit of his stomach. "Yer know him, do you?" the boy asked, noticing the cloud that fell over Linc's face. "He already been scooped onto a wagon, already at hospital, I'd say."

The boy continued talking about the horrid spectacle of all that Bram had brought up from his gut. But Linc had already started running up the street, was already at Pennsylvania Hospital. The hospital had him wait, and then relayed that Bram had already been transported to Philadelphia Hospital, where they told Linc that Bram was not there.

Linc's frustration turned almost to violence when he stabbed two fingers into the chest of a tight-lipped clerk, at which the man pleaded, "Sir, please, I know nothing of your brother. And I need my employment here, and my wages, after all."

Linc was almost relieved when several orderlies converged and surrounded him and proceeded to manhandle him. He could at least punch and kick and curse and push back and wrestle and expend the energy building up inside of him, which was his fear that something devastating had happened to Bram. He'd just lost Meda. Not Bram, too, he wanted to shout, as one of the orderlies said that a constable was coming over to query him.

"For what cause?" Linc shouted at him.

"For assault."

"I assaulted no one."

"I got a hospital clerk that say otherwise," he said, then asked Linc his name.

"What does my name matter?" Linc spit out.

"Because you look like a man with a bounty on his head. And the constable gives us a cut of his commission every time we reel one in. What crimes you committed in the municipality of Philadelphia?"

"Ain't from here." Linc put on his Italian accent. "This is my first time in this filthy shithole of a city."

"Well, the constable got the sketchings of every ugly face wanted in the municipality seared in his brain, and once he looks at you, he shall know, without a doubt, whether yer ugly face is on one of the wanted posters crowding his wall."

Linc continued to no avail to try and wrestle his hands free. They pushed him through an archway that led to a tunnel. Told himself that he surely must be dreaming when he heard a voice penetrate the tunnel's thick black air. It was a woman's voice, smooth and resonant, bouncing around in the tunnel. "Dey taking him to da house named for da one Jesus woken from da dead," the disembodied voice said. "Lazus house."

"Is that that crazy nigger bitch?" one of the orderlies said as the woman came into view, her face practically indistinguishable from the tunnel's air, though her dress certainly was not, her dress a cornucopia of colorful patched-together rags.

"Thought she was warned to stay out of this tunnel," said another.

One of the orderlies pushed her aside. "Get back in the crazy house where you belong," he said.

"Yer listen to her at your own peril," another said to Linc. "She charged with cleaning the shit off the wall in the crazy house, and the stench has gone to her brain and made her crazy, too."

"Only keeps her employment here," said another, "because every time they try to release her one of the head blokes loses a son to diphtheria, so they fear she might be casting around spells."

They joked about that prospect now even as they pummeled Linc until they kicked him through the door into the rear court-yard of the hospital, where vats of burning rags gave off gray plumes that smelled of human waste. "Constable be here in short order to nail yer ugly ass," one of them said, as they laughed, and then silence after the door smacked shut.

Linc massaged his sides as he looked around and saw that he was completely fenced in, the wall at least ten feet high, smooth and unscalable, he thought. Then the woman from the tunnel appeared again, as if the putrid, smoky air had formed her. "You be searching for da one wid da rings, I hid dem rings."

"Rings?" Linc asked, moving closer. "You mean the scars on his forehead? Yes, do you know where he is?"

"Lazas house," she said. "Dat's where he goin'."

"The Lazaretto? Quarantine? Why quarantine?"

She put her hands to her temples and made small tapping motions. "Say he got da fever. Say dey pile him on da boat wit da rebel shitheads."

"Is he alive? Was he talking? Breathing?"

"Dey's shitheads drivin' dat boat. Dey not da ones who usey show up to take a one to Lazus house. But dey say dat's where dey go. I hear it sure as I hear da one shithead call me nigger hag. 'What cho lookin' at, nigger hag,' he say to me? No need for him to talk to me in dat way. Why? Why?" She looked directly at Linc when she asked it. "Dat's why I holds onto da rings." She rubbed her temples in ferocious circles. Her skin was smooth even where the creases were. Linc touched her shoulder, told her that neither did he understand why someone would talk to her in that way, which at least seemed to calm her.

"How did you get out here?" he asked her.

She pointed to a corner of the courtyard cut out in square that the cats used to come and go.

"Where does it lead?"

"The tunnel you just came trew."

He sighed and looked from the cut-out square to the top of the fence, trying to decide.

She seemed to read his thoughts. "I seen rats big as jackals come and go ober dere."

She walked across the courtyard, close to the smoldering vats of trash. Linc followed; he nearly gagged from the smell. He kicked at a rectangle of red bricks stacked against the wall. The bricks separated easily and he was staring at a jagged hole. She sat down next to the hole and crossed her legs in a bow and fixed her hands as if she was praying. She breathed deeply, audibly, and Linc wondered how she endured the stench. He lay flush to the ground and pushed his head through the opening and was staring at a mound of hay. He inhaled a waft of horse manure that was as perfume after the stench of the smoldering trash. He struggled to maneuver through the hole but his shoulders were stuck. "Turn yourself," he heard her say. Her voice seemed to come from the other side of the fence, and he wondered if she was an apparition, though he was certain about the nonexistence of such things. She was leaning over him, pushing against his shoulder. *Do one, den da oder one.* He did. Shards of wood punctured his skin, ripping it, as he thought he heard the door open. He bent his knees and with a final thrust was on the other side. A stable. He rolled through the hay; he wanted to yell from the burn of the hay against his raw skin. He managed to stand and start running in one quick move. He was through the stable, back out on the street. He leaned and gasped to catch his breath. Then he started to run again, looking toward the river. Made his way to the pier. He walked up and down the pier, calling out, "Lazaretto! Any boys pushing off for the Lazaretto?" though he knew he had no money for fare. Had only the contents of his satchel, his timepiece the only thing of worth.

Had he gotten to the pier just a few minutes earlier he likely could have talked his way onto Carl's boat. Carl, still the generous person he'd always been, was ferrying a boatload of people to the Lazaretto for, of all things, a grand wedding celebration for two of Lazaretto's live-in staff. Since high-quarantine season was winding down — ships were already being directed farther upriver to the Port of Philadelphia, and the hospital was all but empty; and since the Lazaretto was a lush backdrop for a wedding, with its stunning overlook of the river and its formal gardens, the quarantine master consented to them inviting a few family members to sit in witness. But once word of the wedding spread, people signed on to attend whether or not they had affection for the couple because the trip would give them the weekend with their own loved ones who lived and worked at the quarantine station. Like Vergie, for example, eager for the chance to see Sylvia; like Miss Ma, because Nevada now worked at the Lazaretto as the head cook; like Carl, who offered to transport them all because, well, because Sylvia was there; like Splotch, who'd been nursing an intense desire for Vergie of late and hoped the weekend away with her might deal him a lucky hand.

But Carl and his crammed vessel had just pushed off. And the few remaining ferrymcn declined Linc's request, his offer of his watch. Until he approached a couple of half-drunk men who said they were moving in that direction. "Gittin' on to Wilmington but got te pause by the leper house to deliver cargo stored below. Show me what yer got." Linc gave up his timepiece. And then he was Lazaretto bound.

■ ■ ■ ■

PART II

■ ■ ■ ■

17

It was later than it should be for a river ride, particularly for a boatload of twenty black people traveling the Delaware in a southerly direction. The sky was already dressed in evening red, its purple and black lining beginning to show. But Carl and his passengers had pushed off from the dock a full hour past their departure time because many had overpacked and it had taken time to accommodate their cargo: their presents for the bride and groom; their own plaid vests and taffeta skirts and crinoline slips and cuffed-bottom pants, and shoes for doing the cake walk; even the attitudes some had managed to squeeze on board because this assemblage was ripe for disharmony.

The groom, Spence, was an orderly at the Lazaretto's hospital whose aunt lived in close proximity to Sylvia's family. The bride, Mora, the facility's processing clerk, hailed not far from Fitzwater Street, where Miss

Ma and Nevada and Buddy lived. So those they'd invited already came from different worlds. The teachers avoided the gamblers; and there was even dissension within like kind: the one didn't like the other because their child outlasted the other at the Coachmen's Association–sponsored spelling bee promenade; or the member of First African felt put down by the church clerk at Mother Bethel A.M.E.; or the one's Virginia-born husband had ruined the new brocaded couch of the native Philadelphian by spilling hot pipe ash upon it. And if they needed yet another strain of contention, those related to the bride and groom resented the whole field of opportunists who had taken the trip just to be with kin. These were trifles back home, where their differences receded in the face of them all being black in Philadelphia. Though in the confined space of the boat, their differences were dramatic and their personalities were popping like firecrackers, and Carl warned that their discord would surely make them capsize.

Fortunately the weather was pleasant and the trip not very long since Carl was worried about the weight. He'd constructed the boat himself over several years from the scraps and throwaway pieces of other shipbuilders down at the waterfront. He called it a schooner, though it was smaller than most schooners, two-masted, with only a small cube of below space, which was now packed with the things they'd carried on board. As the boat groaned and creaked like an arthritic mule on its way down the Delaware River, Carl noticed another boat traveling in the same general direction. The other boat was the one Linc, with the promise of his watch, had talked his way onto. It was a yawl, smaller and lighter, and it had come to within a few meters of the wedding guests and was now floating alongside. When Carl saw that there were white men in the boat, his discomfort mounted over their intentions after their sudden change in velocity. He'd heard stories about black boaters terrorized on this river by white men. He was just about to call to his assembled passengers standing portside to tell them to step back from the rail. The railing was low and he didn't want any passengers tumbling overboard. But they were already waving out how-dos to those in the other boat, and at least for the moment they weren't going after one another. He convinced himself to settle down, reasoned that it was just his day to be on edge. He was on edge about the weight they carried, on edge about the approach of the other boat, and now even on edge about the height of the railing. At least there was a railing, he told himself. Where he stood at the helm, there was no railing. The only place he'd scrimped was the area around the helm, because that was his space, and he knew where to step and where not to step.

Two of the three in the other boat, a river courier and his assistant, raised their tall bottles holding rum-colored liquid in salute to those on Carl's boat; the head man tilted his bottle and gulped. "Fucking darkies," he called after he'd swallowed. "Go back to Africa!"

The river rose up suddenly and slapped him in the face, and Linc, who had sat low against the deck with head hung, lost in thoughts of Meda, and worrying about Bram, called out, "Serves you right. They done nothing that warrants your taunting. Guess the river is on their side today." The head man told Linc to shut his dumb-ass mouth or swim the rest of the way. Linc retorted that he'd more than paid for the trip with his timepiece, and that if he had to swim, they all would be swimming.

The occupants of Carl's boat had not heard the man's insult, except for Vergie, who felt it more than heard it, the way she'd always felt insults from white people. She was certain that anything coming from the ragtag trio in that other boat was sure to be disparaging. "I hope the river swallows you up!" she shouted. She spit into the river, intending it for them, then flicked her hand in the air at them and turned to rejoin the others as their hearty laughter went to nervous coughs over what she'd just done.

"You okay, Verge? What you doing?" Carl asked. He was protective of Vergie, a carry-over from her little-girl years, when he was first courting Sylvia.

"She just enjoying her lovely self," Splotch said.

"I believe *I* asked Vergie." Carl cut him off.

"I was just giving those in that raggedy boat the greeting they deserved," Vergie said.

"Tain't so," said Lena, sister of the bride. "She doing what she got no business doing." Then Lena planted herself right in front of Vergie. She had already tired of Vergie's incessant chatter about how she couldn't wait to see Sylvia, and how Sylvia was promoted to head nurse, and Sylvia this, and Sylvia that. She resented Vergie for not acknowledging the real purpose of the trip, her sister's wedding. And then there was the fact Lena had been sweet on Carl for years but had been unable to capture his attention because he'd had eyes for nobody but Sylvia. Now she pointed her finger in Vergie's face. "Vergie, you know good as me you got no business taunting them in that other boat less you plan on passing today, and if that be the case, you need to be in that boat with them. Otherwise you need to swallow your tongue and sit on your childish actions and stop putting the rest of us in harm's way."

Vergie stepped back to give herself room. "I'll do it to you, Lena" — she flicked her hand in Lena's face, then turned portside, in the direction of the other boat, and made the same move again — "and I'll do it to them. And I have never passed, and I do not plan on passing today. And I defy anybody to declare that I'm not as colored as Blue-Black Bob."

"You ain't colored," Lena said as she pushed Vergie hard, and before Vergie could recover herself there was a rush to get between them. One group pulled Vergie toward the bow, another nudged Lena to the stern; they were both consoled by their factions: "You know you're right, but not worth making a spectacle of yourself by fighting on this river like a hyena."

The separation worked a miracle in that

suddenly there was space in the boat for a sense of contentment to squeeze in right along with everything else they'd brought on board. Shortly, the atmosphere lightened as they marveled at the rainbow floating atop the river, and how low the rapturous red sky was hanging, and how intoxicating was the smell of the sea, which was a blend of fish oil and bergamot and thyme. One man, Skell, short for Skeleton, owing to how thin he was, pretended to be Captain Ahab on the hunt for the great white whale and gave a dramatic recitation. Another blew a harmonica, another shook a tambourine. The married men told wife jokes, and even the women laughed, and had jokes of their own, communicated by their winks. The smell of cedar rose up from Carl's pride and joy of a deck, and a comment about how nicely it was planked made him smile. The sky seemed to be smiling, too, with its curvy red mouth, and now even Carl began to relax just a bit. A near-euphoria draped over them all and hung like the red sky, close and palpable, until the blue and black moved in.

In the other boat the courier-in-charge had watched in disbelief as Vergie flicked her hand at them a second time. He understood by association that she could not be white. He was from the part of Delaware below the Mason-Dixon and not accustomed to entertaining slights from those he reasoned were of the race that should still be bought and sold. He threw his head back and drained the rum from the tall bottle. "Mulatto wench!" he spit as a rage moved through him, amplified by the drink, and he called to his aide to ready his shotgun.

"Why the fuck you calling for the shotgun?" Linc yelled.

" 'Cause I don't tolerate no back talk from no niggers."

"What back talk?" Linc said, trying now to calm the man down. "No need for waving around guns. You know how rum will put things in your head that are far from the truth."

"What are you, some nigger-lovin' piece of shit?" the head courier said as he twisted a wrap of line around the tiller and moved back from the helm as his aide staggered toward him and handed him his shotgun.

"Stupid-ass lug, why the fuck you give him the gun for?" Linc said, horrified as he scrambled to stand to wrestle the gun away before the man could take aim at the schooner. But he'd already taken aim, Carl's head in his sights as Linc lunged for him, and the boat pitched noticeably, and Linc fought with everything he had to shake off the younger man, who had Linc by his neck. And by the time he did, the other had already fired off both barrels and was fumbling to reload before Linc overpowered him and took him down.

The sounds of merriment had been at their height in Carl's boat when the courier took aim. Applause roared for Skell's Ahab soliloquy. The booms of laughter for the one wife's comeback to her husband's jibes were accompanied in time by the harmonica's trills and the jangles of the tambourine. At first the gun blasts seemed part of the merriment, too. But a second later a hole opened in the water and the river exploded in shock and Carl yelled for everybody to get down, though he could barely hear himself as he shouted; the sound of the second blast lingered and shimmied before it fell, and now he felt the sound that was a thunder ball of heat trapped in his leg that was louder even than the screams and shouts as the wedding guests scampered to get low on the deck.

"This all your fault, Vergie," Lena sobbed. "You had no right provoking them. Now we all might die 'cause of it. Why are you even here, you like the albatross in Skell's recitation, just bad fortune strangling us with your white-lookin' self."

The retort that would have been usual for Vergie under any other circumstances sat fully formed at the base of her throat. It threatened to choke her as it expanded, gathering all the guilt and shame she'd accumulated over the years about the way she looked. A plume of whispers and shrieks rushed to fill the hole left by her non-response. Some sympathetic to Vergie, other's pushing Lena's point as the boat rocked from side to side. Then Miss Ma's laughter got in between the dispute and Carl told them all to be quiet, he was managing to put some river between his boat and the other one, and right now his singular goal was to get to the Laz as straightaway as he could, and their discord was making a wavy line of his concentration.

Carl thought that his leg would explode from the noise of the hot metal trapped there, and he gasped on his words, which amplified their power, and everybody swallowed their conversation, and the schooner was suddenly silent. The night sat directly on top of the silence. The red sky had fallen even lower and was now slipping below the boat, exhausted from trying to hold the night at bay.

Vergie was the first to notice the blood that had seeped through Carl's boots and accumulated in a puddle at his feet. He was standing at the helm, but barely. She yelled out his name. He tried to straighten himself up. "Skell, take the helm," he managed to say. Skell commenced to crawl on his belly to get to the bow. Lena tried to beat him there, hollering, "Carl, mercy, he's shot, somebody help him." There was a scramble and a tussle as half a dozen other people tried to get to Carl all at once. The boat tilted and Carl stumbled as he tried to stand straight up; his shot-up leg couldn't bear his weight and he fell forward at the very place where he'd not attached a railing. He grabbed at air to break his fall. The air couldn't break his fall. The river scattered to make way for his entry and descent. Once in the water, he fought with everything he had to stay afloat. His arms did well; it was too loud around his leg, though. A blow horn moved through his calf and he thought that it was the sound that had the power; the sound was pulling him under, multiplying itself in its reverberations. He tried to piece through the sound to get back to the top. Then he thought he heard Sylvia calling his name, saying hold on, hold on, Carl, hold on. Sylvia, Sylvia, such a sweet, soft, soothing sound to succumb to, he laughed to himself, as he thought of other *S* sounds: sumptuous, sensual, simply, surely, yes surely. And then even the commotion in his leg quieted down.

18

The Lazaretto resembled more a country estate than a quarantine station. Gracious walkways hedged with azalea and rhododendron cut a path to the mansion-sized main house where a porch looked out on the splendid river view. The setting gave the workers here something soft and beautiful to focus on when they took a break from protecting the Port of Philadelphia from plagues. It was thick work: receiving and inspecting the steady stream of vessels that had to first stop here to get permission to enter the city's bustling port, then processing the immigrants, holding over the potentially infectious to nurse them back to health or, in the worst cases, rock them as they die. But tonight and for the weekend the relief would be better than even the stunning river view as they prepared to welcome the wedding guests.

Sylvia was especially excited because Vergie was on the way. She'd been in a bright mood all day just anticipating seeing Vergie. Adding to the mood, Ledoff, the quarantine master, was soon to take weekend leave from the Lazaretto along with most of the rest of the white staff. Ledoff had been alarmed that such a large contingent of family and friends of the bride and groom were about to converge on them; he'd consented to a similar arrangement for a white couple the year before and only four people had come. Still, he allowed the plans to stand, as he was from a long line of abolitionists and did what he could for the sake of parity. So for everyone's comfort he directed all of the white staff to take weekend leave except for two people — his nephew, Son, and the Lazaretto's doctor. Son was a hulking, genial man with the intellectual capacity of an eight-year-old. He took expert direction from Sylvia and Nevada and the rest of the staff. Ledoff did the staff a favor by allowing Son to remain. The same could not be said about the doctor. The doctor was next in line to run the quarantine station when Ledoff was away, but both Ledoff and Sylvia understood that in Ledoff's absence, Sylvia was in fact in charge.

She'd been humming all morning as she and Ledoff worked to clear the final ship of the weekend, likely the final ship of quarantine season. The vessel filled with immigrants from Germany appeared in good order; it was clean and spacious, no more than two to a berth. The passengers presented in reasonably good health, no elevated tempertures, no pink-eye, no thrush, no yellowed eyes or skin, no open boils. Sylvia had had to tussle with the mother of an infant boy in order to examine the child. The mother spoke no English, so Sylvia made a baby-rocking gesture with her arms to let the mother know she meant the child no harm. The woman relented, but soon stretched her arms out, reaching for her baby, and there it was all over again, that image of Meda that refused to stay submerged, that would float to the top and invade Sylvia's conscious mind. Even now, more than two decades later, the image carried the whole jumble of feelings associated with that night.

She tried to stifle the memory as she hurried back to her room to get cleaned up and dress for the party. She was approaching the tiny creek hedged with scandalously hued roses, and now Nevada's back was in view as she clipped roses to fill vases for decorating the food tables. Sylvia was glad to see Nevada. She'd missed her. Nevada had been in Philadelphia all week helping her new man friend, Buddy, make arrangements for his sister's burial. Nevada was already dressed for the night-before-the-wedding celebration in a black lacy dress that fell from her shoulders and skimmed close to her hips and flared out around her calves.

"They let the German ship go on, am I not correct?" Nevada called over her shoulder.

"You correct, Nevada, and how did you know it was me?"

"The heavy sighs," Nevada said, a chuckle to her voice.

"I was not sighing, and let me see if the thorns got you."

Nevada looked down at her hands. Her thumb and middle fingers were bloody. "Drats," she said as she put the rose basket down and reached into her dress pocket for a handkerchief. Nevada had no feeling in her fingers. When she was a toddler in Virginia, the wheels of a runaway wagon crushed her spine and she'd been given up first for dead, and then for immobilized from the cheek down. But she had enjoyed a miraculous recovery, claimed to have been brought about by her devastated father who imagined himself to be like Abraham as he'd stretched his baby girl on a warm bed of dirt under Orion's bow and offered her up, feather pillow poised to gobble her final gasps. Then through his tears he saw her feet move, and then her arms, and then, so he swore, Nevada laughed and sat up and began to play in the dirt that was to have been her dying bed. The only lingering effect of the accident had been a deadened sense of feeling in her fingers. Nevada often joked to Sylvia that other parts of her body more than compensated for her no-feeling fingers by having too much sensation, way too much for just one man alone, which is why she had to play the field.

"Why they let the Germans go with swiftness and they held that ship from the West Indies for a year?" She tried to hide her hand from Sylvia.

"It was not a year, and half of the West Indians were hot with fevers besides. Now let me see your hand."

"Felt like a year, burned all their belongings, bet they don't burn that brown whiskey loading down the Irish ships. Have not seen Irish vessels in a while, guess Boston is favoring the Irish, Philadelphia seems to favor Italians of late —"

"Your hands, Nevada." Sylvia cut her off. "Do not try to change the subject with your rant on immigration practice, or quarantine practice, or wherever your mouth is headed."

"You know it true, you said yourself that when they bring in rags or sugar their cargo is as good as burned to ash. Plus, don't you have a life somewhere to save?"

"Maybe yours since you seem to enjoy staying unobservant around sharp things coming in contact with your fingers." Sylvia pulled Nevada's hand to her and lifted the handkerchief. "Nevada, these wounds are ugly and deep. Are you trying to get gangrene?" she chided Nevada as she went into her bag and lined her supplies on the rock serving as a table and a seat.

Nevada interrupted Sylvia's chastising, "Either give me a big wad of cotton to put in my ears to blot out your sermon, Sylvia, or let me stuff it in your mouth to stem it at its source."

"The house ready?" Sylvia ignored Nevada as she dressed her fingers.

"All set up. Son and that one with the broad back, Kojo — Lord Jesus, that man has a good-looking back — they moved all the furniture against the wall so there should be good dancing space."

"What you doing looking at that man's back?"

"Why should I not? The good Lord fashions such a back, He means for it to be admired."

"Admired by his wife." Sylvia laughed as she wrapped a band of the cotton around Nevada's rose-thorn-punctured fingers. "You know his wife coming for the weekend with the others on the boat."

"I know, he told me, we got an understanding betwixt us —"

"Happened that fast, you already got an understanding with the man? Mnh, always happens fast with you, Nevada." Judgment laced Sylvia's tone. "What about Buddy? I thought that was actually going somewhere. He been widowed for how long now? Plus, he seems decent enough, at least to my short but explosive encounter with him that night I tried to deliver your birthday cake."

"But Sister died —"

"And that changes matters how?"

"They were close."

"The correlation is lost on me, Nevada."

"Leave me alone, Sylvia. Go correlate with Carl."

Sylvia stopped and looked at Nevada. "Oh my, seems as if your fingers are not the only thing punctured. Seems I have struck a nerve as well."

"Well, if you claim the right to pick a man

for me, that river runs both ways. You quit Carl for no good reason that I could see, other than the wooing attempts of that high-yellow son of those highfalutin people who run the school down south. You were too pretty for him, besides. And you are pretty. You scrunch your face whenever I remind you of that. I don't know who put it in your head that you had to choose between being pretty and smart, so you decided on smart and then just deny —"

"Stop, Nevada." Sylvia cut her off. "I shall not allow you to turn this table," she said, thinking that it was a fact that she wasn't pretty in the way Nevada was with her soft red-toned complexion and softly formed features. Nevada's eyes were light brown — too light for her skin color, she'd joke when a person complimented her. "These eyes are the symptom of a confused Indian and a colored in love and some kind of mishap with a white man." She knew how to use her eyes for play, the way she batted them around, or held them half-closed, or in a wide-open come-'ere-baby stare.

Sylvia fixed her eyes on Nevada's now. "I am willing to wager that if the one, Buddy, was already spoken for, Kojo's back would not be in your conversation."

"What, Sylvia, are you trying to purport?"

Nevada asked, as she ripped at a sapling with her free hand and threw it in the creek.

"I am saying that you apparently have got some very strong feelings for this Buddy, this available man, but your feelings are so large that they frighten you, so suddenly Kojo, an already-spoken-for man, becomes a sufficient distraction."

Nevada sucked air in through her teeth. "You do not know half of what you think you do, Sylvia."

"I know Kojo's wife set a woman's hair on fire who she suspected of running with him."

Nevada looked stunned.

"Yeah, she did. Hear she splashed the woman's hair with kerosene and set a candle to it. Said the woman had a beautiful suit of hair. Straighter than yours, so it took its time burning." She rubbed her hand over Nevada's hair. "This thick head of hair you got will likely go up like kindling."

"Why you lying to me, Sylvia?" Nevada said, as she pushed Sylvia's hand away. "She never tried to set nobody's hair on fire."

"You can dare to think I am lying. But if I were you, I would wear a hat tonight, something made out of a slow-to-burn material, like maybe cast iron. Maybe you better get on over to the kitchen and find you a pot worthy of decorating to wear on your head."

"You know how full of mess you are?" Nevada said as she ran the palm of her hand over her hair as if considering how combustible it was. She'd rinsed it in henna earlier and it was now pulled back in a bun tied with a red ribbon. She took a deep breath then. "I had no intentions of allowing Kojo to whisper his man-lies in my ear, Sylvia, I swear to you, I did not. But I did think Buddy should have come here on the boat with the rest, and that this weekend likely would have helped with his grief over Sister. I guess when I gave Kojo the time of day, I was retaliating against Buddy for not coming to spend the weekend with me. Lord Jesus, so the woman used a candle?"

"With an extra-thick wick. I'm told she travels with a canteen filled with kerosene." Sylvia's voice shook with laughter, and now Nevada laughed, too.

They both laughed so hard that Bay, head of the cleaning staff, called from the other side of the creek.

"Thought the party was over at the house," Bay said. "Sylvia, you not even ready? They gonna be here directly."

Nevada held up her bandaged hand, practically wheezing from laughing so. "I'm wounded, Bay."

"So I guess I got to carry your load," Bay said, as she made her way across the narrow, shallow creek, stepping from rock to rock that served as a bridge and then picked up the basket of roses.

"Well, I would help her but I got to get cleaned up and dressed," Sylvia said, moving for the creek, then asked if there was still water in the pump.

"I saved you some," said Bay. "You last."

Nevada called out for Sylvia to hurry. "I need you to come out to kitchen and help me coordinate my headdress," she said, and that started another round of laughter that caused Sylvia to almost lose her footing. She laughed through her bath, laughed while she dressed, and even while she helped Bay and Nevada finish decorating. She especially laughed when Kojo showed up with his broad back and big hands. Sometimes she hated laughing this deeply, as if a part of her knew that she'd cry soon and the laughter was cutting a path through her chest to make way for the hurt she knew she'd feel. But right now she needed to laugh. She really did.

19

The boat Linc had been on, but no longer was, arrived first at the Lazaretto. Linc had slammed around and in turn been slammed around by both men, eventually suffering a sound whipping. They threw him from the boat at Hog Island and told him he was lucky to still be alive. Then they made their delivery at the Lazaretto. They were delivering a nondescript crate that could have held blood-red oranges from Florida. They were such shoddy workers, having been hired from the bottom of the list last-minute by the hospital. They kicked the crate onto the Lazaretto's pier and then just left it there. No notification to the guardhouse that stood only yards away, no reattachment of the sheet with the yellow markings to indicate the suspected contagion, no signature from the quarantine master or his substitute certifying receipt of the crate. The steady stream of delivery people who'd earlier deposited the side of steer for to-night's feast, the fresh-killed pig, and double the usual order of meal and potatoes had taken greater care with their leavings than this one dropping off dangerous cargo. Any of the Lazaretto staff would have assumed that the crate was simply the final round of supplies.

That was a poor assumption indeed. The crate contained the lifeless body of Bram. Though the doctors worked feverishly to save Bram's life, they declared him expired shortly after the emergency wagon delivered him to the Municipal Hospital. They sus-pected he'd been suffering from yellow fever. In the prior century, the city of Philadelphia lost thousands of lives to the disease, an ugly disease. Beyond making the sufferers feel that their insides were on fire, yellow fever turned the skin and eyes yel-low, caused severe abdominal distress and incessant vomiting; the afflicted would bleed internally, the bleeding so severe that it would spill out of every orifice, even the eyes. The mere thought of an epidemic could unleash hysteria: the panicked wealthy would surely flee the city; commerce would come to a startling halt; all that thrived about the city would surely be toppled, reducing it to a squat of smoldering rags. A previous yellow-fever epidemic had even caused Philadelphia to lose the honor of serving as the permanent capital of the United States.

So the Board of Health regularly hushed suspected cases of yellow fever and shipped them off to the Lazaretto to be confirmed. As it did so now, with Bram. No toe tag identified Bram by name, no record of death was issued on his behalf. His body was still warm, though barely, when he had been hastily wrapped in thick muslin and packed in a sack and situated inside a non-descript crate.

Here on the Lazaretto, only the doctor knew to expect the crate, that the crate contained the remains of a possibly infectious corpse. But the doctor was too compromised. He was severely addicted to opium. He'd already forgotten to expect the crate.

The doctor had just lain on his side in his office and had Spence, the poor groom who should have been off somewhere practicing the cakewalk for the party tonight, administer the opium-stuffed pipe to him. Spence needed to tend to whisking his suit, buffing his shoes, and otherwise preparing himself for his nuptials. So instead of spending the

266

next hour here, letting the doctor casually pull on the pipe, and nod off and then signal Spence that he was ready for more, Spence jammed double the usual amount of opium into the pipe. He lit the pipe and watched the doctor pull hard. There was no sound after a long exhalation of air save the thud of the doctor's head falling against the cot. The low light of the bedside lamp cast an orange-tinged hue on the doctor's face. His eyes were closed. His mouth gaped. Spence stood, not moving, afraid that perhaps he'd given him too much at once, perhaps he'd killed him. His mind immediately went to Mora, his bride-to-be. He imagined himself telling Mora that the wedding could not go on because the doctor was dead. Imagined the sense of relief he would feel telling her that. He remained motionless as he confronted himself with the guilty thought that he would rather this man be dead than himself have to say "I do." He focused on bringing the doctor to. He sat him up and slapped his face and yelled out, "Doctor! Doctor!" Hissing sounds as the doctor drew breath, and Spence suffered a convolution of relief and disappointment.

"That is it," Spence said as he inspected the hull of the pipe. "Nothing left but ash."

The doctor blinked his eyes, and Spence

commenced to clean the pipe and hide it away in the back of the shed where the leeches were kept. He removed the cotton mask from his nose and mouth that he wore to protect his lungs from the onslaught of smoke. He slid his arms from the white jacket that was part of his uniform and always made him feel more like a house Negro than a hospital orderly. He could feel the sweat draining from his armpits as he inspected the jacket closely for signs of ash, then hung it on the hook reserved for him. He poured alcohol on his hands and rubbed them together furiously to clean them. He hurried through the outer office to get to the outside. The telegraph machine made a commotion as Spence walked past, but he tried to ignore it. He stopped, closed his eyes, as if that would close his ears. He went back into the inner office and grabbed the doctor by the shoulders, sat him up again, and shook him into focus. "Tele's coming in," he shouted in the doctor's face.

The doctor was limp under Spence's grasp. He smiled a sloppy smile. "You're one fine nigger, Spence, truly fine."

Spence slapped the doctor's face again hard. "Tele might be urgent," Spence said as he watched blood rush to the doctor's face and settle under the skin where his hand had landed. "Urgent! Urgent!" he repeated, but the doctor's head slumped into a nod, and Spence stared at his hand as if his hand had acted independently of his brain. The doctor started to cough, and Spence could tell he was trying to get his eyes to focus. Spence was relieved. If he had to hit him again, he thought his hand might totally disassociate from the rest of him and become a balled fist and not stop until the doctor was an unrecognizable pulp. He helped the doctor to his feet and led him to the outer office past the solid oak desk and the shelves with mammoth-sized books to the side of the room where the telegraph machine wheezed and stuttered. The doctor leaned against the table as he squinted to decipher the markings the machine made. "Spence, look at this, crate coming with suspected contents to be examined — holy shit, look at this, Spence." Spence didn't look at the telegraph. He studied his pinky finger instead. His finger was a misshaped mass of bone and gristle fused that way when he was eight years old after his mother doused his finger with acid for reading aloud. Told him that if he was ever tempted to let on to a white person that he could read, just look at his finger and imagine that it was his face. She'd witnessed such a horror perpetrated against her childhood friend where she'd grown up, in western Georgia; she'd been made to watch after he'd been caught reading aloud as sulfuric acid was splashed in his face. His screams, she said, were a part of her fiber after that, remaining with her constantly. The lesson stuck. Though it was twenty years since the Emancipation, his mother had already been a free woman for almost a decade when she'd melted away the skin on his baby finger — and though Spence was a prolific reader, he'd been rendered incapable of admitting to his literacy. He rubbed his finger now and allowed his eyes to retreat to their practiced blankness. The doctor waved him away. And in a flash Spence was out of the room, out of the house.

The doctor mumbled as he maneuvered around the table, stepping with extreme care, as if walking a tightrope. "Ledoff, I must tell Ledoff. Crate coming." He repeated it over and over, walking a line to the door, then onto the porch. He half-sat, half-landed on the porch bench. He vaguely remembered that Ledoff had left for the weekend, so what did it matter, what did anything matter? The mist was hanging in strings and he moaned and angled his face so that the mist could stroke his face and soothe some the stinging place where Spence had hit him hard. He looked out onto the Delaware and marveled at how smoothly the river coursed all the way to the horizon, where the sky and river appeared locked in an openmouthed kiss. "Ah, love," he said, about to descend into another opium nod. But then he jerked up, because suddenly the sky and river parted lips and coughed out two boats. "Two boats?" the doctor whispered. "How many dead men are coming this evening?" He tried to get up. "I must tell somebody," he said. But the mist was too charming now; and, anyhow, his chin was already at his chest as he lightly snored.

The wedding guests arrived, shouting and praying and cursing and calling for help as they disembarked. Kojo was first on the scene and was immediately consumed by the chaos as his mind tried to put together what happened. Had they capsized? Were they all accounted for? His wife, Lil, where was his wife? Lord, please don't punish me thus for taking up with Nevada, he screamed in his head when he didn't see his wife among the first to have staggered in their hysteria from the boat. Then Lena was at his side. She yanked Kojo's arm, and they began yelling at each other as Kojo asked what happened, where was Lil. And Lena just kept saying, "He's gonna bleed to death, get us help."

"Who's gonna bleed to death, and where is my wife?" Kojo yelled at Lena.

Lena pointed in the direction of Carl being carried from the boat and stretched on the pier, and Kojo saw the blood pushing past the wrap around Carl's leg. Kojo grabbed Lena by the shoulders and looked directly in her face. "Listen like you should but usually don't, Lena. There's a bell over there by the guard tower, a thick cord hanging. Get to it as fast as you can and pull the cord with everything you got."

Two barges sat symmetrically at the pier of the Lazaretto. After the sun set, a barge-man emerged on the hour to strike the bell, sending a pleasant series of chimes through the compound. A thick cord hung from one side of the bell, too thick to sway even. When yanked, as Lena did on Kojo's frantic command, the cord activated not only the bell but forced the mallet to strike a massive circular gong. The hit against the gong caused the air to reverberate, releasing an air-splitting, urgent sound that stretched from the pier all the way across the creek to the staff house, where Sylvia had just now finished unwrapping the scarf from her head, and remnants of laughter from her earlier teasing of Nevada still hovered in her chest. She pulled her fingers through her hair. She'd plaited it before her bath to stretch it out, and it was now a thick and full halo. She smiled at herself in the square of mirror glass propped up against her bedroom dresser. That's when she heard the gong.

It had been weeks since the gong had been sounded, and that time a man had jumped from a ship originating in the Mediterranean and swam ashore and was running loose around the Lazaretto. She could tell by the splash of darkness outside the window that it was past time for the boat to have arrived. The boat carrying Vergie. She thought first of Vergie. She froze then. Uncharacteristic of her in the face of an emergency to freeze. Said out loud into the bedroom air, "Vergie, Vergie, my God, please don't let that gong have anything to do with the boat carrying Vergie."

Nevada stuck her head into the room. "What's the gong about?"

"No idea," Sylvia said. Her hands were shaking and she rubbed them along her dress.

"You all right? Sylvie?"

"Yeah, yeah, let me get down there and

see what is going on." She pushed past Nevada and was out of the room.

The creek separated the staff's living quarters from the other side of the compound. Sylvia slowed herself as she navigated the rocks that served as a bridge over the creek. She concentrated on the stew of sounds. The night clatter moving through the trees mixed with the water's loud swishing over the rocks, and now the noisy crickets and frogs. She tried to focus on the frog sounds. She didn't have her lamp, and she'd heard how the nurse who'd preceded her had once been running through this area in the dark and slipped on a frog and split her head wide open. She saw a sliver of light at her feet then. It widened into a band. Heard Nevada's voice. "Don't worry. She is unharmed, I am sure."

"Who?" Sylvia asked, not turning around.

"Verge."

"What makes you think I'm worried?"

"I know you all to pieces is what."

"You do not know most of what you think you do." Sylvia stepped over a frog, grateful for the lamp Nevada carried.

"I know you needing this light I'm shredding over your footfalls," Nevada said as if on cue.

"That would be *shedding.*"

"Actually, my light is falling piecemeal, so what I said is what I meant. And furthermore you should step from outta your shoes and run, now that thanks to me you able to see where the hell you going. You know you want to."

"Yeah, but you could not keep up with me running. And now that I have the benefit of your scraggly lamp, I'm used to it."

"I shan't only keep up, I'll race you. And if I win, I want a piece of white lace to edge my curtains."

"And what I get if I win?" Sylvia asked as she bent to pull her shoes from her feet.

"You already got the light."

Sylvia was out of her shoes, and she and Nevada jumped onto the final rock that bridged the creek. They ran then, through the area they all called "the hemorrhage" because the roses were blood red, then through the tangled understory of berry vines and oak saplings that edged the dead house and the crematory, then the perimeter of the cemetery. The earth was soft and warm under their feet, muddy in places, and they hoisted their party dresses as they ran past the patch of farmland with the hens and goats that kept them supplied with eggs and milk. Then the cook's shed and the main house and the mansions where the doctor and quarantine master lived that looked out on the startling river just beyond the barges.

They were at the top of the clearing. Then they slowed to a trot, their breaths responding in turn, their bodies trained for runs like this because they often needed to get from where they slept to the main house in a hurry. Especially Sylvia. They had an unobstructed view of the pier. The huddled party guests appeared to have been cast down from Heaven, the way the searchlight was turned on them. They resembled a flock of geese, wet and fluttering.

"Sweet Jesus, what has happened?" Sylvia said, as much to herself as to Nevada.

Now she saw the stretcher being carried; her heart stopped.

"They laboring carrying that stretcher. Must be a large somebody on that thing," Sylvia said on a whisper.

"Too large to be Vergie" — Nevada matched Sylvia's whisper with her own voice turned low.

Sylvia watched the doctor staggering ahead of the stretcher, but thankfully she saw Spence holding up the rear. "I'm going over there," she said as she ran ahead of Nevada in the direction of the hospital.

"Yes, go, Sylvie. I'll make sure Vergie's

okay, though I know she is. I woulda felt it in my bones otherwise."

20

The crate containing Bram lay patiently on the pier, having attracted the wedding guests' belongings after someone deposited his burlap sack beside the crate, then another his cardboard box, another her fancy flip-top overnight bag. In short order the crate was obscured as belongings were tossed even across its top.

Vergie sat down on the corner of the crate. She was wet and shivering as she clung to a blanket someone had thrown over her shoulders. Vergie had gone into the water after Carl. She was a strong swimmer, that skill honed on the frequent fishing trips she'd taken with her father from the time before she could even walk, when she'd spend as much time in the water as she did in the boat. She'd gone under twice before she spotted the trail of blood that led her to Carl. She dragged him to the surface and by then Splotch and two other men had also jumped in, and, with the help of the river's perfect push, they'd gotten him back in the boat. She didn't consider right now that she'd saved Carl's life as she stared straight ahead into the gray and silver river and assaulted herself with her thinking. She berated herself for inciting Carl's shooting in the first place. Her inability to rein herself in when she felt disrespected had caused it. Hadn't her aunt Maze told her time and again that every situation was not cause for a fight; that she must learn to distinguish between trifling slights and major injustices; that she must let the small things roll off her back, and save her temper for challenging the more egregious treatment; that catastrophe might result over some insignificant matter because of her tendency to overreact. And it had happened today; the flick of her finger at the white men in the other boat may have cost Carl his life. "Dear Carl," she said out loud, as her chest went stormy and she started heaving. "I may have killed you, ah, I may have . . ." She started shaking uncontrollably and thought she was going into convulsions when she sensed someone approach and at first she thought it was Splotch and she tightened inside. But then she felt the warmest hands moving up and down her arms, the sweetest voice in

279

her ear saying, "Come on, Verge, you need to get out of these wet clothes, come on now before you catch the grippe."

"Nevada, Nevada," Vergie cried. "Carl was shot because I flicked my hand at some white men."

"Don't do that, Vergie," Nevada said as she pulled her up and got her into a complete hug. "That is a devil's trick to make those that have been wronged feel that they are in the wrong. Nothing you could have said, no gesture you could have made, justifies someone firing a gun at your boat. I will not abide such talk from you. Now come on, get dried up. I have a bowl of turkey broth with your name on it." Nevada spoke in a calming voice as she led Vergie toward the house.

Son, the strapping though feeble-minded nephew of the quarantine master, was there with the wheelbarrow to begin transporting the company's belongings down to the storage area in the cellar of the house where the party would be. Son didn't know that the crate was not part of the company's belongings, that there was a corpse inside the crate. He just knew that he'd been directed to haul everything that was there over to here. And that is what he proceeded to do.

Son followed Kojo's instructions and loaded the piles of things left at the pier onto the wheelbarrel and carted them from the pier to the basement of the guesthouse. He'd been back and forth to the cellar, serving each person who called for this or that bag or case or satchel, waiting patiently while they retrieved what they needed, then returning same to the cellar. So far, no one had asked for anything from the pine crate, and he was disappointed, because he wanted to take the empty crate and fill it with rocks and see if he could sink it in the creek. The crate had tiny openings between the slats of wood, and Son got down on his knees and held his candle close to try and peer inside. He thought he could see a thick muslin sheet, thought that the thing inside was shaped like the dead bodies that Son occasionally saw being toted from the hospital. He'd asked his uncle about it once as they'd watched a particularly large man being carried from the hospital to the crematory, and Ledoff told Son that it was a corpse, and that all corpses had to be burned or buried. Son pronounced it *course.*

Right now he hung his lantern on the hook on the wall above him and sat down on the cellar floor. The glow of light fell over him as he studied the thick line of twine

281

that was wrapped around the crate and knotted at the top and bottom. Son's uncle had taught him how to undo knots of all varieties. Do not fret over the tangle, he'd instructed him — just use the tangle, follow it, let it show you the ends. He traced the twine where it was most confused. He picked at the center to loosen the confusion and slid his fingers in and then let out a little yelp when he thought he'd touched the end. He loosened the knot and shouted hooray when he'd gotten through the tangle that had held the crate's lid secure. He repeated the process at the other end. He was proud of himself as he lifted the lid and leaned in and then laughed from the on-slaught of odor that was a mix of pine and bad eggs. Just as he'd figured: there was a body inside. It was wrapped in a loose cotton sack and tucked in with sheets as if it had just been put down for a nap. Son untied the sashes attached to a board at the bottom of the crate that had held the sack in place. He lifted the sack and cradled it the way he'd cradled the foal that had died last year unexpectedly. His uncle had ex-plained that the mother likely killed the foal, that the mother sensed it was sick and killed it to protect it. Son wondered if this one's mother had killed him. He had that same rotten-egg smell that he remembered from the foal. He slung the sack over his shoulder and walked it to the very back of the cellar. He looked from end to end of this section of cellar and picked out an earthen spot beyond the concrete floor. He spread the body out and opened the loosely gathered top of the sack. A thin sheet of cotton covered the face and was attached to an undersheet with a row of silk stitches. Son wondered if someone had closed the eyes. He'd often hear Sylvia talking about having to close a dead man's eyes; the way Sylvia talked it seemed to Son like a kind thing to do for a person. He popped the stitches and lifted the cotton square. This man's eyes were already closed. Son was struck by the thick clumps of forehead scars. He felt sorry for the man that his face was scarred. He traced his fingers over the scars and then patted them lightly. He thought that the man had a nice face, that he must have been a nice man, not the type of man that would yell at Son and call him a stupid lug, a donkey's ass, imbecile, dunce, retard, freak, the way men often did before he'd been sent here to live with his uncle at the Lazaretto. Son bowed his head and made whispering sounds the way he'd noticed others do over the dead. He lightly replaced the cotton square over the man's face. He started to pull the top of the sack back around his head, but then stopped, deciding to leave his head uncovered just in case he might wake up. He removed the cotton square as well and laid it on the corpse's chest. Then he looked up to see what the man's eyes would view should he wake and not be able to untangle himself from the sack. Son was sensitive to such things, having himself been tied down to a gurney, unable to move because of the contraptions attached to his head when he'd cry out in pain and think that it wouldn't hurt so much if he could just look at something of interest. He tilted this one's head so that should he wake he'd be staring at a spider's web that glistened silver in the corner of the low ceiling where it hung. Satisfied, he got up to leave. He heard a sound then, like a muffled blast. He realized the body had just blown wind, intensifying the smell of rotten eggs. That sound always made him laugh. He laughed now. He doubled over, he laughed so hard. When he finally composed himself, he climbed the ladder that led to the yard and re-latched the cellar door.

He took the crate deep into the woods. Then he returned to the cellar to see if the body had moved. He didn't think that it had. He thought now that he wanted to keep the body completely hid from anyone else who might come down here. He repositioned the boxes and bags and trunks that the guests had brought with them so as to make a wall. He added to the stack larger items that had already been down here — a retired potbelly stove that he had to drag because it was too heavy to lift, a desk with three legs that was upended and resting on its side, a cracked dresser mirror. When he was finished he stood back and admired his wall. It was wide and tall and sturdy. He laughed out loud. Then he left to find Sylvia or Nevada or Kojo, to see what next he'd be instructed to do.

The Lazaretto's hospital was a wide, two-story stone mansion-like structure. Sylvia went around to the back door where they kept lye soap next to the spigot. She scrubbed her feet and then washed her hands. A lantern drizzled light from the top of the door and she could see flecks of lavender and rosemary that had been spun into the soap. The sight sparked the smell that went straight to her head with a jolt. She stepped into the slippers always waiting for her here and then hurried up the three short steps that led into the hospital's back corridor.

The doctor was still calling for leeches; his voice reverberated down the hall and seemed to be coming from any one of the framed oil renditions of white men that lined the corridor walls. Spence, the poor groom, was leaving the intake room that was midway down the long hallway. Sylvia was relieved to see Spence. He was smart, a quiet intellect, a gentleman. His aunt belonged to some of Maze's social clubs, and Sylvia had been delighted when Ledoff had asked her opinion of Spence because he was thinking of bringing Spence on as an orderly. She'd even thought for the briefest time that Spence had eyes for her, had settled into the notion of keeping company with him since they practiced the same profession; if anyone would understand her devotion to her work, surely he would. But then as it turned out he'd really had eyes for Mora, or more likely that Mora had eyes for him, bulging eyes the way she'd gone after Spence shortly after he'd arrived, as if God had stopped making men.

Right now she could see the thick creases in Spence's forehead all the way from where she was; he looked up and she watched his expression loosen when he saw her, as if the sight of her dispelled the worry that had been trapped along his brow. "I was coming to find you," he said as he rushed toward her.

"Who's on the gurney?" she asked, standing still to collect herself for whatever she was about to hear.

"It's Carl."

"What happened?" she asked in a whisper, as her heart dropped to a lower spot in her chest.

"Boat shot at, probably by those Petty Island whites drinking moonshine. Carl took a shotgun blast to the leg, then went overboard."

"Sweet Jesus," she said. She wanted to sink to the floor. She started for the intake room instead. "Anybody else hurt? Vergie?"

"No, Vergie's fine, just wet and cold."

"Ah," she said, relieved about that at least. "Vergie went in the river after Carl, right? I know she did with her foolhardy self. How bad is the leg?"

"Shattered."

"Knee involved?"

"No. The knee appears spared." Spence looked down, and then rushed his words. "Can't say the same for the rest of the leg. I fixed a tourniquet mid-calf. Gave him a few drams of morphine in some brandy." He looked back up at Sylvia then. "I think the lower leg's good as gone."

"Is he conscious?" Her voice shook as she tried not to cry.

"Fading in and out."

"Let me take a look at things," she said.

The doctor yelled out then. "Nurse, dammit!" Sylvia motioned Spence away, then took a deep breath and walked into the room.

21

Night had fallen hard over the Lazaretto, especially for Linc. He'd walked part of the way here from Hog Island, where he'd been forced from the boat of the men who'd shot at the schooner filled with black people. Then he'd begged a ride to here from a shad fisherman who'd taken pity on him when Linc gave him a story of having been beaten and robbed, not entirely untrue, and he certainly looked the part. But he'd apparently come in through the Lazaretto's rear because there were no markers pointing toward the entrance, no glow from an overhead gas lamp. There was just an unforgiving non-path through tangled understory of aggressive oak saplings and vines that ripped through his pants and sliced at the skin along his legs. Just a plethora of croaking frogs and a type of mist that seemed to drop and hang as if suspended by invisible threads. Just his anger and his dread and his grief about his own situation, his concern for what damage those gunshots may have done, if anyone on that schooner had been hit, or killed. But now there was also: music.

His ears perked up then, surprised at the sounds. He'd expected maybe the whistle of ships loaded with sugar or whiskey or rags or tea that had to be cleared through here before entering the Port of Philadelphia; or perhaps the disappointed wails of hopeful immigrants detained in quarantine who'd presented with swollen glands, diarrhea, bloodied spittle, hot foreheads, incessant vomiting. But not what he heard: the zoom-zoom of a banjo, harmonica shrieks, jangles from clapping tambourines that shattered the air. It was black people's music, and it worked its way into his bones the way their music always had, from the time he first heard it as a little boy at Buddy's house and Buddy had looked at his badly beaten hands and told him they were the finest hands he'd ever seen. He was suddenly transported to Buddy's, remembering now how Meda would pull him into the dining room, where the women fed him bowls of mustard and kale slick with lard; they called him Sugar; told him he was a toothsome something for a white boy. Remembering how much he loved it there: loved the syrupy ways of the women, loved how the air shook when the men laughed, or cursed; loved the smells of vanilla and baking apples. And then there was the music, the way the air rippled and held the beat. Such a beat tugged at him now, leading him — he hoped — to Bram.

He approached a clearing and now faced a thin creek. The gentle sound of water was no match for the thump and clang of the tambourines. And now there was another sound, a woman's unbridled sobs. She was there by the creek. Her naked back exposed. Her skin the color of whiskey. He turned away quickly, out of respect, disturbing the air around him that smelled of creek lilies and seared duck fat.

Sylvia had just left the hospital. She had cleaned the wound in Carl's leg and packed it, having removed all the buckshot she could find. She'd gotten Carl as comfortable as she could with a tonic of brandy and morphine and then she'd left — left with the doctor drooling and nodding in the chair at Carl's bedside — before her ability to distance her emotions from the task at hand expired. For the span of time she worked on Carl, it was just a limb with a nasty gunshot wound commanding her attention. She'd been efficient because she'd been detached. She'd closed her ears to his cries in ways that she could not have if she'd allowed him to be Carl — gushy, big-hearted, lovable Carl. She would have rushed then, to spare him the pain. She would have rushed and done a sloppy job. And he was alive, she'd told herself over and over as she walked back to the house, where everyone was gathered, her resolve intact to put as sunny a coating as she could on the report she would give about Carl. Then she noticed the splatters of blood on her dress and she stopped at the creek to clean the dress, knowing that the last thing the wedding guests needed at this point was the sight of Carl's blood. Not after what they'd already endured on the boat ride over. She sat on the rock and unhooked her dress and allowed it to slip from her shoulders. That's when she heard the music. She was surprised, but also relieved that they'd decided to go ahead with the pre-wedding celebration, because it would help. But the music wore away at her resolve to be cheerful as the creek water lapped the blood from her dress. She cried, tried to get all of the crying out of her as she felt an anger welling up that she even had to be cleaning Carl's blood away, that a boatload of black people could not even travel the few miles from the docks of Philadelphia to the Lazaretto without harassment. Then she sensed an opening in the air behind her that let in the salty smell of a man's sweat.

"Who is it? I am not decent," Sylvia snapped.

"I'm sorry," Linc said. "My back is to you, be assured."

"Are you lost?" she asked, as she pulled her dress from the creek to cover herself. The dress was soaked and the splash of water shocked her chest. "You must be lost. This side of the creek is for people who live here."

"People live here? Then I must be," he said. "Lost, yes, I must be lost. I thought this was the Lazaretto."

"It *is* the Lazaretto, and the people who work here live here," she said, as she reached around to hook the back of her dress. She stood from her perch on the rock and lifted her lamp. "Turn around," she barked.

Linc did and she raised her lamp, blinding him. "My brother fell ill this afternoon" — he rushed his words — "collapsed on the street in Philadelphia, and I'm told he was put on a boat to be quarantined here."

"And no one on either of the barges stopped you from coming onto the Lazaretto?"

"I — I honestly didn't see a barge. I must

have come in the wrong way. A barge would have been welcome, considering what I have just been through, you know, the woods and the thorns and all."

She moved in closer, studying him, he knew, trying to figure out what he was. He wondered then if she recognized him as a wanted man. Wondered if she'd seen the postings of him over the years detailing his crime. *Orphan Sets upon Housemaster in Vicious Fist Attack: Reward Offered for Information Leading to His Apprehension* is just one of the headlines he could recite after all these years. He started to toughen his expression, but then he relented, just allowed his naked desperation to hang there uncovered.

Sylvia wrestled with the urge to offer him consolation. As a nurse, she routinely doled out consolation right along with a camphor salve or alcohol soak. And she could see that he was ripe for a word of reassurance as she bombarded him with her lamplight. But she did not offer consolation. Right now she was tired of feeling sorry for white people.

"Are you acquainted with those shooting at boats when the people in them are studying their own affairs?" she barked at Linc, even though everything about him suggested to her that he was not.

294

"Beg your pardon?" He reeled even as he stood firm and continued to look into her blaring light because he couldn't look away since that would mean guilt, and he had been in that boat, making him guilty by association. It didn't matter that he'd fought with all he had in him to try and keep the drunken bastard from getting off those shots; he'd gotten the shots off, and Linc had been in the boat when he had, and if she knew that, Linc would be reduced to just another white bigot in her eyes, a disgusting vermin, in no way worthy of her assistance. And he needed assistance right now because he needed Bram. God, Bram!

"A boat was shot at," she continued. "A group of upstanding people coming here for a wedding celebration, innocent of anything that would warrant them being shot at. Shot at as if they were game. Are you connected to them?"

"Absolutely not, I am sorry, that is outrageous, no, I assure you. Was anyone at all injured?" he asked, bracing himself for her reply, and recalling that he had remained low on the deck as they'd passed the other boat, unlikely he would have been seen, remembered.

"Somebody was hurt, yes." Her voice shook, and she swallowed hard, determined not to cry again. "When did your brother supposedly pass out? We never got word. We do get word in such cases."

"This afternoon," he stammered.

"And he was sent here for what reason?"

"I honestly do not know. His name is Bram, short for Abraham, named for the president, as was I. My name is Lincoln."

"Mnh. Is that supposed to sweeten me because you were named for Mr. Lincoln. If I were a rebel would your name suddenly be Jefferson Davis?"

The pained look that came upon his face stopped her, softened her some. She lowered her lamp. "Your brother is likely still in Philadelphia. But, regardless, you are on the wrong side of the compound. So go to the other side of the creek and follow the path up to the main house, and just beyond there you'll see the barges. A bargeman should see you and ask you what your business is. Tell him Nurse Sylvia said for you to wait up there. If he is in a better mood than I am, he should allow it. Once I am able, I will discover what I can about your brother's situation."

"Yes, ma'am, Nurse Sylvia. I am deeply grateful for whatever assistance you render." He thought something about her was vaguely familiar. Clicked through his mental file but could not make a connection, so settled on her familiarity having to do with Meda. Her demeanor was so like Meda's in the aftermath of Meda suffering an affront by a white person. He swallowed the rise of emotion moving up his throat as he thought about Meda, thought about Bram, and what a drastic condition Bram must be in to have been brought here. He followed her directions until he wound out of her view. Then he departed, following her directions, and walked toward the music. It led him to a pair of houses, and he approached the one that glowed with yellow light.

Inside the house they were beginning to have a time. They'd dried off and changed clothes and spruced up and were now gathered in the parlor, its space expanded with the pocket doors parted so that the parlor flowed into the dining room. Their anger was beginning to thin over their ordeal of being shot at for sport. Their breaths came easier as they talked it out, some loudly over top of one another, others by whispering in a loved one's understanding ear. They expressed their gratitude that they'd all gotten here alive, especially that Carl was still alive, and that the river had not claimed Carl and Vergie and the others who'd gone in to save him. Some even

297

claimed that the river had helped with the rescue; that it intentionally rose and provided the lift as Carl's rescuers propped him and made it possible for the hands to help from inside the boat. God and the river, they agreed, had taken their side in the end. Gradually, as they talked it out, they could feel their frayed nerves reconnecting, their sour stomachs beginning to quiet.

Now they nibbled on starter foods of lettuce and cucumbers, eggs mashed and spread on soda crackers, fried mackerel, stuffed tomatoes. The music was starting up as the tambourines shimmied, in a halting way; the harmonica trilled softly; a base drum mimicked the rhythm of a thumping heart trying to settle itself down. The vibrations carried through them; these were calming vibrations. A little laughter then, someone let go with hand claps, another stomped his foot. Hips could not resist swaying. Arms reached out. The chatter grew wings and flitted about. The taste of hell that had been the boat ride over was gradually replaced by the comfort of a community wrapped up in the music that was both worldly and praising.

Vergie, though, was having a harder time. She couldn't reconcile the gratitude that the others were expressing right now with the fact that Carl lay wounded in the hospital. Though it was promising that Carl was at least semiconscious as they'd carted him off the pier, Vergie understood the damage a scattergun's blast to the leg could do. She knew the rivers of arteries running through the leg by name from when she used to hold Sylvia's books for her as she studied. She'd traced her finger over the drawings, fascinated by the complexity, and match the lines to the names Sylvia recited. She knew Carl's wound was serious, and that it was all her fault. Though Nevada had refused allowing Vergie to heap upon herself the responsibility. She'd listened and shushed her as she combed and brushed Vergie's hair to help it to dry. She reminded her, over and over, that the outlaws who shot Carl were the only villains, period.

That talking-to had calmed Vergie, but the relief was only temporary. The sense of guilt was returning in waves, and though she tried to force herself to laugh at Kojo and his wife as they attempted to cut up on the dance floor, she was getting ready to stand up here and cry all over again. Nevada tapped her shoulder then and handed her a pot filled with strawberry punch. "Keep busy, Vergilina Mayella," she said, calling her by her full name.

"God, Nevada, what will I do if Carl does not survive?"

Nevada held up her bandaged finger to stop her. "If any part of him knows Sylvia's working on him, his life is good as saved. You know how much he adores her." Nevada tried not to notice Kojo and Lil on the dance floor, the affection moving with them as they danced. She'd already tired of hearing Bay and the others in the kitchen talking about this one's wife and that one's sweetheart. And when they got to Kojo, Bay said, "He got hisself a cute little ole wife, nice disposition, too, real sweet." "Smiles too much for my liking," Nevada had said, causing Bay to put her paring knife down and look at Nevada and raise her eyebrows. "Just my opinion," Nevada rushed to add. "Y'all can like her much as it pleases you." Then she pulled her attention from Kojo and his wife dancing and focused entirely on Vergie.

"Okay now, I'm countin' on you to keep the punch bowl filled and my table looking pretty. Moving hands hold the sadness at bay till situations change and the sadness flies away."

"You just made that up?" Vergie asked as she took the pot.

"Good, whadin it?"

Vergie nodded and laughed despite herself, and then Bay stuck her head in from the kitchen to tell Nevada that the hourglass on her turkey was done, did she want it turned, or basted, or what? "Comin'," she called over her back, as she blew Vergie a kiss and Vergie puckered her lips in response and went behind the table to fill the bowl.

Linc tapped on the door, to no response. He reasoned that they could scarcely hear him, so he turned the bulbous glass knob to let himself in, telling himself he'd apologize for entering their party uninvited.

Aromas crowded the foyer, sweet and heavy smells, the music seeming to ride on top of the smells like a bent finger saying "Come 'ere," motioning him toward a set of pocket doors. He slid the doors apart. Before he saw anything else: before he saw the twenty-five or so people — the women dressed up in linen and cotton and lace, mostly in high heels, the men in vested suits; before he saw the sideboard groaning under the weight of the roasted ducks and accompanying bowls heaped with assorted greens, carrots, beets, and corn; before he saw the framed pencil etching of Lincoln centered over the brocaded fainting couch; or the roses that seemed to be everywhere, he saw a woman standing behind a long table, pouring a strawberry-colored juice from a pot into a carved glass punch bowl. Her race was ambiguous, her face caught in the light reflecting from the glass bowl. As she moved out of the light, she threw her head back and said "Oh drats" over a splash of juice that fell on the tablecloth, his awareness grew that not only was she black, but that she was the same one who'd enraged the men on the boat by flicking her hand at them. He started to turn around and leave lest she recognize him, then reminded himself again that that was unlikely, he'd not stood and raised a bottle with the other two. Plus, he didn't want to leave; he was drawn to her, her presence provoking a powerful stirring right now. He was ashamed of himself because of it. Not ashamed because he was a white man going weak-kneed over a black woman, but ashamed because he thought his desire somehow devalued her.

He didn't mean to devalue her. He'd spent large chunks of his childhood with Meda after all, and Buddy and his friends. He reminded himself of that now. Convinced himself that since black people had been so familiar to him, that he was surely without prejudice, and that the surge he felt as this woman moved closer to him had nothing to do with the realization that she was black — her full lips the confirmation. But he couldn't deny the surge, the force of it, as it lumbered more than pulsed, rendering him wooden.

"You got clay in your ears? I asked you if you are lost." She was right up on him now, practically shouting in his face.

Linc stared down at his feet. Shyness had never been among his repertoire of traits, especially where women were concerned. But with her standing in so closely, suddenly he couldn't get his voice to work.

"A mess," he stammered out finally.

"I would agree. You are quite the mess. What happened? A frog chase you into the creek?"

He felt mocked, aware suddenly of how he must look, contrasted with the high-buffed shoes and crisp clothes of the people in here. He backed up so that the shadow of the column near where he stood would hide him some. She followed him into the shadow. He took her presence in. She was tall and slender, dark hair, dark eyes — large eyes with a downward slant, eyes that should belong to a timid girl. Her stare compensated; it was a fiery stare. "Or if not a frog chasing you," she went on, "maybe a big old owl lifted you up and dropped you in the manure pile."

"I tracked dirt," he said. "I apologize."

"You ought to apologize," she said. "And you ought to be glad my cousin is not about. Sylvia is the nurse here, she's very serious about cleanliness and does not tolerate mud-trackers."

"If I offer to clean it up, will you save me from her?" he asked, his confidence seesawing back to normal as the thumping from the dance floor and the music wrapped around him.

"Save *you*?" she blurted. "My friends and I needed saving from your kind while we were on the river. Now here you are requesting that I save *you*?"

"What happened to you and your friends?" He feigned ignorance.

"We were shot at!"

"Shot at? By whom? For what cause?"

"By your kind, and for no cause, no provocation." She looked away then. Her profile was stunning, the line of her jaw, the way her mouth protruded. He felt himself going to mush. He tried to convince himself that his reaction to her was typical, that this was the pull he always felt toward a woman when spurred on by his baser instincts. But he could not convince himself, had to concede that he had never been so affected by a woman in this way, such that it involved his entire self. Told himself now that this was his mind playing tricks, a defense to distract him from the fire in his belly over his current situation, over the fate of his brother. If that was the case, it was working: he was distracted.

Glaring at him now, she repeated, "Yes, your kind."

"Not *my* kind, I assure you," he said and shook his head from side to side emphatically. "In fact, had I been in the vicinity, I would have come to your rescue. I swear it on my dead mother's smile — I would have, or I would have died trying," he said, remembering as he said it how hard he had fought those louts on the boat.

"Better if you had saved my friend from getting shot." Her eyes appeared no longer focused on him as she stared straight ahead and talked into the air.

"What is your friend's name?"

"Carl."

"And yours?"

"Vergilina."

"Vergilina," he repeated in a whisper, as if he'd been handed a prize. "How is Carl faring, Miss Vergilina?" He touched her arm; it was a forward move he knew, but he did so to calm himself as much as to console her.

The starched feel of her blouse was warm against his fingers.

She shook her arm away from where his hand touched. She was glaring at him again. "Who are you, besides?" she asked, exasperation running through her voice. "And what is it you want? You never said."

He just stood there, mute, thinking about what he wanted. He wanted to be at a card table right now, enjoying the comforting sound of cards being shuffled; wanted to feel the cards against his fingers as he arranged the cards in a fan; he wanted Meda to be alive; he wanted the afternoon back so that he could follow Bram outside of the tavern and be right there with him when he fell ill. He wanted to discard the threat looming over him like a beast's shadow that he might be recognized. What else did he want? He tried not to look at Vergie's lips, how full they were as he thought of all the things he wanted right now.

"You surely do not work on the Lazaretto" — Vergie filled the silence left by his non-response — "because the white workers were given leave for the weekend, allowing us to enjoy ourselves unhampered."

"Unhampered?" Linc almost shouted to be heard over the music.

"Yes, unhampered. It means we get to

306

enjoy the festivities and be who we are without having to look over our shoulders to determine how our actions are affecting your kind. You never heard that word?"

"I know the word. And surely you would have no need of looking over your shoulder at *me*. You could enjoy yourself to your heart's content and I would likely get enjoyment merely watching you have a good time."

"You are not a normal white man, then." She looked away again as if she were trying not to cry.

"Neither are the ones who shot at your boat and hurt Carl."

"They are in fact closer to the normal that I know."

"I wish you could know me, then," he said. "My name is Lincoln, Miss Vergilina, and, well, I wish you could know me, because if you did, well, you would know with every certainty that I am in fact your kind, every bit your kind." He surprised himself that he'd said that; he hadn't intended to say that.

Vergilina's mouth dropped. "Are you telling me that you are a colored man?" she asked.

He looked around this grand room that smelled of bourbon and sage from the barbecued pork that had just been put out on the sideboard. He stopped and swallowed and in an instant flashed back to that night when he'd just left the tables at a house on an alley of a street on the rough edge of Manhattan's Tenderloin district; he was pushed against the wall by more black men than he could count, a knife held to his throat by one of the men intent on avenging the death of his little brother at the hands of a white man. Linc knew that the fact that he'd had nothing to do with the crime would mean nothing to them — he was white and would do as a fill-in for whoever had murdered the man's brother. So Linc had deepened his voice to save his life and swore that he was every bit as colored as each one of them, had a colored mother, he lied, who'd encouraged him to pass for white that he might make a better life. "I wern't able to try and pass for no white man. Man know his dern soul, den he know his soul. I hail from over on Fitzwater Street in Philadelphia," he said, calling out the block where Buddy lived. "Would a white man be living 'mongst niggers if he was truly white?" He used the inflections in his voice that were so familiar to him from having spent time with Buddy. As his good luck would have it, one of the men knew Philadelphia, knew Fitzwater Street. They'd let him go, even dusting the cement flakes from his back.

He looked at Vergie now, even as he thought about his brother, blond-haired, pale-complexioned Bram. Bram had looked deathly sitting across from him at the tavern, his skin the color of a boiled chicken, his eyes yellow like a cat's eyes, his shirt bleeding sweat. Linc's entire life, he could always sense Bram's nearness. Now he could not. The feel of Bram's absence was like a bludgeoning. He exchanged it now for the feel of Vergie's nearness; the look on Vergie's face, her head tilted slightly, her fleshy mouth pulled to one side in a smirk, her stormy eyes fixed on him, questioning, waiting for his response.

"Yes," he said. And when he said it he felt a lug drop in his stomach as if he'd just betrayed Bram, betrayed the mother who'd died birthing him, the father killed fighting for the Union, even as the words slid out with such ease. "I am telling you exactly that I am a colored man."

He felt dizzy then, as if the earth no longer expressed its gravitational pull and was about to spin away, unhinged. He felt the blood draining from his face, so he coughed into his hand in hope of bringing color back to his face, as the last thing he needed was to appear whiter than he was.

Before he could say more, there was the thump of the front door opening and closing. And now Vergilina was squealing and running and calling out Sylvia's name. "You took so long, Sylvia, I was dying waiting for you to get here. How is Carl?" There was an onslaught then as everyone in the parlor moved at once to the foyer where Sylvia was, even the banjo player and the one clapping the tambourine, only the one blowing the harmonica remained. Linc pushed himself harder against the column, trying to blend in with the vanilla-colored wood as the notes coming from the harmonica fell at his feet and sounded like a grown man crying. Or moaning, about to cry.

22

Sylvia woke with a jolt. The first light of day was pushing through the parlor, and a foul odor had overpowered the air in here. She sat straight up and took in a deep breath, and the odor assaulted her stomach like a fist. Carl, she thought first of Carl. His pain had been considerable when she'd last checked on him, just a couple of hours ago. She'd given him more morphine and left him in the chasm between sleep and delusion, and then returned here and nodded off on the couch, intending to help Nevada and Bay and Vergie and whoever else was in the kitchen, chattering away as they cleaned up after the party; told herself she just needed to sit still, rest her eyes, for the briefest period of time. The last thing she remembered, her moccasins were slid from her feet, her legs pulled up onto the couch, a pillow eased under head, a light sheet draped over her, and her forehead gently kissed. She'd fallen into a soft slumber and dreamed that she and Carl were dancing in the river, and then she was trying to remember why she'd ever quit such a man who could move so in the water. Then a gray octopus tangled her up and Carl disappeared under the water and the octopus began defecating all over her, and though the smell was nauseating, she clung to the octopus because the feel of his droppings was like silk. She threw the dream off with the sheet as she got up from the couch, but the odor hadn't left with the dream. She thought then that the smell was inside her head, a warning to her of Carl's infected leg. He would lose the leg, she was sure. She sighed heavily and slipped her feet into her moccasins and started for the stairs. She'd have to arrange transport for Carl back to Philadelphia as soon as possible. They were too short-staffed here to even consider a surgery as major as amputating a leg. No doctor really to speak of, and since Ledoff had given most of the staff leave, there was really just her, with Spence to assist, and though Spence would be an apt assistant, this was his wedding day, after all; and, besides, she wasn't about to attempt it, she told herself, and that settled it.

She tiptoed into her bedroom, where Vergie was fast asleep. She went to her chest of drawers and pulled out a loose cotton dress. The aroma of pine greeted her, a relief from that other smell, and the dress that she changed into now smelled of the mint oil that Bay would drizzle in the basin where they washed their clothes. It both invigorated and calmed her.

She was halfway out of the room when Vergie stirred and was immediately fully awake, grinning in that way that showed all of her gums.

"Lookout, sunshine, your competition has arrived, because Vergilina is up," Sylvia said, as she came all the way back into the room and laughed in spite of herself.

"Sylvia, you didn't come to bed. I slept small so you'd have room."

"You do not know the meaning of sleeping small. There is still a spot on my back from two years ago when we shared sleeping space at Nevada's people's house in Virginia."

"Awl," Vergie said, feigning remorse, then turned remorseful for real as she asked about Carl.

"Headed over there now to make sure he's comfortable. He was comfortable when I left him, and Spence is with him now."

Vergie sat on the side of the bed with her

313

hands in her lap. She studied her fingers, fighting tears, Sylvia could tell. "Come hook the back of my dress and redo this bun in my hair and tell me about the party," Sylvia said. "Did you behave at the party or were you full of your usual sass?"

"I was my typically well-behaved self," Vergie said as she sniffed and jumped up and ran to Sylvia and hugged her. "Please tell me that he will live."

"Only the Good Lord can make and keep such a promise. But as far as my trained eye can see, he does not appear to be dying at this moment. I'm going to arrange for him to be transported back to Philadelphia as soon as possible. Now hook my dress in the back, and tell me who all is here who I may or likely do not know, and describe who made a fool of themselves doing the cake-walk."

Vergie fastened the dress and Sylvia sat at the vanity as Vergie removed the pins holding Sylvia's bun in place. "Well, of course you know Miss Ma is here —"

"Lord, yes, thought I heard her laughing when I was all the way over at the hospital."

"And Skell —"

"He is officiating the wedding, Nevada says —"

"And that frightful Lena —"

314

"Well, she is the bride's sister, so I guess she thinks that gives her special license to be more intolerable than usual —"

"And there was a strange man who wandered into the parlor last night, tracking up the place with mud."

"Stranger?" Sylvia thought immediately of her encounter at the creek. "Tall? Dark-haired white man? Proclaimed himself named for President Lincoln."

"Sounds as you describe him," Vergie said as she brushed Sylvia's hair and tried to ignore her own quickening pulse. "You two crossed paths?"

"At the creek," Sylvia said, as she closed her eyes and enjoyed the feel of the brush against her hair. "Supposed to have been looking for his brother sent here from the hospital. Though he's either mistaken or loony, the hospital always alerts us. I directed him back to the other side of the creek. How did he end up here? Must have been before he met up with me near the barges. I took pity on him and allowed him to take sleeping space in the curing shack."

"He remains here?" Vergie asked, trying to slow her breathing down.

"Mnhm." Sylvia bent her head so Vergie could brush her edges. She thought she might drift off to sleep, the brushstrokes were so relaxing.

"Well, are you aware that he's black?" Vergie asked on a quick intake of air, giving her voice a breathy sound.

"We are not talking about the same man then," Sylvia said as she opened her eyes and picked up Vergie's reflection in the mirror. "This one is definitely white, tall, dark-haired."

"We are talking about one and the same. Lincoln. Did you just say he was named for the president?"

"And he claimed to be black?"

"He did indeed."

"Explicitly?"

"Yes, and at first I doubted the claim but I spoke of it to Nevada and she confirmed it."

"Does Nevada know him?"

"No, but she said that if the tips of his ears are black, then he is surely colored, and I do recall that they were —"

"What! Tips of his ears are black? Only Nevada could come up with such foolishness."

"Well, she insists that she's known many a light-skinned colored pass themselves off as white, but she's never ever seen it happen the other way around. Which is a fact. Have you, Sylvia? Have you ever known of a white

316

man who claims to be colored?"

"Just because I have no knowledge of it happening does not mean that it has not happened."

"But what would a white person gain by doing such a thing?

"Depends on what they might be after —"

"Well, Nevada said that I should be the last somebody questioning a person's race. To which I had to clamp my lips shut because she is justified in saying it."

"And all of this about the man's race, this matters to you why, Vergilina?" Sylvia asked. She could see even in the mirror the sudden change in the color of Vergie's cheeks, her cheeks tinted the shade of a peach at full ripeness that hangs lower on the branch, begging to be picked. "How well do you know this Lincoln, after all?"

"I do not know a thing about him and I do not care a thing about him."

"Who said a word about caring for him? Now you just went ahead and introduced that prospect. Do you care about him?"

"Sylvia! I only saw him for the first time last night, how much could I know him? And besides, your scalp is dry, where do keep your pomade?"

Sylvia pointed to the vanity drawer and Vergie retrieved the pomade and rubbed it into Sylvia's hair and commenced to give her a vigorous scalp massage. She started at the nape of her neck and worked her fingers all the way to her forehead. Sylvia closed her eyes, enjoying it, Vergie could tell, as she felt the tension in Sylvia's scalp ease under the press of her fingers. Poor Sylvia, Vergie thought. How difficult the whole situation with Carl must be for her. She wondered if Sylvia blamed her the way that Lena and probably most of the people on the boat blamed her, the way she blamed herself. She felt herself about to cry again so she tried to change her line of thought since she considered it unconscionable to put Sylvia in the position of having to console her right now. She dragged her thumbs up and down the center of Sylvia's scalp and then back and forth from ear to ear as Sylvia let go a whispered *ahhh.*

She swallowed the urge to cry and let herself think of Linc instead, and she was seeing him all over again, how sweaty and disheveled he was, and how sincere. She could tell that he was taken with her and she rushed to clarify her race. She was accustomed to white men assuming that she was white and doling out attention that they never would if they'd known that she was black. Accustomed also to the transformation in their demeanor when she'd let them know her true self. Their faces would suddenly redden, they'd cough, squint, their voices suddenly stuck in their throats, their heads drawn way in; then came the full body draw-back, the accusatory stance, the *you, you said* with a wagging finger as if she had committed a heinous crime. One even spit, and Vergie reflexively hauled off and slapped him, knocking a gold-capped tooth from his mouth; to her credit she'd had the presence of mind to run, about as fast as she'd hit him hard. As disparaging as the reaction to her race sometimes was, she was comfortable with it because she expected it. Her feelings never had to flow deeper than the top of her chest where all the loathing and disgust sat at the ready to be summoned. Linc's reaction had been the opposite. He'd seemed to lean in even closer, and his manner was so respectful, so honest when he'd said he would have fought to defend their boat. It was so unsettling. She didn't even know where to begin to piece things together, the opening in her chest for starters that managed to push through the top layer of loathing and disgust revealing a complex of unfamiliar sensations that both titillated and frightened her. And all that while she thought him white. What now that he claimed to be a black man? That should simplify things, she thought. Though it did not. It only made matters more complicated still.

Sylvia snored lightly as Vergie finished massaging her scalp and then twisted her hair in a bun. Vergie whispered her name. "All done," she said. "You look as pretty as ever." She smiled at Sylvia in the mirror and held herself back from asking where the curing shack was.

23

Linc sat up with a start. It took some seconds for him to realize where he was as he looked around in the lean-to of a shack and remembered then that Sylvia had taken pity on him last night when she'd finally gotten to the barge where she'd told him to wait. She'd insisted again that he must be mistaken about his brother having been sent there by the hospital. "We always get advance notification," she'd said. She was civil, professional. But a storm was kicking up below the surface, he could tell. The same was true for him, though he guessed his inner turmoil was more evident because her manner had softened considerably from when he'd encountered her at the creek. He wondered if she'd gotten wind of his claim to be a colored man.

Pink and yellow daylight plowed through the window that was really just a square cut out of the side of this wooden shack. His eyes traced the spot that his fingers had traced before he'd fallen asleep, chains bolted to the wall, chains that ended in wrist shackles. He'd fallen asleep imagining what it must feel like to live chained to a wall. He woke every hour, it seemed, his wrists throbbing, his thinking weighted down by his mounting desperation over Bram's condition. And now he had further complicated his situation by claiming to be a black man. Asked himself now why'd he even made such an outrageous claim. Tried to convince himself that he'd mainly told that lie so that he would not be taken for one of those who'd terrorized that boat yesterday, even though he knew that was unlikely; then told himself it was so, that the people here would take pity on him and help him find Bram; and certainly them believing him black would hamper him being recognized as the violent orphan with the large bounty on his head. He couldn't yet admit to himself that his say-so of being black, the way the words had slid out so soft and easy, as if they'd been greased down with lard, had everything to do with Vergie. Even as he realized that no woman had ever affected him so, he couldn't yet allow his conscious mind to accept that he might be smitten. Now he convinced himself that he was just caught up in a whirlpool of emotion over Meda's death, Bram's disappearance, returning to Philadelphia; it was everything else going on, not this Vergie, not the nearness of her that had made the earth tilt, rearranging everything about him so that he'd said with such ease, yes, I am in fact a colored man.

He rubbed his wrists, thinking that as soon as he found Bram, he'd tell him about how he'd slept in a slave shack. When they were young boys they'd been riveted by Meda's stories of people who'd escaped from slavery and fled north. Their favorite story was about the woman who'd climbed into a pine box and had herself mailed north to freedom. That one at least had a somewhat happy ending, because Meda didn't sugarcoat the stories. She'd once told them about a young woman who looked something like her and had no skin on her back because every night her back was whipped raw. She'd described the whipping in all of its brutality and they started to cry and Bram even covered his ears, saying that he couldn't listen anymore. But Meda insisted that they listen. She maintained that they needed to understand how ugly evil was so that they would never be so ensnared. "You're white boys who will be white men,

323

and on every side you will be seduced to have dominion over colored people in one form or another. Think instead about Mr. Lincoln's heart," she'd say, then she'd go on an extended riff about something Abraham Lincoln said about equality.

Linc sighed at the memory and rolled a cigarette and stepped outside of the shack into the blazing pink and yellow. He could hear the loud churning sounds of the river as it tumbled over itself. He walked farther toward the patch of farmland. More voices, a man and a woman this time, the rhythm of their interaction so familiar to him. The man pulling on the woman, pleading. Her pushing him away, calling him a low-down dirty scoundrel. "Get from 'round me," she yelled. "Go have your wife."

Linc winced as he watched the man go lumbering off, shoulders hunched as the woman stood there, unwavering; nothing about her moved. By the time he'd finished his cigarette, he could hear her sweet-talking the hens as she collected their eggs. Now she felt his presence and turned and squinted.

"Who you?" She threw her voice up the hill.

"Ah, Lincoln, my name is Lincoln. I am here at Nurse Sylvia's invitation," he rushed to say it to prove he had license to be here.

He braced himself as Nevada walked up the hill toward him, dragging the fallen pink remnants of the daybreak with her. He thought her pretty with her round face and light eyes. "You the guilty man?" she asked.

He managed to hold his expression together as he gathered words from the back of his mind, words that he'd held there for a decade. *I am not guilty. I was justified.* Then, shifting his thoughts to the present: *I tried with everything I had to stop them from firing that gun at the boat.*

"The one who tracked mud through the foyer last night?" she continued, as he managed to keep the spread of relief from taking over his face.

"I offered to clean it, I did."

"So Vergie informed me." She was right in front of Linc now; her head tilted, studying him as if he were a curiosity.

"Something amiss?" he asked.

"No, just seeing," she said. "Vergie told me that you are a colored man. So I am just trying to see. Though to my mind, a man is a man is still a man. And you look fairly standard to me, could go either way. No offense. Race a matter of geography, anyhow."

"Ma'am?"

"To my way of thinking, the worth of one

skin color versus another was conjured up by man. The sun darkens the faces it kisses and it kisses the ones closest to it. The sun act just like many a man I come to know, a lazy suitor content to select its lover from the block it live on rather than venturing out of the neighborhood." She moved in closer and peered up at him. "I see that your ear tips are dark, that must be where the colored part of you hides, in the tips of your ears."

Linc resisted the temptation to grab his ears, even as he tried to figure out what she'd just said. "My mother used to tell me the same thing about my ears."

"Did she now? She from Virginia?"

"No, no, ma'am."

"What's her name?"

"Uh, Alma."

"Mnh, I knew a Meda, though everybody called her Sister. Wonder if her given name was Almeda and they shortened it. She just died the other day; her brother's sweet on me, at least he claims to be, though if that be true, I aver he would have taken the boat ride with the others to spend the weekend with me."

"But did you not say his sister just died?" he said, stiffening as he realized that she was talking about Meda, his Meda, and

Buddy. Realized that this was the Nevada that Meda had spoken of, this was Miss Ma's granddaughter. "He may be too grief-stricken to be with people at this time."

"I believe I could have given him respite."

"From what I hear about the boat ride, he may have fared better on dry land. As my mother always said, an unseen protector keeps us from unseen dangers."

"So where your momma from?"

"New York," he said, kicking himself now for saying his mother's name was Alma. A flood of other names occurred to him: Ginny, Martha, Bessie, even Ann, Betty. But Alma? "That is where I grew up, New York," he said. "And I am very sorry about your friend's sister." He lowered his eyes then; he could mostly manage to disguise the sadness he felt about Meda in very short intervals.

"Okay," she said, as she shifted her egg basket from one hand to the other and started walking again. "Lovely talking to you, even if I only take agreement with half of what you said. I still maintain the man should have put himself on the boat. You welcome to breakfast. 'Bout a half hour from now," she called over her shoulder.

"Much obliged," Linc called behind her. "Where should I come?"

"The same house as last night."

"And who shall I say invited me?"

"You can tell 'em Nevada, though I might deny it." She laughed out loud when she said that.

When she was out of range, he let go his pent-up breath, which he hadn't even been aware he was holding in. He thought this farce had gotten out of hand. Particularly with people here who knew Buddy and Meda. He needed to end it. Needed to concentrate on finding Bram, not putting all of his focus into pretending to be a black man. He decided that he'd tell the truth of himself when he went for breakfast. He would explain that he was swept up by their music last night, that he'd just wanted to share their space, just for a while, because he was in the midst of some traumatic circumstances. He'd tell them how Bram collapsed and disappeared, how devastated he was over Meda's death. He would admit that he was not born and reared in New York, that he was the little white boy who was always with Meda on Saturdays when she traveled to Buddy's house. Surely there were others here who, like Nevada, knew Buddy, might even be people here who recognized him. But if he admitted to that, there might also be those here who knew

328

what he'd done to Robinson. Might be people here who were sympathetic to Robinson. Meda had told them on her first visit to see them in New York, after they'd run away, that Robinson's people had spread money around Fitzwater Street in the hopes of getting tipped off about where Linc was hiding out. He walked toward the creek as he thought about what to do. There were advantages both to coming clean and to extending the lie. He decided on splitting the difference between the two. He'd admit that he wasn't black, but stick to his story of being from New York.

He found a remote part of the creek and, shallow though the creek was, tried to submerge himself and bathe as best he could. He tried to shut his thinking down. Bram had told him once that it was possible to find a space of nothingness that existed when one thought ended and before the next began. It was just a dash of space, a spec of sand, but if he could find it, it was possible to elongate the dash into a noticeable spate of time that was supremely calming. Bram told Linc that that's what he did when he reached beyond and seemed to go into a trance. Linc had never been able to be still long enough. Though right now he did try to at least concentrate on the feel of the rocks against the soles of his feet, the splashing sounds the water made, the smell of the lavender and lilies, the croaking frogs, the slant of sun on his chest; he'd never noticed such things before as he reclined somewhat and took it all in. Then, despite his best efforts not to, he thought of Vergie.

24

They set up tables in the shady back for breakfast. The men and women emerged from their separate sleeping houses in their go-to-market-type garb — not Sunday's finest, those were patient for the wedding later, but a notch up from what they'd generally wear around their houses early on a Saturday. They said, "Morning. How you? You sleep well?" in singsongy voices as cheeks were smooched and hugs went around and they waited for Nevada to direct them to their seats. "Ma, you sit here," she said to Miss Ma, "right next to Skell, who appears to be doing preaching duties for the wedding, maybe some of his religion'll rub off on you."

"Not if I can offer up resistance," Miss Ma said to the laughter of those inclined to joke about such things as religion, or those having none, as Nevada motioned the others to the table, careful to seat Spence's relatives — the tailor and his schoolteacher wife, and the milliner, and the record-keeper at Shiloh — far away from her grandmother's end of the table. That end she made heavy with the more raucous crowd who were known to frequent Buddy's house.

Splotch was told to sit at that end, though he countered that he should desire to be placed next to Vergilina. "You old enough for your desires to be withheld, Mr. Splotch," Nevada said, to laughter. Kojo laughed especially hard, and Nevada turned and looked at him. "You find that funny, do you? Does the missus? And where is she, by the way?"

"She wit the bride and her sister, spreading out the wedding gown so the wrinkles will fall away," Miss Ma said, and then she let go a stream of laughter, to the discomfort of those sitting in the refined section.

Plates of food were relayed out to the table then. Shad that had been planked and charred, fried scrapple, bowls of hominy, scrambled cows brain, and the eggs that Nevada stretched with peppers and chunks of ham. Vergie rearranged the settings to make space for the basket of rolls, steam still rising. The food aromas, especially the smell of the rolls, hung in the air.

When they had settled themselves, Skell

offered up grace, taking time to ask for special healing blessings for Carl, and then to touch the hearts of all assembled there that they might not turn away from enjoying the bounty of this day: the weather, the company, the occasion of the wedding, leaving Carl in His hands, working through the hands of those trained to do His work.

Shortly there was the pleasant sound of silver gently hitting glass, weaving in between the chatter that tickled the air, light and sweet, drifting from topic to benign topic: the array of roses on the trellis; the pleasant sound the rolling river made; the elegant table Nevada had set. Splotch made a joke about the waning moments of Spence's life as a free man to a plume of laughter especially from the men. No one mentioned Carl, as if they'd all heeded Skell's prayer that they not fret, but rather trust. And then Linc approached the gathering and the air around the table went still.

Kojo rushed toward Linc. "Sir? May I help you? Direct you?"

"Please, call me Lincoln," he said as he recognized Kojo as the one Nevada had spurned earlier.

"Well, Mr. Lincoln, you'll forgive me if I shan't call you by your first name, seeing as I had a buddy whose daddy was tole by a white man to call him by his first name and the next thing you know my buddy's mother was trying to decipher if the bashed-up dead man presented to her was her husband for sure."

Linc lowered his eyes. "I am sorry. Truly. That certainly would not be the outcome in this case, I assure you, nothing even close, really."

"So, you were saying where you trying to get to?" Kojo asked.

"Well, here. Uh, for breakfast."

"Oh, well, you see, this is a special gathering just for us, Mr. Lincoln, and —"

"Lincoln, please, call me Lincoln. And I have been invited." Linc looked beyond Kojo to those gathered at the table. He looked for Nevada; even Sylvia would do. Someone who could vouch for him.

Now Splotch had walked over to where they were. "You the one my lady told me about, correct?" Splotch asked in a low voice.

"Your lady?" Linc asked, careful to allow just a slight raise of his brows. But his eyes wanted to bulge, his mouth wanted to gape. His heart was in fact beating double time. This was Splotch. Splotch! Unmistakably. Beyond the defining scar that gave him his name, he'd once held a knife to Linc's neck.

The scene came back to Linc in a flash: when Splotch had accused Buddy and Linc of cheating and he'd grabbed Linc and pressed that knife to his throat. Linc could almost feel the vein in his neck pulsing the way it had that day, as if it knew it might be severed. He balled his fists to hold himself from rubbing his throat.

"Yes, my lady, Miss Vergilina," Splotch whispered, though his voice carried a hard edge. "I saw you sharing space with her in the parlor last night. Is it just a habit wit you crashing in on other folks' private times?" Splotch asked, as he moved in closer to Linc. "Soon as I saw you come strutting over here, I said to myself, Here come that white-looking nigger from last night."

Linc turned red. He tried to swallow the words pushing through his mouth, but it was too late, as he heard himself say, "That be the case, then I guess that would make you that black-looking nigger from right now."

"Say what?" Kojo said, as now he, too, moved in closer to Linc. "I shoulda known you wadn't no white man. Why ain't you just say from the first?"

Both Kojo and Splotch had moved so close up on Linc that he could feel their breath against his face. He took a step back, not to retreat, but just to give himself room to size them up, to calculate his chances should he need to take them both on.

"What we got goin' on here?" Nevada screeched at the top of her voice as she walked toward them carrying a jug filled to the rim with strawberry punch. "I invited this fine young man here whether it pleases you or not, Kojo. Everything around here is not meant exclusively for your pleasure."

Kojo turned quickly to look at Nevada, a pleading in his eyes that she not expose their carrying-on, but his movement was abrupt, causing it to appear that Nevada accidently — it was actually intentional — splattered the full volume of strawberry juice right in his face and also Splotch's. There was a collective gasp as both Kojo and Splotch jumped back, letting out yelps and wiping at their eyes.

"Oh my, now that was just so clumsy on my part," Nevada said. "I do so beg your pardon, both of you." She winked at Linc then and handed him a handkerchief to wipe away the splatters of juice that had hit him. He took the handkerchief and nodded a thank-you.

Kojo moved quickly away, walking toward the house. Splotch just stood there, drawing his hands down his face and Linc offered

Splotch the handkerchief. "From one colored man to another," he said.

Splotch looked at the handkerchief and then looked at Linc. "Fuck you," he said to Linc, then he walked away, too. Linc lowered his gaze, focused on a spot where the dew hung on the grass like diamond chips.

Now Nevada was in front of Linc. "Ready for breakfast, Sugar?" she said, and he thought again of Buddy's house, the way the women had called him Sugar, the thought softening him.

"I would love breakfast," he said, realizing all of a sudden that he had not eaten since before this time yesterday. Nevada was already calling for Vergie. And now he watched Vergie emerge from the kitchen. She was smiling in his direction and he imagined what her face would do when he told her he'd lied last night about being colored. He realized now that if his calling Splotch a "black-looking nigger" had not boxed him in to having to masquerade around this quarantine station as a black man, seeing Vergie at this moment surely did.

She walked toward him and he got that surge again. Now she was standing in front of him and he felt dizzy, felt sweat accumulate under his shirt collar. He tried to

337

tell himself that he was not affected by the nearness of her.

"Having breakfast with us, are you?" Vergie asked him. He nodded, and as he glanced for the briefest second at her mouth, her lips slightly pursed. Realized now that glancing at her mouth last night was what caused him to claim to be a black man. Now he was angry at her for the provocation. Angry at Splotch for coming at him like that and forcing him to call him a nigger. Angry at the whole assemblage at the table as Vergie showed him to a seat.

The air was stiff all around him as Vergie introduced him and he bowed in the direction of each name she called. Now he was angry even at the stiffness in the air. He thought that he had his own stiff air to deal with. He was sorry in general about the treatment they likely endured on a daily basis. But he had his own turmoil, too: people looking to string him up for a justifiable punch he'd thrown almost two decades ago, his brother vanished, Meda dead. He had his own joys shattered. Not a single one of them had a monopoly on heartache this instant. Yet he felt guilty for being angry at them for the apprehension his presence unleashed. Then he noticed Miss Ma.

He held a steady face when he looked at

338

Miss Ma and wondered if she recognized him. No, she couldn't recognize him, he thought. He was only thirteen the last time she'd seen him. He was much shorter, his voice still squeaked; his hair fashioned in that bowl haircut that Robinson had dictated all the boys wear; his skin was paler, smoother, having not yet been exposed to the abundant sun that came with his bricklaying work, nor roughened by the hard-living nights. He almost wanted to hug her, wanted to say to her, "Miss Ma, it's me, the little white boy you saved from arrest when you sang your warning song in the yard. He wanted to hear her grunt the way she'd do whenever she saw him, though he could detect the affection she had for him in that grunt.

But he didn't. He had fully retreated behind the lying mask he wore; it was like burlap against his face; the friction of it burned deep wedge marks in his skin. His hot breath had nowhere to go. He was suffocating under the mask. Yet he smiled as he took his seat. "Well, this sure does resemble a table my dear departed mother would have set. I feel myself getting misty-eyed just looking out on this splendid arrangement."

"Colored mama?" Miss Ma asked, and

Linc nodded and noticed a few jaws drop, when he did.

"And you named for the president?"

"Yes, ma'am, my mother was grieving terribly when he was killed, as I guess was every Negro mother in the Union, so she named me for him."

"You got his ways?"

"I beg your pardon."

"Named for someone, you supposed to have his ways, part of being named for someone so he don't ever die. Honest Abe," she said, then she started to laugh, and Linc pretended to be surprised by the uninterrupted stream of sound. Meanwhile a platter of eggs was passed to him followed by grits, a thick square of scrapple, and a healthy portion of planked shad. He lowered his head and whispered a prayer over his food. The aromas danced under his nose, especially coming from the fish and the butter in the hominy.

"Grace been issued aready," Splotch said, returning to the table, clean shirt on. He took a seat at the head.

"Well, I see no harm in giving thanks twice for a meal this fine," Linc said, as he concentrated on the plate of food; the shad's mouth seemed shaped in a smirk as it stared up at him with its one eye. "Plus, I recall my childhood, when a plate would be removed as surely as it was set in front of you if you did not first bow your head in gratitude. I grew up in a Christian home —"

"Ain't none of us can't make that claim," Splotch said, cutting him off.

Linc chewed a mouthful of scrapple before he answered. His palate swooned from the first taste. The outside was crunchy, but just below the crust the meat was soft and moist and infused with sage. He convinced himself now that he would suffer through a sustained high level of discomfort for the privilege of this meal as he cut into the shad, separating the head, imagining for a moment that it was Splotch's head. "I should have been more specific. I did not simply mean a home where Christianity was practiced. That was actually the name of the residence. The Christian Almshouse Orphanage of New Yark," careful to pronounce that city's name the way the black men he'd played cards with did. "My mother worked there in exchange for room and board for the two of us."

"Sound like a white place to me," Splotch said. "You raised white boy or colored?"

"Well, seeing as how my mother was a brown-skinned woman, it would be kind of

341

hard for me to be raised as a white boy." He spit out the words "white boy" the way he'd heard Buddy and others do as he pulled the center bone from the shad, filleting it, and then stopped talking to scoop up a healthy portion. He almost wanted to close his eyes over how good it was.

"From the looks of you," Splotch said, "I offer it would be hard for you not to be raised a white boy."

"Well, good thing all is not as it looks to be," Linc said. "I had one beautiful mother, and I could not even think of being reared by anyone other than she."

"How she look?" Miss Ma asked Linc.

"She was small-statured, but she had a graceful way of carrying herself that made her appear taller, straight back; until the day she died, I never knew her to slouch." He put his fork down and stared off into the morning air that was yellow and then blue as the high trees swayed and let in the sun and then hid it. "She had eyes that drooped a bit, they were a little sad, but her smile compensated. Everything around her brightened when she smiled."

He stopped himself as he bit into a roll, then sopped the roll through the grits and allowed the conversation to shift away from him. Bits of what they said hit his ear and he realized that some were talking about a funeral they'd attended the past week and then that's all he could hear because they were speaking of Meda's funeral.

"I will say that her brother spared no expense on her service," he heard Skell say.

"For certain, that beautiful blue gown and the matching satin slippers and Sister's hair pinned up the way she liked it," Miss Ma said, and Linc felt his insides twisting. "Undertaker had even shaped her mouth in a smile. She had a pretty ole mouth, anyhow. Looked to be seeing the face of Jesus laying up there in that casket smiling. And then it was the most beautiful thing I seen that Buddy got the iceman's horse to lead the procession to the cemetery. That horse walked so proud, like it was his high honor to lead Sister to her final resting place."

Nevada had returned. "Y'all talking about Sister? That sure is timely, 'cause I made this cornbread in honor of her memory." She held up a tray of cornbread cut in squares, the tops so evenly browned they appeared as if they'd been painted on. She leaned in and offered Linc the tray. He took one quickly, had to grab it quickly because he was so filled with contraries right now that he thought his disconcertion would show. He was at once that little boy grabbing for Meda's hands, and this grown man on the run. He was honorable, and he was a fraud. Here with the most selfless of intentions — to find his brother; he was also here to hide out to save himself, to work out his own selfish desires. The cornbread was hot as he bit into it; it was both hard and soft and the flavor exploded in his head. He tasted a hint of lavender; tasted memory; tasted grief, a grief almost overpowering.

"Is it good, Sugar?" Nevada asked him as she passed the tray to Miss Ma. "Sister told me that usually when she gave someone her recipe, she'd kill 'em right after so her ingredients could stay secret, but she said she liked me so she would let me live." They all laughed then — Linc, too, surprised that he did as he imagined Meda saying that. His chest opened then, allowing the grief the space to spread out, to separate, leaving a hole in the center that the laughter momentarily filled.

25

Not far from where they were having breakfast, Son was down in the cellar, enjoying a
hunk of cornbread Nevada had just cut for
him, his reward for being such a good
listener and worker. He intended to offer a
portion of the cornbread to Bram, also
wanted to give Bram a sip of water from his
canteen. Thought the food and drink might
tease Bram all the way awake. Son was sure
that Bram had moved since yesterday as
he'd been careful to position Bram's head
so that it faced the spiderweb. But just now
Bram's head was angled more toward the
wall, his chin almost touching his shoulder.
Son gently lifted Bram's chin so that he
once again faced the spider's web, then
placed his hand over the sack where he
thought Bram's heart should be to see if his
chest was rising and falling. He imagined it
was. But then, Son imagined he could feel a
pulse in all kinds of things: hollowed-out

logs, seashells, the ground after a storm.

"You dead or just 'sleep?" he asked Bram. "If you just dead, I'ma eat all this cornbread." He waved the cake under Bram's nose, to no response. He crammed the cake into his own mouth and closed his eyes over how good it was, the kind of good that filled him up inside and made him want to cry because he thought how much he would miss it if suddenly he no longer lived here. He started crying then. He ate the cornbread and cried. When he was down to the last morsel, he set the plate down. "I'ma leave this for you if you woked up, 'cause you been moving since yesterday. Move again." Son held his own breath so that he could detect any motion. Nothing. Not even the dust down there moved right now. "Water?" he asked as he waved the canteen under Bram's nose. He dabbed water on Bram's lips. "Maybe you are dead," he said, as he sat on the floor next to Bram. "Or maybe not." He patted Bram's forehead and then went to the other end of the cellar and gathered the crates and odds and ends of old furniture to add to the wall to make it even taller and wider and thicker, to further separate Bram from the open space that was the rest of the cellar. Satisfied with his labors, he left.

■ ■ ■ ■

Sylvia felt the onslaught of heat as she pushed open the back door to the hospital. The smell seemed to come from everywhere in here, as if the pictures of white men lining the walls were instead corpses in varying stages of decay. This was that smell she'd dreamt about, intuition warning her of Carl's deterioration, she realized as she pulled a handkerchief from her dress pocket and covered her mouth and nose, and then stepped inside. She collided with Spence, who was on his way out. They seemed almost to embrace as Spence circled his arms around her to keep his balance, and she instinctively wrapped hers around his waist, and they stood this way momentarily under the threshold. When their bodies separated an awkward air rushed between them and they both looked down at the floor as Spence bent to pick up her handkerchief that had dropped and handed it to her as he said that he'd just been on his way to find her. "The leg, Sylvia," he said on a whisper. "It is trying to gangrene already, you believe it?"

"I know, I dreamt of it," she said as she took the handkerchief and twisted it around

347

her fingers.

"So what now?" he asked.

"I go clean the wound, and then I get Doctor, so that he can sign off on getting Carl transported back to Philadelphia as soon as possible," Sylvia said as they started walking down the hallway. "And you go off and do whatever a man does on the day of his wedding — besides change his mind."

"You caught on to my scheme, Sylvia," he said, trying to make light. "I have been all day concocting an excuse for avoiding the altar."

"Well, I can understand how one might try such a thing, marrying into a family that boasts the likes of Lena. But never let my name be pulled into association with your scheme."

He laughed on a whisper, then touched her wrist lightly, stopping her in the hallway midway to Carl's room. "I've already burned the barium salts for peroxide and, uh, about getting the doctor . . . Truth be spoken, I do not know if the doctor is in best form this early —"

"He is usually in the best form that he will be early. He declines as the day wears on." Sylvia cut him off, even as she felt the touch of his fingers against her wrist. "Why?

Have you seen the doctor already this morning?"

Spence looked away. "No," he said. Though in fact he'd just left the doctor, had just put the long pipe to the doctor's mouth and lit the mound of opium in the pipe's bowl and watched the muscles in the doctor's face go slack. "But I was thinking whether the doctor is of use or not." He rushed his words. "I am not scheduled to say vows until this evening. Some cockamamie time my bride-to-be and her crazy-headed sister came up with. And they tell me I cannot step foot on that side of the Laz until wedding-bell time lest it bring all kinds of damnation to our life together. They say I dare not catch a glimpse of Mora beforehand. I am just speaking all this to declare that I am here to help for as long as you need me — and you'll likely need help preparing Carl for transport."

"And I am declaring that you need to be off practicing the saying of 'I do' so you do not stumble over your words when it's time for you to say them in front of all the people who journeyed here for that single purpose."

She gently shook her wrist free and started walking again, in silence, all the way into Carl's room. Spence followed her in. Carl's bed was centered under the screened window that drizzled in the pink and yellow morning light, the moisture from the dew, and the splashing sounds the river made. It would have seemed a beautiful scene to Sylvia if not for Carl's leg, swollen, the wound oozing its substance clear through the bandaging. Carl was soundly asleep, snoring lightly.

"Well, hear me out on other points, Sylvia," Spence whispered, as he doused a cloth with alcohol. Sylvia held out her hands and he wrapped them in the cloth, pressing lightly. "Carl is a big man. You need strength to hold him down should his pain throw him into a delirium."

"You mean the doctor needs strength," she said as Spence pulled the cloth from her hands, wiping the tips of her fingers as he did.

"If favor is smiling down on us, then, yes, of course I mean the doctor." He held a gown open for Sylvia and she pushed her arms in. "But maybe favor has turned her back on us, and the doctor cannot perform the duties they pay him a whole lot of money to perform."

"What are you trying to say, Spence?"

He looked out the window, a glaze of perspiration coating his forehead. "I am saying that if a major surgical procedure is required, then you will need me to assist."

"Spence, there is no way that I am attempting a major surgical procedure on this man," she said as she moved toward the bed. She undid the wrapping that loosely surrounded the wound. The sight of it merely confirmed what the smell had already indicated. Infection had surely taken hold. She leaned in and turned the leg slightly and peered in at the wound. She called for peroxide, and Spence was already handing it to her. She poured the peroxide into the wound. The wound seemed to cry out, though Carl appeared unfazed in his narcotic sleep.

Spence stood beside her, leaning in, too. His breath stroked her neck.

Sylvia asked as she palpated the length of Carl's leg below the wound, "I surely do not dispute the severity here." Sylvia stood up from the bed and turned to face Spence. "But, again, my plan is to get him back to Philadelphia as soon as humanly possible, certainly before the end of this day." She pointed to the bands of cotton that Spence handed to her.

"And what if it must be sooner than transportation can be arranged? Today is Saturday, Sylvia, the ferries are irregular today."

"We are not at that bridge, so no need to contemplate its crossing," she said as together they rewrapped Carl's leg. Their shoulders touched, and then their arms. They were efficient, the movements of each in time with the other's. When they were finished, they stood back, surveying their work. Spence broke the silence.

"I know the sight of Carl like this must trouble you mightily. I know you and Carl share a past. Believe me, Sylvia, I inquired about you over the years."

"Before or after you inquired about Mora?" The question slipped out before she could call it back.

"I have no response to that," he said, as he looked down, "other than to say that should I have had my first choice —"

"Let us agree," Sylvia interrupted him, redirecting the conversation, "that our plan is to get him to Philadelphia as soon as possible. If his condition becomes dire before then, we will adjust as the situation dictates."

Carl began to stir, gasped out her name. She went to the head of the bed. "Hey, sweet cakes," he said, "my sweet little honey pot, you look to be an angel in all that white, you not here to lead me to glory, are you?"

"No, baby, 'course not. And leave the rest of us on this evil earth? You not getting off that easy." She ran her hand along his cheek, and kissed his forehead. She sensed Spence leaving the room as she focused fully on Carl.

"But, but, Carl, it is your leg —" she whispered.

"That is some mighty fine brandy y'all serve at this place," he interrupted. "I would have looked to get shot a long time ago if I knew I could sip on some good liquor that did not come from corn, and have you standing over my bed —"

Sylvia put her finger to his lips. "Carl, you got to listen to me, baby. You got to hear what I must say to you —"

"Only thing I want to hear from you is that you will accept my hand in marriage. I know that last time I said it would be the last time, but a man is allowed to reverse himself when he is staring death in the face."

"Carl —"

"I shall be true, so true, I shall never ever make you blue," he tried to sing, and then laughed a morphine-tinged laugh.

"I know it," she said, as she stroked his cheek some more.

"So true I will be to you, just say you too" — he continued his attempt at song.

"Infection's taken hold, baby —"

"Da-da-dee-du." His voice rose in degrees. "If we do not stem it, it will —"

"Kill me," he sang. "Put a dagger to my heart and just kill me." He closed his eyes. He was no longer singing. He was talking, pleading. "Just kill me, Sylvia, please. I would rather be dead than be a one-legged man. You remember how we danced. Life is not worth the living if I cannot dream of you and me dancing again." His voice was raspy; water drained from the corners of his eyes. She dabbed Carl's eyes and encouraged him to sip the morphine-tinged brandy. She whispered love words and watched him smile a sloppy smile. She stroked his cheek and spoke softly until he faded again into sleep.

26

At the appointed time for the ceremony, everything was nearly as it should be. Kojo had built the trellis of pine that would form an arc over Mora and Spence as they spoke their vows. Vergie and Miss Ma and Bay draped garlands of roses around the trellis, and affixed bows to the chairs, and otherwise transformed the area behind the house into a wedding chapel. Fine white linen covered the tables set with the best china and silver and candleholders on display. The gifts dutifully delivered from the basement by Son were shaped in a high and wide pyramid and formed their own display. The corn had been husked and grilled; the turkey baked and resting; the spirits ready for uncorking; the cake, all five tiers, iced and swirled.

The guests were assembled in their going-somewhere-special garb. Skell donned a collar and a crucifix — he was a recently ordained minister and as such was legally allowed to officiate. He carried his oversized Bible with the pages edged in gold, the appropriate verses concerning holy matrimony already marked.

Lena and Mora stood at the window of the upstairs-bedroom-turned-bridal-parlor, waiting for their cue to begin the procession down. Vergie and Nevada sat next to each other, and Vergie leaned over and whispered to Nevada, "I heard from Bay that the bows on Lena's dress are about the size of Virginia and North Carolina conjoined." Nevada let go a laugh but then swallowed it as Skell fixed his face in a grimace. Skell stood next to Kojo, Spence's best man. Nevada refused to look at Kojo.

The guests chatted and waved their sachets scented with rosemary oil to hold the mosquitoes at bay. Every now and then someone turned to the back of the yard, looking for Spence. The one on the harmonica blew a few toots and they all came to attention, expecting that Spence had finally arrived, but it wasn't Spence. It wasn't Spence again when PD, the soloist who would sing the Lord's Prayer began to stretch his voice out. Nor was it Spence at every new sound that followed over the next half hour. People started to fidget and whisper to aisle-mates that something must be amiss — it's supposed to be the bride that holds things up, definitely a bad sign when the groom is late. Finally they heard fast-moving footsteps and there went up a collective sigh, followed by an even more unified groan: still no Spence. This time it was Son. He ran straight to the aisle where Nevada was. He reached in the pocket of his overalls and pulled out a finely textured linen envelope. "For Mora," he announced. "From Spence to Mora."

"Oh shit," Nevada said under her breath as she moved quickly from her seat and took the envelope and ran into the house.

"One does not need to be a soothsayer to guess at the contents of that envelope," Kojo's wife, Lil, said as she fanned herself ferociously.

"Well, no sense in jumping over a puddle when the ground is dry," Miss Ma said.

"I agree," Skell called from up front. "We should at least wait to hear a report."

"Smells like a bad report to me," said Splotch. "Man thirty minutes late for his own wedding. Where might he be?" Splotch got up from his seat and walked toward the rear of the gathering space. "Let me try to hunt him down. I did not come all this way to play with my thumbs."

Vergie watched Splotch leave. She was relieved. He'd hovered around her after breakfast, and she could not walk two steps without him right there: smiling at her; offering his arm for a walk; a bench so that they could sit and chat; his assistance clearing the breakfast dishes, cleaning the ash from the stove, stoking the coals in the barbecue pit. At home, his attention was tolerable, but here on the Lazaretto it had become so concentrated it approached unbearable, especially since she had been so preoccupied with worry over Carl's condition. And added to that, she'd sensed that Linc had lingered after breakfast, hoping to say a word to her, but Splotch had made that impossible. She'd felt her stomach sink with disappointment when she watched Linc exit the gathering after breakfast. Nevada added to her disappointment, going on and on about what a charmer Linc was, that he had her grandmother eating out his hand, Nevada said, and Vergie knew that Miss Ma did not suffer fools lightly. "Perhaps he might call on you when you return home," Nevada had told her. "I did tell him that you live on Addison Street with all the high-siddity Negroes, but he should not be thwarted by that, as Sylvia and I have managed to be close as sisters despite that."

Nevada had come back into the yard and the chatter hushed and all sat up to hear an explanation for Spence's absence. She positioned herself up front, but not directly at the center of the trellis. All eyes were on her as she smoothed out her dress, which was cinched tightly at the waist and matched in color the palest of the pink roses adorning the trellis. Her hair was pinned to one side, and Vergie thought that she'd never seen Nevada more beautiful as when she folded her gloved hands lightly in front of her as if she were about to sing an aria. She cleared her throat, then said, "Spence has sent word to Mora that the wedding must be postponed. I cannot say for certain when — or even if — it will take place. However, we still must eat, whether they say 'I do' or 'I do not.' We will be serving dinner the next hour."

A stunned silence followed, even though they'd just been chattering on about the possibility of this very outcome. Now they looked at one another in disbelief. "What? Why? Really?" they said in a run of voices.

"This must be related to Carl," Skell said. "No other explanation."

"Dear Carl," Miss Ma said in a whispery voice.

Then Kojo asked what had Spence's note

359

said, exactly.

"I am not at liberty to speak on it," Nevada replied as she looked out onto the gathering.

Then Lil asked how was Mora taking the news?

"How would you take it?" Lena said, entering the fray as she walked slowly down the center aisle. She held her bridesmaid bouquet as if she herself were the bride, and Nevada and Vergie looked at each other and smirked. "I just want to know where Sylvia is."

"Well now, Lena," Nevada said slowly, "where do you think she is? She is at the hospital. She is the head nurse here, after all."

"Do not get huffy with me, Nevada," Lena said, now at the front of the chapel area. "I am just proffering the observation that we have barely seen Sylvia at all this weekend. No Sylvia. No Spence. And now no wedding . . ."

The air rippled with gasps that Lena would pose such a notion. Nevada bristled. "I suggest, Lena, that you leave Sylvia's name out of your misshapen mouth."

"Make me!" Lena pushed her chest out at Nevada.

Vergie rose from her seat. "I will make you

if she does not," Vergie said, and she started to move toward the aisle.

The schoolteacher, Ella, whispered to her cousin that Maze would be mortified if she saw Vergie conducting herself in such unladylike ways.

"Well, not as if this gathering is exactly high society," her cousin whispered back.

They snickered among their group; then Miss Ma unleashed a stream of laughter. And then the yard-turned-chapel went still.

Two white men entered. Both in suits and top hats, both with billy clubs braced as if they were coming to quell an uprising, as if they had license to be here and the ones already here needed to ask permission of these white men to take their next breaths.

Kojo stood, his eyes on the one walking down the center aisle, his eye really on his billy club. He'd been hit with one before for no good cause other than they'd been searching for a thief and he was as good as anybody to use for their whipping boy. "Sirs?" Kojo said.

Then Skell stood, too. "May we help you?"

Then the husband to Ella's cousin stood; the soloist who'd been prepared to sing the Lord's Prayer stood; the one holding the harmonica stood; one by one, every man in the yard-turned-chapel stood, their faces ashen as if they were watching their own deaths approach, but standing nonetheless, ready if necessary to fight for themselves, to defend the women assembled here.

Vergie wanted to yell and curse at the white men intruding on their gathering, wanted to tell them to take their damn billy clubs and beat their own asses, wanted to fling her hand at them the way she'd flung her hand at the white men in the other boat. But she did not. She considered what the result would be the way she rarely considered the consequences of her unbridled temper. If she expressed how she felt this instant, one of the two would surely move in her direction, putting Skell and the other men in jeopardy because they'd be compelled to defend her and might end up with a head-bashing or worse.

She eased from her seat. She walked to the back of the yard-turned-chapel as she heard Miss Ma say, "Praise the Lord," which stopped Vergie in her tracks, as Miss Ma was not known for making such proclamations. "You have come to investigate how we was shot at and nearly killed on the river. Praise the Lord, I say." Then Nevada also joined her grandmother's chants of "Praise the Lord," then Skell joined in, then Kojo and his wife; one by one the entire gathering joined the chant, and Vergie marveled at the wiles of Miss Ma as she turned to leave the yard. "Praise the Lord," she whispered to herself — the saying it helped wrestle down her temper, which had so wanted her to shake a fist at the white men who'd barged in on their sacred time. She walked away from the yard. Wished she'd been able to reason with her temper when they'd been on that boat the way she'd done just now. Everything did not have to be a fight, at least not her fight, her aunt Maze had tried to impress that on her. Sometimes it was better to turn away, walk away, as she was doing now.

She was walking in circles, she realized, because she'd come several times already to this part of the shallow creek where the rocks made a bridge. She decided this time to cross — slipped her shoes from her feet and lifted the hem of her dress and stepped from rock to rock. She could see tadpoles just below the surface of the water shimmying like fast girls. A floating bloom of coral honeysuckle served as a raft for a family of hummingbirds. Their journey kept her occupied until she reached the other side. She walked past the main house and the mansions that served as Ledoff's and the doctor's private quarters. She stood on the pier, flanked by the barges. The sun was sinking lower in the sky, leaving a trail of red and yellow. The air smelled of wet pine and fish oil. The blue-gray river lurched in spots as if it was trying to reach up and steal some of the sunset's color, as if it was tired of being blue and gray and wanted the feel of orange.

She started walking again. She was passing the hospital, but she didn't allow her head to turn in that direction, lest she fall into despair all over again about Carl. His condition must have deteriorated for Spence to miss his own wedding. She was falling into despair anyhow. Now she faced the curing shack, where Sylvia had told her that Linc had spent the night. She peeped in. The sight of the chains bolted to the wall drew her all the way in. The ceiling was low and she had to practically stoop once she crossed the threshold. It smelled of mud and mint, and she guessed the mint aroma came from the sheet folded neatly on the cot. Bay, who did the laundry here, had a penchant for drizzling oil of peppermint into everything she washed. Just above the cot were the chains. Vergie had grown up with stories about the liberators of the enslaved and as a child she would fantasize that she was the most famous liberator of all, Black Moses. She'd imagine herself shooting down the overseers trying to foil their escape; taking hatchets to chains such as these. She fingered the metal, it was hard and cold as death. She tried to imagine these chains bolting her to the wall, but she couldn't. A knot of guilt rose up in her throat and she swallowed hard. She knew that had she been born as she was four score sooner and two states south, she still wouldn't know the feel of these chains. She'd know the big house. The beds there. Welt marks on her spine not from a whip but from the rough friction of the sheets, the proprietor's breath pushing in her ear like knife stabs, his sweat like acid burning through her skin all the way to the bone.

She put both her hands through the circle the chain made and sat on the cot and swung her feet around and reclined. She closed her eyes. She still couldn't imagine it, even as the metal dug into her wrist and the pain of it shot through her arms and the line of anger widened. "How dare they!" she said out loud. "Hate-filled ravagers." She saw herself again, flicking her hand at the two on the boat because she knew they'd said some disparaging thing about them. How many disparaging things had she heard, even from the ones who covered their prejudices under the veneer of politeness? Her flick of the wrist had been for them, too; for every time she'd moved seamlessly through the parlors when she'd assist her aunt and uncle as they catered lavish affairs for one of their white clients and they thought her white and she'd had to endure overheard talk about the smaller brain, larger teeth, penchant to steal, animalistic, work-averse, rhythmically proficient, overly natured, the dear, sweet, loyal, mammified Negro. She'd seen them crammed into that other boat, too, when she'd flicked her wrist. And right now that might be what was costing Carl his life. She pressed her wrists deeper against the cold metal that dug into her skin. She knew that she could pull her hands from these chains at any time, so she allowed the hurt and pressed them deeper still.

27

Linc was preparing to leave the Lazaretto. He'd just met with Sylvia, who'd taken him into Ledoff's study and shown him the meticulously kept log and assured him that Bram could not be there. She asked him again who had directed him to the Lazaretto. "It does not matter," he said as he looked out the window and watched the river lapping by. She offered him transportation back to the city on a ferry due in shortly. "If not that, there will be another shortly after, though that one will be an emergency run to get Carl to a hospital in Philadelphia." He accepted her offer. Then she excused herself, said that she had to ready Carl for transport. He thanked her again, started what felt like a long trek to the pier to await the ferry. He patted his shirt pocket, then looked through his satchel and realized that he'd left his tobacco in the shack where he'd slept. He reversed course.

The trip back to Philadelphia without knowledge of Bram would be even more of a torture without a smoke.

He breathed in deeply as he walked toward the shack. Given the circumstances, he thought that at least the open space here had done him some good. In New York his room faced a crowded alley that smelled perpetually of burning rags, or wood, or charcoal. When he thought about it, gray predominated there; as if he lived in only two dimensions. At least until night caught and he made his way over to the Tenderloin section with its sensory deluge and he'd see color everywhere: in the clothes, and the food, and the drink, and the way the conversation splashed in unanticipated directions — even the danger had a color. And every night that he was up there, he was thrilled by it. It reminded him sometimes of Buddy's house, except that Buddy's house had the added bonus of familiarity. He felt as if he was part of a family at Buddy's. Even though he wasn't really, he felt that he was.

As he approached the shed he noticed for the first time the pop of yellow and white wildflowers that bordered the path to the entrance. Birds chattered away, and he thought he even heard a woodpecker as he stepped inside. He stopped then. There was

Vergie, stretched out on the cot. Her long dress hung in volumes over the sides of the cot and in the second that it took his eye to move from the hint of her ankle along the length of the dress, he imagined himself covering her even more perfectly than the endless fabric did. He asked himself why was she here like this if not to entice him to do what he'd been yearning to do since their first encounter in the parlor. Imagined it now as his eyes took in her slender waist, the mild elevation of her breasts, her hair, which was spread out in waves on the cot, her eyes closed, her mouth pursed. He thought he would explode when he looked at her mouth — that mouth that had caused him to say he was a black man, her substantial lips, the tilt of her chin. Then he saw the chains, both of her hands inside the circle of chain, and he gasped. He was paralyzed at first as he told himself that he could not be seeing this. She could not be chained to the wall. And yet she was. He ran to her then, calling her name as he did.

She opened her eyes with a jolt. "Oh my God," she said when she saw him standing over her. His expression was frozen and horrified, not unlike Nevada's and Miss Ma's that morning when she'd chopped away at her hair.

"Who did this?" he asked, as he pulled her hands from the circle the chain made. He stopped then as he held on to her hands, his face a mix of relief and confusion when he realized that the chains had not actually held her shackled.

"Please tell me you stretched yourself here like this," he said, as Vergie slipped her hands from his hold and swung her feet around and sat all the way up. "Otherwise tell me who did, so I will know who I am about to stomp to his death." His voice was low as he struggled to keep an even tone. The sight of her like that had made a wavy line of his breathing.

Vergie rubbed her wrists. They were blue in places from the chains' indentation. "I feel foolish," she said, concentrating on her wrists. "Please walk out and come back in again and pretend that you are seeing me for the first time."

"The first time this hour? Or the first time ever?"

"Does it matter?"

"Well, if it is the first time ever, I must find an owl to drop me in — what was it? Cow dung? Is that not how you characterized my appearance when we first met?"

"That was unkind of me," she said. She shifted on the cot. She looked down at the dirt floor. And then she cried. It was a hawking cry. When she was younger, her aunt Maze had tried to teach her to cry pretty. Had told her that one day she'd find herself needing to cry in the presence of a handsome man, and she should lightly dab her eyes with her handkerchief and allow only a wisp of a soprano sound from her throat, not all the nose-snorting that was her custom. That lesson had been lost on Vergie. Right now she made gagging, slobbering sounds as she spit and blew her nose.

Linc just stood there in the middle of the shack, partially leaning so his head wouldn't scrape the ceiling. His feet were plastered to the dirt floor because he didn't know what to do. He considered going to Vergie to attempt to comfort her, but he was wary about her mental state. For all he knew she could be an absolute loon. Why else would she purposely shackle herself? But then he couldn't just stand here and watch her cry. "Fish or cut bait," Bram would say. He felt a pang as he thought about Bram. He wanted to do as Vergie was doing right now, he wanted to weep. But all he could do was grab his smokes and leave, head back to town and start his search for Bram again there. For all he knew, Bram could be back in New York by now. He could be in his room, in a trance, talking to the dead. The image comforted him as he looked around for his pouch of tobacco and saw it peeping under the sheet he'd folded. Vergie was practically sitting on it.

"Uh, Vergie," he half-spoke, half-whispered her name.

She made a honking sound as she blew her nose and then looked up. He thought the sound provocative because it was so unexpected, so unladylike that it reached all the way inside of him.

"My, uh, my tobacco — it is there." He pointed right at the spot where her hip met the cot.

She followed Linc's eyes to the outline of her hip. She removed the pouch from under her. "I do apologize," she said as she handed him the pouch. "And my display of hysteria is unforgivable."

"Unforgivable only because there's nothing to forgive," Linc said, as he took the tobacco and dropped it in his bag. His sleeves were rolled up to his elbows, his arms were dark with hair, and Vergie's gaze followed the length of his arms.

"I should not be here, intruding on your space, such as it is," Vergie said, as she dabbed at her eyes — finally. "I saw the chains and I was drawn to inspect them.

The thought of the awfulness wrought by those chains."

A field mouse darted through the shed, just avoiding the hem of Vergie's dress. Vergie pulled her foot back to allow it to pass. Linc had never been in the company of a woman who reacted so calmly to a scampering mouse. Nor one who looked at him as directly as she did now. No demure lowered head, no batting of the eyes. Straight on she looked at him as if they were equal in every way. He felt a surge then, like the surge he'd gotten when he'd seen her for the first time. The intensity of it weakened him and he needed to sit. "May I?" he asked as he pointed to a spot on the cot.

"It is your mat," Vergie said as she pulled her sprawling skirts in to accord him space.

Linc sat. He tried to relax, but he felt wooden, back erect, hands on his knees, looking straight ahead to where a spit of light pushed in between two slats. "You are right," he said, "about the awfulness wrought by chains like those. My mother told us stories when we were young that brought us to tears. Now it just evokes rage that rises up in me. Once I heard a white man calling two orphan kids river rats spawned from niggers. I was across the way and I barreled over to him and I told him

373

that I was offended, that any upstanding person should be offended, and I hit him so hard, I knocked him into a coma. He has survived to this day in quite an unholy condition." He didn't know why he told her that skewed version of what truly happened, didn't know why he was telling her such a thing at all.

"Good," Vergie said. "Good for you." She sat up and punched her fists in the air. "I guess that they thought you white. I imagine how they would have strung you from a tree if they knew that you were a black man. My error has been that I have expressed my rage without hiding the fact that I am a Negro, and I have paid dearly as a result."

"And you should not have to hide your race, Vergie. You should not," he said it with emphasis, the irony not lost on him.

She sighed. "I just wish — ah, dear Carl . . ." she said, and then she went quiet.

"Tell me about Carl," he said, practically whispering. "How is he faring?"

"I cannot. It will cause another outburst."

"Is he alive?"

"He is."

"Well, there is hope then. As long as there is life, there's the possibility that life can continue. Life wants to keep on drumming to the living beat." He quoted Meda as he

374

felt the tightness in his muscles ease a bit. He sat back some and concentrated on a single ant he saw marching across the wall, trying to replicate the movement of its colony so that it could find its way home; it leaned back as if it had made a great discovery and then disappeared into a seam of the wall. A woodpecker knock-knocked just outside of the shed; a breeze pushed the leaves to a melody of whooshing sounds.

"That is a nice thought," Vergie said, "life wanting to keep on drumming to the living beat. Sounds like something my aunt Maze might say."

He looked at Vergie and smiled. Vergie thought his smile honest the way it involved his entire face; a sadness hung in his eyes, though, and she asked him if he had located his brother. "My cousin told me that she saw you at the creek and that you were looking for someone and she told you to meet her at the barge."

"She did," he said, as he sat up straighter. "Though I confess, the sound of the music drew me to your party, plus I sensed that was where the beautiful women were."

Vergie stared at him straight on and pulled her full lips to one side in a smirk. Her reaction was different from most of the women he'd complimented like that; they'd giggle or turn red or at least lower their eyes.

"I apologize," he said. "I could not resist. You are beautiful. And did the wedding go off without a hitch?" he asked. Asked it quickly before Vergie could react.

"Can you fathom that there has been no wedding?" she said, relieved that he'd moved beyond calling her beautiful.

"No wedding? What happened?"

"The bride was jilted. Well, not actually jilted. The groom had official business. I suppose the result is the same."

"The groom? Spence?"

"Ah, yes, Spence. So you were observant during breakfast?"

"Well, Spence I did not actually meet, I just know of him because of his absence. Mora is the bride, Lena is her sister who has a penchant for one-upmanship and a special affection for Carl. Miss Ma is Nevada's grandmother. Skell is the voice of reason. Kojo is the strongman. And Splotch is a, a —" he stopped himself. "So what was the reaction of the folks who traveled all this way for a wedding that got put on ice."

"As you might imagine, the reaction went from confused to disappointed to livid, but even that got cut short when we were rushed by the police."

"The police?" Everything about Linc

376

tensed. "Why are the police here?"

"Well, I suppose actually they are constables. I don't know. I was wary of my ability to restrain myself, so I left."

He stood quickly, not even trying to hide his angst. "I must go, Vergie, they are very likely here for me."

"For *you*? Are you a wanted man? For what crime?"

"The crime I just told you about," he said as he grabbed up his satchel. "The man I punched when I was defending the orphan boys had high reaches. He will not die, nor will his family's want of revenge."

Vergie was looking at him straight on again. He tried to avoid the sight of her mouth; her pouty lips scrambled all semblance of logic in him. He might well stroke her face, put his lips to her forehead as if they were accustomed to one another in that way. He reminded himself that he'd only seen her for the first time last night, yet he reached forward anyhow and touched her cheek with his thumb. She jumped then, though not from his touch. Someone was on the other side of the shack, and Linc jumped, too, with balled fists, poised for a fight.

"Who are you?" Vergie asked, agitated.

"Begga pardon," he said, "but I am trying

to hunt down Nevada — can you tell me where she might be?"

"First, can you tell me who are you?" Vergie asked and Linc restrained himself or he would have answered for him. It was Buddy. Buddy! He looked exactly as Linc had remembered. Same coloring that used to remind Linc of the hens the Benins' cook roasted on Sundays, same stature, same eye that hung lower. Linc felt as if he'd been hit with a sandbag, all the air left him and he turned his back and pretended to wipe his face. He couldn't let on to Vergie that he knew Buddy, he was supposed to be from New York, after all. He listened to Buddy identify himself to Vergie, explain that he'd recently lost his sister and had gone fishing to grieve, but he realized suddenly he didn't want to be alone.

"Buddy?" Vergie said. "I am Vergilina, and I have heard Nevada mention your name once or twice."

"Believe none of it," he said and laughed. "You the nurse's kin, right? Met her one time years ago, she threw a cake on my floor — long story for another time. I probably could not pick her outta a crowd today. Nevada goes on and on 'bout her, about the two of you, and ain't none of it good." He laughed again.

Linc pretended to be looking for something on the cot, his conscious mind finally grabbing a hold of where he'd first met Sylvia, even as he tried to process Buddy's presence here and now. Sylvia was the nurse who'd treated his wound the night Splotch put a blade to his neck. "Hey, there, partner, sorry 'bout the intrusion" — Buddy was addressing Linc, so Linc had no choice but to turn around. Buddy's hand was extended. "My name is Buddy, but you can call me Buddy."

Vergie laughed. "You're funny," she said.

Linc shook his hand. "Lincoln," he said, making his voice go deep again, to sound more like the black man he was pretending to be. Buddy's grip was strong and tight as if he was trying to get Linc to look at him, but Linc did not.

"Now, where is Nevada, Miss Vergie? I do hope it is in that direction," he pointed toward the guesthouse. "Place seem to be swimming with the law. And nothing worse than a colored man in the woods with some police on the loose. Though they claim to be looking for a white boy, so that counts me out. Don't count you out, though, partner," he said to Linc.

"I am headed for the ferry, so it does not matter one way or the other," Linc said.

"And he's not white, besides," Vergie said.

"No? Sure look it," Buddy said. "But who am I to say? Drop of colored blood, and so forth." He had his good eye trained on Linc, a deep crease in his forehead. "I think the constables are waiting to take that same ferry. I wonder if it works the same as when they hunting down a colored, any one of us will do under those circumstance. But they probably more particular with white folk. They look to get the exact one they looking to get. So you may fare just fine. Me? I would lay low. Catch the next ferry. Now where did you say I could find Nevada?" He turned back to Vergie.

"I will walk with you to the guesthouse," Vergie said. "Lincoln, you should walk with us as well, catch the next ferry. Let the police have this ferry to themselves," she said, stressing her words.

Linc stood a moment, thinking what he should do. He honestly could not tell whether Buddy had recognized him or not; though Buddy had always had the knack of holding his face exactly as he wanted to hold it — at cards, for example. He'd told Linc that it helped to think about not hiding whatever it is he might be trying to conceal. The thing you try to hide the most is the very thing you expose, he'd preached to Linc back when he'd instructed him on how to bluff at the card table. "Especially your hands," he'd drilled into Linc. "Your hands give you away, because you not considering them, and they must close up to protect the lie you trying to tell."

"I do not know about you, partner" — Buddy directed his words toward Linc — "but a pretty miss such as Miss Vergilina requests that I stay in place, I surely would stay in place."

Linc forced himself to smile. "I suppose I will remain and catch the last ferry out."

28

There would be no next ferry. Earlier, while the guests sat waiting for the wedding ceremony to begin, a series of telegraphs had come in that stunned Sylvia, mortified her. She blinked, thinking her eyes deceiving her. The first asked for confirmation of a Code Yellow corpse, to which she replied in the negative. The second indicated that such a corpse had been delivered, to which she requested further details. The third stated that an unlicensed courier confessed to leaving a body on the pier contrary to protocol, to which she replied with a request of further description. The next described the crate, to which she replied in the negative regarding receipt. The next was an official directive that the Lazaretto be placed on lockdown until further notice.

Lockdown! she shouted in her head. With the infection in Carl's leg growing by the hour, with two dozen people here who did not even belong here and who surely did not want to remain past tomorrow. Lockdown?

No, no, no, she thought, as she tried to reason as much as one could through the confines of a telegraph machine. Just allow her the ferry she had already arranged to get this one critically wounded man back to Philadelphia. Please. Could she pile the guests on said ferry as well. *Negative.* Imploring. What about food, supplies? *Confirm receipt of directive.* Could she hear from Ledoff first. *Confirm receipt of directive.* Ledoff is the quarantine master, the doctor is indisposed. Might I hear from Ledoff? *Confirm receipt of directive.* Confirmed. *Await message from quarantine master.*

Spence had come into the room, a handsome groom on his way to be married, making a stop first to do his duty and feed the doctor the pipe. "Sylvia?" he said, surprised to see her leaning over the machine, her face stricken, her color drained.

"I came to summon the doctor on the off chance that he might be right-minded," she said. "The machine was clicking away." She collapsed in the chair. "I cannot fathom that this is happening on my watch."

"*What* is happening?"

"Seems a body was delivered the past day

sans protocol. We have not received it, but regardless, the Board of Health has declared us in a state of quarantine."

"Us? The Lazaretto?"

"Do you believe it?"

"What about Carl?"

"Dear God, what about Carl? That is all I can think of beyond the twentysome people now trapped here. We are even running short on morphine! Dear Carl . . ."

"We have to get him back to Philadelphia —"

"There is no way out. Do you understand, Spence? Nothing in, nothing out. Not people, not supplies, not food." She shook her head back and forth as if in a daze.

"Do they understand Carl's condition?"

"Do they care? They would sacrifice him in an eye twitch. They would sacrifice any one of us, or all of us, to save the populous of Philadelphia from another yellow-fever outbreak."

"Hogwash about the populous. More to save the commerce, the reputation, the wealth of Philadelphia. The rich might flee, and where would that leave the city!"

"They have their priorities, we must establish ours," Sylvia said, as she pulled a sheet of writing paper from the drawer and dipped the pen in the well of ink.

"So what we got, we got staff plus the twenty on the boat, the constables —"

"Are the constables still here?"

"Just saw them out the window, standing there, scratching their heads, I guess, since the ferry they planned to board has not arrived."

"The ferry was likely held back in the port of Philadelphia when word of the missing body first broke."

"Well, did the constables find what they were after?"

"I do not know, Spence. Right now I have much larger concerns than theirs."

"Sylvia, part of your concern must be for the well-being of all of us suddenly locked in here. Those white men lurking around will throw everyone into even more turmoil."

"Everyone, or you?" she asked, as she dipped her pen in ink and started writing again.

"Me, yes, me. I do not trust them. Any of them."

"Well, they are here, we are here, no one is going anywhere —"

"What about that white-looking colored man?"

"Lincoln?"

"I do not remember his name. Although

Kojo swears he is up to no good."

"I believe he was on the last ferry goin' out of here," Sylvia said, as she wrote furiously now on the paper. "Least I hope he was. I would hate to be the one to break it to him that the brother he is here to locate is likely the missing corpse."

"So for how long are we quarantined?"

"They will not say. Unless we can locate the body and determine that it was not yellow-fever-contagious, or, if it was, that it posed no threat —"

"What about the doctor?"

"What about him?" Sylvia looked at Spence as if he were a lunatic for mentioning the doctor right now.

"Protocol says he is the next in line absent Ledoff."

"Do you want to explain that to him? Better yet, are you prepared to acquiesce to any plan he should put in place?"

Spence breathed in deeply, then looked out the window at the river, which seemed to languish suddenly. He felt his stomach drop. As if being quarantined was not bad enough, he was thinking also about supplying the doctor's needs; with no shipments getting in, he wondered how long he would be able to fill that long, heavy pipe. "What is your plan, Sylvia? What do you need for me to do?"

"The first thing we need to do is gather everyone in the guesthouse and I will do the dishonor of informing them of this drastic situation. I have made notes of what I will say. But we will not — I emphasize, we will not — mention the missing corpse. We will say only that a crate with potentially infectious contents was scheduled to be delivered here, and its whereabouts are not known, and as a result we are quarantined."

"So we are committing the sin of omission?"

"It is better than a sin of commission. To cause hysteria around here over a missing dead body would be a sin indeed. Half of them will suddenly claim to be seeing ghosts."

"And then what?"

"Then we discreetly query each one about anything they may have noticed suggestive of the errant crate. Beyond that, we need to inventory our stocks of medical supplies, of food, of other necessities, and determine how long, how far, they will stretch. Through it all, Spence" — her voice shook — "we do all that we can to keep Carl alive."

Spence just stood there, nodding, after Sylvia had finished. "I am with you, Sylvia," he said with conviction. "I will get word to

Mora that we have to delay our nuptials."

"Your escape hatch finally opened for you," she said, not looking up from her paper. If she had looked up, she'd have seen the sudden sense of relief widen across his face.

After Nevada made her announcement and the two white men with billy clubs came and left, the jilted wedding guests streamed into the house. They looked ready to sashay in an Easter Parade: the ladies in their taffeta and lace and silk, the bustled dresses, cinched at the waist and spread out wide, many to the floor, their hair in high bouffant styles with curlicue bangs; the men in finely cut dinner suits with silk-faced lapels, meticulously ironed, their shoes buffed, their hair trimmed and stricken with a boar-bristle brush to encourage their waves to show. The parlor was done up, too, in anticipation of the wedding feast that would now just be dinner since there had been no nuptials. The bows that had adorned the outside seating hung from the archway between the parlor and the dining room. Roses in a variety of arrangements dressed the tables and the side board and were gently strung around the chandelier and lent a heavy sweetness to the air. Most everyone whispered in groups about the travesty of the white men barging in on their gathering. "We might have been having church for all they knew — unconscionable!" said the tailor's wife, Ella, to her cousin, as they marveled, reluctantly, at the quick thinking of Miss Ma — of all people — to lead a chant of Praise the Lord that had confused the white men. They later learned that the men were constables. They'd shown to Skell and Nevada a paper affixed with an official seal. Nevada had looked at the paper and said an emphatic no. Skell did the same, while Miss Ma's laughter provided background sounds. Now Ella and her cousin, along with everyone else, tried to guess at the contents of the paper. Nevada would only say afterward that she was not obliged to speak on the contents of the paper, with Skell divulging only slightly more when he said they were hunting a bandit who was not in their midst.

So they had this on their minds, and also the fact that the wedding had not taken place, and they whispered about the propriety — or lack thereof — of taking their gifts back home.

Vergie had taken Buddy out to the foyer to try to locate Nevada, and Linc stood alone in a corner of the dining room. He sensed that some of the whispered chatter might be about him. He felt awkward, lowly, like a field hand amidst gentry when he measured his dress — he was even without a jacket — against their own. He balled his fists in response to the way that Splotch looked at him from across the room. He looked down at his hands; his knuckles were prominent, white, too white, and ugly. He was remembering all over again how Mrs. Benin used to tell him that he had the ugliest hands she'd ever seen, that he'd never excel at piano the way Bram did because of his short, ill-formed fingers that lacked any hint of grace. Said he must have been spawned from a gorilla with those fingers. She would hit his hands with her pointer. Standing here now, his knuckles throbbed as if the skin had just been stripped, over and over, from the landing of that stick. He unballed his fists and hid his ugly hands behind his back. Now he thought he looked like a thief. His discomfort was swelling to overwhelming. He walked through the dining room and into the kitchen. The air was warm, aromatic with an intermingling of sage and rosemary and burnt sugar. Bay softened the space with the low melody she hummed, "Go Down Moses." The sounds of the spoons hitting the oversized kettles as she filled bowls with string beans and candied sweet potatoes kept time with the melody. Linc started to ask Bay if he could help her with anything, such as cleaning ash from the stove, bringing in wood, lifting heavy pots. But then he looked around the door and saw Buddy heading in the direction of the kitchen. He walked through to the outside, where he'd left his satchel. The air was sappy. He reached for his pouch to roll a cigarette. The back door opened and now Buddy was out here, too.

"Getting crowded in there," Buddy said.

Linc nodded.

"And you ever look at me again like you don't know me, I promise to whup your ass."

"Damn, Buddy . . ." Linc felt his voice shake.

"And you cry right here and now, I will whup it even more. I thought I raised you that a man do not cry. You a man, or a little boy?"

"Meda's gone, man, it hits me all of a sudden like a typhoon and I am drowning all over again." Linc was crying, he was shaking as he tried to get matches from his satchel. Buddy took the satchel and fished out the safety matches and lit the smoke Linc had rolled. They were quiet as they passed the smoke back and forth between them, save the intermittent sniffing sounds they both made.

Buddy broke the silence first. "You look good, Linc. God, Sister loved you, both of you."

"There was talk of her at breakfast, and I barely held myself together. I did not expect to show up here and be met with people who knew her."

"How did you show up here? Bram is missing? Is that what I half-gathered from Vergie?"

Linc sighed. "He is."

"And you got these people here believing you a colored man?"

Linc hunched his shoulders. "It just happened, Buddy, I do not even know how."

"Well, I looked at you out there in that shack and I knew you had a reason for pretending not to know me. So, like any cardplayer worth his salt, I played along with your bluff. I figured it had sumpin to do with Robinson's people still hunting you. So tell me about Bram."

Linc told Buddy all of it, beginning with how he'd come to Philadelphia to be with him, to stand over Meda's grave and say his last goodbyes. Buddy listened intently. When Linc had brought him up to the point when he arrived at the Lazaretto, Buddy asked him if he and Bram had traveled to Philadelphia together."

"We did not. He came the day before."

"The day before? For what purpose?"

"He went to the Benins', he wanted to spend time in Meda's room. He converted, you know, to the world of spiritualism."

"So Meda told me," Buddy said, as he got that pointed expression on his face he'd get when he was figuring out an opponent's hand based on the cards that he himself held.

"What are you thinking, Buddy?"

Buddy blew a long stream of smoke and then finished the cigarette and crushed it under his foot. "And no sign of Bram here at this place?"

"No." Linc looked down.

"Something else going on, Linc."

"What?"

"For one, my sense tell me that those two white boys traipsing through here was lacking the fervor of Robinson's kin. Surely they not the ones who broke down my door. I passed by them just before I come up on you and Vergilina in that shack. The whole of what is going on here is not in my line of sight just yet —"

Nevada had just stepped through the door

393

to the outside. "But my my my, look at what *is* in my line of sight," Buddy said, and Linc watched everything about Buddy change. It was as if Buddy was no longer operating under his own strength. His characteristic lean to one side that marked him as a tough guy had vanished, replaced with perfectly balanced shoulders; the muscles in his face softened, and even his bad eye seemed fully opened. "The sun is right now breaking through the storm clouds of my life," Buddy said. And Nevada unleashed a smile and Buddy had already left Linc's side, had already opened his arms wide, Nevada already laughing as she fell into them.

Linc walked past them to return to the house. He was happy for Buddy. Though he was sad for himself. Missing Meda all over again, missing Bram. He was thinking he would go inside and find Vergie and say his goodbyes. Sneak back to Philadelphia on the next ferry out of here and pay Mrs. Benin a visit. She'd always had affection for Bram, at least. Might give him assistance if it meant it would help Bram.

29

They had just completed dinner. Vergie had convinced Linc to remain for the meal and promised that she would walk with him to locate Sylvia and find out when the next transport out would leave. Linc and Buddy pretended to size each other up the way two men who'd just met likely would. And Splotch whispered to Buddy that he did not favor Linc at all. Buddy asked him why, and Splotch replied that something about Linc just did not sit right with him. To which Buddy said, "Well, *nothin'* about you sits right with me, Splotch, so if it is just *somethin'* about him, he appear to be a length or two ahead of you."

Then they heard the gong. Everyone turned at the same time, it seemed, looking up, then around, and the movement and the noise seemed even to sway the chandelier in the dining room. Kojo announced, "I work here day in and day out, and that gong means that trouble is all around us." Which elicited near hysteria as they began to call out, *What is happening? . . . Mercy. I knew I should not have come to this godforsaken place. I'm leaving. . . . Where is that big white fellow in charge of our bags?*

Nevada banged a pan to get their attention. "That gong also mean to keep calm until we determine the status of the situation. Kojo also knows that, but he left that part out."

Then the front door opened and the two white men entered, more like were pushed in by Son, followed by Sylvia. Buddy stood and positioned himself so that he was standing in front of Linc, shielding Linc from being seen from the parlor. Then he tilted his head ever so slightly in the direction of the kitchen, and edged himself in that direction with Linc moving in lockstep behind him until he was at the archway of the kitchen door. Linc quickened on through to the outside and stood along the side of the house. He picked up his satchel that he'd left out here earlier. Now he was looking down, at the square of wood that was the cellar door. He lifted it, and descended the ladder into sweet darkness.

Sylvia had met first with the two constables

and explained to them the situation of the quarantine. They'd huffed and barked that they were exempt from any order that they remain on the Lazaretto. She heard in the one's speech, saw in his demeanor, felt in his essence, which seemed to ooze from his pores, that his resistance superseded a normal resistance that anyone would display when told they could not leave a place. His resistance was magnified, she knew, because a black woman was looking him in the eye and telling him that he was not free to leave this place. She steadied her voice; she was nervous. She'd been in the position before when she'd had to detain entire vessels skippered by powerful, wealthy mariners. Though it was part of Ledoff's official duties as the quarantine master to verbalize such orders, Ledoff would cede that authority to Sylvia because he maintained that was the direction of the world and the world needed to get used to a black person in charge. Sylvia would handle such assignments with aplomb, knowing that Ledoff was always on hand to back her up. Who should back her up now? Son, who stood next to her, simply waited to be told what to do; and Spence had left the room because his hatred and fear of white people was so large that he pretended to be illiterate in their presence. "I am empowered to enforce the order of quarantine by any and all means, including use of physical restraints if necessary," she said, directing her words at the one she sensed was the leader of the pair. When they'd stormed the office earlier, flashing a warrant with an official seal and she hastily read the description of the person they sought and assured them such a one was not in their midst, one of them had accused her of lying; the other had raised his hand to stop him, had politely asked Sylvia if they could take a look around. That one cleared his throat now and replied that physical restraints would not be necessary. And Sylvia spoke only to him when she said that confidentially, they had information that the potentially infectious matter that prompted the order of quarantine was on the other side of the creek, so after they sat through the meeting that would be held once the gong was sounded, they could help best protect themselves from contamination by returning to and remaining on this side of the compound, and that they should find comfortable quarters at Ledoff's residence. The part about the infectious matter wasn't true, but she reasoned Spence had been correct when he'd said that Sylvia must also manage the emotional well-being of everyone now trapped here. In this situation, keeping white men with billy clubs, particularly the one with the air of superiority, confined to this side of the Lazaretto would help.

After she met with the constables, she sounded the gong, and then went to the house where the (hysterical) wedding guests were assembled. She began by complimenting them for their refreshing attire. She was sorry, she said, that she was not similarly dressed. "I feel like a weed among lilies," she said, knowing that would disarm the best of them. She turned serious then as she apologized for all that they'd endured, the boat ride over, the lack of a wedding ceremony, both certainly outside her sphere of influence, she said, "but as second in charge by the power vested by the seal of the mayor, and governor, and since the doctor is currently indisposed, I am the chief authority here." She went on to tell them that Carl was stable, and to please keep him in their prayers. Then she cleared her throat. "I must now deliver news that may bring you displeasure."

She told them about the missing crate. Everybody listened raptly trying to determine what this had to do with them. "The reason we did not know that the crate was delivered is because the courier delivering it did not follow protocol and informed not a single person here that he was depositing said crate."

She breathed in deeply again. She questioned her ability to manage this crisis absent Ledoff. Though she had received a telegraph from him finally. *If I should be allowed, I would be there. Since I cannot, there is no one better suited than you, Nurse Sylvia, to take the helm.* She'd wanted to cry when she'd read it. If there were ever a white man that she loved, she thought it would be Ledoff.

She picked up the eyes of the people gathered here as she scanned the room and explained that the missing crate was at the heart of the most unpleasant news she was pained to have to convey right now. "The crate may have contained infectious content," she said. She was determined that "infectious content" was as specific as she would get. She would not mention yellow fever. However, she herself was not given to hysterics over the spread of the disease since Ledoff had shared with her a paper that theorized that the disease was spread by mosquitoes, not by person-to-person contact. Prevailing thought did not embrace that theory, and the folks in this room surely would not, either. "As a result," she continued, "the Lazaretto has been declared under quarantine, and that quarantine extends to every person here. Those now here, must remain here. Those not here, will be barred from entering."

She stopped talking then to allow the impact of what she'd just said to settle in. She glanced at her notes. She'd written down the likely progression of their reactions. There would be a stunned silence, she knew, followed by a collective gasp. After the initial shock, calls of *For how long?* would crowd the room and would range from whispered murmurs to shouts, some begging, some demanding. Then the other questions would surely begin to mix in. *What was in the crate? How was it lost? Have we now been exposed to it? Is it the fever? Yellow fever? Will we all succumb to yellow fever?* That would be the loudest, most sustained outburst, until the smaller, more practical concerns would break through the hysteria as they began to consider the lives they needed to lead come Monday morning: teaching at Bible school; spreading fabric at the shop on Fourth Street; opening doors for the rich on the Square; writing copy for the pamphlet on improving Negro life; unloading crates at the waterfront; midwifing; serving as notary public; setting up the night's card game; preparing the lecture to be delivered at the Institute for Colored Youth; caring for the arthritic elder; rocking the colicky baby; keeping house; scrubbing steps; making hats to be sold at the milliner's shop; making soap to be packaged with an exotic French name; baking bread; clipping hedges; cutting leather for shoes; embalming a corpse; dressmaking; planning lessons for September's start of classes.

Sylvia checked off her sheet as each phase presented itself. Next they'd try to come up with alternate ways of getting out: sneaking out under the cover of night; swimming away; trekking to the river through the backside of the woods. After Sylvia described how surrounded they now were with vessels meant to enforce the quarantine, there would be one more spate of angry outbursts. Miss Ma would surely laugh, others would surely cry, more crying, more cursing, accusations that Sylvia knew more than she was letting on. Then finally they'd give in to the circumstance they were in. It would be a craggy yielding, Sylvia knew.

She allowed them time to vent, understanding as she did the importance of letting a thing run its course. She listened to it all unflinchingly, answered what she could, promised only what she could deliver: that they would be fed, and kept as comfortable as possible; that she would communicate the critical messages they needed to send home by way of telegraph, starting with the most urgent, and that they should decide among themselves which was the most pressing and present her with a list; that she would update them as soon as she knew more. She got up to leave. Said that Carl's condition and the need to stay in communication with the city required her to hurry back to the hospital.

She glanced at her paper. It had all happened just as she'd sketched it out, except for one detail, which arose now as she felt Lena's voice at her back. "Can you tell us the status of things with Spence, please." It was more a demand than a question.

"As you can imagine, Lena, the sudden extraordinary circumstance of the quarantine has rearranged everything, including, obviously, Spence's wedding plans. Though he can explain to you better than I about that. Right now he is working to keep Carl comfortable, as we had every intention of getting him back to Philadelphia today."

She addressed the whole room then and said again how sorry she was that they all had to endure this situation. She glanced at Nevada, who winked her approval at how well Sylvia had handled this awful situation. Then she left. Vergie ran behind her and caught her as she was about to cross the creek. "Is it a corpse they are looking for?" she asked.

"This matters to you why, Vergilina?"

"Just tell me, Sylvia. Please. I promise not to breathe a word. Is it Lincoln's brother? It is. I know it is. I could fill in the detail by your expression."

"We cannot say for sure who it is until the corpse is located. So, yes, it is a corpse. Do I think it is the young man's brother? My intuition tells me so. Why are you so concerned? Has he not already left? I arranged transport for him on the last ferry before we were quarantined. I only wish I had arranged a way for everyone out of here before this. But who could have predicted?"

"Who indeed?" Vergie said.

"So, has he?"

"Has he *what*?"

"Departed. I did not see him among the stunned faces in there."

"He has," she said, as she hugged Sylvia to hide her own face. "When will you be back to get some rest? I worry that you are not getting enough sleep."

"As soon as I can get back, I shall be back."

Linc could hear the footsteps gathering upstairs as he rummaged through his sactchel for his safety matches, then lit the lamp that had rested at the foot of the ladder. He held the lamp high and was struck by the mountain of bags and boxes and suitcases and furniture stacked in the middle of the floor, reaching almost to the ceiling. Now he heard the cellar door crunch open. He put the lamp on the floor behind him, allowing most of darkness to return. He listened to the sound of wood creaking as someone descended the ladder. The frazzle of light that he could not manage to obstruct barely illuminated a man's boots, large boots, and now his hands came into view and Linc could see that this was a white man. In a quick move, he reached for the lamp and held it high to blind whoever this was. The man let out a yelp and started to cry. Linc lowered the lamp some, confused. He recognized the man to be Son; he'd seen him earlier when he was with Sylvia, had heard Sylvia giving him instructions; had thought the instructions strangely drawn out, as if she were talking to a child, but he'd not given it much thought, in view of his larger concerns. Still, he felt his muscles uncoil as he watched Son sobbing, Son's face smeared with cake crumbs. Linc realized right now what he should have guessed earlier if he'd given it any thought, that Son was but a child in a man's body.

"Do not tell on me, please do not tell," Son managed to say between his sobs. Linc nodded and looked down, out of respect for this display of emotion from a man.

"What am I not to tell?" Linc asked, trying to find a soothing tone of voice and coming up short.

"I was not supposed to have more cake," he said.

"Well, I am pretty sure that that's forgivable. What's your name?" Son told Linc his name, and Linc told him his. Then he asked Son if he wanted to play a game with him, told Son that he was down here playing hide-and-seek and he needed to get a message to someone.

Son nodded and Linc asked him if he knew which lady Vergie was.

"Yes," he said. "The one with white skin."

"Can you whisper to her where I am?" Linc asked. "But only to her. I will keep your secret if you will keep mine." Son said that he would.

He climbed back up the ladder. But he

was disappointed because he had wanted to check on Bram. He'd crept down here after he'd delivered Spence's note and had seen a thin stream of liquid shining along the side of Bram's face. He'd thought at first that something was dropping from the ceiling, but then traced it to Bram's nose and gently wiped it. He'd talked to Bram and told him what he was doing, the way people would talk to him when he was strapped to a bed. "I am wiping your nose," he'd said. "Do you think you can blow for me?" Bram did not blow, but he did open his eyes and stare straight ahead. "I am over here," Son had said, trying to get Bram to look at him. He figured out then that Bram could not drink, lying flat on his back, so he'd propped him up and tilted his canteen to his lips and watched the ball in his throat move. He heard a sound then, as if Bram was trying to cough. He wondered if Bram had a cold. Bram's eyes were wide open again. They were the color of the river when it was its bluest blue. Son could tell that Bram was really looking at him. "You can cough now," he said. Bram tried to cough but seemed to choke instead. Son quickly leaned him over and slapped his back. A rope of black fluid spilled onto the sheet and Son said, "You spit like a frog." He eased his head back

407

down, then asked him if he wanted water. Bram lowered his chin slightly, which Son took to mean yes, so he opened his canteen and sat him up straight again and helped him sip. "You thirsty," Son said as Bram continued to sip the water. "And you sleep a lot." Bram practically emptied the canteen, and Son lowered his head again; Bram's eyes were closed, and Son wondered again if he had died. He used the hem of the sheet to wipe Bram's mouth, then folded it under so that the blackened mucus didn't show. He patted his head and told him to get some sleep, he would come by later. But now he could not, because Linc was in the cellar. He did not want any part of Linc's hide-and-seek game. But he played anyhow. He found Vergie and whispered to her what Linc had told him. He was happy to, because maybe then Linc would find another place to hide and he could go back down to look after Bram.

30

By early the next morning, Sylvia and Spence had done all that they could to stem the advance of dead tissue in Carl's leg. They'd cleaned the wound, drained it, wrapped and rewrapped it; they'd consulted and fretted and prayed and even applied maggots. They'd watched the flesh go blacker still. Nothing left to do but what they'd dreaded doing.

The doctor was in the room and Sylvia wanted to slap his useless face. He was sitting in the chair next to Carl's bed, head all the way back, as if pondering the ceiling; his mouth was wide open. She kicked the leg of his chair. He let go a loud snort and then sat up, suddenly awake. His pupils were dilated like a cat's eyes.

"So is it your opinion that the leg cannot be saved?" she asked him, the senselessness of asking him anything at all brutally apparent to her. She'd tried to inform him of the quarantine, and he smiled and started humming.

"He'll lose them both, for sure. Legs are sympathetic," the doctor blurted to the mix of apprehension and disdain spreading across Sylvia's face that he would suggest something so preposterous. "One goes, the other quickly follows. Didn't they teach you that at that fancy colored nursing school you attended?"

"I must have been absent that day," Sylvia said, swallowing the sarcasm so that it wouldn't coat her words.

"Well, get Spence over here to prep me," he barked, as he stood and then leaned against the wall. He was sweating so heavily that she thought his body might leave its print on the wall. He motioned to his forehead.

Sylvia clasped her hands in front of her.

"My forehead! Dammit, Nurse, swab my damned forehead!"

"With all due respect, I am only obligated to swab your forehead in the midst of a surgical procedure, sir," she said.

"Well now," the doctor said as he straightened himself from his slouch, seeming suddenly returned to his right mind, "Spence is assigned to me and works when I say he works."

"Yes, yes, Doctor," Sylvia said.

"And since your obligations do not begin until a surgical procedure, mine certainly do not start with weddings."

"Sir?"

"I am only obligated to perform surgery on those here officially, either sent by the city's health administration or a part of a manifest seeking entry to the port. Amputating the legs of colored wedding celebrants, Nurse Sylvia, is not part of my obligation. Send him back to Philadelphia, let them treat him at the dispensary if he's got a patron, if he even lives that long."

"Yes of course, Doctor," Sylvia said as she looked down and loosened some the clasp of her hands. She was relieved. She didn't want him any closer to Carl than he was right now lest he also maintain that other parts of the body were sympathetic, like the manhood, and dismember that of Carl's, too.

"Furthermore," he said, "I have got to leave. That dying leg is making it unbearably hot in here, and the damned smell, nothing worse than the smell of death."

Sylvia flinched. "Yes, Doctor," she said in a whisper, as she saw the shadow of Spence approach the door. She stepped out into the corridor and with her eyes told Spence to make himself scarce in a hurry. She'd noticed how the doctor had a knack for corralling Spence's time, Spence disappearing for stretches after the doctor would summon him. Spence observed the look she shot him and darted into the room next door. Sylvia turned back to the doctor. "Yes, it is cooler in your house, Doctor," she said. "I will see you out and then try to locate Spence, though it might not be easy with the quarantine."

"Quarantine?"

"Yes," she said, that's all she said as he offered her his bent arm and Sylvia ground her teeth so hard she thought they'd break. She slipped her arm in the crook of his and led him down the corridor toward the front entryway. He dragged his feet and began singing "Row, Row, Row Your Boat." Sylvia sang along with him so that he wouldn't hear Spence as he crept back into Carl's room. Time came to a standstill as she ushered the doctor through the grand marble of the hospital's foyer. The infection was moving through Carl's body with greater speed than the doctor moved through the foyer right now. Sylvia wanted to yank him by the arm and fling him through the front door so that she could return to tend to Carl. Instead, she sang along with him and walked in baby steps.

Finally they reached the outside and she unlinked her arm from his and nudged him in the direction of his house. He walked a few feet and then turned and acted as if he would go back into the hospital. She grabbed his arm again and reversed his direction. He laughed a sloppy laugh. She sang louder still so that the irritation she felt for him, the pity, the revulsion, wouldn't choke her. The river sent up streams of silver and snagged rainbows. The air smelled of thyme and cod and mint. It changed her tune all of a sudden. Now she sang a song with no recognizable words, just a run of notes without order. "Za de bra da bre de de da dun," she sang. The sounds centered her as she led the doctor up the hedge-bordered path to his house. She opened the door and encouraged him in. "Take a good nap, Doctor," she said, then forced herself to smile. He blew her a kiss and she resumed her wordless song.

She walked trancelike back to Carl's room. Neither did her hands shake nor her knees buckle as she turned into Carl's room with its heat and foul odor and the sweet sad sight of him snoring, water draining from his eyes. He was tied to the bed, held securely under a straitjacket Spence had

413

fashioned out of sheets. It was as if Spence had read her mind, knew that it had to be now, right now.

She cleared her throat and watched Spence's back stiffen. "It looks like it falls to me to do the —"

"Amputation," Spence finished her sentence.

"Amputation," she said with finality. He turned and faced Sylvia, his mouth and nose already banded with cotton; she could only see his eyes; his eyes like sweet drops of black molasses. She was a jumble of emotions as she nodded, tried to pick through the noise of all of her thoughts right now, to quiet them some. Suddenly rage predominated as she thought of the hate-filled men who'd done this to Carl. Too much rage. It was debilitating. She breathed deeply to try to calm herself. Spence had arranged the implements she'd need, the knives and scalpels, the saw, tenacula, artery forceps, even a hatchet. What a smart man Spence was, Sylvia thought to herself. How wise. Too wise to be marrying the likes of Mora, with her trite conversations about such things as who has the prettiest hair between the Indians and the Italians, or what complexion somebody's new baby was; before Mora even asked the gender, was it healthy, did the mother survive, she'd first ask: What color is it? Now Sylvia's rage found a more manageable object in Mora. She couldn't stand Mora for the way she had gone after Spence so shamelessly. He had barely arrived on the Lazaretto before Mora was making him tea, batting her eyes in his direction, asking him to walk with her to the creek so that she could gather pond lilies to make perfume, feigning a sprained ankle so that he would carry her in his arms to her room. Sylvia had watched and held it all in. Didn't even mention to Nevada how maybe she herself would have liked a chance to know Spence better. Didn't even realize, until this second, as Spence held open a surgical gown and she allowed him to slip it onto her arms. He tied the gown in the back in neat bows, and then cleaned her hands. Finally the cap over her head, and the mask. "Damn you, Mora," she whispered, almost inaudibly, as she studied the leg, the markings Spence had drawn.

"Pardon?" Spence said.

"Nothing, just checking your work," she said as Spence stood next to her, and she now felt a wide swath of heat rising from his body. Part of her wanted for him to gather her in his arms and comfort her, to prepare her for what they were about to do;

415

part of her wanted for him to take the lead, while she followed his instructions. Part of her wanted to suddenly become the type of woman she'd typically disdain, a woman who'd subjugate her own talents in an effort to snag a man. She'd never known that part of her existed until now. Though even now she couldn't allow it free reign, as she called for a scalpel and he asked what size.

"You going in from the side, I take it," Spence said.

"Of course, lateral, what do you think?" she snapped. "First I need to make a slit so they'll be a flap of skin left over to cover the stump."

He handed her the scalpel and she pushed and dragged it along Carl's skin. Carl cried out and tried to move, but the straitjacket-sheet kept him secure.

Sylvia turned a deaf ear to Carl's moans; she knew that the slit she'd just made was the least of it, like pulling back a flap of a turkey's skin to push a sage leaf under for flavor. It was easier to think about Mora right now, it helped her get to the part that she had to get to. "Bitch," she muttered under her breath as she deepened the incision and blood leaked out in a line, then a puddle. Carl's moans gave way to choking sounds as Spence encouraged his swallows

416

of morphine-laced brandy. Then Spence was next to her, sopping the blood as she cut and pulled, moving through the pulpous layers of flesh and fat and muscle. "Thread ready?" she asked.

"Here and waiting."

She lifted an artery. It was warm and pulsed softly. "Right here, quick," she said to Spence, who was there with a length of thread, wrapping, then knotting the artery with the thread as Sylvia severed the tied-off vessel and moved deeper into substance of the leg, and together they tied and snipped the other principal arteries, then the veins. Then Sylvia scraped through the flesh to get to the bone.

Carl's cries were higher-pitched now, and more desperate. Though Sylvia was entirely disassociated from Carl right now — who he was, what he meant to her — just as Dr. Miss had taught her all those years ago; he was a life she was attempting to save, and life had moments that, when they arrived, they did so with naked brutality. "Hatchet," she said.

Spence looked at her quizzically, his eyebrows raised. "Hatchet? You're going all at once?"

"All at once," she said. And Spence placed the handle of the hatchet in the curve of her fingers. It was large and cold. It felt right, cold. She focused on the separated flesh and aimed beyond the separation, beyond the leg. She aimed for the floor, the foundation, the creek that rushed beneath the Lazaretto. Then she went all the way down, hard, so hard that she felt it in her own chest. "A-*hack*," she said out loud, mimicking the sound the blade made.

"A-*hack*," Carl responded, drunk and high and in shock. "Ahhh, *hack*, ha, yah," he said as he slid into blessed oblivion.

Sylvia stood back as Spence used a sheet to soak up the blood. "The bone's still intact," he said.

"You lying to me?"

"Wish I was."

"I coulda felled an oak with that strike."

"It was a beautiful strike, for sure, but you pulled back."

"Did no such thing," Sylvia replied as she stepped back to give him room to wipe away the accumulations of flesh.

"I'm not criticizing, but as hard as you started down, you coulda gone all the way through the table if you had not pulled back."

"Is it possible you handed me a dull blade?"

"There are no dull blades among the

instruments I spread out for use. You pulled back."

"I guess you suggesting you could do better?"

"Not for me to suggest a thing," he said.

"I wonder if you would accuse Mora of pulling back. What do you and Mora even converse about?" she said then, surprising herself.

"We find our topics," he said as he whisked away the blood-soaked sheet.

Sylvia moved back in toward the bed and pondered the half-severed leg. The bone glistened. "I need more light," she said. "Get me more light."

"Cannot improve much on what is hanging already," he said as he motioned overhead, to where light from a canopy of lanterns flowed unimpeded.

"It's not enough. It feels dark in here. I need more." She felt her stomach spinning, as if a storm was brewing in it. She couldn't look at Carl's leg for the moment, couldn't bear to see the way she was botching the task. She watched Spence walk to the other side of the room to get a lamp from among several lined on the bottom shelf of the supply case. He had a nice back, sturdy, the outline of his shoulders pressed against the white jacket he wore.

"Is Mora with child?" she called across the room.

"Need oil," he said, as if Sylvia hadn't said what she just said. "Every last one of these lamps is empty of oil. You'd think those aides could at least keep oil in the lamps, at least they could do that."

"Mora's with child," she said then, with a certainty to her tone, "and you have been feeding the doctor opium. That's why he summons you so often." But she was speaking only to the air; Spence had already left the room, and now she allowed herself to lean against the edge of the table. She pressed her eyes shut. When she opened them she could see that the room was well-lit and she wondered if perhaps she'd had her eyes closed all along so that she wouldn't have to be her own witness. She was, after all, amputating the leg of the man she'd once purported to love. Loved him still, it was the desire that had always been absent. Or maybe Spence's presence, her focus on Spence, her desiring Spence, had dimmed her view. She situated the saw's blade in the ridge the hatchet had made. The ridge was shaped like a smile, and she widened, deepened the smile with the saw as she drew it back and forth, back and forth, back and forth in a steady rhythm. And then the snap.

As with the first hatchet strike, she felt the snap first in her chest. She gasped. The fibula completely severed from its contiguous self. "Help me, Jesus," she muttered as she moved on to the more formidable tibia. She grunted in time to the saw, putting the full force of her body into working the blade. Bone pieces swirled around, and then bone dust. The dust darkened the more she worked the saw and she knew that was good, she was all the way into the marrow. Lord Jesus, she thought — the marrow. Her shoulder was on fire; her wrists throbbed; her fingers ached. She could no longer see, the bone dust having found its way into her eyes, making a storm in her eyes. She couldn't even tell how far into the bone she was. This bone was impenetrable. Where the hell was Spence? She needed her eyes flushed. "Shit. Where the fuck are you, Spence?" She called out.

And then she felt the thick heat of Spence's hand covering her hand, his breath pushing into her ear. "I'm here, right here," he said.

"My eyes —"

The words were no sooner from her mouth when she felt the light swabs of cotton against her closed eyelids. His touch stunned her with its realness. He moved the cotton gently over her eyelids, then up along her brow, then her forehead, pushing and dabbing and smoothing. His breath was soft and hot as the fine mist of it landed on her skin. "Did I get it all?" he asked. "What do you need next? Just tell me everything you need."

It was better that he'd asked what she needed and not what she wanted. She'd always been adept at distinguishing between the two, her success had been predicated on that ability. She wanted Carl's leg attached and healthy; she wanted for Spence not to be affianced to Mora; she wanted to be in another space, even the room next door would do, wanted Spence to untie the back of the surgical gown and move his hands under the gown and lower his lips to the hollow of her neck. But her wants had no place here and now. In this moment, only her needs mattered. And all she needed right now was to have the dust cleared from her eyes so she could see.

"My eyes, Spence," she said sharply. "I need them flushed. I cannot see."

He pulled himself away from her, straightened himself up, even as he seemed to collapse as he stood. "I am sorry, Sylvia, I didn't know what — I am sorry — of course, there is water right here," he said as he poured water from a jug onto a cloth and then tilted her head and rung the cloth so the water rained over her eyes.

She squinted and took the cloth and pressed it to her eyes. "More?" he asked. She shook her head no and slowly opened her eyes.

"I cannot get through the bone. You might need to work the saw some."

"Looks to me as though you got through it five minutes ago," Spence said and Sylvia looked down and saw the bone completely severed, feeling a confluence of elation and devastation.

She stepped back. Spence covered the lower leg with a sheet and lifted it from the bed. The effort it took for Spence to carry the leg was evident as Sylvia watched the muscles in Spence's shoulders tense in and out, and listened to his sharp inhales of breath as he tried not to grunt. He moved to the other side of the room, where a vat waited, and slowly lowered the leg. She could see the relief in his body when he was free of the weight — though she thought now that surely what remained on the table, the empty space where the leg had been, was heavier still. No weight more crushing than absence, she thought; it held memory, sensations that would never, could never, leave. What a torture it would be for Carl to drag that painful absence around from here on. She stopped herself. To indulge a sentimental mood was not only useless right now, it was detrimental. The bones yet needed shaving and smoothing, threads had to be snipped, antiseptic salve applied. But all Sylvia could see right now was that absence which took up the space on the table beneath Carl's knee. How would he ever balance that absence with his remaining leg? She knew only one way that would even approach what he'd need. Her hand in matrimony. Spence was standing next to her again. "Should Carl live to once again seek my hand in marriage, I shall oblige," she said.

Spence sighed.

"And you?" she asked.

"I plan to follow your lead, Nurse Sylvia. As soon as I can get up the nerve to make my way to the other side, I plan to do right by my bride-to-be."

After Sylvia and Spence completed shaving the bones and snipping the threads and wrapping the stump, Sylvia left Spence to perform the rest of the cleanup. She walked outside of the hospital's back door as if in a trance. She sat on the bench and took in deep gulps of air, as if she'd stopped breathing while she was inside and was now attempting to replace what she'd missed. It was not yet a night sky, the air blue and red, heavier than it looked, and warmer, too. She sensed motion in the air, knew who it was even before she caught the whiffs of lavender. "Yes, Nevada?" she said, as she felt her sit next to her on the bench. "It must be important that you came over here. Meal preparations should be at their height right about now."

"It is important, Sylvie," Nevada said in a whisper. She took in Sylvia's appearance, how disheveled she was; splatters of blood up high around her neckline, and low around the hem of her dress, the places the surgical gown had not covered, Nevada reasoned. She knew Sylvia well enough to know that there was no need asking her if she was all right; Sylvia would resist consolation until she was ready to be consoled. "I just came to tell you that you were right. I made a big mistake being with Kojo. And now that Buddy is here . . . it was Buddy all along. Kojo was just a substitute. A very poor one at that."

"You are lying to me, Nevada," Sylvia said, staring straight ahead.

"I am not lying. It is Buddy I want."

"Yes, but that is not what brought you over here."

"You think you know me all to pieces. Okay, I confess. I came to tell you I think Buddy might ask for my hand." She giggled like a schoolgirl. "I know you always thought he was the one for me anyhow —"

"I am glad about that, Nevada" — Sylvia's voice was wooden — "but you have one more chance to tell me why you are really here."

"Drats, Sylvia. Okay . . . I want to know how Carl is doing."

Sylvia swallowed hard. "He has got a better chance of surviving now than he did this morning."

"He had you working on him, how could he not?"

"He lost the leg. And of course the doctor being the doctor, the surgery fell to me," Sylvia said as she blew into the air. She could hear Nevada trying to swallow a gasp, saw the pale pink of Nevada's sleeve move through the air as she put her hand to her mouth.

"I guess I cannot see him just yet?" Nevada asked when she had recovered herself.

"Not just yet." Sylvia sighed. "I shall give you one more chance to tell me what really brought you over here," she said, struggling to keep her voice steady.

"I told you why —"

"I know you better."

"Well, since you got so much knowing, why don't *you* tell *me* why I came here?"

"Just being your busybody self. You had the sense something happened and you are trying to determine if I am holding up okay."

"Are you?" Nevada asked, taking the opening Sylvia had finally provided.

"No," Sylvia said. "As a matter of fact, I am not." Then she put her hands over her face and cried into her hands. She cried for Carl, that he'd have to go through life as he now was, though he'd begged her to kill him instead. She cried for his mother and pictured her sinking to the ground when she was told. *No, not my baby's leg,* she'd wail. She cried for Vergie, who'd fault herself; for Nevada and the others who loved Carl as if he was their own brother; she even cried for Lena, petty, spiteful Lena. And then she cried for herself as she struggled to reconcile the slashing and the saving. Yes, she'd severed his leg from the rest of him; she'd saved his life. Those were the hard tears, oppositional, wrestled. She thought the cavity of her chest would crack wide open, she cried so hard, thought the hacking sounds she made were swaying the earth from side to side. She realized then that Nevada was rocking her. Dear Nevada. Was there ever a woman more righteous when righteousness demanded its due? Nevada had put her arm around Sylvia's shoulder, and their shoulders moved as one, as if the two were sitting side by side on a church pew as the choir sang, or even if there was no music, just souls stirring. The river swished by, as if keeping time. It was a soothing combination now, the earth swaying, the push-pull of the river. She closed her eyes and went with the rhythm until she no longer cried.

Spence broke the silence between Sylvia and Nevada as they swayed shoulder-to-shoulder on the bench. The night had crept all the way in, and he placed a lamp on the ground next to the bench. "Ladies," he said. "I guess you will need this light for the trek back over."

"Nevada may," Sylvia said as she sat all the way up and dabbed her eyes with her handkerchief. "I'll stay on this side of the creek. Carl will be waking soon."

"No, you go ahead on back, I'll tend to him," Spence said. "Delay me having to face the music likely waiting for me over there."

"I don't think music's gonna be your problem when you finally make your way over there, Sugar," Nevada said. "In fact, if it's just music you facing when you get back over there, you ought to count yourself a truly blessed man."

"That bad?" Spence asked as he sat on the bench.

"Worse than that bad."

"Mora threw a fit?"

"She threw a fit, her shoe, her comb, brush, lamp, and was about to pull her mirror from the wall, but I had to step in at that point."

"Hush, Nevada, you are exaggerating," Sylvia said.

"You can think I am exaggerating if it pleases you, and I have not even gotten to Lena. If you value your life, Spence, Lena's the one you must avoid. She was hell bent on coming over here, but I told her this is where the yellow fever germ is." She laughed. Spence joined in, and then Sylvia, too, and it seemed that the crickets also knew of Lena because suddenly their outburst made a contribution to the levity trying to gather around the bench.

Nevada asked Spence then if he had thought about an alternate date for their wedding ceremony. "The area behind the house is still decorated," she said. "You could still do it since we are trapped here together anyhow."

Spence sighed. He stood and jammed his hands into his pockets and paced a couple of steps in either direction. Said that he and Mora would work out the timing based on everything else going on.

Nevada stood, said, "Let her know, but right now I best get back over and set the food table for those greedy Negroes, they are discontented enough since they came all this way and didn't witness two joined in holy matrimony *and* they cannot even leave."

Spence insisted that Sylvia go, too. He would stay and keep watch over Carl.

31

The quarantine was in its third day and Nevada had managed to stretch the food. The hens had been generous with their eggs as if they knew the situation. The cornbread and grits were plentiful, the goat supplied just enough milk, and, city boy though he was, Buddy was a sure shot with the geese, and the ducks, but declined to go after the wild turkey Nevada told him about. The white men stayed to themselves on the other side of the compound, though they did manage to show up around mealtime. Generally there was a spat just about every evening, and Lena was usually somewhere near the center. But the groups had started to mix in, too. Ella found herself in conversation with Miss Ma, someone she'd otherwise disregard. And Nevada thought Kojo's wife pleasant after all, though that was probably helped along by Buddy's showing up, surprising Nevada, delighting her. Not so

with Buddy and Kojo. Buddy mispro-
nounced Kojo's name when they were first
introduced, called him Fojo, so Kojo called
Buddy, Buffy, and their interactions only
went downhill from there.

Linc would hide out in the cellar during
the day. After the sun had dropped under
the river and the Lazaretto went dark, and
after the constables had eaten and belched
and returned to their plush quarters at Ledoff's house, and when most had retired to
the parlor to listen to soft songs played on
the harmonica, or to the corner of the dining room for Bible study led by Skell, or to
hear an impromptu lecture by Ella on the
improvement of Negro life in urban areas,
then Vergie would sneak away to the cellar
with a plate of food for Linc. She'd check
to make sure no one was about in the back
of the house and Linc would emerge from
the depths, and they would run toward the
woods, holding hands, giggling like five-
year-olds. They would take the long way
around to the shack where Linc had slept
that first night. They would sit together on
the lumpy cot and fondle out each other's
pasts: Vergie told Linc how she'd chopped
off all of her hair, how she was almost
snatched by a rich woman whose pink
feathered hat matched the embroidery on

Vergie's petticoat. She talked about how much she loved her father, and her ideas about her mother, whom she'd never known. "She was gypsy, a wanderer. I suppose that is why I've stayed so close to Sylvia and my aunt and Uncle Levi. Perhaps there is a part of her in me — that fear has stilted me in some ways."

Linc in turn talked about that first job he and Bram had in New York, where they were groundskeepers, but they were bored beyond measure so they got jobs in the guts of the city. Told her about the night Bram was burned, how he faulted himself, how Bram turned away from the piano after that and it broke Linc's heart. Vergie would stiffen whenever he mentioned Bram. She wanted to tell him what she knew. She just did not know how. So she'd just listen to him sigh, and enjoy the feel of his shoulders as they nestled side by side, talking the way that people did when they were falling in love.

Tonight the air was dark and heavy and smelled of the sweet corn grilling in the charcoal pit. Vergie lifted the door to the cellar and called, in a whispered voice. "Linc, it's me, Vergie. I am coming down." He helped her down the ladder and she handed him his platter and sat with him while he ate. Afterward, instead of going

433

outside, she opened up the spread that she'd borrowed from the top of Sylvia's closet and propped the pillow against the wall and they sat like that and talked. Tonight they laughed about the situation Linc had first observed between Nevada and Kojo. "When I saw him covered in red from the juice Nevada dumped on him, my first instinct was to help him, I thought he'd been stabbed. But then I reminded myself that Nevada does not seem like a knife-wielding woman, what do you say?"

"No, definitely not," Vergie said, trying to catch her breath and settle herself down. "Nevada has no feelings in her fingertips, so she must take care around knives."

"No feeling in her fingertips?"

"No, she was run over by a carriage when she was a baby."

"Oh, that's awful," Linc said as he winced.

Vergie held up her own hands. "I have tried to imagine what that must be like."

"I suppose the rest of the body compensates," Linc said, noticing that Vergie's fit of laughter had closed up the space between them on the spread.

"That's what Nevada says, too. But imagine, if I could not feel anything, I could not do this," she said, as she drew her finger along his arm. It was a forward move for her, she realized, as she felt his arm stiffen. She'd never tried such a move. Most of her moves with the men at home had the purpose of holding them at bay. She didn't think about her intentions here. She might stop. And she did not want to stop. That trickle of a sensation she had first experienced when he'd appeared in the parlor had grown to a river and she otherwise had no idea how she would ever contain it. "Well, of course I could still do this," she said, as she continued to lightly stroke his arm. "But without the tactile sense I would not be aware of what I was doing."

"*I* would be aware," he said as he looked straight ahead at the line of lamplight hitting the wall.

"Well, Nevada did say that her malady gives her a greater insight. And I am inclined to agree."

"I would say that is a safe inclination," he said, practically whispering.

"She told me about you."

"Nevada told you about me?" He spoke haltingly, all play gone from his tone as he prepared to deny that he was Linc, the little white boy who was always with Sister.

"After the first night in the parlor, Nevada told me that we were doing a love dance, that she had watched us from the kitchen

435

doorway. And I told her she was loony, we had not danced. And she said that we had, we just were not aware of it, but the air was, because it swirled around us in big red sashes that only she could see, because she allows herself to see such things which most people do not. She told me that you had eyes for me. Is she right? Is she?"

"I've only been acquainted with Nevada for the briefest time, but my sense is that she is generally right." He looked at her mouth as he spoke. Her lips were painted red and parted, and he ran his thumbs along the side of her face and then pressed his lips against hers. He couldn't believe the jolt that moved through him at the feel of her mouth. She leaned into him with such ease. Felt to him as if she was made to lean into him this way. Her eyes were closed and her face had the intensity of someone fervently praying, and he thought that he heard her whispering. She made small crying sounds from the back of her throat as he pushed against her in circles.

He'd managed to unhook the back of her dress, then pulled it from her shoulders. His lips found the spot on her neck that she thought must be her weak spot. His lips were hot and wet against that spot on her neck and now she was crying the way she'd always cried when she'd craved something this intensely.

"Are you all right?" Linc whispered. "Vergie, are you?"

"Oh God, uh, yes, Father have mercy, yes."

Linc reached behind him to spread the quilt out more. He reached back for the pillow but kissed her before he did as if she might disappear from him in the slice of time that it took for him to grab the pillow. He stood facing her now; he kneaded the pillow. He raised his eyebrows, asking her with his eyes for permission. She looked behind him at the ladder that led to the cellar opening. He read her look. He tossed the pillow on the quilt and went halfway up the ladder rungs and grabbed for the rope that hung from the door handle. He tied the robe around the top ladder rung. He knotted it and tied it again as if this were the most important thing he'd ever had to do in his life. He was sweating by the time he got back to the space where Vergie was. She had allowed her dress to fall away, her restrictive petticoats too. He grew dizzy from the sight of her. He tried to speak, to tell her how beautiful she was but he was babbling, he was babbling and slobbering and now he thought he might cry, too, as he freed himself from his own clothes. He had never ever felt as he did right now as he drew her to him and their skin touched in places that should be taboo given the length of time they'd known each other. And yet he'd never remembered feeling this pure. He was a liar and a fraud, a throwaway orphan boy; still there was a sense of innocence about their skin touching right now. He felt more than worthy, he felt exalted, ordained, as they lowered themselves on the quilt, first on their knees as if they were praying, and then all the way down, moving together in a frenzy the way the holy sometimes did when the Spirit hit.

Afterward, they lay swaddled in the quilt, her head against his chest, his hands stroking her back. Her heartbeat was settling down, the tingle slowly leaving her body. The air was soft as it fell over them like a smile. This could be the most perfect moment she'd ever lived if not for the fact that she had yet to tell Linc about Bram. She turned and angled herself on her elbow. "Do you believe in God?" She asked it in a whisper.

"Why, are we damned to hell for what we are doing?" He kissed her forehead. "If that be the case, I can go with no regrets, because I have surely been to Heaven these nights I have spent with you."

She laughed in spite of herself, felt the laugh all the way to her toes. "Heaven? This cellar is certainly a new twist on Heaven."

"I think that Heaven will likely be a twist on my sense of what is — if it is."

"Did you go to church a lot growing up? I guess they were fairly strict about that sort of thing at the orphanage."

"They were indeed."

"And what about since you've been grown?"

"Mnh, occasionally." He thought back to the Sunday mornings when he'd just left an all-night card game and would fall in on a church service where Bram was earning money playing the piano.

"Do you enjoy church?" Vergie asked, as she ran her finger along his nose.

"Why? Are you thinking about a ghastly large church wedding when I make an honorable woman out of you?"

She held back a gasp. Felt a flutter in her chest when he said that, though she'd never fancied herself the type whose single purpose in life was to get married. "Maybe I like my state of dishonor," she said. "But my aunt Maze would settle for nothing less than a big church wedding, just so you know."

"Really?" he said, a laugh to his voice. "I

actually had the Lazaretto in mind. Splotch could be my best man."

"And Lena could be my maid of honor."

They both laughed then; they laughed so hard that they shook and gasped, and had to sit up so that they could breathe. Linc kissed her forehead again and said, "Though of course Bram will be my best man."

"Aw, Linc." She lay back down and pulled him against her. She wrapped her arms around his neck as tightly as she could. There was no way to say it other than to just say it, she told herself. "Bram's dead." Her voice warbled when she said it, and at first Linc thought that she was laughing still about Splotch and Lena. But then he heard the words, her voice distorted as it moved through his ears.

He sat up with a jolt. "What did you say?"

"I am so sorry, Linc —"

"What did you say?" He spoke each word pointedly.

She sat up, too, and stared straight ahead. "They put us under quarantine because a man who stumbled out of the tavern where you and Linc were died from what they think was yellow fever, but his body never arrived but it was delivered and —"

She tried to pull him back down, to squeeze him to her, to comfort him.

"No!" he shouted as he jumped up.

"Linc, aw, come —"

"No." He put his hands to his head, as if by doing so he could suddenly undo what she'd just said. He started picking up his clothes, starting pulling his clothes on. "Where's his body?"

"They do not know."

"They do not? This is horseshit. Somebody must tell me something —"

"Lincoln, they cannot tell you more than I just have. Plus, everyone thinks you are no longer here, and the constables are still here in quarantine, too."

"Fuck the constables. Your cousin or somebody has got to tell me something. How can they claim such a thing — that Bram is dead — with such certainty? They do not have a body, how can they say he's dead?"

Vergie started gathering her clothes around her, as well. "I know this is hard for you —"

"You do not know —"

"Well, I can imagine —"

"You cannot imagine!"

"Aw, God, Linc, do not —"

"Do not *what*? Do not go find some answers?"

"Actually, I was going to say do not be a

441

donkey's ass."

"Bram is all I have," he said, as he stuffed his feet into his boots, the effort masking the sobs fighting to take over his voice. "You have all these people — Sylvia, Nevada, your aunt Maze, your daddy. Bram is all I have."

"You have me," she called to his back.

"It is not enough," he said as he untied the rope that had served as a makeshift lock. And then bounded up the ladder and was out of the cellar.

"Yeah, well, go to hell yourself," Vergie said after she heard the door slap shut.

She had wanted to say it to him directly, but the words had caught in her throat. She looked up now at the closed cellar door, then back at the crumpled quilt on the floor. She folded the quilt, set the pillow on top. She swallowed hard to get rid of the ball in her throat, felt it drop to her chest like a hard regret. She'd rushed things; rushed telling him about Bram, rushed opening herself for him to move inside of her the way he just had. She picked up the pillow and squeezed it to her. It smelled of the beeswax Nevada had smoothed on her edges to keep them from frizzing up. She was grateful at least that it was not his scent that lingered but her own.

32

Linc staggered toward the creek like a drunk. Vergie's voice still boomed through his head. Bram is dead. Bram is dead. Bram is dead. "No, no, no, no," he said out loud, "you cannot be, Brother, dammit, you cannot." He could hear wings flapping, and the call and response of night birds as they hooted and cackled, now squeals and clicks moving through the grass as if the nocturnal life out here was mocking him. Even the sound of the creek washing over the rocks that had been so soothing since he'd been here now sounded like a storm crashing through a caved-in roof. He had reached the boulder-sized rocks that served as the footbridge across the creek. He stepped out on the first boulder to start his trek across. He forced his eyes to focus, to no avail; he lost his footing anyhow. The shock of the water felt like an assault as he cursed and flailed about. He punched at the water. He thought he threw his shoulder out. He kept punching. His fist hit hard against the rock and he punched still. He punched until his breath could no longer sustain the punching. He leaned against the rock, gasping. A frog perched there, croaking, its eyes bulging, fixed on Linc. "What the fuck are you looking at?" Linc said. "He's dead, my brother's dead." He cried out Bram's name then. Then he just cried.

Linc sat on the boulder, hung his head, his breathing close to settling down. He could just make out the crunch of footsteps. He thought that it might be Vergie. He hoped that it was not. He knew he couldn't process Vergie's presence in his current state. Her presence would only confuse him. He might soften, even as he felt his resentment toward her growing wide and hard. He had denied who he was for Vergie. Had pretended to be other than a white man. He'd stepped out of himself, like a stage actor pulling on a made-up character. Left his true self drifting alone on an island moving farther and farther away, almost unreachable. By denying himself, he'd denied Bram, and had denied Meda, who'd told him, in the end, he and Bram had really just each other. Now he had nothing; now he was utterly alone, disconnected. He called Bram's name over and over in his head, louder and louder, as if the sound of his brother's name booming in his head might summon Bram from where he was, might bring him back even from the crater of death. Was this not the Lazaretto? Was not Lazarus the leper who was raised from the dead? *Live out your fucking name, Lazaretto!* he shouted in his head.

The footsteps were right at his back now. It was Sylvia. She had been at the hospital all evening into the night. Spence had told her that he thought tonight was as good a night as any to say his wedding vows and Sylvia had wished him well; he'd kissed her forehead that burned with regret. She didn't tell Spence that she planned to debride the flesh around Carl's stump because she didn't want him to keep delaying his wedding. She figured she could do it on her own, and she'd come outside to get a gulp of fresh air before she started.

His back was to her, but she recognized it as Linc. He appeared to be ranting silently and she stood there and watched. He turned around then as if he knew she was there. She put her lamp low so as not to blind him. She thought about how she'd blasted the light in his eyes the first time they'd met, how rude she'd been, how she'd intentionally withheld a word of consolation because her heart ached for Carl and she was angry about the unprovoked attack on the boat. She'd burned through the moment when she might have said or done something to let him know that no matter the current situation, it would all work out in the end. She believed such moments were tests sent by the universe to measure her propensity for good. She'd fallen short that first time. So right now she did not pepper him with questions about why he had stealthily remained on the Lazaretto. Did not ask him if he was in fact a wanted man, or where had he been sleeping. In the woods? With Vergie? She didn't say that she had suspected his continued presence here all along. That Vergie's demeanor had betrayed it, given the way she sauntered more than walked during these days in quarantine; the way she lost her way in the middle of a sentence; the way she smiled into the air as if the air had just begged her: Pretty lady, make a smile for me. Instead, she pushed through all that was indictable about him at the moment so that she could see clear through to his need.

"I get to return the favor," she said, right up on him now. "You walked up on me as I sat at the creek, crying, so I guess it is only fitting that I interrupt you in the moment of your despair."

"I'm not crying."

"Well, you would certainly have cause, given the condition of your hand." She directed her light toward it and he looked at his hand and grimaced, his hand still formed in a fist, the skin worn away in places, exposing bloody patches, and he became suddenly aware of its throbbing.

"So I have smashed it," he said. "Perhaps it should be smashed, perhaps I should smash the other hand as well. They are ugly hands, apelike hands, despicable."

"That would be your assessment, not my own," Sylvia said, as she moved all the way to the edge of the creek. "Are you able to straighten it? May I see you wiggle your fingers around, please?" He did. "Flex your fingers for me," she said, and she situated her lamp on the boulder and inspected his hand and then palpated his wrist, asking if it hurt. Here? Sharp pains or just soreness? She pulled on his fingers, then said that she was satisfied he had not broken anything. "Though I might suggest that all of that energy throwing your hands around should be put to better use getting yourself into dry clothes."

"I have no other clothes, nothing to change into," he said, and he began to shiver even as he held himself stiffly so that it would not show. "I have nothing, nothing at all. My brother is dead and I am empty."

"I am very sorry about your brother, Lincoln, I truly am. It was dreaded news when I learned of it, and I thought that you had made it out on the last ferry before the order to quarantine was issued or I would have found you, to tell you. How did you learn of it?"

"It does not matter."

"You are correct. It does not. Although I must also tell you that the remains have yet to be located. So nothing has been confirmed. I tell you that neither to give you false hope, nor to add to your torment. It is just the fact of the matter that you should know." She watched him begin to shake. "Are you getting chills?" she asked.

He hunched his shoulders. "I have told you I am empty."

"Well, I regret that I am wholly incapable of treating your professed state of emptiness, but I may at least offer you some dry clothes. I must go over to the hospital. Walk with me. You can dry up and change over there."

Linc was too spent to protest as he pulled

himself from the creek and followed Sylvia toward the hospital. Blackness surrounded them as they walked, except for the broad streak of yellow pouring from Sylvia's lamp that painted just enough of a path for them to see their way to the other side.

The smell was even more pronounced. Sylvia took in the air. This was the smell that flesh gave off as it died, the body screaming to be relieved of what it could no longer use before the uselessness consumed it. "You smell that?" she turned around and asked Linc.

Linc had been staring at the paintings of the white men that lined the walls. Was noticing the point of this one's chin, the cut of that one's nose; he'd look at men sometimes, measuring their features against his own, checking for similarities.

He turned around and sniffed when Sylvia asked him if he smelled something. "Other than the wet fabric clinging to me, I cannot say that I do."

She started down the corridor. She pushed open a door and told him he could use that room for changing. "Pump for water at that basin; towels, hospital garb, on the shelves. Gowns and shirts and slacks and the like. You should find what meets your needs. You should also pour some alcohol on your hand."

She pulled the door shut and he looked down at his hand. He had not even realized that he'd been landing his fist against the rock. At least it throbbed less right now, looked less misshapen now than it had at the creek; the blood had even begun to dry, trying to form a hardened protection over the tender places. He remembered how Meda had dressed his hands the time Mrs. Benin had beat them raw, remembered how Bram had cried on Linc's behalf because Linc refused to cry; Bram's screams had grown louder with each hit as if he and not Linc was the one getting beat. He stared off into space, his mind here in this hospital supply room and simultaneously years away. He tried to imagine how death would feel. "Ah, Bram," he said. Then he put his head in his battered hand and wept.

Sylvia eased open the door to Carl's room. He looked over as soon as she entered the room and said, "Hey, sweet baby." His voice came from the top of his throat, but at least he was alert, she thought. Oriented.

"Carl," she said as she kissed his forehead. "You the best thing I've seen all day, you know that, don't you?"

"Must be early," he said as he tried to laugh but let go a loud, long moan instead. Sylvia quickly mixed a cocktail of morphine and brandy and helped him sip. "Ah, thank you, sweet cakes," he said. "My leg is giving me a fit. I try not to complain, but it hurts like the dickens."

"Whereabouts does it hurt?" she asked as she went to the foot of the bed and looked at the wrapping around the stump. Spence had attached a cup to catch the drainage. She really missed Spence right now.

"Hurts all over."

"Above or below the knee."

"Below, from my ankle all the way up my calf."

She was relieved about that at least, phantom pain was normal. She was praying for no involvement above the knee. "Let me take a look and see what's going on," she said, as she looked around for scissors, more light. She saw Linc walk past the door. "Hey!" she yelled, and Carl jumped. "Sorry, baby," she whispered, then cursed under her breath when Linc didn't reappear. Then she saw Linc's head at the door again. He peeped in, his eyebrows raised in a question. She motioned with her arms, big, urgent motions, and he walked all the way into the room.

451

"I need your help," she said as she concentrated on unwrapping the stump. "See those lamps over there on the bottom shelf, light two and hang them from this railing above my head, please. And how is your hand?"

Linc looked at his knuckles as he picked the lamps up from the shelf. "Better," he said.

"Good, before you get the lamps, hand me that magnifying glass, and after you hang the lamps, clean your hands real good for me, please. There's soap by the basin. Water in the pump. Douse your injured hand in alcohol after that. Then look on the second shelf and you'll see strips of cotton, wrap your hand and then come over and I will secure it. You're not squeamish, I hope," she said, as she held out her hand and he placed the magnifying glass there. She leaned in and peered at the stump.

Linc lit and hung the lamps and washed and doused his hands as Sylvia had instructed. He wrapped the cotton and went and stood next to her and looked at Carl and nodded awkwardly. "Hello, sir," he said, as Sylvia secured the cotton around his hand.

"Sir?" Carl said, and then laughed a syrupy, morphine-inspired laugh. "I must be getting pretty close to Heaven, white

452

man calling me sir. Am I, Sylvia? Tell me, sweet cakes, am I getting ready to die?"

"No, baby," Sylvia said as she stood from her lean. "But that joy juice is starting to kick in. Say hello to Lincoln."

"Lincoln? You named for the president?" he asked.

"Uh, yes," Linc said, trying to concentrate on Carl's face so he didn't have to look at what was left of Carl's leg.

"Parents favored the president?"

"Yes, sir, they — I mean, my mother did."

"So that means you not from rebel stock?"

"Not by a little bit," Sylvia said. "He's got a colored mama."

"You got a colored mama?" Carl asked, squinting at Linc. "I should have known no white man would be addressing me as sir."

Linc hunched his shoulders. Asked himself how much longer could he continue this farce. Sylvia tapped his shoulder then and said, "I need a sheet folded about yea wide." She separated her hands. "I am going to raise his leg, and I want you to situate the sheet under it, please."

Linc pulled a sheet from the shelf above the lamps and folded it as per Sylvia's instructions. He moved gingerly toward her. He still avoided looking at Carl's stump, concentrating instead on Carl's face. His face agreed with Vergie's description of him. "You just look at his face and you know that he is good through and through," Vergie had said. He told himself that's why he'd focused on Carl's face, not because he was at all apprehensive about looking at the stump. But he was apprehensive. And now that he was looking at it, he felt as if someone had just punched him in the gut. The worst, he thought, as he fixed the sheet under it, were the threads that hung and which he guessed tied off the blood vessels. He supposed he was holding his head back at that point because Sylvia whispered, "It's not going to jump up and bite you."

"I know," Linc said defensively, straightening himself. "I was trying to position the sheet."

"Well, now I need you to get him to drink the rest of what is in that glass. You'll want to help him sit a little higher up and hold the glass to his lips and tilt his head," Sylvia said as she went to the basin and began drenching her instruments with alcohol.

Linc picked up the glass and moved quickly to the head of the bed. Carl's head was leaned to one side, as if he were trying to decipher some important thing. "So, you named for Lincoln. Guess your mama loved Lincoln like all the colored women did

454

'round the time he was killed." Linc nodded as he moved in closer to the bed but Carl waved him away. "Hey, Sylvia, how 'bout the woman you told me about who loved Lincoln so much? Seeing this'un buck here whose colored mama named him for Lincoln making me remember her over again."

"Drink your medicine, Carl," Sylvia said as she laid the instruments one by one on a towel. "Furthermore, I have no idea who you might be talking about."

"Yeah you do, the one you told me about when I asked for your hand that day on my boat when I was bringing you here and you turned me down and then told me about the first baby you delivered. *You* know, Sylvia, the woman who was always drawing pictures of ole Abe Lincoln and claimed to have served him tea."

Sylvia dropped her scalpel when he said that, and she said "Drats" out loud and leaned to pick the scalpel up with a big commotion, hoping to distract him from the story. She didn't want the details of the story to come out with Linc here, that she'd participated in separating a mother from her baby in the way that she had. She motioned to Linc, making a cup of her hand and putting it to her mouth, and telling him to get Carl to drink, thinking that he was useless to her right now if he couldn't even do that.

Linc approached Carl again. "Uh, sir, let me help you drink this," he said.

Carl grabbed his arm this time. "I'm *talking,* partner," he said. "You had a colored mama, I know she trained you not to interrupt people older than you when they talking."

"It's the morphine," Sylvia said, between her teeth, directing her words to Linc. "He needs to finish what's in the cup, else he won't go under anytime soon."

"That was like something you see on a theater stage," Carl continued. Some no-count rich lawyer white man with his fancy gold watch with bridges on it gonna force you and the midwife into telling the poor mother that her baby girl was dead —"

"Carl!" Sylvia said sharply as she scrubbed the scalpel with a ferocious back-and-forth motion. "Drink your medicine and drink it now. And your assistance would be more than appreciated this instant, Linc," she said, irritation coating her words.

Linc's hands were sweating and he felt dizzy as he shifted the glass from his bandaged hand to the other. Now he tried to convince himself that it was in fact the ap-

456

pearance of the stump making him feel woozy, and not what Carl had just said about the woman who drew pictures of Lincoln and served him tea and had a baby! Told himself that surely Carl was not speaking of Meda, not his Meda. Surely Meda never had children. Surely Meda was not the only woman to have sketched drawings of Lincoln during that time. Half of the colored women in the Union likely indulged such a hobby. Many probably filled whole sketchbooks with their own renderings of Lincoln. Probably white women sketched Lincoln, too. And certainly other women may have been called upon to serve the president tea, any one could make that claim, whether or not it was fact. Besides, surely this man in a state of near delusion from a combination of the pain and the morphine could not even be fully aware of what he was saying. Linc thought that he could discount it all, but for the detail about the watch. Benin had owned such a rare gold watch with bridges on the face.

Still, he convinced himself, it was likely all a coincidence, and he tried to approach Carl again, tried to put the glass to Carl's lips, but Linc's hands didn't seem to accept that it was a coincidence; his hands were trembling. "You got the shakes?" Carl asked then. "Sylvia, you best come help this boy. What the matter is, partner? You coming down with something?"

Linc could feel sweat pouring from everywhere, his scalp, under his arms, the backs of his legs. All the blood seemed to drain from his head and settle in his stomach. He looked down at the glass in his hand; it seemed that he'd dropped the glass a thousand times by now.

Sylvia moved quickly to the bed. "Lincoln? Do you need to sit?" She took the glass from his hands. "There is a stool right there behind you. Sit and put your head down low and take deep breaths."

He shook his head. "I'm well enough," he said, though he did sit.

Sylvia took over the task and helped Carl sit up higher and got him to sip.

By the time Carl had drained the cup, Linc had recovered himself and was standing again. Carl smiled at him drunkenly. "Hey, hey there, buddy." Carl's words slurred. "You feeling arright? The shakes let you be?"

Sylvia patted Carl's forehead and told him that she needed to do a procedure on his leg. "Anything for you, sweet cakes," he said, as he smiled a sloppy smile. "But tell me, Sylvia, why you lie to me about that woman's baby?"

Sylvia talked over him as if she'd not heard the question. "Now Lincoln is going to wrap your arms nice and snug to hold them down just in case you start dreaming about any number of the pretty misses lining up to be your sweetie and you try to get up and get out of the bed —"

"Why you lie to me, Sylvia?" Carl asked again.

"I have never ever lied to you, Carl," she said, as she turned and motioned to Linc and mouthed the word "straitjack" and pointed to the hook where the one Spence had fashioned earlier hung.

"You did, on my new boat that day when you would not accept my hand and you told me why —"

"I was as honest as I know how to be, every fiber of my —"

"Most of it, but not all of it, Sylvia. You broke my heart that day, Sylvia." He started to cry.

"It's the morphine, sweetie, you're not thinking —"

"It is *not.*" He said it with determination, his eyes suddenly focused, his voice suddenly clear; the morphine-induced stupor seemed suddenly lifted and Sylvia got a chill at the dramatic transformation.

"I believed every word you said when you explained why you could not be my wife. I accepted how important you being a nurse was to you being alive. I felt it, Sylvia. I felt your whole truth, but then you let a lie sneak in. And I felt that, too. And it hit me that I wasn't up to the high standards for your whole truth. You couldn't trust me enough —"

"Carl —"

"Let me finish, I might die before I ever get off this Lazza place; I had a lotta years to think about this. And a lotta hours laying up in this bed with nothing else to think about 'sides the fact that I got to go through the rest of my life a one-legged man. I have always thought if you coulda just admitted the whole truth of that story, and trusted me enough to say what really happened — I mean, it was a small thing, after all. I remember it clear as day: the nice flow of the river, the gulls playing around in the sky, that nice cedar smell drifting up from my new boat. 'What happened to that baby?' I asked you. That's all. Such a simple thing. Not that it mattered to me one way or another what happened to one little baby. But it mattered to you, Sylvia. It mattered so much that I thought I could hear the clamps falling around your heart when you said you didn't know. But you did know. I felt your knowing, that's how large it was." Carl was straining to keep his eyes focused. His voice came from higher in his throat. "And I'm of the mind that had you kept the truth going in that instant — just a simple question, Sylvia, so simple — you also woulda accepted my hand. All you had to do was hold the truth with us in that boat, that's all." He repeated the words "that's all, that's all," and gave it tune and tried to sing. But then he could not. His mouth drooped as he yielded to the morphine and Sylvia breathed a relieved sigh.

Linc cleared his throat then and Sylvia turned around to find him standing there, holding the straitjacket. His eyes were round with curiosity, and that irritated Sylvia as she thought, *What does it matter to him?* She told Linc that they had but a small window of time before the morphine wore off. She showed him how to tie the jacket and knot the ends around the bedpoles. Then they hung a sheet from the poles over the bed so that it fell to Carl's waist and acted as a curtain to block Carl from seeing what Sylvia was doing should he wake. She told Linc to bring over the towel that contained her instruments, and the mat for catching the debris. She pointed to each instrument and

461

whispered its name and said that she would call for them as needed. She had him tie a mask to cover her nose and mouth, said the last thing they would do would be to wash their hands once more. Linc surprised himself with his deftness, given his bandaged hand.

Sylvia moved right into the gangrenous portion of Carl's leg, snipping away at the rotted parts. Linc found the stench almost unbearable as he handed Sylvia each instrument she called for, and Sylvia congratulated him for being such a fast learner. Still, he found it easier to look away, up at the hanging sheet rather than at what Sylvia's hands were doing. Blood-tinged detritus had accumulated on the mat and Sylvia motioned to him to get rid of it. He did and was on his way back to the bed with a clean mat when he glanced on the other side of the sheet and saw what Carl's face was doing; his face was contorted, and Linc placed the mat down and whispered to Sylvia that Carl appeared to be waking up.

"Drats," Sylvia said. "Not already. There's more here than I expected. I need you to talk to him."

"Me?"

"Either that or I shall, in which case you can finish cutting the infected tissue away."

Carl let out a yell, then a full holler, then a rumbling moan, and Linc rushed to the head of the bed even as he tried to close his ears to the sound of a man in such anguish. Now Carl was trying to sit up, and Linc checked the ties against the bed to make sure that they were secure. "Uh, sir," Linc said.

Carl gasped and moaned and writhed as much as the straitjacket would permit, and Linc could see that Carl was trying to focus. "Sir," Linc said again. "You hurting. I know. But I'm gonna stand here with you and help you through this." Carl squeezed his eyes shut and Linc grabbed a square of cotton and wiped at the fluid draining from Carl's eyes.

"Where is Sylvia?" Carl gasped. "I cain't see her."

"I am right here, baby, just behind this curtain at the foot of your bed."

"What did she say?" Carl asked. "I cain't hear her."

"She said to tell you she's right here," Linc said, as he dabbed away the sweat crowding Carl's forehead.

"Oh Jesus," Carl said and then let out an extended moan.

"It will be over soon," Linc said.

"Not soon enough," Carl managed to say

between gasps. "Tell her, tell Sylvia" — his words filled with cries and mumbled expressions of pain and he struggled to talk. "It was such a simple thing. The baby, that's all I asked her. What happened to the baby?"

"He's asking what happened to the baby?" Linc said, relaying the question, because Linc himself needed to know. "He says he's dying and he doesn't want to die with a lie between you." Linc watched Carl drift off to sleep. "Well?" Linc said now to Sylvia's silence. "He is waiting. No, do not try to move," he warned a sleeping Carl, as Carl's breathing yielded to a light snore.

"All right then," Sylvia said, her voice filled with agitation. "All right." She took a deep breath and started to talk; she went back to the beginning, describing Meda that day, without saying her name, what a pretty woman she was with her polite nose and sad, dreamy eyes, her soft hair pulled back in a bun. Described how poised she was, saying that she carried herself as did the girls who had gone to finishing school, and that her speech had that quality, too, like the girls in Sylvia's social clubs who would put on French airs or otherwise display their learnedness.

"Had she?" Linc interrupted her.

"Had she what?"

"Gone to finishing school, uh, Carl is trying to ask."

"Oh, he can hear me now?"

"Can you hear her, Carl?" Linc spoke to Carl's closed eyes, and hoped that Sylvia could not hear Carl's gentle snores. "He is nodding," he said to Sylvia, and then pretended to talk to Carl: "I know it is painful, sir, but it will not be much longer. Yes, I will ask her to get on with the story."

"I am getting on with it. Stop interrupting me and I will be done with it. And, no, she had not been to finishing school, she was a poor girl, but she had been well schooled by the Quakers, and apparently she'd absorbed it all. In any event, she arrived too late for the procedure she was scheduled to have. She was much too far along."

Linc started to interrupt her again to ask if the woman had arrived alone, but then he thought better of it, so he settled in to hear the story in whatever circuitous way Sylvia chose to render it. He dabbed the sweat from Carl's forehead and then Sylvia answered his thoughts anyhow.

"She arrived with her employer in all of his fancy livery," Sylvia said, her voice gaining momentum, "his impressive two-horse carriage, his finely threaded topcoat, his showy gold watch with bridges on the face

465

that he kept pulling out and looking at as if he had someplace more important to be. It was a despicable display of wealth, given the circumstance. But that young miss was composed throughout as I led her back to the whitewashed room that we reserved only for those other procedures. I knew as soon as I helped her out of her cape that she would in fact be having a baby that day and no other procedure. She had already dropped. And she seemed happy about it as she chattered on about having felt it kick, and that it was likely a boy because she had not had heartburn, and heartburn, they say, means a girl. She was talkative, telling me personal things the way that those who came into that whitewashed room often did, a consequence, I suppose, of knowing that I would see all there was to see about their physical person, and that I was to be party to an act that they would be able to share with no one else, so they may as well reveal their other parts as well, their feelings, their pasts — oh, their pasts, the stories I have heard!"

Sylvia stopped to catch her breath. She could see a mass of gangrenous flesh. It was tough as gristle as she snipped at it, then tore it away with her scalpel. Just beyond that she thought she had finally reached healthy tissue, but this section, too, was blackened, yellowed, fetid. *How deep did it go,* she wondered. Beyond the knee? "Drats," she said, thinking that he might need to lose even more of the limb. She tried to calm herself; forecasting doom would not help her with the task at hand. She resumed the story then. The telling of it calmed her at least, took her over as she cut through the essence of this dead and dying tissue, cut to the retelling of the story as she moved beyond the descriptions of the flickering candle, the astounding darkness once the baby slid into her hands, the heat of the baby's first breaths against her neck, the assaulting emptiness when Dr. Miss snatched the newborn from her arms, its tiny fingers reaching, reaching toward the sound of its mother's voice; then the trembling of the lawyer's hands as he touched the midwife's elaborately carved desk, to support himself, as if he might pass out otherwise, Dr. Miss's head wrap that had come undone, and the long sash that fell down the side of her face and moved back and forth as she stood there, deflated at the knowledge that she would not be the one to decide the baby's fate.

Sylvia rebalanced the scalpel in her hands, her hands so bloodied she could not tell where her fingers ended and the living substance of Carl's limb began. She looked around for the salt solution. It was not on her cart. It was on the other side of the room, next to the basin. She started to fault Linc, but of course she could not. He was just a confused young man, a tortured soul; he was hiding from himself, she could tell. How could she expect for him to put the salt solution on the cart with her other supplies if she had not specified that to him? She walked across the room. Her movements were wooden, as if they were being managed by a novice puppeteer. She rinsed her hands and retrieved the salt solution. She did not glance beyond the sheet as she walked back to the bed. She did not want to see his face just yet.

She poured the solution onto the remains of Carl's leg. "The midwife had been such a beacon of power to me until that moment," she said, as she watched the solution work its way through. "But at that moment she appeared crushed, broken, though I wanted her to fight for the baby, to say no, we will handle its discharge. To tell him that he was the one in a compromised situation. That he had been paid well to have the woman he'd escorted here to be no longer with child. And that result had been satisfactorily

468

accomplished. I wanted her to tell him to take his damn carriage and political connections and be gone, that we would send word when she was well enough to travel back to his fancy house and do his bidding once again. That child had been my first. So of course I wanted her to fight for it. But I knew that the midwife would not as I watched the sash of her head wrap swing back and forth. Perhaps on another night she may have, but this night we had just learned that the president had been shot. Who can say how that may have sapped her ability to push back?"

Sylvia paused. The mat had filled again with the morbid cuttings she'd excised from Carl's leg. She did not want to call out for Linc to empty it, did not want to interrupt herself to walk it to the vat. She just wanted to get through the mass of seemingly never-ending dead flesh. She dumped the contents of the mat on the floor. They would clean it later. She slowed herself; she flexed her fingers and repositioned her scalpel. Her cuts into this section of flesh were precise as she snipped away at more deadened flesh, and then more, and then more still.

"Since Dr. Miss would not take charge, I knew that I must," she said as she resumed her narrative. She could feel her voice

469

change as she talked, her tone lower, coming from a deeper, an almost haunting place now. "Yes, I knew that I must," Sylvia said. "I knew that I was risking my employment with the midwife, perhaps all future employment, as she would never produce a letter on my behalf if she knew, and would likely tarnish my reputation any way that she could, but I followed behind Dr. Miss when she went to deliver the baby to the waiting carriage. It was already full morning, so I kept my distance, that she would remain unawares. The streets were bustling with further news of the president's death. A crazy chorus of church bells rang out willy-nilly, and the cacophonous clangs matched the scratchy, grating feel in the air as women cried and men pushed their hands against their brows, and there was a palpable sense in the air of what will happen now, what will become of things, of us. Through it all I could hear the baby cry.

"I watched the midwife tap on the carriage door. The door opened and I crept around to the other side. She did not see me; my hooded cape was around my face, and besides, there were too many people about. I crouched on the side of the carriage until I reasoned she had slid the cradle onto the seat next to him. I waited until I

470

thought she was likely gone. The blood pulsed through my head, and with the sound of all the church bells crying I thought my head would explode. I pulled on the carriage door then. I pulled on it with all of my might, but I could not open it. I heard the horses begin to pick up their feet and I ran to the front of the carriage and signaled the driver. 'Please, please,' I called to him. 'I must speak with your mister. It is a matter of life and death.' He peered down, and I could see his eyes soften for me. He whispered to his horses to hush and be still and then climbed down from his perch and walked to the side of the carriage where Dr. Miss had just been. He pulled open the carriage door for me and extended his hand to help me up. The baby had a rousing cry going, and the lawyer seemed almost relieved to see me. I lifted the baby from the cradle and pushed the cradle to the carriage floor and sat. I rocked the baby and cooed that everything would be fine. Dr. Miss had thankfully packed a feeding bottle in the cradle, and I offered it, and the baby pulled it hard and drank.

"I focused on the baby. The baby was so easy to look at as it settled into contentment and drank. It opened its eyes and looked at me, and its eyes were dark as tar.

But then I turned to look at the lawyer. He was staring at me, waiting, but when I looked at him he turned away, though not before I saw the torment in his eyes; his eyes held dark circles beneath, and the whites of his eyes were red and almost, but not quite, washed clean of their true color, which was an ocean blue. I told him that the baby was special to me because it was my first and I just wanted to know that it would be well cared for.

"He looked straight ahead, seemingly not affected by anything, not by me, by what I'd just related, the baby I held, or the commotion just outside of his carriage. His words were wooden as he spoke. 'And what would you do should I release it to you?'

"I told him that I knew of a home for orphaned children where my classmate used to work after school. He asked its location and I told him it was less than a mile from where we were. And he leaned forward as if to prepare to signal his coachman. But I told him I would transport the baby right then. I was afraid he might change his mind in the time it took to travel that mile. I promised him that I would give them an acceptable story. I swore to him on everything that I held dear in this life and the next that I would never speak of his identity, of hers, of the baby's to a living soul. He flicked his wrist in my direction as if saying, 'Be gone,' and I did not wait for him to change his mind. As quickly as I could, I pulled open the door and propped the feeding bottle under my chin and nestled the baby so close that I could feel its fast heartbeat. I climbed down to the ground and ran. I ran away from the carriage, away from the direction of Dr. Miss's house. I ran and cried and held the baby close as I listened for the sound of the horses as the carriage sped away. A group of women had gathered near the corner, and one of them reached out to me. 'And you with the newborn. To have to learn of the president's death when you have not long ago issued forth life. Come settle yourself down, child.'

"I tried to explain that I had not just given birth, but I was crying too hard, and in any event she had already pulled me to her, she was already swaying from side to side, and it felt good to be rocked in such a way at that moment. I just fell into the rhythm of her motion, and even the baby stopped crying. When I had settled myself, I walked the rest of the way to the home.

"The woman who'd opened the door was tall and thin and with a mass of dark hair that fell into her face and I was startled by her appearance. She apologized, said that she was so distraught over the president, she'd not concerned herself with even combing her hair. I just pushed the baby into the woman's hands, and at first she would not accept it. She said that they were beyond capacity and had just taken in another infant not two days before. But I pleaded with her, told her the story I'd contrived, that a constable had been setting up a blind in the alley a block away to catch tax cheats and had heard this baby's squeals and thinking it a rat had almost bashed its head with his billy club. That the baby was otherwise unwanted. The woman's eyes softened and filled with tears. She called into the house then and an older woman, squat and graying, ambled to the foyer, and gently took the baby from me. She spoke with a brogue so thick that I could hardly understand her, but her tone was calming, sincere, as she cooed at the baby and held it close, and that satisfied me, so I left."

The room was completely silent save for a lone drop of water that fell into the basin as if it had been hanging at the mouth of the spigot, waiting for Sylvia to be done. She picked up the magnifying glass and inspected the stump. Her breaths were slow and she inhaled deeply. That deathly smell that had pushed out from the stump in wide swaths seemed reduced to mere ribbons of a scent, seemed to grow fainter even as she stood there. She used tweezers to pull away at a dot of flesh. It appeared pink, healthy. She nipped at it and cut it off just as she'd done with the gangrenous sections because she thought it wise to sacrifice a bit of what was good to make sure she'd gotten all of what was not.

Linc cleared his throat then and Sylvia jumped. She had forgotten he was there, even as she'd been sorely aware of his presence. She could see his silhouette on the other side of the sheet. She'd not realized how tall he was until just now. One of his shoulders seemed fashioned higher than the other as he stood there with his elbow resting in the palm of his unbandaged hand, his chin resting atop his fist. His chin so pronounced she could almost see the cleft there. "Mnh," she said, as she walked to the basin and freed herself of the gown and the mask. "Carl is resting comfortably?"

"He appears to be, yes."

"I am grateful for your assistance."

"May I ask —"

"I may choose not to answer," Sylvia said, as she scrubbed her hands.

"What of your promise to not say the

names —"

"It is a promise I fully intend to keep."

"And what of the drawings she made of the president such as Carl described?"

"What of them?" Sylvia said, dismissively, as she pulled the broom from the closet.

Linc had come from behind the curtain the sheet made. He sighed and leaned his head back and stretched. It was such a long lean that Sylvia could see the scar on his neck and she almost asked had someone held a knife to his neck. But then he took the broom from Sylvia and began sweeping the scraps of dead flesh. "I knew a miss who also sketched the president. No other reason."

"In New York?"

"No, in Philadelphia," he said, as Sylvia turned away to get the dustpan.

"So you have spent time in Philadelphia, besides this time?"

"I have, yes."

"And are the constables here in fact looking for you?"

"They may be," he said, as he took the pan and leaned down to scoop up the putrid remains and walked them to the trash vat.

"Are you the guilty party?"

"In some ways I am guilty, but my actions were completely justified."

He turned to face Sylvia then and she saw that same sadness, that stark vulnerability she'd seen in him their first encounter, though it was even more pronounced now. His eyes appeared even darker, deeper, his cheekbones even more prominent, as if a storm was raging there, his mouth pursed. "Mnh," she said. "Well, you may keep to the room next door, then. I shall put a quarantine sign there so no one will enter, though no one will come into the hospital anyway, except for Spence, whom I will alert, and the doctor, who is not a threat. Just tell the doctor to go back to his house and you will bring him an opium pipe and he should do your bidding" — she smirked — "provided he thinks you are white."

Linc flinched when she said the part about him being white. He looked away, looked at the window, where blasts of gray and yellow were throwing themselves at the night, the night fighting back by growing darker still, even as it had already begun to yield. "Was it a girl or a boy?" he asked then. "You never said."

"It was a girl of course. As I stated at the outset."

"No. You spoke only of 'the baby,' or 'it.' "

"It is easier for me that way. It — she was my first." She balled her fist for emphasis, and to settle it once and for all. "You should find everything you need in the way of bed linens in the supply room."

"Thank you," he said, though he seemed to be speaking more to the display outside the window than to Sylvia. "I am grateful to you. Most grateful."

33

The grounds of the Lazaretto were still as winter as Sylvia walked back to the house. She felt as though she were sleepwalking, and then she thought she felt a shadow behind her and turned quickly, but no one was there.

Though someone had been. It was Son. He had fallen asleep outside, under the porch, waiting for Linc and Vergie to leave the cellar so that he could go down and give Bram water and make sure that he had not died again. He did not know for sure whether or not they had left, but he would take his chances. He lifted the door and took the ladder stairs slowly, and the quiet told him they were gone. He didn't even light the lamp. He knew this space like a blind man as he walked behind the barricade. He could see Bram there wrapped in the shroud, his head to one side. He opened his canteen and sat next him and propped his head to give him water, and then he started to cry.

Sylvia crept up the stairs and eased into her bedroom. Vergie was sprawled across the whole bed and Sylvia thought, *I am not fighting for sleeping space with this girl.* She changed quickly into her nightgown, wanting her head to touch the pillow before the daylight did. She went into the top of her closet for her quilt and extra blanket, prepared to sleep on the parlor couch. She looked instead at an empty shelf. Vergie woke then. She sat up all at once. "Sylvia, you are back, how is Carl?"

"He has survived another day. Each day he lives, chances improve that he will continue to live. He is in the good Lord's hands, as we all are. And where is my bed linen?"

"For what? Are you not sleeping in here? I promise to sleep small," Vergie said, remembering that Sylvia's extra pillow and sheets were down on the cellar floor.

"As exhausted as I am, and as my extra bed covering has disappeared, okay, yes. But the first instant I feel your foot in my back, you are on the floor."

Vergie waited for Sylvia to kneel and say her prayers, then she moved over, excited.

She felt like a little girl again, sharing the bed with Sylvia, the way they'd shared sleeping space when they traveled on family trips with her aunt and uncle. She wished she were still a little girl right now as she thought of how she'd bungled things with Linc. She should not have ceded her passions so quickly, should not have told him about Bram when she did, how she did. "So what exciting thing happened over here tonight?" Sylvia said in a voice that sounded half-asleep.

"Well, Spence and Mora finally tied the knot."

Sylvia sat up. She'd almost forgotten. "How was the ceremony?"

"Where shall I begin? If you subtract Lena and her frightful self, and the fact that Skell's pronouncement of man and wife turned into a long-drawn-out Baptist sermon, and that Kojo couldn't find the ring for a full half an hour, and the one playing the harmonica was having problems with his instrument and missed every other note in his Lord's Prayer solo, and Mora cried nonstop, and Spence looked liked a sad, wet dog, then I suppose it was a very nice wedding."

Sylvia chided herself for taking such pleasure in Vergie's description, and then she let herself laugh out loud. Vergie laughed, too, then said that the one thing that held up to near perfection was the food. "I never tasted duck so juicy."

"Yes, Lord. Yes, Lord, that Nevada can surely cook."

"And I had no appetite, but I was cured with the first bite."

"Why did you have no appetite? Are you not well?"

"I have had a difficult time this night, Sylvia," Vergie said, and then she said no more. There was a tap on the door and Nevada peeped in. "Hey, Sylvie. I thought I heard you. How's Carl?" She found her way to the chair.

"He is comfortable. He is alive. I believe I got all the infected tissue."

"Thank God, I have been praying. And they tell me the Lord pays special attention to a sinner's prayers."

"And you have been sinning, right?"

"Let us say that Buddy is having very few complaints about being quarantined."

"Well, close your mouth, please. I can see you grinning all the way from the other side of this dark room."

"Speaking of grinning, I guess Vergie told you about that fiasco masquerading as a wedding. I am still trying to decide which sounded worse, the never-ending harmonica solo or Mora's bawling. And then when Kojo dropped the ring as he tried to hand it to Spence, mercy —"

"Come on now, Nevada" — and Vergie jumped all the way up to sitting. "Tell Sylvia how Kojo got down on his hands and knees to look for the ring under the fainting couch and, and —" Vergie could not finish talking for her gasping laughter.

"And what?" Sylvia insisted. *What?*

"He blew wind," Nevada said.

"No, he did not!"

"Oh yes he did so," Vergie said. "It was so powerful and loud we thought his pants would split."

"And Spence turned up his nose, 'cause he was standing closest to him, and then he said, 'Jesus!' "

"Out loud, he said it?"

"Out loud," Vergie said.

"And Mora and Lena started fanning themselves —"

"And Miss Ma was near the back, and she did not know what was going on, and she asked, 'What happened?' and Splotch said, loud enough for all to hear, 'We appear to be in the midst of a quite smelly situation.' "

Sylvia hollered then, they all did. They laughed soundly for what felt like the better part of an hour. They laughed convulsively; and as soon as they felt that they could laugh no more, Vergie would add to the fun starting them up again.

"I needed that laughter," Sylvia said when they had finally settled down.

"You did, Sylvie," Nevada said. "Being on the front line with the quarantine, and then keeping Carl alive. Nothing better than some laughter to chase the worry away. I myself been trying to keep the jokes coming with Buddy since he's still broken up over Sister's death."

"They were real close, huh?" Sylvia asked.

"They were. Though you would hardly know they were related, because she was a very refined type. And when you'd hear her proper speech alongside of Buddy's how should I say, improper speech —"

"Like Daddy and Aunt Maze?" Vergie laughed.

"Y'all woulda liked Sister," Nevada said. "But no chance you woulda possibly met her the way your mama, Sylvia — or your aunt, Vergie — measured the time you were allowed to spend on Fitzwater Street with us lowly Negroes."

"I have to beg to differ," Sylvia said. "I actually went inside of Buddy's house once, on that fateful night I tried to deliver your birthday cake and ended up throwing it on the floor. What a scene that was!"

Nevada chuckled. "I heard of that from my grandmother, but the shock was not you throwin' the cake, the shock was that you had actually stepped inside of a house where cardplaying was going on."

"You *threw a cake,* Sylvia?" Vergie asked. "Why?"

Sylvia recounted the story. Then Vergie asked who the white boy was whose neck Splotch wanted to slit. "And why was he even there?"

"I don't think I ever knew. Handsome little something with the darkest eyes," Sylvia said, remembering how she'd cleaned the knife wound on his neck, picturing the scar. "I could not get a clear answer about who he was when I asked back then. Why was he there, Nevada?"

"I never knew much about him. I think he was just some boy from an orphanage Sister had got attached to."

"Which orphanage?" Sylvia asked, and her voice caught in the top of her throat as she pictured the wound on the little boy's neck, imagining the scar it would leave, measuring her recollection of it against the scar she'd noticed on Linc's neck. Now she compared their eyes — both had eyes black as tar.

"Sylvia, you asking me questions I cannot answer. I am sure Buddy will be glad to oblige you when you can finally take yourself a breather and let me cook you up a special meal and serve it to you. I want you to get to know Buddy, besides; tell me if he is as good a catch as I think, or if I am kidding myself. 'Cause I hope to high Heaven I'm not kidding myself."

"Well, he is at least unattached, so that's a good start," Sylvia said. "And what was Buddy's sister's name?"

"Sister — right?" Vergie offered.

"No, she was *known* as Sister. At least that's what everybody called her on Fitzwater Street," Nevada said. "But her given name, which I didn't even know till just last week, when she died, was Meda."

"Meda," Vergie repeated it. "That is a nice name."

"It is," said Sylvia. Though Sylvia did not know how it was even physically possible for her to speak right now, because she was sure her heart had just separated from her chest cavity. She thought she could hear the separation as it pulled away. Vergie and Nevada chattered on in the background. Bands of pink and yellow daylight had begun their tumble in through the tall windows, and Sylvia closed her eyes, and Nevada whispered, "Aw, poor thing is exhausted. I am about to go see what the hens have done for me this morning." And Vergie whispered that she would come with her, and soon the room was silent as a crypt except for that painful sound coming from Sylvia's chest. It was the sound that a starched muslin sheet makes when strong hands rip it in two to fashion a swab for a slit neck, a tourniquet to save a limb, a life, a secret; to use as a head wrap of the type Dr. Miss wore, wrapped around and around, such a tortuous wrap — Sylvia did not know how it had come undone that morning. But it had, first when they spoke with Benin, and then later when Sylvia returned to the house after depositing the baby at the orphans' home.

Dr. Miss had met her in the foyer, asked her where she'd been, why did she have the appearance of one who'd just run from blood hounds trained on her scent. Sylvia told her that she'd gone for a walk to try to calm herself after the combined events of the baby and the president being shot. She'd gotten caught up, she'd said, in a throng of hysterical people reacting to a deep-voiced man on a soapbox proclaiming that they must all, that day, take flight for Canada because Lincoln's assassination signaled that a new revolution was afoot that would see every colored person bound and chained no matter their status as already free. "Could that be true, ma'am?" Sylvia cried and shook. The tears, her trembling, were genuine, even if the reason for them was not, and afraid that Dr. Miss would detect her lie, she added a truth: "And I am so distraught over the baby, and us having to tell Miss Meda that her baby died."

Dr. Miss took Sylvia by the hand and led her into the parlor and sat her down on the couch. She placed a pillow behind her back, a warm towel on her neck, and gave her a handkerchief doused with lavender oil and told her to sniff. Told her, in the softest voice Sylvia had ever heard her use, that she had experienced grave occurrences the past night into the day. That she could best help herself by finding a place within herself to discard the parts about the night that would ill serve her by remembering. She had Sylvia look at her, and repeat after her that the baby died. She died. The baby girl died. Like the refrain of a song. Sylvia had watched the sway of the sash hanging along the side of Dr. Miss's face as she repeated the words back to Dr. Miss. The lavender felt like cotton puffs filling up in her head, felt soft, pure. The repetition, the motion of the sash, the lavender — it all lulled her. Enchanted her. She felt as if she'd fallen asleep as she sat there, wide awake, repeating over and over: The baby girl died, she died, the baby girl died.

Right now Sylvia could feel the daylight touching her face, pushing against her closed eyelids, causing the darkness to shatter into a thousand loose threads. She realized now that Dr. Miss had tried to hypnotize her, work a spell on her, had tried to imprint a different reality in her mind to override what she'd actually lived. And had Sylvia not already just taken the baby to the orphans' home, she might have allowed herself to be convinced that the baby died. But the part of Dr. Miss's spell that had worked, *had.*

She could hear a sparrow now on the other side of the window testing its new song. It seemed to come from far away, from years ago. And just like that, the ripping sounds stopped, and there was otherwise an astounding stillness as if even the earth had ceased its spin, the same stillness she'd felt when the baby had slipped into her waiting, wanting hands; the candle had died and the room was black. She was so tired that middle of the night, having tended to Meda the length of her labor. As she was tired now, having been the whole night excising the infection from Carl's leg. And yet then as now there was exhilaration, too. She'd been extraordinarily present, had taken her place where she felt she was meant to be in the grandness of life's to and fro. Delivered her first baby; saved a man to see another day. It was a between state back then, and right now, when the mind is too exhausted to fight its own terrifying clarity. And in that speck of time so brief that it had no name for its measure, so brief that she wasn't even aware that she'd seen what she thought she had not seen; she saw it now. That tiny lump of its maleness. It had been a boy. It had been her first.

34

Linc stood on the pier and looked into the river. The daylight churned itself yellow across the sky and he tried to recall the exact instant during Sylvia's recounting when he knew she spoke of Meda. He thought that it may have been her first descriptions of the woman's polite features and sad, dreamy eyes, or the fact that the woman sketched President Lincoln, and claimed to have served him tea. Likely it was the sounds, the discord of notes jumping from everywhere on the scale as Sylvia spoke: notes so high they could shatter starlight; lows that could stir the buried dead, flats that might scorch through iron; sharps that cut like acid-tipped knives. And suddenly there was sound conjugated, music being made, a wordless song, a melody that he thought he knew, a tune he could sing. Meda had in fact had a child. Tom Benin, Linc knew by the description of the watch, had been the father. A girl; she had a girl. That is what Sylvia had said.

But it was not a girl. Linc was certain. The earth had not tilted to make him know this truth; the heavens had not opened to a thousand angels singing; the river had not reversed its course, or turned to blood, or wine, or run dry. He'd known it by his hands. He remembered Mrs. Benin's scorn that long-ago day when she'd stood in the porch entry as he and Meda and Tom Benin must have made quite the picture for her. Meda reading nonchalantly, her legs crossed, a peek of her ankle exposed, as if she were the lady of the house sitting on her own porch; Tom Benin listening to him count, even laughing when Linc applauded himself; Linc squeezed into the chair with Tom Benin, so relaxed with him that he'd pulled his hand out so that they could play a clapping game; he'd situated his hand on top of Tom Benin's, and Tom Benin had commented on the nice form to Linc's hands. Linc had noted that both their hands jutted in an odd way along the sides. After that, Mrs. Benin's irritation with Linc's inability to sit still on the piano bench turned to sudden wrath. Her insults toward him grew venomous. Her violence against his hands, he now knew, was an attempt to beat away the familiarity, the truth that his hands told.

Buddy had always maintained that it was impossible to know if a person was bluffing by looking in their eyes. The eyes are built for charming and seducing, they lie with ease, Buddy always said. "Look at what the hands do. The hands will act on their own accord to tell on what you don't even know you know."

Sylvia's eyes had looked at him directly when he'd questioned the baby's gender; her eyes were unflinchingly sincere. He'd watched her hands, however, furl into a fist; but it was the softest fist. As if her hands alone knew what a tender secret they held.

Linc turned and started walking in the direction of the hospital. Then he kept walking beyond. His steps were deliberate, purposeful as he reached Ledoff's house, where the constables lodged. He would tell them who he was: the son of Meda and Tom Benin. He would tell them what he knew: that Robinson had violated his brother on who knows how many occasions; that he himself had punched Robinson senseless as a result. He didn't think of the consequences as he turned the knob and pushed the heavy door wide open, as if this were his house, as if he were the landlord come to oust errant boarders. He was remembering how Robinson had called them throwaway little nothings. Spawned from alley rats.

He stepped into the foyer, was stopped by a scene in the foyer. Broken glass from smashed vases and lamps, and even paintings pulled from the walls. One of the constables worked to restrain an old graying white man who shook convulsively and yelled, "Get Spence, get that nigger here, he knows what to do." Linc recognized him as the doctor Sylvia had alluded to who would do anything for the promise of an opium pipe. The second constable stood calmly in the archway between the foyer and the parlor and the one tussling with the doctor yelled out to him, "Whadder we do wit 'im? Bloke has gone mad."

"Tie 'im down and lock 'im in one of the rooms till the nurse comes back. Nothing else yer can do till he comes through his need of the pipe or the need kills him before he do."

That one managed to secure the doctor's hands with leather cuffs and forced him toward the back of the house. The doctor sobbed and tried to shake them off. "Tell Spence I will free him, I swear it on my dead mother's soul. I will sign his papers if he comes to me now."

The remaining constable looked at Linc and shook his head. "Man on the hip sucking that opium pipe is a pitiful sight when there is nothing left to smoke. Guess the quarantine keeping more than sickly immigrant people from coming here," he said as he walked into the parlor and Linc followed. "Luke-the-constable" — he extended his hand and Linc shook it. "And what might I be doing for yer? I thought that other than my boy, who came wit me and who cannot keep his lips from the brandy cork, and that slobbering excuse of a doctor, and the one who acts like a dunce, that we was the only white on this place. Do not bode well for us if this is how we stack up when the colored is left to run things. Make a man think them equalatists know what they talkin' about. Though I will say that colored nurse sure proves the point. She makes a regular visit over here to keep me up on the status of the quarantine and so forth. She is tough as iron and is holding up to the task." He went to the sideboard and commenced to pour brown-colored liquid into a sizable goblet. "And the quarantine happens not to be the worser of things to come down in my life. Better lodging here than I keep back in the city with the wife and kids screaming in my ear the whole live-long day. Might investigate if the nurse can get me hired on here after they open the place to ships again. Now, what can I do fer yer? Might I offer you a sniff of brandy in the absence of the head man of this island, who got fine taste in his drink and his apparel."

Linc looked at Luke-the-Constable and realized that he was attired in what he guessed to be Ledoff's clothing, a nicely threaded high-collar shirt, perfectly seamed pants, supple leather slippers. Then he looked out on the mess in the foyer. He could hear the doctor crying and ranting from a far corner of the house. He felt a sensation moving up from deep in his gut, felt like a ball of heat gathering parts of himself as it rose toward his chest. He'd come over here to turn himself in, finally. Expected that this man would have taken one look at him and had his minion wrestle him to the floor and shackle him. And yet he was offering him a drink instead, and the doctor was the one in restraints. He'd been lying this whole time on this island about being a black man, and yet the lie was actually the truth. The sensation had burned through to his throat uncontainable and he opened his mouth to release the fire trapped there. What came out surprised him. It was laughter. It doubled him over as it blazed out. His eyes ran and he made snorting sounds.

"Jesus," the constable said. "What is happening to all people of the white persuasion at this place?" And Linc laughed harder still. He gasped for breath. He collapsed into the wing chair. He tried to compose himself, to explain himself. And then he did compose himself because the door opened and Sylvia walked in and the constable jumped up — almost pulling himself to attention — and ran to the foyer.

"Good day, Nurse Sylvia," the constable said, and Sylvia looked around as if in shock, rendered speechless. "It does appear that the doctor is having a rough go of it. Made a ready mess of the place."

"Where is he?" she asked when she found her voice, which sounded like a growl coming from the back of her throat.

"My boy got it handled, he got 'im in cuffs and barricaded 'im in one of these fine rooms."

Sylvia appeared to be reeling, and he asked her if he could help her to a seat. She waved him away. "Thank you, I shall be well in just a moment." She took deep breaths as she stood there, looking at the holes in the wall where pictures had hung. Realized now what she'd begun to suspect the day that she and Spence amputated Carl's leg. Realized that Spence had in fact been feeding the doctor the opium pipe, and now that the quarantine had likely prevented a fresh supply, coupled with Spence's own absence, owing to his wedding last night, the doctor was in a manic state of withdrawal. "I shall send Son over so that he can begin picking things up," she said. "Although I am tempted to leave it all as it is, so that when Ledoff returns he will understand the urgency when I implore him to request the doctor's replacement."

"On the opium pipe pretty bad, I'd say," Luke-the-Constable agreed. "I'd be much inclined to putting in my word on what I seen of the doctor's egregious manner if it be a help to you, Nurse Sylvia."

Sylvia looked around, still in shock. "The glass, though, is a hazard. It must be cleaned up."

"I will get my boy to throw in a hand. Not as if he is otherwise saddled with work to do."

Sylvia nodded. Then she scanned the foyer again in disbelief. She leaned and tried to upright one of the framed pictures lying facedown. She knew which one it was by the gilded frame, Ledoff's favorite. It was heavy and Linc had come into the foyer and was now leaning with her, telling her to watch her footing, not to fall on the glass. Together they lifted it, and Sylvia said, "In the parlor," and Luke-the-Constable swept away glass and debris with his foot to make a path for them. They propped it on the divan. It was a portrait in oils of Abraham Lincoln. Sylvia was explaining that Ledoff had told her that he'd paid a king's ransom for it because he felt that it was so lifelike, that it captured not only the president's likeness but also his spirit. She was glad that at least the glass that encased it had not been shattered. They stood back and viewed it. It was not the typical rendering of Lincoln, nothing stoic, bland, or contemplative about it. He appeared to be staring back at them as if he took delight in what he saw, and Sylvia remarked that for all the criticism he suffered about his looks, he was not unpleasant to gaze upon. Linc nodded, thinking that's what Meda always said. Tried to tell Sylvia that now. "A similar position was maintained by my uh, my uh, uh, my —" He took a deep breath. He could not yet say the word.

"Mother." Sylvia finished the thought.

They were quiet. The glass encasing the painting caught the daylight and acted as a mirror. Sylvia saw on their faces the struggle to come to grips with what they now knew that they'd always known. Sylvia reasoned that Tom Benin had called out the command that morning to tell Meda that her baby girl had died so that Meda would never figure out who her baby was. Sylvia now believed that Benin had likely always planned that the baby would be a part of Meda's life, and — peripherally — his own.

Sylvia cleared her throat to try to begin to explain to Linc that she'd not intentionally lied when she told him it was a girl. But then she couldn't say anything because just then Spence pushed through the door. Out of breath, he pulled up short as he took in the chaos in the foyer. "What in tarnation has . . ."

"Well, look who it is, Mr. Newly Betrothed," Sylvia declared as she went out into the foyer and stood in front of Spence, her arms folded across her chest. "It is all too apparent that you could not simultaneously satisfy both your bride and the doctor whose needs you have apparently been fulfilling for some time now. Have you not, Spence? Admit it and then take a good look, Spence. This is the result when your services end too abruptly."

"I know, Sylvia," Spence said, his dark

skin many shades lighter from the shame swathed there. "I deserve all the tongue-lashing you can give, but right now you must come with me. We have a situation."

"What situation? I just left Carl. He is resting comfortably."

"Nothing to do with Carl, it is on the other side of the creek. I can explain it on the way over —" And with that, Spence was out the door, with Sylvia following closely behind him.

Linc turned to Luke-the-Constable, who seemed surprisingly unfazed by any of this. "I shall take you up on that offer of a drink," Linc said. "And then I'll tell you why I'm here."

35

Linc took the long way around from Led-off's house to the other side, his head crowded with thoughts of the conversation he'd just had with Luke-the-Constable. Buddy had been correct when he'd told Linc there was something else going on with the presence of the constables. Linc had just learned that they were not here for him. They were here for Bram.

From what Linc gathered, as Luke dappled his explanation of the warrant against Bram with complaints of his own home life, Bram had gone to pay Robinson a visit. He'd told the housekeeper that he had been one of Robinson's favorite boys at the orphanage, and that it was unforgivable that it had taken him so long to stop by, but here he was. The housekeeper had allowed Bram in and even ushered him up to Robinson's room because, according to her, he seemed such a gentle soul with the bluest eyes, and she felt sorry that he was so damaged with that horrific scar on his forehead. He seemed so trustworthy, she said, that she took advantage of his time upstairs with Robinson to run a brief errand. When she returned she found Robinson propped in his chair just as she'd left him, though he was showing more than his usual palsy, and his eyes were red as if he wanted to cry but was unable to summon tears. The real damage, she said, had been done to the room. The room had been ransacked — drawers pulled open, their contents strewn about, closets in disarray. She could not say for certain if anything of value was missing. She had managed to fish through the chaos to find all of his expensive timepieces, his gold rings and such. But there had been a box of trinkets in the drawer of his chest that his kinfolk boasted had been given to him by the boys at the orphanage as evidence of the high esteem they'd held him in. She did not know if there was any value to the box, but she was fairly certain that that had gone missing. Linc had stopped listening at that point because he knew what was in that box: the jewelry Robinson had confiscated from all of the boys shortly after he'd taken over; the rings Meda had given to Bram and to him were surely in that box. Linc's head was spinning as he flashed back to the rag-draped woman at the hospital who'd asked Linc if he was looking for the man with the rings and Linc assumed her to be talking about Bram's burn scars. Then he was remembering that afternoon when they'd squeezed into the hidden compartment of Buddy's cellar closet and Linc had asked Bram, "Did he?" That's all he had asked. And Bram had sniffed and then simply said, "He promised he would return our rings." Bram had gone and got their rings.

He'd almost said that out loud to Luke-the-Constable as he managed to pull his attention back to Ledoff's parlor, where Luke was droning on about his unhappy wife. "Why," Linc had pressed Luke, "would a pair of constables be sent here to apprehend Bram when by the housekeeper's own admission nothing of any value was taken?"

"Murder," Luke had said with a drunken smile. "The Robinson chap finally gave up the ghost."

Linc felt his blood go to ice. "But you said the housekeeper said —"

"I know it, I know it, I know it. He was alive when the vandal was still there, but he has since died, and the warrant states that the violence against the man's domicile contributed to his death."

Linc tried to explain to the constable then that he himself was the one who had pummeled Robinson so many years ago, not Bram. Bram had never touched him. Bram was entirely innocent. Bram would give his last crust of bread to a hungry child, or fight a man twice his size to defend a lady's honor; he could play the piano such that you'd think the heavens had opened and a thousand angels were singing, whether or not you believed in such things as Heaven, or angels, you would still look up because surely there was some beatific force at work that allowed him to play that way. He'd stopped himself; he was breathing hard, trying not to cry.

Luke had drained his glass and sat back and said, "Ah, this brandy, this is the life on this quarantine station." Then he told Linc that all of what he'd just spouted about his brother being a saint was either true or it was not, it did not matter to him one way or the other. The only thing that concerned him is that they had lifted the bounty from Linc's head and placed it on Bram's. "I wager they figure they got a better case if they dwell on what happened just now, than somethin' what happened years and years ago. No offense, but you worth nothin' to me, yet I would be willing to give you a healthy share of my bounty if you let on about your brother's whereabouts."

Linc had stared at him straight on. "Are you trying to make a joke? My brother is dead."

"All right, now that is a start at least. Can you lead me to his body, the commission is not as much if I bring him in dead, but it will be enough to at least quiet the missus's complaining for a week."

Linc had pressed his lips together and left.

So now Linc was crossing the creek — to go where? he asked himself. To do what? For starters, he needed to find Vergie. He needed to apologize for his outburst. And also — he just wanted to see her. He didn't know how much he would tell her just yet about what he had come to know about himself, who he truly was; he just wanted to talk to her, wanted to feel the intense sweep of her eyes, the way she listened with her eyes and how her gaze followed his every word as if there was a meaning to what he said that her eyes alone could decipher. He wanted to hear the timbre of her voice hitting his own ears, the pauses, as when he'd listened to her speak as they'd snuggled under the quilt on the cellar floor, and she'd pause at the end of a phrase and he could hear her swallow. Even that tiny sound, it had astounded him the way that it moved him. He'd thought at such times that he was beginning to understand what love was, when the most insignificant thing about a person — the sound of saliva sliding down the throat — becomes as magnificent as the sounds of angels singing.

He was on the other side of the creek. The path was lush with wildflowers and berry bushes and smelled of lavender and recently turned earth. He spotted Kojo and Splotch then. They were carrying a coffin-shaped pine box and seemed to be struggling with its weight. At the sight of them Linc's world stood still. "Hey!" he yelled.

They turned and Splotch said loud enough for Linc to hear, "Keep walking, nobody but that white-looking nigger."

"Hey!" Linc called again as he ran to catch up with them. "Is that my brother in there? Is it? Is that Bram?"

Splotch and Kojo looked at each other. "Yes, it is your brother," Splotch said. "We on our way now to lower him into a hole."

Linc stopped where he was and fell to his knees. "Do not bury him yet. Please. Put him down, let me see him. Let me say goodbye."

They set the crate down in front of him. "All right," Splotch said as he dusted off his hands. "But I am warning you, it is not a pretty sight in there."

Linc buried his head in his hands and whispered Bram's name. Then he sat up straight and ran his fingers along the groove of the crate's lid. A family of hummingbirds seemed to cry just above as if they, too, wanted to offer final goodbyes. The crate smelled of pine and wet dirt, it was intoxicating as he lifted the lid — or was he just drunk with grief? His brother. He could not look in the crate. Could not open his eyes just yet to see Bram stretched out lifeless because once he saw him that way, he would have to accept his death as real. He clenched his eyes tighter and tried to think of a prayer he could say. He could think of none, so he settled on: "I shall see you on the other side." He did not fully believe that, but right now he also did not *not* believe it, and he thought that at least the possibility of seeing Bram in some Heaven was a comfort right now, so he said it again, louder this time, with more conviction. "I shall see you on the other side, Brother." And then one more time he said it, this time shouted it as if he might actually wake Bram with his shout. Then he opened his eyes and looked in. He jumped up. "What the fuck!" he said. The crate was filled with rocks and grass and dirt.

He could hear Kojo and Splotch laughing from very far away, though they stood right there and were practically laughing in Linc's ear. "You dumb donkey's ass," Splotch said, between his howling laughter. " 'I shall see you on the other side, Brother,' " he mocked Linc.

Linc turned around and punched his fist through the air, through the years, and landed his fist against Splotch's mouth the way he'd wanted to when he was a small boy and Splotch held a knife to his neck. They fought then. They cursed and punched each other, and Kojo stood by, yelling, "Get 'im, get 'im good, Splotch." They rolled in the dirt and Linc appeared to be getting the best of Splotch, and Kojo pushed up his sleeves and commenced to move toward them, but a voice stopped him.

"I would not do that if I was you." It was Buddy. " 'Cause if you do, it will have to be me and you, and nothing would give me more delight this instant than to whup your ass, and I reason your goal is not to make me a happy man."

Kojo turned to face Buddy. He walked toward him and squared his shoulders and snorted. "I did not know he was a friend of yours —"

"Well, this is a case where what you do not know can cause you grave bodily harm."

"Call off your boy, I will call off mine."

"Hey, Lincoln," Buddy yelled into the cloud of dust Linc and Splotch had stirred up, his eyes still fixed on Kojo, as if daring him to make a move. "Save some for the card table. That's where you really gonna give him a whuppin'. In the meantime, come with me — Sylvia got something she need to say to you."

36

Had Linc not taken the long way around through the woods; had he not stopped every few feet in the woods to grapple with all that had happened, to smoke tobacco and talk to the trees, to pick up rocks and hurl them through the air, to stomp fallen branches, to release the coil of rage and regret and amazement, he would have been privy to the activity at the guesthouse. He would have heard the news by now.

Vergie surely would have told him. Vergie was a natural storyteller — the way she'd give life to the tiniest detail, and go back and forth in time, all the while keeping the hearer oriented; she'd imitate the voices of the people she described; she'd wear what their faces did; she'd even venture into surmising their interior worlds. And at first, when she started in with her recitation of the monumental thing that had happened, Linc would have been distracted by the sight of her as his eyes fell to her mouth — that mouth, those pouty lips, both fleshy and firm as they'd moved against his own mouth that first time they were together in the cellar.

The air carrying the sound of her voice would have been confused by the time it reached the part of his brain that handled hearing, because the first sight of her would have redirected all of his nerve impulses first to his lower, baser self — he was just a man, after all — and when he recovered from that he would have felt a jolt to his heart, like a mild shock that brought heat and light with it and opened him up. It all would have happened in a mere speck of time, but it would have felt like a millennium until the impulses rightly routed to the part that deciphered words and he could hear what in fact she'd said.

"Nevada and I went looking for Son because Nevada had not caught sight of Son of late," she would have begun. "While we were searching we came upon the crate filled with dirt and grass and stones, and I confided to Nevada what I had managed to pull from Sylvia, that the crate supposedly held a deceased man, your brother, Bram." She would have said the name slowly, blowing the name out to make it lighter than air so that the sound of it could get a lift and rise and rise higher still. "Nevada said that the crate had Son's markings all over it because he loved to fill empty containers and try to sink them to the bottom of the creek." She would have imitated Nevada's face then, making her eyes pop as Nevada's had. She would have yelled out Son's name the way that Nevada did, too, extending the word so that it stretched from one minute fully to the next. Then she would have replicated Nevada's rapid-fire speech, waving her hands up and down as Nevada did, gasping in between her words. " 'Mercy, it is Son, he musta found the body. Lord, who knows what he did to it, where he put it, he been acting strange lately, running in and out of the cellar at odd times, I thought it was to get the company's needs stored down there. I told myself I was gonna go down there and see, but I am a scared little lamb when it comes to dark cellars, I do not descend into one ever unless I absolutely have to. I should have, Lord, but then Buddy came, and, mercy, I could hardly think straight, and then I got so sad over Carl losing his leg, and with trying to keep all these people fed in quarantine, stretching the food like Jesus did the fish and the loaves, not that I am making myself equal to Jesus, but, hell, I have performed a bit of a miracle, and no one has even noticed that the eggs been scrambled with meal to make more of less, that the cornbread been buttered with duck fat, that the chicken and dumplings was mainly dumplings. Lord Jesus, we got to go in the cellar, Vergie, come with me, we got to go down there.' "

After imitating Nevada, Vergie would have slowed the telling, would have paused to describe how Miss Ma was sitting out back with her sewing basket spread around her, making one attempt after another to thread an embroidery needle, allowing the tension to rise as she imitated Miss Ma licking the thread and trying to get it through that needle's eye, only to have the edge of the thread split, trying it again and watching it bend back, and again missing the needle's eye completely. By the time she'd gotten through that description, Linc would have been rooting for Miss Ma to thread the needle, would himself be damning the needle because she could not.

" 'Ma, put the dratted thread and needle down' " — Vergie would have resumed speaking in Nevada's frantic voice. " 'We got to get down in the cellar. Come on now, I need you, and I know nothing scares you. I watched you stare down a rabid possum back to its hollow in backwoods Virginia, so going in this cellar will be child's play for you, but it is no playing matter. Come on, Ma.' "Vergie would have pulled Linc's hand to demonstrate how Nevada had pulled Miss Ma's, and he would have tried to hold on to her fingers; though she would have yanked them from him, softly, she needed her whole self to get through to the end of the story she needed to tell him.

As she told of them walking down the ladder into the cellar, she would have walked thusly herself, stooping with one knee, then the next, and he surely would have felt as if he was walking with them. "The darkness fell around me with a sudden warmth against my skin that was at once rough and soft as a blanket filled with nubs, and my other senses became so acute I could hear Nevada's heartbeat, and Miss Ma's, too. I knew exactly how many steps to take to get to the lamp. And I felt ashamed when Nevada said to me, in a voice laced with judgment, 'Know this cellar well, do you, Vergilina?' Then Nevada gasped and jumped when I struck a match to light the wick, because that quick swish of a sound was magnified since it was dark, and it was a surprise, and even the otherwise fearless Miss Ma jumped at the sound. Nevada and

Miss Ma were stymied by the barricade of furniture and such that seemed to cut the cellar in half." She would have lowered her eyes when she said that, and Linc would have tilted her chin up so as not to lose the warm feel of her eyes on him. He would have cupped his hands around her face, traced the arc of her cheekbones. "And then what happened?" he would have asked her.

Now it would have been her turn to be distracted, to lose herself in the middle of her telling as his breath hit her face and she could taste the mist of it that smelled of brandy and longing, and at that moment she would have been rushed with the urge to cure his longing, but she would not, because she'd come to understand, after all, that she could not. His desire she could satisfy, but not his longing; his longing sprang from the whole of who he was, as did her own. Each person had the responsibility to concoct their own cure specific to their own essential self — so she had come to realize.

"And then what happened . . ." She would have repeated his question back as a statement of fact and just gone to the end of it, because his thumb stroking her face would have kindled a heat that by then would have spread all the way to her toes. "We heard

516

movement coming from behind the barricade, and Miss Ma went fearlessly there and peeked to the other side, and then she pulled her head back quickly and let out a laugh; it was her most piercing laugh ever, and Nevada started to cry: 'Is it that bad, Ma, what is it?' And I could not wait for her to finish laughing so that she could explain, and I looked back there myself. And the first thing I saw was a trail of ants organizing around the tiniest crumb of cornbread. I did not want to see the rest, as I imagined that the ants had got to Bram as he lay there decomposing."

Vergie's eyes would have begun to fill and she would have barely been able to keep them from spilling over when she got to this point. And Linc would have pulled her to him; he would have rubbed her back and squeezed her so close that she would be able to feel the sobs trapped between his ribs. He would allow her to comfort him, too, the way he'd not been able to do when she'd first told him that Bram was dead.

He would have barely heard her as he pressed her head against the strength of his chest and she talked into his chest and described what she saw. "Son was sitting there, dear Son, sweet Son, man-of-wonder Son. He had propped Bram to almost sitting. I was sure without a doubt that it was Bram by the scar you had described. Son had his canteen tilted to Bram's mouth, and I saw the ball of Bram's throat move as he swallowed, and he swallowed, and he swallowed." She would be sobbing now, so affected by the scene as she retold it. And he would have gently pushed her shoulders back to look on her face, to make sure that what he'd heard was what she'd said. That Bram was alive.

But Linc was not privy to the rising up of activity at the guesthouse that had the sound of a thousand geese flapping their wings to take flight. He was not there to hear the story as Vergie would have told it. Nor the aftermath, the screeching hysteria as the guesthouses came to life and the news spread. *A dead man has been found in the cellar* was the first report. *Fossilized; no, eaten by the ants to the bones; no, it was a ghost; no, a warlock; no, a deity; no, a man brought back to life like Lazarus, Jesus did it, he is here, he is waking the dead. You better get right with God, people, Jesus has come again.*

The commotion woke Spence from his marriage bed and he pushed through the crowd that had gathered at the cellar door. There was a hush when he reemerged from

518

the cellar and set the record straight. "The hospital erred in sending a man here who was neither expired, nor hot with fever. He is yet alive. I will go get Sylvia so that we can keep him so. And then it will be my greatest pleasure to send all you people home."

But Linc was unaware about all that had transpired as he'd tarried in the woods, and then prayed over a crate of rocks and grass. He had fought, been helped to his feet by Buddy, shook the dirt off, swallowed the blood from his busted lip. Now he walked with Buddy toward the house. "Do you know what Sylvia needs to speak to me about?" Linc asked.

"For her to say, not me." Though Buddy had wanted to tell Linc about Bram, Sylvia insisted that she would. Buddy and Sylvia had gone back and forth just outside of the hospital room where Bram was resting comfortably. Sylvia said that she couldn't say for sure if Bram had yellow fever, though it was possible that he'd been pronounced dead in the acute stage of the disease, people were known to survive even from that point. Buddy said then that he'd recalled Bram having bouts of some kind of ailment from the time he was a younger boy, according to what Meda used to tell him. "It could be a liver ailment. Now I am beyond curious and will investigate this as soon as I tell Linc that Bram is alive."

"Whoa, hold on there, Miss Lady, I'm telling him. I practically raised that boy."

"Well, these hands ushered him into the world," Sylvia countered, as she proudly waved her hands in front of Buddy's face.

"What world?" Buddy had asked as he looked at Sylvia's hands dancing through the air.

Sylvia laughed. "Let it suffice that I'm calling in your pledge of years ago. Remember? You promised me you would return the favor —"

"For throwing the cake and saving the day. I fold, Miss Lady, you win," he said. "But, what world?"

"Now, that I'll leave for Linc to say to you."

Linc and Buddy had reached the house. The sun had dipped low in the back of the sky and sent up red streaks to be remembered by. They pushed open the door. The lights were all lit and laughter crowded the parlor and blended with the harmonica and fiddle and spilled over into the dining room. The air smelled of mint and sage and fizzed with expectation as Nevada came in from the kitchen and set a basket of rolls still steaming in the center of the table. They had begun to gather around the table and claim seats, and Buddy left Linc's side and went to Nevada and pecked her cheek and whispered in her ear and she laughed like a naughty girl. Skell held out chairs for the unescorted ladies to sit. And shortly they were saying grace and digging in to eat.

Vergie walked in from the kitchen carrying a jug of punch. Linc looked at her and thought of Meda. He wondered what Meda would have said about all of this, about him claiming to be a black man before he knew that he was, about hiding out in the cellar, about Vergie.

He imagined her having him sit under one of her Lincoln sketches and asking him to explain what *he* felt about all of this. He pictured himself saying, "Ah, Meda, there is a pretty miss who has reached her hand through my chest and touched my heart." He thought that Meda would wink then. He could see it, Meda tilting her head, smirking the way she did when she really wanted to smile but hid behind a stern face, her cheekbones even more pronounced, her eyes sweeping him in that way that made him feel as if he was the best boy to ever walk the earth. Saw her letting that one eye close slowly in a playful wink. Saw himself, too, trying to keep from blushing as if he were ten.

Vergie was involved in a dispute with Lena over place settings and had not yet looked up to see him standing there. Then Sylvia came in from the kitchen and motioned Linc toward the foyer. When he joined Sylvia in the foyer she asked if he would take a walk with her to the hospital. "Is it Carl?" he asked, desperation clinging to his voice.

"It is not, but it is a matter that is better seen than talked about."

Now Vergie stepped into the foyer. Linc held her gaze, and he got that same surge as on the first night he'd laid eyes on her. "I should be happy to come with you to the hospital . . . if Miss Vergilina would also agree to walk with us."

Vergie nodded her consent. He held the door for Sylvia, then took Vergie's hand in his own. He leaned his head back into the dining room. The red of the evening sky cut a slice through the parted draperies. He felt connected suddenly to this hodge-podge assemblage gathered around this table, laughing and sniping and ultimately agreeing. What a community this was.

"I trust everyone is well this evening," he

said. This time he did not have to make his voice go deep when he said it.

AUTHOR'S NOTE

Although the people, situations, and plot lines that comprise the *Lazaretto* are fully imagined, the Lazaretto did, in fact, exist as a quarantine station. Its historical significance is indeed great, even as it remains relatively unexplored. Penn's David Barnes has called the Lazaretto "Ellis Island's great-grandfather." Mr. Barnes's important research and writings on the quarantine station were helpful in stoking my imagination and shaping the *Lazaretto*'s fictional world.

ACKNOWLEDGMENTS

I have not included acknowledgments in the four novels following *Tumbling,* my first. It felt redundant. The people in my universe have consistently provided the vital support and encouragement, the critiques, the space, the understanding, the distractions, the patience, the laughter, the love. But it's been twenty years since the first novel: twenty! My first agent has been replaced by the tenacious Suzanne Gluck, who knows what to say, and when, to keep me steady on the course. Claire Wachtel has continued to persevere through draft after draft; her assisting associate editor, Hannah Wood, is so efficient, so smart, as is Caroline Upcher, who contributed her editing prowess as well. Mary Rhodes, at ninety-four years of age, continues to serve as my wisdom well. And James Rahn is still helping writers like me push the material until it sings. Two of my siblings, Gloria and Bobby, are no

527

longer here in the flesh, but their spirits are, and when my nieces, Robin and Celeste, smile, Gloria *is* here. Paula, Gwen, Elaine, and Vernell, are still the best sisters — and friends — a person could ask for; I'm grateful to their spouses, Charles, Jim, and Jerry; Celeste's husband, Jean; and my nephews, Aaron, Gerald, Paul, and David. My twins — my daughter, Taiwo, my son, Kehinde — are all grown up since that first novel; their insight regarding my work is amazing. And yes, their laughter is still my greatest joy, a nice chorus when Kehinde's wife, Teresa, and Taiwo's partner, Aaron, join in. Okay, so I'm being redundant anyhow. Though redundancy can be a beautiful thing, because Greg is still Greg, my soul mate and truest friend.

Blessings and love.

ABOUT THE AUTHOR

The author of the critically acclaimed novels *Tumbling, Tempest Rising, Blues Dancing, Leaving Cecil Street,* and *Trading Dreams at Midnight,* **Diane McKinney-Whetstone** is the recipient of numerous awards, including the Black Caucus of the American Library Association's Literary Award for Fiction, which she won twice. She lives in Philadelphia with her husband, Greg. For more on Diane McKinney-Whetstone please visit www.mckinney-whetstone.com or follow her on Twitter @Dianemckwh.